Divine Born.
The Spirit Callers Saga #5

OJ Lowe.

Contents.

"We have one directive that takes precedence above all other. The Aerius. Find it. It's in Premesoir. The Thunder Mountains. However long it takes, we must find that ship and its precious cargo."
Directive from Claudia Coppinger to the recently promoted Captain Svalbard of the Eye of Claudia.

She sat, and she waited, lost in her own thoughts. It was, rather worryingly, becoming a more frequent occurrence these days. Amid the buzz of activity and thoughts that her mind had become, it felt like she was the only one to whom she could truly listen. Not the case, of course. Domis had his uses as a tactician and a blunt instrument. But could he truly know the depths of her mind? She felt that he fell too short in that department. A shame, to be sure. He could never know what she knew, feel what she had felt. They were worlds apart. Always would be. She loved him like a son, he was about the only man in the kingdoms she'd give the time of day to. But it wasn't enough. Ditto Rocastle… That man she'd cheerfully have set on fire given half an excuse. Ever since he'd lost his leg, no since she'd taken his leg for his insubordination, he'd been sulky and withdrawn. She'd not let him leave the Eye ever since then. Couldn't trust him, not in public. His obsessions were unbecoming. More than once she'd considered having Domis remove him from the whole equation, yet her hand had been stayed in that regard. Rocastle did have his uses. His Angels had taken to the Quin-C final to wreak havoc and they'd managed that considerably well. He'd trained them to hate, inflicted his own petty angers at the world on them and now they were all ready to be set loose when the circumstance arose.

When. When she was ready and not before. The pieces were all coming together now. She had Mazoud running the house over in Vazara, a house filled with people who were growing to love her more and more. She'd done more for the kingdom than any other person, alive or dead, certainly more than that fool Nwakili who'd always peered down his nose at anyone shorter or weaker than himself. His death had been more than necessary; it had been delicious. She'd taken a hot, sandy kingdom that for too long had been raped of its resources by the other four kingdoms who'd bundled it into an alliance with them, a forced marriage of the worst sort, and she'd made it fertile. Treat somewhere like a cesspit long enough and it won't disappoint you.

She'd given hope to those who had none. More than that, she'd made sure they could sustain themselves. Food. Water. Healthcare.

Despite the trade embargos that had already been thrown up across Vazara, something she knew would hurt the newly minted Four Kingdoms Senate more in the long run than it did the Vazarans, all this stuff taken for granted elsewhere was coming in. She'd needed the people for that, people who knew how to smuggle. This had been part of her thinking in approaching all those criminal masters those months ago and though most of them had been apprehended, their top people remained with her. The word from the top hadn't changed, they were still very much with her. That they'd been snatched off this very station had rankled as an insult. It wasn't one that she'd allowed herself to be drawn on though. What was in the past couldn't be changed. Circumstances had conspired against her for that to happen and it was vital that it wasn't permitted to happen again.

Claudia Coppinger didn't like to think about what might have been. In a way, Unisco's intervention had been a blessing. Had they not found out her plan and attacked her where she was supposed to be strongest, she might still be playing cautious. She wouldn't have Vazara, that was for sure. That potential conflict that had been brewing between Mazoud and Nwakili for years might finally have spilled over into open war and she wouldn't have been able to intervene as easily. Those two had hated each other bitterly. Nwakili resenting the Vazaran Sun's power, Mazoud hating Nwakili's guts and that he'd actually had the nerve to oppose Mazoud's plans on general principle.

She certainly wouldn't have had the chance to grandstand at the Quin-C final, she knew that much. Claudia dragged back the sleeve of her shirt, looked at the small dull-coloured stone embedded within in. If she touched it, tapped it with her nails, it didn't even feel like a foreign object.

That day, she'd felt it. When every eye around the five kingdoms had been on her and what she'd gone on to do, she'd felt the stone flare with every emotion that had been felt about her. If they'd feared her, she'd felt drunk off that feeling. There had been those who'd admired her and respected her around the kingdoms, those who'd thought she had the right idea. She'd felt them all inside her, their belief coursing through her. For so long she'd wondered what it was like to touch divinity and now she'd been granted the chance to find out first-hand. It had been everything she'd expected and more, leaving her breathless in the heat of the moment. Given she'd pretty much been off her head given everything that was pumping into her system, it was amazing she'd been able to survive long enough to get away. A lucky shot, she might have caught one in the head in the shootout and that would have been the end of it.

Except that wasn't going to happen. Something was changing in her, she couldn't say what or why, but she knew that the days of normality had left her long behind. She'd never been natural before, had always felt different to everyone else. Most aspire to greatness. She knew that it was her right, it would not be something that might come to her, but only a question as to how. Somehow, she'd known and now that it had come true, she was realising for herself just exactly how right she'd been.

The stone had been in her wrist ever since she'd walked through that doorway in Hoko, since Wim Carson had ripped a hole in reality using the Kjarn and she'd slipped through it. The memories of that trip were hazy at best, thoughts that died out halfway through her head, a lot of bright lights and a deep encompassing voice that spoke in words that made no sense to her in hindsight. Sometimes the pictures came, sometimes the memories flowed and other times they made no sense, broken bits of thought that broke around her brain. All she could remember was what she'd chosen to. The Aerius needed to be found, the directive burning in the forefront of her brain. She'd paid a high price for that knowledge, it had better be worth it.

Still considering the stone, she still didn't know the full extent of what it could grant to her. She'd allowed Doctor Hota to examine it when she'd returned, and he'd told her the only way he could see to irrevocably remove it would be to cut her hand off. It was, he'd explained, consistent with wounds suffered in wars where shrapnel had been blown into someone, too small to be removed easily, and the wounds had healed up around it. Of course, given the time it took for that to happen, it begged the question how long she'd been in there. Carson had told her she'd only been gone a few hours before coming back but it felt like it had been longer for her, something she found more unsettling than she wanted to admit. She'd lost a lot of time somewhere, could feel it in her body and see it in her face. For the two hours she'd been gone, she looked maybe five years older. Maybe more if she aged well.

More than that, she felt the way her flesh was failing. There'd be occasions, fleeting at first but becoming more and more common that she'd glance into the mirror and fail to recognise herself. Who she was? Why she was set out to do this? Her eyes would be blank, something would be missing, just for a second and then it'd return.

Perhaps this was what being reborn felt like. To grow anew, the old had to be scrapped. It was hard to stand in the way of progress.

Progress. A small word but it could mean so much to so many different people under drastically different circumstances. For her now, it was like looking at pieces on a board. Seeing the moves, seeing how each could pan out and adjusting strategies accordingly. She knew where she wanted to go, what she wanted and how to proceed. So why was this turning out to be harder than she'd expected it to so far?

Unisco weren't rolling over for her, they were proving to be surprisingly resilient a foe. She'd launched attack after attack at them, hitting them where she could. Their well-known buildings were too well defended, their agents too scattered and well-hidden to execute en masse. However, in a way, that worked for her as much as it did against her. Alone, they were insignificant. Her attentions would be far better served against the targets she could see removed.

Her forces were growing every day, the longer she waited to go full out on her attack, the better her chances. The clone tanks were working overtime to produce new recruits, the education programs filling their heads with tactics and weapons knowledge, stamping out any hint of rebellion, instilling in them the desire to obey her. That was progress. A shame that she'd been found out, she could have made a small fortune selling the technology to the five kingdoms. A large army however, made the use of it inevitable. Too long they'd relied on local police forces and Unisco to ensure that the peace was kept. Now they were recruiting, a desperate attempt to catch up. Admirable but ultimately foolish.

When she won, in her mind it was already a sure thing, she was going to see everything torn down and rebuilt. These kingdoms were tepid, floundering and it killed her that she'd subjugated herself to the system for so long. She had bowed when she should have stood tall over the rest of them. Her time to do that was now. Claudia leaned back in her seat, examined her fingers like she'd never seen them before.

She would be divine. Worshipped. The top page in a new history book for the kingdoms. All she'd ever wanted, and it was so close to her. She'd sweep through them like wildfire, grant those who wanted it the benefit of her illumination. Those who opposed her would be crushed. Unconsciously she reached out, gripped the arms of her chair suddenly and felt the metal give beneath her grasp. A gasp escaped her, almost pleasured in its release. A hidden secret, there wasn't anything more pleasurable. A secret shared, however…

Claudia hadn't come back from the other side the same. She was better. Improved. Twice the woman she'd been before. All that worship, all that emotion directed towards her, she could feel it and she loved every second. More than that, she loved what it did to her. The old her had been weak. Insignificant. Hiding behind a book of credit cheques. Now she was slowly earning the right to be front and centre of her entire new world order. Still the assassins would keep coming. The Senate had seen to that.

She'd been amused at first when she'd seen how they'd been quick to put the credits up for her death. She'd been even more amused when they'd realised how strong she was now and how their weapons did very little to affect her. She'd shrugged off laser blasts with little more than a smile. Broken them herself even. Domis had fretted, he was unnerved. Rocastle was sulky about the whole thing, she could feel him just as she could everywhere else. If she knew who to look out for, she could hear, if that was the right term, the individuals and read them like books. He feared her and rightly so. She wanted him to be terrified of her. A scared Harvey Rocastle was someone less likely to go out of his way to fuck things up for her. He was a coward, she knew that, and she hated him for it. Her other lieutenants bore everything she'd expect from them, a mix of awe, respect and a little fear, everything a leader could ask for.

This must have been how the original Divines felt all those centuries ago, she'd thought more than once. The theory had been that they were just ordinary men and women who'd become something more. They'd become notorious and ultimately the people around them who they'd stepped over to reach the top had worshipped them. They'd become their own gods. Of course, back then it must have been a lot harder. All this modern technology at her fingertips had made the whole process one she'd laughed the way through. That brief ten-minute appearance at Carcaradis Island had to have done more than ten years of campaigning and war many hundred years ago. The self-fulfilling prophecies were the best kind. They drew power from the belief their worshippers held in them, became more than human, became harder to kill and with every failed blade and arrow, their legend grew that little bit more.

And how would they remember her in centuries time? The one question she wanted to know more than any other and at the same time, one she was looking forward to finding out. Because if they remembered her, it'd mean she'd succeeded.

Of course, there were problems that she couldn't have foreseen with Divinity. Gauging the limits of the whole thing were tough, she'd think she could go on forever only to find herself suddenly exhausted by her exertions. It didn't come with a manual, working out the kinks on the job was more dangerous than she wanted to admit, least of all to herself. Better that she'd discover her limitation now than at a time it could cause her serious harm.

Some of the clones had already been set aside to be formed into units with the intention of challenging the Vedo. Again, Rocastle had done just enough to prove his worth was justified. He'd produced a sample of blood which he claimed had come from a Kjarn user. Now they had the raw material, everything should have been so simple. And yet, there had been complications, although things were looking up in that respect. They were close, Hota informed her, to producing a working Kjarn clone, a prospect that filled her with excitement.

Her glee had been tempered by the reaction of Wim Carson to discovering the process. As annoyed as he had been, there had been something in his reaction that did explain the reasoning behind the failures. The Kjarn, he'd bellowed, couldn't be quantified and replicated in a lab. To try and do so would be disastrous beyond belief. Given the clones that had died in the process, perhaps it wasn't a million miles away from the truth. He might look like a beggar and act like an eccentric but always it was worth remembering Wim Carson did hold surprising depths of knowledge. Whenever he did offer thoughts on a subject, he knew what he was talking about. She wouldn't have gotten this far without him. Couldn't have. His presence had made the whole enterprise one set on a path to success.

Claudia drummed her fingers into the grooves in the arms of the chair, those that had been left by her earlier grasp, stared into space. Being left alone with her thoughts should have been something to worry her. She'd never been this introspective before. Always thought meditation was a crock of shit. Now it felt increasingly like she was going through it more and more. Keeping her own company. Being reclusive. Of course, being the most wanted woman in the kingdoms made it a little hard to appear in public these days. Perhaps that was her biggest regret. She'd already missed her daughter's wedding, although with the way she felt about Meredith these days, that was hardly a loss. Ungrateful little bitch. She'd been informed the little cow was spending time with her uncle these days, the two of them building the sort of relationship she'd dreamed of having with either of them. They'd spurned her, they'd found each other. Her blood and they didn't want to know her.

Screw them.

Maybe one day they'd all reconciliate. Be a family again. They were blood. Her and Meredith anyway. Despite what had happened, despite all that had been said, she had to believe that. Meredith's words on her wedding day had hurt, not least because of the ring of truth to them.

She'd come around when she was tired of playing Happy Common People with that harlot. Of that, Claudia was certain. Collison on the other hand, he needed to die. She couldn't tolerate betrayal like that. Once they locked down his location, he'd be a dead man.

Around her the lights dimmed and once again she was alone in the darkness. Hold the lights too bright and they hurt her eyes these days. Couldn't be doing with that. She missed natural light. Maybe she should go to the bridge, enjoy the feel of some sunlight on her face. What was the point of it all if you couldn't enjoy life's smallest perks. They were in the best place for it, a few thousand feet above the clouds in the Eye of Claudia, one still boasting several hasty repairs still not entirely fixed following the Unisco attack months ago. The on-board maintenance staff had done their best with what could be brought up in frequent trips, but ultimately it felt like it might be a losing battle. They'd already gotten lucky enough that they'd been able to construct it in secret in the first place.

Even as she considered leaving her chambers and going for a walk, the apathy gripped her limbs and any thoughts she might have had of it left her. She sank back deep into her seat, folded her feet underneath her and rocked back and forth.

Show to me the future and I will play upon its tune a ballad of victory and glory…

That was a future she wanted to be part of. Any other would be a waste, of both her time and effort. If she could not succeed, then she would tear it all down. If she could not have it all, then nobody would. Either her golden future would stand across the kingdoms, or the rubble would.

The time for inaction was over. They'd get her gifts or her wrath. In the end, it was down to them. The spirit calling competitions might have resumed, but things weren't going to return to normal if she had anything to do with it…

A few weeks before…

"Order! Order!"

Thomas Jerome, known both formally and informally to those around him as the Falcon banged his fist on the podium in front of him and did his best to restore some calm to the baying masses all around him. Every member representing one of the local governing bodies of the ICCC had turned out for the long overdue vote. One that they needed, for they'd been without a leader for far too long ever since Ritellia had been killed.

For as long as unification had held across the kingdoms, the ICCC had always had a president at top, an executive committee directly below him, simultaneously a deterrent and a subservient to the big boss, while then came the kingdom councillors, effectively in charge of calling on a national level in their kingdoms. Each councillor had their own committee directly underneath them consisting of those in charge of the regional bouts across their kingdoms. Some were larger than others, some therefore had more on those committees. Each of them was king in their own region, a lord of their own domain, yet everyone answered to someone else. The way it should be. It worked. Or it had worked, rather. For the moment, it had stalled drastically without someone at the top of the pile making it work.

That someone would have to be him. He'd already decided that. Better him than someone else. In theory, anyone on the executive committee could be sworn in as ICCC president. In reality, some had no chance. Getting onto the committee was a closed shop unless someone died. Those who got on to replace them had always been checked and double checked, every assurance had needed to be made that their views would be compatible with those around them. That their face fit the bill. Change was messy, it led to the issues being clouded. On the executive committee currently… Nobody would challenge him. Those that could, wouldn't. He'd made sure of it.

Kwan-Sun had declined without much pushing, citing ill health. He hadn't wanted to end up like Ritellia had towards the end, a walking credit cheque for any doctor who saw him coming. Klaus Zynski would have put in for it, only for his past to come back and haunt him. The man liked prostitutes. Jerome knew that. He'd hired them for him in the past, he'd even procured drugs for him. He'd also had the foresight to record all of it for posterity, an act he didn't regret at all. Zynski no doubt thought he would have been in the top job by now, untouchable. He was in the same position now as he had then. Ten years and Jerome had flourished while Zynski had stagnated. One star rose while one faded. It was only natural which of them would win. Zynski would still stand but not in a manner that made him any sort of credible alternative. On the off chance he was voted in, he was to decline it. Again, Jerome had prepared for every eventuality. Of the others… Raul de Blanco had no chance, they knew he was too good at what he did to be replaced. Adam Evans showed no design of wanting the job. Tomihiro was happy where he was. Christopher Armitage probably would like it, but nobody would vote for him, the man lacked a personality or any sort of decisive bone in his body. He'd won his seat by default and was sleepwalking his way towards the grave. Alizaire was a credible choice, yet she hadn't shown up since Vazara had been annexed from the rest of the kingdom, rumour had it she'd been killed in the attack on the capital. They didn't know for sure and as such hadn't replaced her yet, but he'd look into it on the quiet as one of his first jobs. She wasn't here now though. Ergo, a walk in for him into the job he wanted so badly.

It was, he'd noted many times to himself, a hopelessly corrupt system. That was why he loved it. The difference between himself and everyone else, he acknowledged that. More than that, he worked it. Everyone knew how to overstep the lines; he knew when not to. Perhaps that made him weak in the eyes of some, overtly cautious… He'd laugh in their faces should they ever say it to him. Caution might not figure much in the ideas of these colossal morons, but he'd abide by it. Ironically given his nickname of the Falcon. It wasn't one he'd chosen but he liked it. It had stuck. It was a good name. Better the Falcon than the Sloth.

Slowly the uproar died down from the crowd and he cleared his throat, craning his head closer to the microphone. Always his plan. They always liked the look of those that might defer to them. It wasn't how he said it, more like what he was going to say, a train of thought that hadn't failed him before and wasn't going to start now.

"Ladies and gentlemen, rulers of the International Competitive Calling Committee," he said smoothly now that he could be heard above the noise. "Thank you for all seeing your way to gathering here today. It's been too long since we were last all together, we were more in number then. And before we do, I'd like to ask just a moment to remember our last president. Ronald Ritellia is gone but we will always remember him. He gave a lot to this organisation, including ultimately his life. That we could all do as much as him, our legacies would be secure. But the dead have no need to carry on, it is the living who must pick up the slack. And we have slacked. Because we have no leader to guide us, we have failed the five kingdoms…" They were four now but that was irrelevant. Unlike Alizaire, those Vazaran members who'd been able to make it had. Vazaran senators had been ordered to vacate, no such order had come through to the ICCC which made him smile. They were the enemy and they were deferring to the ICCC law. Fantastic! He couldn't remember the last time he'd felt pride like he did at that knowledge. "… and we must arrest that failure. We have allowed excuses and apathy to creep into the work that we do and that cannot be allowed to continue."

He smacked his hand into the podium once again, a nervous twitch more than anything else. He'd have to fight to avoid doing that again. It looked childish and petulant, neither of which he wanted to be tagged with.

"People across these kingdoms depend upon us to ensure that we see a service is provided and it is a service that in these times of strife that is sorely being missed. That should be our first aim. And our

13

second…" Jerome paused for dramatic effect, let a big grin slip across his face. It might have been a bit sleazy to some but for him, it was an honest representation of how strongly he felt. It was the signal of the hope for the future that lived inside his veins.

"… We cannot continue as we are. We all know what we do and there needs to be change. As much as it pains me to speak ill of the dead, the worst of our number for courting their excesses has departed us. We cannot follow in his footsteps. Should we do that, our days are soon to be numbered, particularly with all the anti-governance propaganda coming from that deranged individual terrorising our beautiful kingdoms. In short, we need to be whiter than white. We need to set an example and as terrifying as that might sound for some of you, you can either buck up or fuck off!"

That brought a cheer from some sections of the crowd, he'd misspoken, he considered his words and decided that he liked what he'd come out with. It sounded like he'd intended it rather than it being a slip of the tongue.

"You all know me as Falcon. My name is Thomas Jerome and I would be your leader. I would be the one who takes us into the next generation. I would be the one who guides our good ship through the troubled waters we find ourselves sailing. I was Ronald Ritellia's closest friend throughout the years I spent on the executive committee, I learned more about governance from him than I ever thought could fit in my head. Whatever his problems might have been, he was an effective leader. I am not him…" Another pause, he could see them hanging onto his every word and he had to admit that he was loving the attention. They were adoring him, even if it might not last. That job was in his grasp, all he had to do was close his fingers around it and squeeze. "… I will be better!"

This time near enough the whole chamber cheered and he grinned again, larger than before, much more confident and relaxed that everything was going to work out for the best.

"If there is anyone in this room who wishes to stake their own claim for the job, now is the chance to speak up or forever hold your peace."

Several long heartbeats. His own rose, all until the moment Adam Evans stood and cleared his throat.

"I believe any chance of peace we might have has been broken," he said genially. "I'd like to offer a speech of my own. Perhaps after hearing it, you might consider my own candidacy."

All eyes were on him as he strode up to the stage, staring at Jerome with a steely gaze that made him want to flinch. Unlike the other men of the executive committee who looked like they'd gone to seed and been happy to settle that way, Adam Evans was still in as good a shape at fifty as he had been at thirty. He moved with a feline grace, covering the distance in no time at all, each step keeping his eyes locked on Jerome as if daring him to say anything.

Truth be told, Adam Evans was the only one on the executive committee who Thomas Jerome feared. There was something behind those eyes that he couldn't explain. He'd been told that Evans was a handsome man with his mane of silver hair and those bright blue eyes but still he didn't trust him. And in here, that was really saying something.

"Welcome, Executive Evans," he eventually said. "If the rest of our delegation truly believes you to be the right man to lead us forward, then they will make their choice. I for one, look forward to hearing what you have to say."

To anyone else, it would have been laying down a gauntlet, challenging them not to screw up. Putting the pressure on. Considering the nature of his job, Evans still didn't look like he'd experienced a day of pressure in his entire life. He let out a chuckle, an easy light sound that made Jerome want to blanch. He really hadn't counted on this. All indications had told him that Evans didn't want the job… Evans had told him that himself, hadn't he… He tried to remember their conversations, felt the sweat dribbling down his neck when he found he couldn't. Just remembered that smooth voice telling him not to worry about it. Everything would work out. That hadn't been a denial, had it? So why had he gotten the feeling that this was a foregone conclusion?

More and more he was feeling privy to the sensation of realisation that maybe he'd been set up to take a fall here. Jerome didn't like it at all, he tried not to let it show on his face.

"I thank you, Executive Jerome," Evans said. "And I applaud you on your tribute to our late leader. I think wherever Ritellia's soul went, he would have appreciated it. Moving words. And on the subject of moving, I think perhaps everyone has missed the point of all this. I know you certainly have."

Not a single face in the room was deviated from him, Jerome noticed with dismay. He'd caught their attention and now he was holding it tight, striding around the stage with all the confident charisma of a born showman. Everyone wanted to hear what he had to say. This didn't bode well for him, he felt, the first sensations of unease churning in the pit of his stomach. "Pray do tell."

Why did he get the feeling he was playing right into Evans' hands? Even if he'd wanted to decline a reply, he wouldn't have been able to. Those three words fell out his mouth before he could stop them.

Something wasn't right. He wasn't this sloppy, he wasn't this slow-witted.

"The world is changing," Evans said. "The five kingdoms are not five kingdoms anymore. Vazara has split, there are people who would actively cease to end us out there. Claudia Coppinger has vigorously cited this organisation as everything that is wrong with the kingdoms. The decadence, the gross corruption, the ineffectiveness. We all know it is to be true, I know it, my opponent knows it, you all know it even if you won't admit it beyond the realms of your own conscience." He paused to clear his throat, gave the crowd a big grin. In the press area, picture boxes snapped images of him and Jerome knew that come win or lose, Evans was going to be the biggest story around the next few days.

"But it's not too late. We can change. Everyone can change if the need is great and our need is the greatest. For six months, we have been without a leader. Our last one was slaughtered like a pig and quite frankly, I don't miss him. In the last few years, what had happened to this organisation under Ritellia's leadership was nothing short of farcical. That he actually chose to enter alliance with someone who would destroy us causes me to worry about whether we should have moved to remove him from the post. Perhaps if we had done so, he would still be alive. We should have acted. If Executive Jerome was a true friend to President Ritellia, he would have pulled him back from the edge before he overstepped his authority."

Another pause, just to let that sink in. He clasped his hands underneath his chin, an apparent gesture of prayer. For a moment, he looked genuinely sad and full of regret. Where there should have been outrage and disgust at his words, the other members of the ICCC were all still listening in rapt attention, like he was saying the things that they'd all secretly believed and were too frightened to say before out of fear of reprisals.

"That, my fellow members, is the greatest tragedy out of all this. We cannot go on as we have done, I agree with Executive Jerome on that. We must change. We must do more than change, we must evolve, become the premier organisation that we are capable of once again. Where there is stagnation, we must breed success. But if you want to entrust that to someone who was the chief crony of Ronald Ritellia, then by all means go for Executive Jerome. Their politics aren't a million miles away from each other. He's spoken of their friendship. He will preach change but in reality, it will take very little time for things to go back the way they should be. Because it is the easy way out.

"Privately, you all might want that. You won't admit it in the light of day, but you do. I do not. Right now, we are at war. There are more important things on the minds of the people out there than spirit calling. By ignoring this and thinking things can resume as normal, Executive Jerome is deluding both himself and at the same time trying to throw the cover over your eyes as well. If we wish to survive the end of this war, no matter who wins, then we must change. And I don't care how hard it is to deny our own natures or the risks involved, we must evolve in order to be part of the future. I for one don't want to spend my last days thinking about what might have been. We survive as one or we die alone. Those are your options. Survive with me or die with Jerome." His voice took on a silky forceful tone as he stared across at the room for one last time. "Vote with your hearts. Do what deep down you know is right. I will do what is best for the future of our organisation. It's a promise you've heard before, but don't doubt my words. I will make the ICCC great once again."

That bad feeling had intensified as he'd stepped back away from the crowd to rapturous applause, even to cheers! Jerome felt sick to the stomach, like he'd just been played like a fool. He wished he had the right to reply. But no. This was how it went. One pitch. One chance to appeal to the crowd. As a process, it had been slated and mocked in the past. Mainly by those who it went against. Now he was on the wrong end of it, he truly felt in accord with those views.

Still he'd done his best, and it might still be enough. Maybe. He didn't feel the confidence he'd felt ten minutes earlier though.

He didn't remember the vote. Every seat had a control pad built into it, the entire function of which had been to give an answer in the event of a vote, any vote, not just this one. They were there with a choice, him or Evans. One or the other. He didn't remember the vote, didn't remember the numbers flooding into the big screen at the top of the stage, couldn't recall the numbers themselves. Just the result. The horrible truth of the result and the sounds of cheers mixed in with very scant jeers, applause and sounds of acclaim filtering all the way up to the stage.

As Adam Evans had been elected president of the International Competitive Calling Committee by landslide margins, Jerome was the first to stride over and shake his hand, even if deep down he wanted to be as far away from here as possible. This hadn't been how he'd intended today to go. To look into that face and smile politely when he wanted to do nothing more than punch him out hurt. Evans' smirk hurt.

"Take this as a hint, Thomas," he said in his ear as the two embraced. "You can fool some of them some of the time. Not all of them and never all the time. They don't want your brand of lies any more. All I want is your resignation on my desk first thing in the morning."

His heart fell further. Inside, Jerome felt like weeping, something he'd not done since he was a small child. He doubted anyone out there would feel pity for him. Worse, he was touched by Evans' words, felt the desire to follow through on them, to please him. That sickened him and yet he knew he was going to do it anyway. His time in politics was over. His power had eroded. How much of his life would he have left after this?

"Your meeting with Supreme Commander Criffen has been approved on the following date at the allocated time, in regards of Prisoner RU-Ten-Forty-Two-X. Please be assured to follow all appropriate security procedures in place (listed below) for failure to do so could be met with fatal consequences should you ignore the warnings given. Please find coordinates enclosed within.

P.S, I look forward to seeing you again."

Message from Command Liaison Natalia Larsen to Unisco Agent Nicholas Roper ahead of a scheduled meeting.

The new offices of the Supreme Commander of the Allied Forces of the Four Kingdoms weren't entirely what Nicholas Roper had expected as he stood outside them, hands in his pockets. They never were. The building was old, gaunt and grey, probably built fifty years or more but it looked like it'd survive a heavy assault from the air. They usually did. Under the edict of the Supreme Commander, they moved the facility every few months, everything they erected for the time they were there simply temporary. That which couldn't be moved was left behind. An interesting situation, to be sure and the antithesis of Unisco. When they settled down, they were there to stay come what may.

Still he had to back the man's judgement. He'd cut everyone out of his inner circle who he was sure he couldn't trust. The legends about him told that he was a deeply paranoid man who despite his military genius wasn't entirely trusted in the circles of which he would have been expected to move. He didn't do the popular thing; he did the thing he thought was right at the time. In another life, he might have been a crusader. Hells, he might have been a straight-up hero of the kingdoms.

The flip side was it had made him the ideal choice to lead the fight against the Coppingers. His orders had been simple, wipe them all out on a military level and he had moved to oblige. He'd already set up several skirmishes on the Vazaran coastline which, while they hadn't done much to remove full Coppinger control from the kingdom, had at least made them think twice about immediately moving in on Serran. He got the feeling that was much more of a priority to the Senate than the reclaiming of the kingdom they'd had taken from them. Nick Roper also owed him his life.

It was an interesting prospect having that sort of debt to someone, an occasional hazard of duty. He wondered if he'd ever be in the position to repay it. Not as impossible as it might seem. Doubtless Claudia Coppinger had her own list of targets, just as the Senate had put up its own kill list of high ranking Coppinger affiliates in the aftermath of the Carcaradis disaster. Bounty hunters had tried, and they'd failed miserably in bringing in any of them so far. That thought made him smile. Rank amateurs were not going to get the job done here. They should just let Unisco do the job and claim the rewards. The professionals would succeed where the novices had failed.

As old as the building might look, he found it hard to miss some of the more up-to-date security measures present about it, early warning systems, alarms, he was sure he even saw the tell-tale outline of a pair of sentry cannons above the porch entrance. Anyone who came through this way was going to have a nasty surprise if their intentions were ill. The door had no lock or handle on the outside, only a card reader currently bearing an ill red light. Nick rolled his eyes, reached into his pocket and drew out the card, holding it against the reader. Too many long seconds passed, and the red light turned green. The door swung open silently and he stepped through into a dark reception, the lights dimmed and the shadows deep in every corner. The one solitary light that was on full glare flickered sporadically up above him. Someone had a flare for the dramatic, Nick thought as he moved several steps forward.

He saw her eyes before he saw the rest of her, saw her perched behind a desk like a cat. One hand was flat on the desk, one down behind it and he wouldn't have been surprised to discover there was a blaster currently trained on him. She wore glasses, a faint red hue glimmering about their lenses and he wouldn't have been surprised to hear they had a thermal lining to detect body heat in the dark. She could see him a lot more easily than he could see her. Second line of defence. He couldn't have hit much in this light, short of firing blind and hoping to get lucky.

"Good morning," he said pleasantly. "I'm here to see the Supreme Commander first, the prisoner second."

She said nothing, just studied him with eyes that were almost malevolent in their fixation on him.

"I can go straight on through, if you like," Nick offered mock-helpfully. He found himself deliberately trying to be disarming, always an important trait he'd found when facing armed women in a dark room. "Or I can show you my ID, we can do the small talk and you could not shoot me in the spine. Does that sound preferable?"

"You can suit yourself either way," she finally said. It was hard to make out much about her in the dank, much less get a read on her. "Both work for me." It didn't sound like she was joking. "Although, I don't feel much like cleaning blood out the floor again."

"Well I'd hate to make more work for you," Nick said. "Wait, they make you clean up after you've shot someone? Guess being short staffed doesn't work for you in that regard, am I right?" With a big grin on his face, he slowly pulled his jacket open and reached inside. "I'm going for my ID. My name is Nicholas Roper, I'm with Unisco." He found it, held it open and flashed it in front of her eyes. He even thumbed the print pad to activate the vocal confirmation.

"So, you want to see Supreme Commander Criffen? And then the prisoner?" A repeat of what he'd said several moments earlier, a confirmation he nodded his head to. "That can be arranged." Her fingers danced across an unseen keyboard, the clacking of the keys the only proof that it was there. "Agent Roper, your appointment has been confirmed, he will see you immediately along with the presence of Ms Larsen. One of your own."

He'd already guessed that but nodded in agreement. "Lovely. Lovely. Is that Soren Larsen or Natalia Larsen?"

She visibly relaxed, both hands came to the desk, he could just about make them out in the half-light. "I'm glad you said that. Wouldn't have liked to have shot you."

"That makes two of us, ma'am," Nick said. He'd been urged to ensure he said that when prompted and now he was glad he had, no matter how ridiculous it had come across at the time. "Some people and their code phrases, huh?"

"The Supreme Commander appreciates his security," the woman said. Behind her, the door slid open under its own steam. He didn't appreciate automation. Too much could go wrong. "Enjoy your visit. Up the stairs, second door on the left. It'll be open for you."

"Well if I'm due this sort of welcome at every checkpoint..." Nick quipped.

The security was impressive but never to the point of impenetrable, he had to note. Granted, he did have permission to be here. If he didn't, he might not have quite fancied it. Always he got the impression that he was being watched on his trek deep into the building. Black eyes of monitoring devices lurked through the gloom. If he looked carefully, he could see the glint of their reflection.

Inquisitor Larsen was waiting for him in the small room he'd been directed to, her expression patient but her eyes exasperated. As to why, he couldn't say as he gave her a smile. She was part of Daniel Kearns' liaison department as best he remembered, despatched to work with the Supreme Commander's office to smooth the way over in case of events like this.

"Inquisitor Larsen," Nick said pleasantly. He'd thought her presence was just part of some silly code, hadn't truly expected to meet her here.

"Agent Roper." Her tone wasn't anywhere near as pleasant, she sounded tired and harassed. Not unlike the last time he'd seen her nearly a year ago now, back in Belderhampton. She'd come up in the organisation since then. "Good to see you again."

"Likewise." Natalia Larsen was not a bad looking woman, older than him with caramel coloured hair and deep brown eyes, managing to look formal in a blazer and skirt above a white shirt. A large ostentatious ID card hung around her neck. She finally managed a smile at him. "Wish it could have been under better circumstances."

"No point wishing for those," Nick said. "You'll be wishing a long damn time and be part of a big bloody queue."

"Truth there," she replied. "You're here to see the Supreme Commander?"

He nodded. "I am. Him first, the prisoner second." Nobody saw the prisoner without the permission of the Supreme Commander. Criffen was that convinced the prisoner was the single most valuable piece of intel they had on the whole Coppinger operation and he wasn't going to let him be lost in the murky depths of some faceless prison somewhere. Nick wasn't entirely convinced by the belief but what the Supreme Commander wanted, the Supreme Commander got. As far as the Senate was concerned, he was their best chance and he was being indulged with everything he needed.

"Good luck with that one," Larsen said. "He's not being cooperative again?"

"Criffen? Or the prisoner?"

Just for a moment, he saw the smile in her eyes, fleeting but there. "Both," she said simply. "By the way, are you armed?"

He'd been expecting this. "Yep. Two blasters, one under the arm, one on the ankle. Want me to remove them?"

"Dear Divines, you're carrying two weapons?" She sounded appalled by it. "Are you preparing for war?"

"If I was, I'd have three," Nick said. He wasn't joking either. "Want me to remove them?"

She finally nodded. "Yep. Nobody the supreme commander doesn't trust gets to carry a weapon in his presence. He's very clear on that."

"So, it's true that he's that paranoid then?" Nick asked. He reached into his jacket, removed the new X9S and popped the power pack out the butt. Ever since Ross Navarro had moved into Alvin Noorland's old job, he'd been making recommendation after recommendation for better weapons. The X9S was infinitely superior to the old X7, agents were already discovering. It improved on firepower and charge capacity while maintaining that sense of reliability that had been the staple of the X7. Not for nothing had it been the weapon Unisco agents had used for so long.

"Prefer to describe it as careful," Larsen said. She took the weapon off him, watched as he removed his old X7 from the ankle holster. She put both weapons in a locker off to the side, gave him a ticket stub which he pocketed.

"Well no harm in that," Nick said. "Agent Larsen, I think things are going to get worse before they get better. A second weapon might save your life one day."

"Who says I don't already have something up my sleeve?" she said with a playful wink. "I might show you it one day. If you can get through the day without antagonising Criffen."

"Now why the hells would I want to do that?" Nick asked. "I mean, antagonise Criffen. Not see your second weapon. It's probably a good choice." He smiled at her, shifted a little uneasily on the spot. He and Larsen had some history. She was still a beautiful woman. Definitely more than a little intimidating. It was part of the reason she'd made such a good inquisitor. Those eyes saw through you. "I mean, if you're not doing anything at the end of your shift…"

It was the first time he'd ever actually met Gary Criffen, but he knew what to expect. He'd read his dossier before coming out here, a lot of very distinguished career behind him, no doubt leading to his appointment to this office. He was the first man who'd led a naval engagement against the Coppingers and in the face of unknown odds, he'd managed to avoid defeat. He'd only been an admiral then. Promotion had followed soon after for 'exemplary conduct on the battlefield.'

The man looked tired, he noticed that immediately, especially when compared to the photograph that he'd seen of him. It was only a few years old, but it looked like the stress had since taken a toll on his body. Criffen was only a slight man, not quite the physical build you'd expect of a man who'd devoted his life to serving his kingdom and later all the kingdoms, with cropped grey hair balding in patches across a weathered scalp. He sat behind a desk in just his shirtsleeves, his uniform jacket hung over the chair behind him, a tabac roll resting next to him, smoke rising up from the smouldering edge.

"Supreme Commander," Nick said as he entered the room. Criffen's gaze rose, one hand halfway to his sidearm before he relaxed visibly.

"Ah you must be the Unisco agent," he said. "Another one. I think I have too many of you people in my offices sometimes."

Nick ignored the comment. "Agent Nicholas Roper, Sir. And might I say, it's a pleasure to meet you."

"I'm sure it is," Criffen said. "A lot of people say it, I'm not entirely sure how many of them mean it. Just as I'm not entirely sure you mean it."

"Well probably more than most, if I'm honest," Nick said. "See I probably do owe my life to you in some respects, so I think being false with you would be rude at worst and churlish at the very least."

"You owe me your life? Well I do appreciate your sense of drama, son."

"That engagement against the Eye of Claudia some months ago," Nick explained. "When you arrived, it was to cover the entrance of a Unisco team intending to rescue one of their agents. That agent was me. So yes. I'm very grateful."

Criffen peered at him. "And it's taken you six months to say that?"

"Well I imagine we've both been busy. And you're not an easy man to get hold of, are you?" Nick kept his tone level, not accusatory, just a statement of fact.

"It has been an uncommonly busy time," Criffen eventually said. "I do have to give you that. These bastards never want to give up. But we'll beat them. Of that, I have no doubt. Eventually they'll fall."

"I wish everyone had your confidence," Nick said. "Unisco analysts predict that…"

Criffen waved a hand dismissively. "Don't tell me what your analysts think. I had one in here a few weeks ago quoting to me all sorts of predictions and I had him banned from the building. You're lucky I decided to let you in. Never heard so much Dei-damned horseshit in all my life."

You kept Inquisitor Larsen around though, Nick thought, hiding a smirk. Arguing that point felt like a waste of time, he decided to keep it to himself. "Indeed. Anyway, the reason I'm here… I want to see the prisoner."

"You're not alone there," Criffen said thoughtfully. "A lot of people want to see him; it doesn't mean they get in to do it. That man is a valuable asset. It's taken us six months to get this close to breaking him but we're close and by Divines, we're going to damn well do it, even if it kills him."

"Part of my Unisco training included interrogation," Nick offered. "Maybe I can tip him over the edge, persuade him to be a lot more cooperative than he's been so far. We're running up blank on anything lately. Nobody knows anything or at least not anything they're willing to share with us. That man is the last solid lead we have. Plus, I was the one who took him down. I'm the reason you have him in custody."

He hated bringing that up, Criffen did too by the shade of crimson that his face quickly went but by the same token, he was right. He had been the one who'd taken down the prisoner in that whole fiasco at Carcaradis Island, when everything had gone to shit, and he'd gone through the ringer to try and see the right people were brought to justice.

"Look, Supreme Commander, I'm not entirely sure what harm it can do. It's a win-win situation for you. I talk to him, maybe he breaks, you get intelligence you can use. Or I talk to him and he doesn't break, he doesn't tell us everything he knows. But at least you get that good feeling of inter-department cooperation the Senate keeps rabbiting on about." He was sick of hearing about it personally. None of them liked sharing what they had, he got the point, no need to keep bringing it up. "We're all on the same side, don't forget that. We're all trying to win this war. We're going to do it a damn lot quicker if we work together."

Those watery eyes studied him for several long moments, thoughtfully pensive as they took him in. The back of his neck itched, he shifted where he stood in discomfort, but he bore it out for the time being, kept the gaze locked. Even tried to hold it tight. Criffen didn't appear to blink, just studied him coolly and impassively.

"Okay," he said. "You can have time with him. That is acceptable to me. Just don't break him too badly. I need him still in one piece. Wringing information out of him gets a lot damn harder if we've got to pick up what you left us with."

Nick nodded amicably. "I won't lay a finger on him. I just want to talk." As much as whaling on a Coppinger prisoner might be satisfying, it wouldn't really help this time. If it had been Rocastle...

Yeah, if it had been Rocastle, chances were he probably wouldn't be let anywhere near him. Arnholt had already made that much clear. Tales of his brawl with the spirit dancer on Carcaradis Island were already turning into a mini-Unisco legend and not one he was particularly proud of. Not with hindsight and having had the time to reflect. Yet at the same time, he still held the opinion that he had done everything he could possibly have been expected to do in that situation.

They'd run him through a full body scanner before letting him down into the bowels of the building, Larsen taking him down. She'd glanced at the readout with an appraising eye, a little smile on her face. The more time he'd spent with her, the more pleasant she'd slowly become, like she was happy to see him again. Given he was probably responsible for the elevated position she found herself in these days, his work on the Hobb and Carling case in Belderhampton, he couldn't exactly blame her.

"Nah you're clean," she said. "Good. Not letting you in there with a weapon."

"You know if I wanted to kill him, I wouldn't need a weapon," Nick said pleasantly. "Ditto for old man Criffen upstairs."

"Yes, but Criffen did have a weapon," Larsen said. "If you were to attack him, he'd fancy his chances of being able to at least get a shot off. At which point, we enter the room and kill you. But why would you want to attack him?"

"Just pointing out flaws in your security plan," he said. "In case it was something you hadn't considered."

"Well don't. Assumption never was one of your better habits, Nicholas. I've been doing this for a long time, how about you assume I know what I'm doing?"

When she used his full name, she sounded like an irate schoolteacher and he had to laugh, the response not quite drawing the reaction from her she'd expected. One moment she'd been frowning, the next she was laughing too. She looked like she didn't know why either. Maybe she needed it, the chance to let her façade slip just for a second and relieve the pressure.

"Sorry," he said. "Not many people call me that anymore. It just came across unsettling. You know when you don't expect something?"

"I'm just surprised you managed to get Criffen to acquiesce to this visit. He likes to restrict access to this prisoner. Less chance of someone getting in close to silence him or free him that way."

"I'm a persuasive guy, Talia," he said loftily. "You should remember that. You taught me a lot of it after all."

"Mmmm," was her only reply as they came to a halt outside an ominous looking door, sturdy and triple locked, card reader, padlock and fingerprint access. They weren't joking about when it came to prisoner security, he saw it and he appreciated it.

"Is moving him around all the time really the best idea? I mean surely Claudia wants him back or at the very least, she probably wants him dead. Criffen's probably a massive target for her as well so putting the two of them together, that just feels like it might be a bit reckless."

"Criffen wants him close," she said simply. "And what he wants, he gets. He doesn't want him in some secure facility where a lot of people have access to him. I don't agree with it, for the record but by the same token, I can see his logic. It is just a massive pain when it comes to moving him. He has to be sedated heavily, strapped down, kept under heavy guard…"

Nick nodded. "Okay. Look, I'll talk to him after, see if I can get him to acquiesce to move him into Unisco custody. It's surely got to be better than what he's currently doing, dragging him around like some sort of trophy. Not that I have a problem with him doing that but still you've got to see how mad it is. Sooner or later, it's going to backfire on him."

She only shrugged. "I've told him this and it's not happening. Criffen's a stubborn man and there's no getting past that."

Larsen had unlocked the door and he'd stepped through it, hearing the locks close behind him. His first thought was that Reda Ulikku had seen better days in his prime. The formerly coiffed Varykian had run to dishevelment, a scruffy beard masking what had been a smooth face before, not a hint of makeup covering him this time. Nick remembered him from the Quin-C, he had been engaged in a bout with Sharon, after all. He'd spectacularly kicked off in the media about the way a bout had unfolded between her and her brother. An action, Nick had later surmised, that had brought him to the attention of Coppinger and set him down a path which had led to him being locked in this cell.

At least he couldn't criticise Criffen's choice of restraints, though human rights campaigners might have. He'd read the file, Ulikku had been handcuffed, straitjacketed and under constant sedation to cut out violent outbursts which had been the norm when he'd first become incarcerated. He could see the drip in his neck, could see the pack attached. Already it was half-empty, his irises were little more than pinpricks amidst the messy pools his eyes had become.

"Good morning, Mister Ulikku," he said. There was nowhere to sit so he stood leaning against the wall, keeping his eyes locked on the mans. If he was overtly aware of him being here, he didn't show it too much. "It's been quite a while, hasn't it?"

No response other than Ulikku baring his teeth. Another change. Some of them were missing. He wondered if that had been an act of violence on the part of someone guarding him or if he'd only worn dentures in the past that were now being denied to him. Hard to say. Didn't really matter. Maybe it had even been him. They'd fought at the final, Ulikku had tried to shoot him, Nick had dropped him. Hard.

"Do you remember that day on Carcaradis Island?" he asked. "That was the day that they locked you up and threw away the key. I hope Coppinger was worth your freedom. Because she's running around there like a lunatic and you're rotting away in here. You know what she just did? She took Vazara, she's living like a Divine over there. They're building shrines to her." Enough of the truth seeded his words to sell the lie. "And nobody remembers who the hells you are!"

"Every sacrifice is its own price," Ulikku said finally, the formerly high voice now low and raspy. "We knew that some of us would cease to live, yet we chose the cause to die for."

"You're not dead yet."

Ulikku's grin only grew. "No. And that's your first mistake. You should have killed me when you had the chance. But you didn't. You showed mercy. You played by the rules and that means you'll all lose. Because we don't do rules, we don't do niceties, we won't stop until her vision has been achieved."

"They," Nick said. The level of sycophantic devotion in that voice sickened him. He'd have given Ulikku a slap if he'd thought it'd do a damn bit of good. "They won't stop. You on the other hand, well you're not going to see daylight ever again. As it stands, they're going to break you open like a giant egg, make you spill your secrets. It's not a case of if they do it, it's a case of when. Sooner or later, you'll sing. You'll sing and sing and sing and when you can't carry a tune any longer, they'll drop you then and there. Be nothing left of you to bury, just an urn of cold grey ash and a wasted career."

"So, if they're going to do that anyway, what's my motivation to talk willingly," Ulikku said. He didn't sound impressed. "Might as well make them work for it. Longer they do, the longer the glorious mistress can run around unchecked. By the way you keep bothering me, I take it that you're no closer to stopping her than when she announced her glorious magnificence to the kingdoms… You said you lost Vazara… That was careless of you all. How do you lose a kingdom?" He tittered manically at his own joke. He might have been six shades of high, but his mental faculties didn't appear to have taken the hit. That, Nick found worrying.

"I'll tell you your motivation," Nick said. "Because you can make a choice. You don't have to die. It'd be a massive waste. Do you really want to die for her, deep down? I mean what has she actually done to get you out of here?"

"When she wins, she'll welcome me back for my loyalty…"

"Not really worth it if they've got to wheel you out in a chair though, is it?" Nick said, fighting the urge to roll his eyes at the comment. "Or if you're too busy drooling to realise what's happened. You really think you'll have a place close to her if you're brain damaged by all the drugs they're going to pump into you? They're going to cut into your mind and they're going to shatter every little window to your sanity they can in the name of answers. And when they're finished, either you'll be shunted off to a place not unlike this or she'll give you what she calls mercy and have Domis kill you. You've already lost some of your teeth to this place…"

"Oh, that wasn't this place!" Ulikku hissed, venom suddenly in his voice. Nick studied him, raised an eyebrow in curiosity. The first show of emotion was always an interesting one.

"Do tell?"

For a moment, he looked to be considering it and then just came out with it, his eyes a little uneasy. "That was my father. I…"

A hesitation and Nick leaned forward. "You can tell me, you know. It's not going to give anything up to Coppinger. I'm just curious."

"… Absolute bastard!" Ulikku wailed. "You'll not get me to talk like this! More of us are coming! Sooner or later they'll find me, and I'll be welcomed back as a hero! I'll be the one who didn't give up the glorious Mistress, the light of order and justice in our heavens!"

"That's a new one," Nick said dryly. "You come up with that one in here or that one you've been keeping to yourself?"

"Mock all you want, but soon you'll be in here and I'll be taunting you. That is if she doesn't kill you first. She really hates you, you know that?!" Ulikku shouted. The bag of drugs on his arm contracted and he let out a little moan, relaxed back in his seat as more of its contents pumped into his system. The acrid smell of urine filled the room, Nick fought the urge to react. "She really fucking hates you. You know what you did to her. Betrayed her. Spat on her kindness. Messed up any chance of her doing this bloodlessly."

Nick actually laughed at that. "Yeah, of course I did. You do know there was no way she was going to be able to do this without blood, don't you? She wants a revolution, there's always those that fall in those. What about when she killed Ritellia? Are you honestly telling me that was never always on her cards? What about Nwakili? He'd have died before giving up Vazara and she duly obliged. If she didn't want blood, she went about it the wrong way. I don't know why she does it…"

"She wants the kingdoms to become a better place! They're broken, and she wants to fix them!"

"… Beyond that soundbite we've all heard before," Nick said, his voice calm as if Ulikku hadn't interrupted him. "I've never gotten that, truthfully. If she wanted to do that, there are better ways of going about it than building an army of clones, souped-up spirits and highly trained callers to command them and declaring war on them. I think you're being lied to, Mister Ulikku. More than that, I think you're deluding yourself. There's definitely something else going on here and you may or may not be complicit in a great deceit. Whether you're happy with that or not, I don't care. I really don't. But when people are dying for it…"

"Are you appealing to my better nature now? I went through the Coppinger training. Twenty hours a day connected up to the program, they hooked it right up to my brain. I don't even feel compassion any more. They kicked it all right out of me. I don't have a better nature anymore. It wasn't that good to start with!" He bared his remaining teeth in a savage mirth at his joke, if that was what it had meant to be. Nick couldn't tell.

"Way you kicked off in the media like a little bitch because things didn't go your way, I'd say you never did," Nick remarked. "I mean, that one little thing led you here. Just think about that. One life choice. You lost it. I really hope she was worth it."

For a moment, Ulikku looked thoughtful, pensive even, his face contorted into deep thought. And then the visage cracked, his ruined teeth bared in mirth. "She is. More than you'll ever know. Because you have nothing in your life now. We all know what Rocastle took from you and you'll never get it back…"

Nick whistled, hid his hands behind his back to hide how his fists were suddenly clenched together, his knuckles white from the pressure. He kept his face calm. He'd heard it before from other Coppinger sympathisers. And he'd made a promise to himself that he wouldn't react by smashing their face back up into the rear of their skull. That would have been unprofessional. Satisfying but unprofessional. And he very much wanted to stay involved with this whole thing, rather than being cast aside for making it personal.

"Death is only the start," he said thoughtfully. "You know; she was a Vedo. They don't believe it's the end but a new beginning. One day I might see her again. I might not know her, but they have a thing about cycles. What happened before will happen again." Best way to deal with an insult. Remove any power it might have over you. Honestly, he didn't believe it himself. But Baxter had. Baxter had told him it all, maybe in some attempt to make him feel better but definitely had told him it.

When two souls form a connection, they are forever bound through the Kjarn, the Vedo master had explained. That connection cannot be severed simply by death, it takes real work, real betrayal and torment. And when a connection such as that exists, it will endure. In one way or another, two will become one again. He'd asked if it was like reincarnation, Baxter had considered it for a long moment before explaining that it wasn't entirely the same but nor was it entirely different either.

"Now who trifles with delusion," Ulikku said scornfully. "Dead is dead. End of."

"I find your lack of faith disturbing," Nick replied. "You'll believe in a leader who is going to go five for five in terms of wrecking the kingdoms to pieces and yet you don't truly believe what she does. She keeps Wim Carson by her side."

"Ah the wizard," Ulikku said. His voice hadn't lost that edge of scorn. "Things were better before he came along."

"Unlikely. Our intel suggests that because of him, she was able to get where she has. I think she'd disagree with you."

Ulikku was too busy studying the ceiling of the cell to give him an answer, head lolled back, glancing high up. Nick wondered if there was something he could prod him with to get a reaction. Nothing looked close to hand.

"What do you miss the most?" he asked suddenly. That got a reaction, Ulikku snapped back to attention, shaking his head like a dog as their eyes met.

"Honestly? Decent food. Cheeseburger. Never used to eat them, had to watch my figure for the circuits but..." He laughed bitterly. "What's the point? I'm never getting back there. I've made my peace with that."

Nick didn't laugh. "I wouldn't say that, Reda. I'd say you've got a long time to make peace with whichever deity you believe in yet. You're not going anywhere so don't get any plans about it."

He was glad to be out of there. A wasted trip but it might not have been. Only time would tell. He'd stopped by the catering van down the road, bought a cheeseburger and asked them to deliver it to one Mr Ulikku care of Mr Roper. A token gesture but it might appease him some more. It might only cost him the credits. It stank of boiled fat and greasy cheese, but it was the sort of thing someone living in a five by five cell might appreciate. Small gestures. You want someone to act like a decent human being, you treat them like one and you act like one yourself. Simple things.

For a few hours, he paced outside the building until he saw her leave. Natalia Larsen saw him, smiled and inclined her head towards him. In seconds, he was by her side, didn't take her arm or her hand, just followed her through the streets without hesitation. The block of apartments had a sign advertising rooms for rent up, she walked inside like she owned the place, he followed her up the stairs and into a first-floor room little bigger than a large closet. All it had was a bed, a bathroom, a table and an even smaller closet. It stank of takeout, too many varieties for his nose to distinguish.

He didn't care as he took her in close and kissed her. Still didn't feel anything but numb as the buttons of her shirt came undone revealing a black bra underneath supporting sagging breasts. Still his mouth worked hers as the rest of their clothes came off, they didn't even hit the bed, just lay intertwined on the carpeted floor, their limbs a mess of each other. It wasn't the first time. From the moment they'd stopped being partners, they'd had an arrangement. As long as they were both single, as long as both were willing and available...

He didn't love her. Sometimes he just wanted her. Sometimes she just needed him. It worked for both of them. She wasn't his first since Sharon had died. But she was the first whose name he knew, the first he cared for. She always smoked after they were finished, always lay with her head tucked into the crook of his arm. This time was no different, he could smell the tabac as she lit it with a match.

"I never thought I'd do that again," she said softly. For a moment, he thought her eyes were rimmed with tears and then realised that maybe he'd imagined it. Larsen didn't cry. He wasn't even sure she had ducts in her eyes. You hurt her, she'd hurt back. Tough old bitch.

"You and me both," he said. It was different to that last times they'd been together. Larsen was older. They both were. She was in her forties now but wearing it well. She was keeping in shape, but it was probably getting harder he'd guess. She was going a little soft around the stomach, the thighs. It wasn't her. She wasn't the reason that he felt cold inside. "Nice while it lasted." The lie came easy. Way too easy.

"You miss me?" Too matter of fact, he noted, her voice sounded like it was trying to conceal something.

"Honestly?" he asked. "Yes." As blatant a lie as he'd ever tell. If she had anything about her, she knew it as well. Inquisitors policed Unisco agents, they could pick out a lie amidst a hailstorm of bullshit if the urge took them. Before she'd been promoted to liaison, Larsen had been one of the best, second only to the deceased Stelwyn Mallinson in terms of notoriety.

"Ulikku," she said. The subject was changed. She knew he wasn't going to talk. Not about whatever it was that they had. Maybe they'd both moved on from convenient arrangements, become different people than they had been when they'd started. He'd have to ask Steinbru at some point, the next time he saw her. "He enjoyed his burger. Ravished it down."

It sounded like Ulikku had gotten more out of the meeting than he had, he thought with distaste in his mouth. Some people just had all the luck. "Uh huh?"

"Yeah," she said, scratching at her stomach. "He said he had something for us to pass onto you?"

That caught his attention. "Go on?"

Larsen shook her head. "Nuh-uh. Not yet." She pointed down to her groin, cupped his chin in her hands and gave him an admonishing smirk. "You can do it bloody right this time. Then I'll tell you."

Despite it all, Nick had to grin. "Oh, you bitch!" He didn't mean it. "They teach you that negotiation tactic at Unisco training?"

"Some things," she said, "are all picked up on the job, Nicholas."

"Approval of mission based on the intelligence accrued from captive Reda Ulikku has been granted by both myself and those above me in the Senate. Act swiftly, but with great care for they have despatched an impartial observer to witness the mission. Ensure that Unisco is not embarrassed in the presence of our friend from Arknatz."

Message from Terrence Arnholt to Acting Operations Chief Nicholas Roper.

Nothing about this whole thing felt right. Still there wasn't a whole lot he could do about it now. Nick found himself thinking as he watched the black-clad figures moving through the night on the screen. They moved as a unit, perfectly coordinated in their formation, absolute silence. Even their breathing would be kept to a minimum. They were in heavily hostile territory and even the slightest mistake would be punished. That couldn't be allowed to happen.

Part of him wished he was with them. It'd be easier than standing here watching them possibly go to their death. It was unsettling, his heart was pounding in his chest, almost beating out a need for attention. He wished he could ignore it. Too many wishes, not enough of them threatening to come true. This watching thing was torture. In the past, he might have gone with them. Now, he'd been told he was too important to send on a mission like this. He blamed that therapist they'd assigned to study him, if he was honest. Covering for Brendan while he was out in Vazara was a dream assignment, one he couldn't have dreamed of months ago. Or it would have been more enjoyable if things were different. If they'd been a lot different, he might have been enjoying it.

The thoughts of Sharon hadn't faded with time. Nor had he expected they would have. How long does the hurt take to fade? Even his little reunion with Natalia Larsen hadn't done much to abate the guilt. It was eating him up inside, a carnivorous little parasite devouring his insides and spitting them out before starting the process again. Some memories weren't leaving him. Just when he thought they were behind him, something would remind him of that hotel room on Carcaradis Island.

"Do you feel guilty about what happened with Agent Larsen?" Doctor Steinbru had asked, looking over her clipboard at him. Through her glasses, she resembled a giant owl perched on the edge of a leather seat, he always thought.

34

"Should I? I mean... Look Natalia is a great woman. Do I want to be with her? Honestly? Well I think she can do better for a start. But right now, I don't... I don't know. I don't know what I want." He'd laid down on the couch, purely for the sake of playing the game then they couldn't level that against him. He didn't want to be here. They'd made him. It was nigh-on almost the first thing they'd made him do when he'd returned to active duty.

Nick, Brendan had said, all fatherly and with a hand on his shoulder. It didn't suit him. Nobody took Brendan King seriously when he was trying to be friendly. When he was sternly barking orders, you knew where you stood with him. This had been... unsettling, he'd found. You need to go see someone.

"When you say you don't know what you want..." Steinbru pressed, focusing in on him with those large-rimmed eyes. He didn't want to stare at them for too long. Instead he'd focused on the ceiling, examining a large crack that ran the length of it. If there was going to be something she wanted to add to what she'd started, he was going to let her. He stayed silent while she studied him. The silence weighed on him like a chain.

"I don't know where I go from here," he finally offered. He wanted to be out of here as fast as possible and sitting in silence wasn't going to do him any favours. It was supposed to be confidential. But he didn't know that he entirely believed that. Unisco didn't do confidential when it came to their agent's medical reports.

"That's natural. Where did you think you were going before all of this?"

"Honestly? I did think of leaving the agency for a time. I mean some agents manage to juggle the family and job, manage to do both. I don't think I could. I wouldn't have wanted to lie to her like that. Keep lying anyway. I know its kingdom security and all that, but it puts me in an uncomfortable position. I wouldn't have liked to have leave but sometimes you have to do what's right, you know?"

"You spent a lot of time apart before she died, am I correct?"

"I wouldn't say a lot," Nick admitted. "We tried to catch up wherever we could. Those weeks at the Quin-C, they were... bittersweet."

"I imagine that it never felt like the best way to have a relationship though, never mind one running to marriage. Being pulled apart when you wanted to be with her."

His voice caught in his throat and he tried to clear it away with a cough. "That was why it should have all come together when I left Unisco, but it was ripped apart. Guess some people just don't get happy endings."

"You found out she had a secret herself," Steinbru then said and Nick glared at her despite himself.

The building was a good distance away, a kingdom from him. The pictures were good quality, video drawn from the headcams on the operative's helmets. What they saw, he could see. This had to go well. He'd gotten the intelligence from Ulikku, he'd given up the location of a Coppinger storage facility in the south of Premesoir. To say he was suspicious about the whole thing was an understatement. There had to be some sort of catch. All initial efforts at scouting it out had been inconclusive. Recon had reported it to be mostly abandoned. He'd had some of Will's staff go over hours of security footage. They'd studied the blueprints of the building so many times he saw the outlines of it when he closed his eyes.

And yet, he had a feeling.

Nobody had gone in or out for too long according to local records. That didn't feel right. Even abandoned buildings had someone by to check on them every now and then. And it felt like too random a location for Ulikku to specifically give up. To the best of their knowledge, Ulikku had never been to Premesoir. There was no motivation they could see for this address to be random.

Nick rubbed the bridge of his nose. His head ached, and he hadn't slept well for a long time. It wasn't nightmares, but something else he couldn't describe. Nightmares he might be able to deal with.

It had been Will Okocha himself who'd cottoned onto a reason for them to act. The sort of one in a thousand spot that had made Okocha so good at his job for so long. He'd glanced at the footage while in the room, observed and then rewound and fast forward it several times. His attention had been locked on that one bit of footage for the best part of an hour, his eyes never wavering, sometimes not even to blink. There hadn't been anyone go in or out, at least not where the camera could see them. But…

He could still remember the sound of triumph Okocha had made as the credit had dropped, as he'd made the moment of realisation. Some sort of strangled cheer, he'd jabbed a finger at the screen, showed them the glimpse of the furthest wall. How every six hours, like clockwork, the glow of a light shone against the back wall, a reflection in one of the other windows. Not bright, had to be quite a distance away from the actual window, but it was there. Someone was moving around in the building. They were security conscious, he had to give them that. But they weren't as good as Unisco. Which meant there had to be another way in. Maybe an underground entrance, maybe through the sewers…

So many ifs and maybes. The blueprints of the warehouse showed no other entrance but that didn't mean anything. It could have been modified. Records of the place showed that it had long since been bought by a company several times removed from Reims itself but still a very distant subsidiary. That in itself should probably have been enough to convince them that something was wrong.

Regardless, the team was on their way in. They'd find something. They had to. With how much effort it had taken Ulikku to cough it up, they better find something worth crowing about, otherwise none of them would look particularly good.

Right now, they needed a win. They couldn't afford anything less. The fall of Vazara hadn't done anyone any favours at Unisco. The Senate was asking questions of them, like how they hadn't seen it coming. As if anyone could have seen that move coming! Anything to hide their own incompetence, like refusing to aid Nwakili, probably more of a factor in the kingdom falling than anything Unisco had or hadn't done.

"Yeah, Sharon's secret... I was keeping stuff from her, so I really can't complain about her doing the same, can I?" It sounded hollow as he said it, he knew that. Steinbru knew it as well judging by the way she looked at him over the top of her notes. She had a way about her, something that hinted she didn't believe much of what he said to her.

"It wasn't entirely the same thing though, was it?" she said softly. She said it with a lot more conviction than he'd managed to say his bit. Still he had to try and drag it out. They both knew he was doing it.

"How do you mean?"

"Well, you did it as a job. National security, international protection, you had to keep it a secret. Not just for your sake but for hers as well. We all know how Unisco operates, what you have to do. We all know why we ensure that our operative's identities are kept as secret as possible."

He did know that. Part of the reason he'd not been out in the field much since the whole event at the Quin-C final. There'd been a lot of videocams about there, most of the carnage had been recorded for posterity. And given his lack of a muffler, he'd been caught running around, kicking arse and outright murdering a whole bunch of Coppinger grunts. Granted, they'd deserved it. He'd been able to explain it away partially as self-defence training, an excuse that wouldn't fool anyone who knew even the slightest thing about fighting but the media had bought it in the immediate aftermath.

There was a great deal of magnitude between being able to defend yourself against someone trying to kill you and proactively putting them down before they could try. At least what had happened between him and Rocastle and Coppinger down at the docks after hadn't been widely witnessed. If Scott Taylor wanted to talk about it, he hadn't done. Gratitude perhaps. The director's daughter hadn't died. Taylor was screwing her, everyone knew that now. It wasn't a secret. If he'd ratted out Nick, it would hardly have been charitable given he'd spared him from cold nights alone.

He'd kept out of sight. Lived off his funds, done some low-key work for Unisco. Worked hard. Shadowed Brendan in his new role, slowly gone through the role of re-inventing himself. Made himself indispensable. Even worked on his shooting and his hand to hand. He'd spent more time in the training facilities the last several months than the last several years, throwing hours every day at it.

"You kept secrets because you had to," Steinbru continued. Her voice commanded authority. Before she'd become a psychiatrist for Unisco, she'd been an agent, but the stories told she'd been glad to get away from it. Some people didn't take to the lifestyle which wasn't as glamorous as was made out. "What was her excuse?"

Many, many times he'd wanted to talk to Ruud Baxter about Sharon, he'd never quite found the nerve. Baxter likely knew her better than any man alive, as much as it pained him to admit. He'd seen the side of Sharon that she'd kept secret from Nick for so damn long. He had the answers. More than once, he'd made to approach Baxter in the halls, when he deigned to appear at headquarters and yet the moments had passed, his motivations had failed him.

Perhaps, just perhaps, he didn't want to know. As hard as not knowing was, the truth could be so much worse.

The moment had arrived. Nick knew it. The team knew it. Everyone in the ops room knew it. And yet, it'd be up to him to proclaim it. He was sweating, his brow covered in the stuff. He felt hot and damp, uncomfortable where he stood. There was a difference. He'd been on these missions himself. He'd survived them. Statistically, there was something like a one-in-six chance of a fatality on them. Twenty-seven missions he'd been on like this. Against the statistics, he'd done well. He'd beat the odds. That was all you could ask for. He'd come through unscathed, at least physically. Mentally, he'd probably have had to get Steinbru's opinion on that and he doubted it would be anything approaching perfect sanity. Functioning might have to be the best description of him these days, at least on the worst of them, and that was all he needed to be. On his best days, even Brendan had said he was up there with the best of them. Not to his face admittedly.

Not that Brendan would ever know that he had viewed those files. He didn't even know Nick had long since worked out the secret way into his office. Forewarned is forearmed. A little bit of knowledge was always a handy thing to have in a crisis. One day he might need it. He didn't want to go into thought about why that may be or when that day may come but better knowing it and not needing it than the reverse.

Aurora Team were in position, ten highly trained Unisco operatives, two groups of five, one at each end of the building and ready to enter on a count of five. Already right now, they were readying their breach charges. Across the ops room, feeds ran live across viewing screens from the minicams on their helmets, real-time views on everything that they saw. They were armed up to the teeth, they knew what they were doing. Every inch of him knew that they should be confident here.

Something felt off. Truly off. A feeling he couldn't explain in his gut, tiny, nagging, just a hint of distrust. A hunch, nothing more but one that demanded his attention relentless in its nag.

"Clear to proceed?" came the request over the comms. The words echoed inside his head, he repeated them over and over again. The smart thing to do would be pull them out of there right now. If you weren't sure, then don't risk it. The first damn thing Brendan King had always said to him. And it was always the best thing to go with your instincts. They could be misguided but rarely wrong. If something looked bad, it probably was.

He reached down to the Abort button on the console, hovered his finger over it. Everything told him he should do it. If he pushed it, they'd slip away into the night, the op would be over, and he'd have to deal with the consequences. If he didn't push the button, he'd have to deal with the consequences, but the team might well not survive.

"Don't do it."

He wasn't alone. Of course, he wasn't. Aside from the techs and the various others doing a dozen little jobs around him, Walter Swelph had come down himself, the new head of the management department. He didn't know him that well. They moved in different circles. He was in theory, only second in command in the entire organisation to Arnholt, his department dealt with internal appointments, disciplinaries and indiscretions as well as running the inquisitors. The command hadn't come from him. He'd remained silent, watching with impassive curiosity.

No, he recognised the voice. Ragwort. Colonel Alvaro Ragwort, the Senate representative of the war effort. He resented the presence of the man here, not least because of his background. Ragwort was a Serranian but hailing from the icy north of the region, an insular people in Nick's experience. They didn't think their way was right, they knew it was right and to hells with what everyone else thought. Ragwort was balding blond, heavyset and carried himself like a fighter. He looked like a killer, even before you got to the leather patch that covered his right eye amidst a mess of scarring. In short, if you needed subtlety, he wasn't the man you selected for the job. His presence here was a message, everyone knew that, and they were on eggshells around the man. Not least because of his Arknatz background.

Arknatz itself was a bit of an anomaly in the way the five kingdoms had structured itself over the last fifty years. Ever since Unisco had been founded by the five premier intelligence agents of their day, it had been recognised as the dominant force in maintaining law, order and peace across those kingdoms. It had very quickly reached the top of a hierarchy that needed building and maintaining. The people had been gotten in place, the missions had been undertaken, the lines in the sand had been drawn. Before Unisco, there had been more than a dozen independent agencies running their own agendas over increasingly lawless kingdoms, refusing to share information with each other, refusing to work together. They spent as much time fighting each other as any actual villain. Arknatz was one of those organisations that had been there before and about the only one still clawing out an existence at the table. They had their secrets, their people were trained well and because of some side deal made many decades ago, they'd not only survived the cull of all those other organisations but managed to thrive in their absence. Nobody at Unisco liked them but they tolerated them by decree.

And as a senior senator from Serran had once commented, sometimes you needed an organisation out there to do things that Unisco might find distasteful. Nick had often considered the Unisco situation over the last several months. It tried to be everything for everyone, running from specialised law enforcement backup to intelligence gathering to its own military taskforce to covert operations and assassination when the need arose. Sooner or later, it'd trip over itself, overreach. Sooner or later, every Unisco agent found themselves involved in a situation they found themselves uncomfortable with.

With the war against the Coppingers breaking out when it had, Unisco had been reorganised, Arknatz had been given a larger role and they were being forced to cooperate. Ironic, given their previous lack of desire in that department going back many years. Nick certainly didn't feel comfortable enough with the way Colonel Ragwort was feeling confident enough to start barking out orders to it. It was the sort of voice that implied it expected the order to be carried out and quickly.

"I'm sorry," he said mildly. "I didn't catch that, colonel." He smiled politely enough, aware it might piss him off and not even really caring. Even wondered if it was worth pushing it further. "Sounds like you're catching something. Been some of the wild coughs going about the building lately."

"Agent Roper," Ragwort said with a look of disgust. "Your concern about my health isn't needed. I'd rather you gave the order for your team to begin their mission."

Finger still above the Abort button, Nick clucked his tongue. "I've got a bad feeling about this." He might as well lay it all out on the table. "Something doesn't feel right."

"Or it might be empty warehouse," Ragwort said with disgust. "Ulikku is a known deviant, he sounds convincing but maybe he's a liar. Only one way to find out."

Nick wasn't going to argue with that. His opinion of Ulikku wasn't something to be repeated in polite conversation. Ragwort's accent was thick, but understandable. It wasn't overtly dissimilar to listening to Derenko, if Nick was honest. No doubt, they'd each claim there were subtle differences to where they came from, but he could hear the northern influences in their tones.

What he was going to argue with was the way Ragwort had brushed away his concerns, not that he cared really what the Arknatz colonel thought. He was in charge here, not Ragwort. This was a Unisco operation. "Something doesn't feel right here," he repeated. "Anything you know about this place that we don't?" He let an easy relaxed tone slip into his voice, nothing accusatory. They were supposed to be sharing information after all. Trust but verify.

Ragwort replied as much, the disgust palpable in his voice. "Agent Roper send them in for Divine's sake."

Nick took a moment further to consider his position one final time. Ignoring the bad feeling, there were three outcomes he could see ahead of him. One, that Ulikku had been lying and they would find an empty warehouse. That would be acceptable to him personally, none of his team would be hurt and they could come back. His bad feeling would be unfounded, only the waste of time and resources but Ulikku was someone else's prisoner and people above him had chosen for the information to be acted on.

Two, Ulikku was telling the truth and they'd catch a Coppinger operation unawares, make a whole bunch of arrests, maybe gather more intel and the whole thing would be a massive success. Maybe there'd be casualties but that wasn't always unavoidable when the choice had to be made. Worst case scenario, it would only be a minor Coppinger facility but taking it off the board would be a victory no matter what, it'd be something to cheer about. Best case scenario, they'd remove a whole bunch of scientists and weapons and people who could tell them more about Claudia's grand plan.

Three, Ulikku was telling the truth and sending them into a trap. If he examined the bad feeling and searched for any possible source behind it, this would likely be it. He had personal experience of what the Coppingers could bring to bear when they wanted to make a statement. He'd seen their soldiers, he'd seen the creatures they'd created, and he wouldn't want to be on the receiving end of them, never mind sending a team to face them. He'd fought one or two before, the one she'd called Cacaxis according to her brother, he still had the container crystal containing Unialiv on his person.

Three options, two good, one bad. Statistics said that a two out of three chance of a positive result was worth going through with. And he had faith in the team, he'd overseen some of their training himself. They were new recruits in the role, experienced in other areas but raw in this. Add the knowledge that they couldn't have been trained any better to that two-in-three chance of it all going well…

"You have clearance to proceed, Aurora team" he said. "Good luck."

Sometimes the silence that these sessions passed in was the most bearable thing of them all. Sometimes he didn't want to think about the consequences of what Steinbru was suggesting to him. Something about what she said managed to stick in his head, lay down ugly roots and branch out.

"I'm sure it wasn't like that," he said eventually. He didn't have any sort of conviction in his voice, he wasn't sure if he believed it himself. He knew exactly what it was she was doing, trying to make him think about it, but that didn't make it any easier to ignore it.

"She concealed all this important stuff from her past about you," Doctor Steinbru continued. "And it was all in her past. From what we now know, the Vedo were extinct. They weren't coming back. She was out, even if they did. So why keep it a secret."

"It feels like we've been over this before."

"Because you're not perhaps hearing what I'm saying. You're hurting, that's right, I can tell that. Director King could tell that. I think you're screaming out in silent pain and you just want someone to hear you."

He shook his head. "Doc, I'm fine. I'm fine."

"Which in itself isn't right. Your traumas have been many. I think you're working to actively suppress them."

Nick wasn't impressed, he raised an eyebrow and glanced towards the door. Wondered if it was too late to stop these sessions. Maybe like a rolling boulder, they'd now started, and they weren't stopping any time soon.

"Let's talk about the island."

That didn't sound promising. Ever since the Quin-C, he'd done too much talking about that whole damn island. The very thought filled his stomach with bile, made his head ache and he threw his hands up in frustration.

"Doc, I've done nothing but talk about the island over the past few months," he said. *"Believe me, I don't want to bring it back up. I want to put that behind me."*

"It's not going to go away though, Nicholas. It happened. I think you're remembering it all too vividly and I think it's suffocating you. Talking helps…"

"And I've spoken enough about it!" He was surprised by the venom in his voice. *"I've spoken to Arnholt about it, to Brendan, to people who I trust, the media's asked repeatedly about it. Even spoke to Claudia fucking Coppinger about the whole damn thing. And now you're making me do it again! Seriously…"* He let his voice tail off, a little out of breath from the suddenness of his rant.

It probably wasn't the first time Steinbru had had to hear a rant like that, she just smiled slyly and leaned forwards in her seat. *"And on that subject of Claudia Coppinger… Going undercover like you did with her. That was reckless."*

"It was something that needed to be done." That was what he'd said to himself at the time and it was what he'd continued to repeat after the event. He believed it as well.

"It didn't need to be you."

"I think it exactly needed to be me. I think everything just fell into place there for the perfect trap. Right there and then, I was everything they wanted and everything they needed. There are still spirit callers out there who joined up with Claudia Coppinger who we can't account for. Divines know what they're doing! But it can't be anything good."

"Nicholas, you shouldn't have been anywhere near anything like that at that point. I've spoken to some of the people who were around you at that point. William Okocha said you looked like you were on the verge of some manic breakdown when you and he put it all together."

43

"No, he didn't," Nick said. "You may be paraphrasing it, but I'll bet you any credits you like, he didn't say it in those exact words. Will's my friend."

"And your friends want you to get help. As for attacking Ritellia in front of everyone…"

"That was satisfying."

"You could have killed him."

"I pulled my punch. His dignity probably took the biggest blow. And right now, I imagine he's too dead to care."

"And then, what happened at the stadium after… I've seen some of the footage of you tearing around like a one-man army. You could have been killed."

"I might have been killed if I'd hidden under my seat. Least doing that, I gave myself a fighting chance. I did what I'm trained to do. And I saved lives. I mean, do you know how many people were at risk? All of them!"

"And I think the most at risk person there was you. Nicholas, you didn't run after Harvey Rocastle for altruistic reasons."

"He'd kidnapped the director's daughter…"

"People were dying," she pointed out. "One spirit dancer in the scheme of things is no more or less important than anyone else in that stadium. Nobody would have blamed you if she'd died."

"Rocastle was someone we needed to capture," Nick said quickly. "He already escaped from Unisco custody once already. An embarrassment we needed to put right, if nothing else."

"You didn't try to capture him though. What did you actually do, Nicholas? Beating him senseless wasn't the best thing for anyone involved."

"One of his spirits was ready to kill a hostage. It was the first thing that I could come up with that'd distract his attention. You know what happens with the bond between spirit and caller when the caller is in danger. At least, I assume you do. It's an old tactic, I've used it before myself." That last remark was unnecessary, he knew that, but he'd made it anyway. He didn't like the way he'd done the job being questioned.

"I've seen your notes on the Lucas Hobb incident," she said. "That's a whole new set of circumstances that we might discuss at a later date."

He said nothing. That felt like a bloody long time ago and he didn't want to go over old ground with it. "Can we get back to where we were before? I don't want to talk about Hobb or Carling for that matter. One's dead. One's not going anywhere from jail. They're not important!"

"Okay, Rocastle killed your fiancé. I don't think you'd have shed too many tears at the prospect of beating on him," Steinbru said slyly. "Apparently you gave him quite a painful one. Several broken bones, the reports say. Mia Arnholt described it as brutal. Scott Taylor described it as vicious."

"Did what I had to do. I doubt either of them were complaining too much at the time. You know, because of the situation that they'd found themselves in."

"Nicholas, if you'd shot him through the head, there'd be one less Coppinger in the world," she said. "Do you ever think of that?"

He shook his head. "Not an important Coppinger. And besides, that's not our way. Shooting him then would have left at least two bodies. Minimum. More if his troll had rampaged. I don't regret the choices I made that day."

"And yet, a lot of people would have made different ones. Not even regular people, a lot of Unisco agents would have done the same. I'm worried if I'm honest. In fact, do you want to know what I think, based on your actions in their entirety, since you discovered Sharon died?"

The room went into silence as everyone watched the screens, all different angles of the same view, the doors to the warehouse, followed by the flash and the bang of the breach charges forcing them open. They all saw the weapons rise, as the two teams of five broke into the warehouse, saw the dirty green linoleum on the floor, dust covered and disused barring the faintest trace of days old footprints. Shelves of aged products lined the walls, their labels too faded to be read, not with the swift glances the minicams gave them.

Probably the first sign that the place wasn't abandoned was the way the lights flickered on above the teams as they entered, humming slowly into brilliant life. Nick remembered seeing somewhere that this place had been used to store foodstuffs before it had become abandoned. If the old packaging on the shelves was anything to go by, it probably stank in there. Somewhere in the corner of one cam, he was sure he saw a rat scurrying away into the murkiness of the mezzanine. Maze looked like a good description of the place, not too many wide-open spaces so far, not huge clear lines of sight. That had its perks if it came to a firefight.

He still didn't like this, couldn't help but feel uneasy. He wouldn't have liked going into this situation if it were him going into the unknown. He'd done it plenty of times but that feeling never waned.

Across the room, Ragwort was clucking his tongue in his mouth, he looked as unsettled as Nick felt. Probably for entirely different reasons. They both wanted this to work well. From Ragwort's perspective, they needed a result, something worth taking back to their high command, absolutely nothing would be a bad result for them. From Nick's perspective, he'd be happy if none of the team were wiped out. That wouldn't reflect badly on Unisco. A bust would suit Unisco fine. Wouldn't look great but they'd survive it with ease.

He hated politics. On the screens, the team were approaching the middle of the first floor, one of them audibly confirming what they could all see...

"... Approaching stairwell, ready to secure..."

They'd suspected as much. There was more below the surface than first met the eyes. One of them reached the stairwell, peered over the railings, far into the darkness below. Either it was deeper than it looked, or the feed was screwy. Far in the distance, he was sure he could see some pinpricks that might be lights.

"Aurora team, you have clearance to check it out," he said, unable to help himself. His curiosity had been piqued. Nick looked to Ragwort, then at Swelph. "Looks like it's something at least. That wasn't on the building plans."

Swelph said nothing. Ragwort rubbed his hands together, his face splitting open into a grin. "Looks like Ulikku was partly telling the truth, no?"

"That's the foundation of a good lie, in my experience," Swelph said finally, a little testily. "A little truth to hold up the bullshit."

Nick had to smirk at that as he turned away from the two of them. As curious as he might be, he didn't like stairwells. Going up was a bit of a bitch, leading with your head, vulnerable to someone on the high ground... Going down was easier, but still an ambush was possible at the bottom. If what was going on down below was an active Coppinger operation, they had to know someone was here by now.

"Aurora team, you see any signs of surveillance?" he asked. A chorus of negatives came back to him. That assured him but not completely. These men and women were professionals. They knew how to spot any sort of known recording implement. Didn't mean one hadn't been invented yet that could give them the slip. He'd seen the sort of technology Claudia Coppinger had been pushing her people to invent. Nobody did business with Reims anymore, the company had been effectively disabled, forbidden from operating in the business world, but most of the brilliant minds had vanished into the void. A worrying prospect.

46

A team of Unisco accountants had gone over the company books, discovered huge profit holes across their margins, billions of unaccounted for credits swimming into holes and not reappearing again. In that respect, they'd had a little luck in finding out what was going on when they did. Coppinger wouldn't have gotten away with it forever, but another year or two might have been feasible. Earlier was always better. She might have been able to squirrel away even more funds for her war, even more technology and firepower to give her a better advantage in the long run.

Of course, now that she'd gotten in bed with Mazoud and had a say in how Vazara was run, she in theory had access to the wealth of the kingdom, which while not infinite was definitely not insubstantial. Any hope of bankrupting her was gone. Vazara might have been plundered for years, but the well of minerals there wasn't dry by a long shot.

On the screens, the team had left two men on the top of the stairwell. He approved that decision. It meant that they wouldn't be flanked from behind easily. The chances of two Unisco operatives being dropped without them giving any sort of warning were low. Not impossible, but difficult. Very difficult. Their minicams showed the rest of the team heading down into the darkness, headlamps lighting up the other eight to show a sterile stairwell, a dirty brown colour cut down deep in the foundations of the earth.

"You ever see anything like this?" Ragwort asked. "Before or after this war started?"

Nick shook his head. On the screens, the bottom of the stairs panned out into smooth floor, a plain grey door cut into a dull metal wall a few metres away. It looked out of place, diminished as if it didn't belong, the door misshapen and not quite the same size as the gap it covered. "Expected something a little more high-tech if I'm honest," he said. "Nice to know that they're rag-tagging it just as much as we are sometimes."

Ragwort looked confused. "Rag-tagging?"

"Putting it together on the fly," Nick explained, rubbing the back of his head. The first man had reached the door, they could see his hand on it, ready to yank at the handle. Those behind him readied their weapons, they could see the faint glow of summoners being activated as spirits were brought into being. They were ready to go to war. "Not well thought out, a bit of a mess… You know what it doesn't matter."

The team were all using the same spirits, large saxcion hounds from the west of Serran, a little town called Saxca which Nick had only ever been to once and had no desire to do so again. Unisco had a training facility there, used to work on squad-based spirit combat.

Probably where Aurora team had been put together before being shipped off to be based here in Premesoir. Those dogs were bloody massive, vicious and loyal.

The door opened in front of them, Nick wasn't sure what to expect, but already the dogs were through the gap before the first man, BRO-80 aimed and ready to fire. First sights of the other side, he got the impression of some sort of huge chamber, he was trying to watch eight screens at the same time to get a view of the whole, eventually gave up and focused on one of them.

Chamber wasn't a million miles off the mark, he guessed, on first impression. Cut out of the earth underneath the warehouse, something had definitely gone on here, though it was hard to tell what from the poor quality of the feeds. Sometimes underground, the reception wasn't great. Dirt floors covered in a grey mesh that gave it minimal covering at best, leading up to a great groove in the ground ahead, a groove that as the minicams moved closer, turned into a pit.

That was when the first minicam went black and suddenly there were only seven screens active. Nick forced himself not to close his eyes, he needed to see this. Credit the team, they reacted swiftly enough, spinning to face the threat, already the dogs were snarling into attack, weapons were coming up and muzzle flashes were filling the remaining views, roars of blaster fire ripping through the speakers.

Behind him, Ragwort was shaking his head. He only saw it out the corner of his eye, didn't react, not as he continued to move his eyes from screen to screen, trying to make out what was going on. A dog went for something, came crashing down with two bleeding puncture wounds in its side, wounds the size of plates. Something swept back, he briefly saw a flailing… he wanted to say limb… sweep out and catch one of the team hard, something solid and golden coloured. Not quite a pure gold, a sickly gold tinged with a crusty green filth.

"Divines!" Swelph exclaimed. "What is that?!"

Nick didn't have an answer, saw the flicker of one giant white eye sweep past a minicam before claret splattered across the lens and the connection was lost with the sound of the owner screaming his lungs out as he died.

"Holding team, move in to back them up," he quickly ordered. "Something's wiping them out down there. Proceed with caution!"

Three were down, another went down screaming, eyes went to him and Nick paused, caught his breath in his mouth. That wasn't right. He'd gone down and there wasn't anything there, nothing the eyes could pick up. The two guys who'd been left at the entry point were already hurrying into battle. Part of him knew they'd be too late. At this rate, they'd be little more than the encore to this thing ripping through the entire team. He should have ordered them to retreat. They threw the door open, this time accompanied by the full contingent of spirits they had about their persons, not just saxcion hounds but accompanied by the presence of a bear, a horse, a lion and a wolf, as well as a huge bee that would probably have caused an entire ecosystem to collapse if it grew that big in the wild.

Bees should not grow that big! Somewhere that thought danced about his head amidst the chaos of battle. For the first time, he saw something, that same great golden-green shape bursting out of nowhere and crush one of the team in its jaws, crunch-crunch snap and a scream as brutal fangs split him apart at the top and the bottom of his torso. He managed a spatter of blaster fire into it, not that it did him much good. If the thing felt it, it didn't show any signs of emotion.

It was huge, heavy and thick with girth, he didn't know how something so big could remain so hidden, not at least until it came to a stop and then vanished from sight again.

Oh...

Part of him realised 'snake' just the same as another part of him twigged onto 'oh camouflage'. Those two initial thoughts snowballed until the realisation dawned that it wasn't any sort of ordinary spirit. They'd all seen ones like it before, if not this particular one.

All spirits out on the screens piled into its last known position, tearing and biting, the dogs had to smell it! The snake didn't seem to really care, bursting up out of them as if they were insignificant, all six eyes burning into the lens' that were focused on it. Now the team knew what to look for, they were firing onto it, six blasters singing in unison as they targeted the huge serpent.

If being shot bothered it, it didn't show as it lowered its head like a bulldozer and burst straight through the lot of them, bones breaking and screams ripping out over the feed. The spirits of the dead men took one final punt at the snake, determined to avenge their fallen masters, savage attacks that left no concern for themselves. They didn't last long, crushed in the coils of the snake, savaged by the fangs.

Fresh blaster fire burst onto the scenes, one remaining minicam showed a few of the spirits go down, shots to the head. A man stepped onto the screen in front of them at an awkward angle, Aurora Four's neck looked broken at Nick's best guess. His face couldn't be seen, up in the shadows but they saw the glint of his eyes, pale and sparkling in the darkness.

"Bang," he said playfully, putting one hand on the scales of the snake, rubbing it firmly. "If that's the best you've got..."

The blaster reported, they saw the flash and the feed went dead. The moment it did, Nick ripped his headset off and slammed it down into the table in front of him, felt it break under the force of his blow.

"Son of a bitch!" he swore, smashing his palm down into the mangled headset again and again, not letting up.

"You know what I think? I think you've lost someone you were willing to give everything up for. I think that's the sort of thing that changes someone. I think you've realised that nothing is going to be as it was. And I think right now, you're so consumed by revenge that you're past caring if you live or if you die in the process. You're just concerned with the fight. That's why you've been training, I think. You've been putting it all in, ready to either go out in a blaze of glory or to come back a hero. I don't think it matters either way to you."

Steinbru paused, looked at him over her glasses. "Can you really tell me I'm wrong?"

"Of the early life of the man known affectionately to his admirers as King Bren, there is little to be said of Brennan Francis Charles Frewster. Most people think he appeared in the public life as a pioneer of spirit calling, of various shows on the viewing screen where his outgoing presence and vivid public persona made him an instant star. He brought with him a knack of making those around him comfortable. Without a doubt, he is perhaps one of the most famous living men from Canterage, a national treasure whose death will doubtless bring about a period of national mourning."

Opening monologue from Living with Brennan, a documentary about the known life of Canterage celebrity Brennan Frewster.

Nick had heard the stories about this man before. There were so many legends about him, it was almost impossible to tell which were real and which were deliberately seeded falsehoods to improve his own reputation. Not all of them were good, some of them made him out to be the sort of man that you didn't mess about with.

Back when Unisco had been set up around the time of the unification of the five kingdoms, there'd been five initial agents, one from each kingdom who'd been there to set it all up. They'd sworn under oath to be the first of many, to protect and serve in the best interests of the citizens of those kingdoms. Wherever there were those who abused the spirits in their position, used their power to deny the freedoms of those people, Unisco would step in with harsh and swift retribution.

Four of the five were dead. Their names remained in legend, they'd been the best of the best back in the day. Ricardo Laszlo from Serran. Thomas Walker from Premesoir. Yukio Singh from Burykia. Nwankwo Boateng from Vazara. Time had conquered all of them. They'd been in their prime some fifty odd years ago. Nick had seen the statue of them outside the main Unisco offices in Premesoir and Canterage. It was the least they could do. Once the last of them died, he'd be added to the pantheon. Yet he'd stubbornly refused to go quietly into death. Worse than that, he'd refused to quietly retire as well. He'd done just about the opposite, building on his notoriety as a spirit caller to jump screaming into the limelight. He could sing, he could dance, even a few sleight-of-hand tricks that looked incredible if you didn't know that Unisco sometimes taught them in the academies.

That had been Brennan Frewster. One hells of a showman and a personality that you could light up a room with. He'd been the youngest of the five of them, but even now he was well into his nineties and

51

acting like he wasn't a day over fifty. Whenever Nick had seen him on the viewing screens, the energy of the man was something to behold. He'd have bet a lot that he'd been one hells of an agent back in the day. One of the best. Whatever he did, he did with a smile on his face, his teeth strangely prominent with his best salesman smile.

His orders had come in. He wasn't going back into planning and overseeing operations any time soon. Not without supervision. The reprimand had been polite but pointed. They blamed him for what happened to that assault team that had been torn apart. He couldn't hold that against them. He blamed himself. He should have pulled them out. They'd still have been alive if it wasn't for him hesitating. He probably hadn't reacted the best way after either, smashing his earpiece. Especially in front of Ragwort as well.

He felt like he'd been in this position before. Had to have been nearly a year ago now. He'd been on an operation in Serran with Lysa Montgomery and she'd been stabbed by a particularly vile specimen named Bertram Avis. His knife had gone straight through her vest, Nick had shot him and invoked the ire of the senior agent. He'd been suspended, had gone back to Canterage for a while. He didn't want to think too much about the misadventure that had followed in Belderhampton but suffice to say that he'd felt as responsible now as he did then.

His fate would be decided when Brendan King returned from his ill-timed jaunt to Vazara. Privately, Nick felt it had been a mistake for him to run off there with David Wilsin right now, with the way the war was going. King might not even come back. So much for being groomed for a command. It was something he wasn't even sure he wanted, something he was sure had been offered to him as a bone for saving the director's daughter from Harvey Rocastle. That hadn't even been his concern at the time, hence it felt hollow. He'd just wanted to murder Rocastle in as painful a manner as he could. He'd wanted to get his hands around the fat fuck's throat and squeeze and squeeze until he felt the life drain out of him, despite what he'd been telling Steinbru.

Still, it had kept him out of the field for a while and he hadn't realised how much he missed it until he was on the road walking up to Frewster's mansion, leaving his rented speeder at the gates. The man himself had gotten in touch with Unisco, said he wanted to talk to one of their best agents about a sensitive matter. He'd been flattered they'd sent him, at least until he realised that Icardi wanted rid of him for the time being. Davide Icardi had stepped up to fill in for King while he was away, he got the impression that Icardi would be happy if he wasn't around. That suited Nick down to the ground. He didn't like the man, so what if the feeling was mutual? Icardi's opinion meant nothing to him. It was his position that was a problem.

Getting his hands dirty again. That was an ideal situation. For the longest time, he'd mourned Sharon. He'd missed her but now he felt like he was ready to start living his life again. He needed this. He needed to smell the air, especially out here in the Canterage countryside where the mansion had been erected. Somewhere he'd seen a story that Frewster had designed it himself and he could believe it. It looked like a child's imagination of what a house made entirely of candy would look like if it had been magnified times ten. He'd never seen so many pinks and browns together. Some might call it an eyesore, Frewster had named it Withdean, an old Canterage word meaning happiness and contentment. He thought it was charming in a strange sort of way. It didn't so much look like it had been built as thrown together piece by piece over the years, a smaller house made larger by addition and addition over time. Today, it looked like it could house a dozen people easily.

He doubted that Frewster had bought it with what Unisco had paid him over the years. More likely it was what being regarded as a Canterage national treasure got you. He'd been given a special award for services to the kingdom some years earlier. He'd presented everything from spirit calling tournaments to game shows to events letting people showcase their talents that weren't related to spirit calling. The joke used to be, before he'd known the truth about him, he'd do anything for a handful of credits.

The joke still applied. When you considered his Unisco career though, it took on a slightly more sinister complex. The Unisco of then wasn't the Unisco of today. Back when they were starting out, their objectives had covered a wide scope of things the agency wouldn't touch today out of fear of soiling their hands beyond cleansing. There was a much stronger media presence today than there had been back then. All it took was a hint of a rumour about something unsavoury and they were all over it. There was no stopping them. Parasites. Nick had made quite a good living out of being someone in the public eye, it didn't mean that he had to like it.

There'd been too much of that when Sharon had died. Too many people wanting an interview, he'd declined them politely at first. Then he'd ignored them. He still remembered that there'd been one guy and his big bruiser of a cameraman doubled as bodyguard who'd refused to take no for an answer, had followed him for two days straight.

He hadn't done it for three. Nick wasn't proud of what had followed on the night of the second day, but he'd made his point in suitably demonstrative fashion. Brennan Frewster wasn't the only one who knew a few useful sleights of hand tricks. The journalist still didn't know to this day how Nick's wallet had wound up in his pocket. He hadn't been detained for long, but it had done some damage to his reputation. When you've got a previous record for petty theft, it was the sort of thing that hangs around your neck.

Frewster's door was the sort of door that the average millionaire loved, very big and heavy, a big golden knocker in the shape of a lion head. He doubted it was real gold but still found it quite impressive. Probably gold-painted brass. He clutched it in his hand, felt the weight with an appreciative smile. You knew where you were with heavy things. He crooked his arm, pushed it back hard into the door with a satisfying thud-thud-thud.

The buzzer to the left of it kicked into life. "Yes?"

No frivolities, no signs of welcome. Just a question.

"Nicholas Roper, here to see Brennan Frewster by his own request," Nick said. "Said it's a six-six-one-four." Unisco directive. Roughly translated. Agent requires assistance.

"Hold one moment."

He knew it wasn't Frewster speaking. Everyone knew that voice, if you'd grown up in Canterage. Nick always remembered it from the competitive Ruin championships he used to watch. Frewster had been a celebrity player, later hosted the event. You got to know the voice. It always gave the impression that Frewster was slightly befuddled by what was going around him, slightly plummy but nobody could ever accuse him of ignorance. The man had been a Unisco agent. He'd learned the hard way that you didn't go far in the organisation if you didn't have something about you, despite appearances. There'd been a corrupt senior agent a year ago whom he'd believed to be a fool yet had managed to manipulate the events around him almost to getting away with a whole catalogue of crimes.

In the aftermath of the Lucas Hobb and Nigel Carling fiasco, he'd made the decision right there. Never again. No matter what Frewster might say or do to make out that he was just a doddering old man, he wasn't going to buy it. In fact, he'd expect him to lie through his teeth. When you were with Unisco for a good chunk of your life, the habit became a hard one to ignore. Some professions drove you to drink, some to drugs. Working for Unisco, lying became the hardest habit to kick. It seeped into every fibre of your being, made it absolute second nature. To lie was the first instinct, not just to your enemies but to your friends as well. He should know, he'd done it enough himself. He'd spent years lying about what he did to the love of his life and she'd died with him still telling those same lies.

Probably why that brief reunion in Natalia Larsen's bedroom had been so satisfying. There'd been nothing he'd held back. No secrets beyond the trade ones that they were keeping. He'd known what she was. Former inquisitor turned liaison. She knew what he was. Agent of Unisco. Nothing more. Not right now. Very little of the man he'd once been. He didn't like to think of the deaths that could be accredited to him.

What of Frewster? Did he have those same thoughts now he was reaching the end of his life and the end was close for him? Boundless energy and enthusiasm or not, there was no denying that he had to be coming close to the end of a very long life. He doubted Frewster had expected to live for as long as he had. Nick had always privately felt he'd be lucky if he hit forty, never mind ninety. That was part of the attraction he'd had for the thoughts of leaving the agency and living out his life with Sharon. He'd loved her, he'd wanted to spend the rest of his life with her, he wanted that life to be longer than it could be.

He still had her engagement ring in his pocket. Hadn't removed it since the day the coroner had given it him back. He'd bought it at the Belderhampton carnival, shortly before the stall had been blown to hells. That had just been one of those nights everyone had occasionally.

The door opened, he saw the stiffly-stood woman in a high collared shirt, her expression one of quiet aggravation at the change to the days schedule. Years of playing Ruin had left him with the ability to conceal his expression at will. They taught it at the Unisco academy to cadets who had problems with that very act. Nothing helped like the prospect of taking credits from people. She wore a suit that probably cost more than he'd made in the last year from Unisco, almost military in her bearings and she might well have been for all he knew. Her hair might have been blond once, now there were hints of cloud mixing with the sunshine. Nick already had his Unisco ID out to show her, she glanced at it with more interest than she'd shown in Nick himself, studied it for several long seconds before turning her attention back to him.

He'd never seen a female butler before, but it didn't surprise him in the slightest. Frewster was a well-known eccentric, he'd do stuff that nobody else would even think of doing and he'd come out looking a lot better for it. Rumour had it he could throw a pile of credits into a viper nest and come out wearing a delightful pair of snakeskin shoes and a fetching belt.

"Please follow me," she said, her voice as stiff as her posture. Over the intercom, he hadn't been able to tell it as female. Now, he could. Just about. It was the sort of voice that commanded respect and compliance immediately. "The master has deemed your presence acceptable. I will take you to him."

She studied him, gave him a final withering look and then turned on her heels and allowed him to pass. As she turned, he caught a glance of her neck and the hint of old scarring there startled him. He managed to regain his composure before he offered her some grave insult.

"Thank you," he said, bowing his head.

She said nothing, closed the door behind him and looked him up and down again. "Are you armed?" she said.

He was. He considered lying for a moment before realising that this was one circumstance where it probably wouldn't be smart to do so. "Yes. X95 blaster pistol in holster on my left hip." He decided to be more honest than he probably needed to be. "X7 blaster pistol in ankle holster." He hadn't turned the weapon back in. Very few agents had done so. They'd been made to upgrade their primary sidearm but in times like these, a second weapon wasn't a terrible idea. He kept quiet about the knife in his pocket. That might be the sort of trick that saved his life.

"Nobody takes a weapon into the presence of Master Frewster," she said. Again, her voice was neutral but forceful. It wasn't an order, it was a suggestion. It was a suggestion that didn't impress him but a suggestion regardless. "Unisco or not."

"And yet, it's Unisco he asked for," Nick said. He wasn't surrendering his weapon. That was a big no-no as far as the agency was concerned. The only time you give up your weapon is if it is taken from you by force or at by request of a superior agent. You don't give it up to servants who want to throw their authority around. "It's Unisco he wants. And he should know exactly what sort of people they tend to employ."

She inclined her head, not unlike a large bird. Her eyes gave nothing away. It was like trying to stare out a stone statue, just as unreadable in her appearance, her eyes expressionless. "Therefore, if he expects me to give it up before walking into his office, he can wait until they send another agent. Don't expect it to be quickly. Unisco was a bush he burned a long time ago, he doesn't have the damn right to whistle someone up whenever he wants some help." He turned, made to go for the door handle. "I'm sure he'll be pleased at having to…"

"You pass."

She said it without blinking, he felt he did a good job of managing to hide his surprise. Another test? He remembered his previous thoughts about underestimating Frewster. They'd been more apt than he'd thought.

He'd tried small talk as they walked through the mansion, following her at a respectful distance. Talk had never come easily between him and the help, especially not ones that looked to be as loyal as Frewster's butler. She gave the impression that she'd fight to the end to ensure that his wishes were carried out, his privacy prioritised, and his life secured. An interesting scenario. To devote your whole existence to someone, not even someone you loved in the traditional sense, was something he couldn't entirely get his head around.

"Worked here long?" He never liked that, the words sounded hollow in the corridor. The home was a lot less opulent than he'd expected from a man like Frewster. Given the exaggerations of the outside of the house, he'd expected the inside to look like a pauper's wet dream, gold to line the walls and silver across the floors. In that, he'd been sorely disappointed. Frewster's taste in décor extended more to the sentimental than the valuable, the walls covered in various pictures and news reports about what he'd done in the public eye. There were articles about him winning tournaments, meeting royalty, presenting awards as well as accepting them. A life well lived, Nick had to say.

"Long enough," she said. Didn't offer more. He wasn't sure he wanted to go inquiring. Already his mind was wandering about what Frewster might want to see him about, none of the possibilities were good. He'd heard the message that had been recorded when the old man had called the director's office direct. Word had it that Arnholt, back in the office and resuming his duties, had not been impressed. Out of respect though, he'd seen that it had been passed down and down until it had wound up at Nick's feet. He didn't have anyone to pass it along to, he'd had to deal with it. He'd thought about that conversation several times already, anything to avoid dwelling on the painful silence that pervaded the corridor.

"Hello there, my dear. Can you put me through to the director…?" Amicable. Polite. A voice that made sure the listener knew that the speaker had absolutely nothing to hide. They knew that they belonged where they were.

"Can I take your name please?" Arnholt's secretary didn't miss a beat. He'd met Ms Luccisantini before, it was the sort of experience you didn't forget. She looked adorable, at least until you remembered that a lifetime at Unisco had knocked most of the kindness out of her. The favourite office rumour about her was that she'd skinned the flesh from a man's hand after he'd pinched her ass, a rumour never proven.

"Certainly, darling, certainly. Name is Brennan, that's four N's, not in a row, make sure you spell it right, Francis Charles, Frewster. If

you want to do a background search on me, make sure that you…"
Frewster sounded more amused than anything. He'd probably been
through the dance before, knew enough of the processes to make an
educated guess at what would be going on. Anyone who'd been at
Unisco for as long as he had, kept their mind whittled sharp to a point.

"Mr Frewster!" Lola Luccisantini's voice took on an indignant
tone here in the conversation. When her voice rose several octaves, it
was time to worry. *"Background check is not necessary, we all know
who you are. What we do not know is why you feel the need to assume
that your celebrity is enough to gain you direct access to the director of
Unisco. We have proper channels for this, you know."*

*"I'm all too aware of that, my dear lady. I set most of them up
after all. Now, what was the code I believe I'm supposed to give you…
You'll have to forgive an old man, especially one whose memory isn't
what it once was… Six-six-one-four."* Agent requesting assistance. That
had been one of the first directives they learned, never forgotten, never
taken out of fashion. There was a reason for that. Unisco or not,
sometimes someone needed some help.

"Mister Frewster, I'll put you through." Luccisantini wasn't
hesitating now, Nick could imagine her moving into action to ensure
that the call was put through quickly. Sometimes everyone needed
reminding of their history, even if forgetting who Frewster was and
what he'd done for Unisco was close to a cardinal sin. A brief pause as
the call was put through before he heard the mildly surprised voice of
Terrence Arnholt.

"This is Director Arnholt. Hello Brennan." Again, polite.
Amicable. Not even close to being mistaken for friendly.

*"Heh, heh, heh. Little Terry Arnholt now in the top job, how
about that. Would not have seen that coming twenty years ago."*
Frewster sounded amused. Probably not the best way to go about
getting help, Nick thought. When you had an insider knowledge into
something growing up, he supposed it was easy to comment on what it
had become.

*"Yes well, we all change and sometimes not for the better,
Brennan. We grow, we evolve, I think you'll find."* Cheap shot from the
director but by the same token, one probably deserved. He could give
out the sarcasm just as well as any performing showman.

*"Indeed, you are right, of course. Director. Wise beyond your
years, it would seem."* It sounded like Frewster had decided not to let
him get away with what he was saying.

*"What do you want, Brennan? You left the agency, you said
you'd had enough of what it had brought to your life. I remember that
all too well."* Nick could well sympathise there. He'd had enough of

that himself. Sometimes getting away from Unisco seemed like a great idea not just for your health but your sanity as well. Frewster hadn't done too badly out of the experience.

"We sometimes say things that in the cold light of day we'd like to partly take back." At least there was some hint of apology there in Frewster's voice, even if the words weren't uttered. He gave the impression he knew that the verbal sparring couldn't continue like this. Even if Arnholt's next response sounded like he wasn't entirely finished with the former agent.

"You can't partly take something back, Brennan. Either you take it all back or you own it. There's no standing with your feet in two worlds."

"I'm calling with some vital information and a request for aid. I still have some eyes and ears in places…" That had been it then. The real reason that he'd chosen to call in. He needed help and it had sounded like he didn't know where to turn.

"You're a game show host!" No mistaking the sound of incredulity in Arnholt's voice. Nick couldn't blame him. It sounded like the sort of thing Frewster might have called in thirty years ago. And even then, not to the director of Unisco.

"Which doesn't mean that I forgot everything that I learned. I've forgotten more than most of your agents today will ever know, Director. Believe me on that." Probably just about cryptically mysterious enough to get Arnholt's attention.

"What sort of information?" Now the intrigue was there, the director had found his curiosity to go with it and he could hear the glee in Frewster's voice as he spoke next.

"Ah uh, I'm afraid that's Unisco's favourite word, my friend. Classified. Need to know. You will want it though. They'll go to any length to ensure that I don't share it out. It's a real game changer."

"Brennan go to your nearest Unisco office and…" He could hear the urgency in Arnholt's voice, it was the tone he used when he was about to give an order he expected to be obeyed and quickly.

"I'm going to have to decline there, Director. There's something I need to do first. Something I can't do alone. I'll need help. Specifically, the kind that you're able to have one of your agents provide. You know where I am. I'm sure you'll do the right thing. Ta-ra."

"Damnit Brennan wait!" At that point, the line had gone dead, the recording had cut out before Arnholt could complete his sounds of exasperation. Nick had a feeling they'd been quite explicit.

He would have laughed at the sheer absurdity of it, if it didn't have the potential to reflect badly on him. What was it that Icardi had said to him? An annoyed Frewster had the presence in the media to make things uncomfortable for Unisco, especially given the way the war with the Coppingers was faring currently. Avoidable negative publicity would do them no favours. It might not be fatal, but it would be a wound they could do without. Those were the worst type of wounds in his experience. The type that were self-inflicted due to lack of care.

The order had come. Go see him. Find out what he wants. Assist him. Get what he needs. Four orders made simple. If only the mission was as simple as it sounded. Frewster had six decades of operational knowledge behind him, he knew what he was doing, and on top of that, he had the credits to hire in any help he needed. What he might need Unisco for didn't bear thinking about.

Maybe it was a simple matter, but he didn't want to pay for it. That information he claimed to have for them best be worth it.

"Nice place," he said aloud. He'd been thinking it; didn't realise he'd spoken until the butler gave a look at him. "Not at all what I'd expected." He'd already started to put together a plan of how he'd deal with Frewster when they came face to face and this had thrown him. He'd expected him to be some sort of egotistical arsehole, the taste in his décor didn't point to that. What people surrounded themselves with, it usually said a lot about them in his experience. All the pictures and the articles, they said that he had an ego about him, just that he didn't necessarily place a value on things that other people considered important. Maybe his memory was going, he was an old man after all, and he wanted to remember the past for as long as he could.

"Master Frewster likes to surprise people and challenge their expectations," she said. "He's a remarkable man, one must say."

"I've heard," Nick said. "Is he like he appears on screen?"

She gave him a withering look. By looking at her, he'd apparently crossed some sort of line, but he found it hard to care entirely. He'd faced down worse. The hired help wasn't on the top ten of scary things he'd faced down. Wasn't even in the top ten of things he'd seen this year given he'd faced down Claudia Coppinger and Wim Carson and survived them both. Even on a smaller level, it had barely been twelve months since he'd faced the deadly Lucas Hobb in combat and walked away from it. He was still here. Hobb had been a world class assassin and he wasn't with them any longer.

"Let me get one thing straight with you before you go in there, Roper." Not even the Agent now. He bit his tongue. They'd come to a halt outside a grand-looking door, the inlays gilded and a plaque bearing Frewster's name stamped to the top of it. She jabbed a bony finger at him. "I have a great deal of respect for the master. I've devoted the rest of my days to ensuring he lives out what time he has left in peace. Because he doesn't have long." She leaned her head in close, lowering her voice. He noticed an air of sadness in her eyes. "He's not long for this world. He's an elderly man. His heart isn't what it used to be. He can't last forever, unfortunately. You know what he used to do. Every year he's had has been one blessed with time he might not have had."

He nodded his head. "I understand that."

"You cause him undue distress and you should prepare for the worst. Because you wouldn't be the first Unisco agent to come foul of me. You don't scare me in the slightest."

Nick made a mental note to look up who Frewster's butler had been before she'd come to work for him. He had a feeling that it might make interesting reading. Sounded like she'd led an interesting life, unless she was full of bluster which somehow, he doubted. She didn't give the impression she was a fantasist. Nobody was that scary unless they had the ability to back it up.

"I'm not here to cause him distress," he said. "I'm here to see what he wants. I'm here to help him with it. Nothing more. If everyone leaves happy, I'd consider it a job well done."

She relaxed, just an inch but noticeably. With it, he let himself relax. If she wasn't tense, she wasn't going to be an immediate threat. He got the impression that she'd at least let the meeting go ahead now.

"I'll be happy when you're gone," she said eventually. "I think what he's doing is a mistake. I've offered him that opinion but he's a prideful old man. He thinks he knows best."

"If we all didn't think we knew best," Nick said. "None of us would do anything ever. It's probably not a helpful view but I think it's a necessary one. Self-belief is a marvellous thing."

"Except when it gets you killed," she said. She raised a hand, rapped on the door three times, paused and then twice more. Some sort of code, he wondered. A sign that things were okay? Interesting.

"Enter, dear."

She gripped the handle, twisted and Nick caught his first glimpse of Frewster's inner sanctum as the door swung open. He blinked several times, allowed a few moments to take it all in. He wondered how many people had seen this room over the years. Any sort of wealth that had been devoid of shown in the corridors was present here, all sorts of trinkets and trophies that Frewster had accumulated over the years present here. When he'd had the house in Belderhampton, he'd had a room just like this. The house had had to be gotten rid of. He hadn't wanted to live alone in it, not without Sharon. He'd had all the stuff packed into storage, all the Unisco equipment that had been there sent back to the closest office. Even that had been tainted, it brought back memories of Alvin Noorland, the man who'd designed most of it. He missed Noorland. He'd been a good guy. A little strange, rough around the edges but a good guy regardless. The sort of person you could rely on when things got tough.

Some of the trophies were from competitions that didn't even run any longer, their value alone had to be immense. Back in the day, they had been solid gold, rather than gold plated lead. He almost felt the urge to shield his eyes from their radiance, they'd been polished frequently and recently, judging from the gleam.

"Come in, come in, son," the weary voice said from somewhere about the centre of the room. He dragged his attention away from the contents of the room, focused it on Frewster who'd risen to his feet, one hand resting on a cane and the other on a rather new-looking X7. He wondered how long he'd had it and how he'd come by it. The old man stood by a pair of plush couches in the centre of the room, a fire roaring away at the far wall. He'd smelled the burning the second he'd walked in, the warmth a pleasant respite from the chills outside.

"Mister Frewster," Nick said. He covered the distance, offered him a hand which the old man studied for a moment before inclining his eyes towards his own hands. One with the cane. One with the blaster.

"You'll have to excuse my rudeness, but I'm afraid my hands are rather occupied right now, you see."

He had to smile. He'd heard Frewster say that on a Winterheight special episode of Face Your Ruin some years ago. He'd loved that show, where they made famous spirit callers who hated each other play Ruin against each other for charity. Frewster had been immense on the show, frequently baiting the contestants against each other until the atmosphere had reached a fever pitch. Mistakes were made, errors were ensured, and everyone went home happy bar the loser.

"You could put the blaster down," Nick suggested. "I'm not here to harm you. Unisco sent me. Agent…"

"Nicholas Roper, I know," Frewster said. He gestured with the blaster, Nick glanced around and winced a little at the surveillance feeds he could see on the monitors. Every room of the house by the looks of it. He'd passed most of them on the way here. That was interesting. Frewster was clearly worried about something. "We all have our little eccentricities. Mine is paranoia."

Nick said nothing. Just let him continue.

"You're keeping quiet." Frewster holstered the weapon inside the silken robe he wore above a faded suit, time tearing most of the colour away from the grey. "That's smart." Now he shook Nick's hand, pumping it with a vigour that belied his age. "Not many do that these days. Just hear them talk and talk and talk and they never say anything, they just want to hear what they've got to say and if others hear them, then well that's just a big bonus for everyone." He smiled, reached up and patted Nick's cheek. It was a strangely paternal gesture he wasn't sure he was comfortable with. He tried to recall Frewster's file, particularly his personal life. Widowed twice, five children and eight grandchildren. One hells of a life he'd led.

Frewster glanced behind Nick, nodded to his butler. "You can leave us now, Helga. I'm sure that Agent Roper wishes me no harm. Not yet anyway. He might when he's heard what I have to say, but that aside…" That roguish grin had filled viewing screens for years, Nick recognised it for what it was and had to smile himself. "We have important business to discuss."

Helga bowed her head, strangely submissive at the sound of his words. Nick wondered what had happened to the brusque, threatening attitude, the confident prowl of a cat alone in its own kingdom he'd seen earlier. She slid back out the room, closed the door behind her with a click.

"You'll have to forgive Ms Carlow," Frewster said. "She's a pussycat normally but a tiger when I want her to be."

Nick blinked. Carlow. Why did that name sound familiar to him? Frewster carried on as if he hadn't said anything out of the ordinary, just gestured for him to sit and Nick obliged, sinking down into the couch with relief.

"Nicholas James Roper," Frewster said, giving him his full name, which surprised him. "The hero of Carcaradis Island. I didn't expect them to send their latest celebrity." He let a note of amusement into his voice, Nick tried to brush it off. He'd heard them all before. "I've seen the footage of you running around. Good form, to be sure, but I'd say your efforts at secrecy could be better."

"I think we could all have used more secrecy that day," Nick said, his voice soft in the firelight. "I didn't want to do what I ended up doing that day. I saw people die. Not all of them deserved it either." He thought of Noorland and Fank Aldiss to name but two of the many, the two that had cut the closest to his own life. "We did what we had to. Coppinger wants to play the game by her own rules."

"Can't be having that," Frewster said, a note of sympathy ringing in his voice. "Are you having any luck in finding her?"

"That's classified," Nick said automatically. He shrugged. Might as well tell it like it was, the secrets were open amongst the agency. "You keep track of the news. It's about as accurate as it gets unfortunately. Nothing on Coppinger or Rocastle or Wim Carson or

Jake Costa. Mazoud is out of reach for the time being. Domis Di Carmine hasn't been seen since he murdered Nwakili and there's no guarantee that we could kill him even if he did poke his head out the ground. Any victories we get, they're small. You'll take them when they come but you'd trade the lot of them for the chance to take one of the bigger players off the board."

"Out of a thousand small cuts, even mighty beasts may bleed to death," Frewster said sagely. He inclined his head towards the drink's cabinet. "Do you require a drink? Take your mind off things?"

Nick shook his head, gave the room a slow glance. How much history had been witnessed in here? Frewster had had the house for years, this was his private office. Everything in here was the symbol of another time, one that had long since died and they weren't getting back. Even if Coppinger was killed tomorrow, she'd have achieved her goals to devastating effect.

The kingdoms had changed beyond recognition. Unity would have gone. Removing her might not even remove the threat that she offered. There'd been too many fractions. Nations were gearing up for a war in the first stages of full bloom. Vazara under Mazoud was ready to pick a fight with anyone who stepped up to take the challenge. They might not win, especially if the other four kingdoms united and smacked them down, they wouldn't surrender without blood.

Going back to what they had wasn't even entirely an option when some parts of Serran and Burykia were already talking about whether she was right or not to do what she'd done. They were talking about the merits of it in the Senate.

If those thoughts weren't enough to drive him to drink, he didn't know what would. He had to remain strong though. Rise above it. He'd never been a big drinker, the last thing he wanted to do was get legless in front of Frewster when he was supposed to be being professional. He shook his head again.

"Sorry," he said. "But thanks. Got a speeder waiting outside. On that note…" He was pleased with the way he'd managed to change the subject rapidly. "Mister Frewster…"

"If you'll allow me to call you Nicholas, I'll permit you to call me Brennan." Another toothy grin, another small chuckle and the hint of rose in the cheeks that made Nick want to smile.

"Okay, Brennan. I need to ask you before we descend further into small talk. What do you want with me? What can Unisco do to aid you in your times of trouble?"

Frewster sighed, got to his feet and rose towards the drink's cabinet, poured himself a large measure of firebrandy and shook his head.

"Nicholas, I've lived a long life. I've seen things that ordinary men should never have to see. I've seen the fantastic and the horrific, great beauty and terrific ugliness in a world threatening to break apart for a long time now." He brought back his glass, drained the contents in two large gulps. Nick was privately impressed. Drinking firebrandy like that without choking was an impressive achievement. That stuff could sear the muscle from the throat given the chance.

"I want you to do something for me," he said. "I want you to listen to my story, then I want you to help me. The last request of an old man who isn't long for this world." Frewster glanced at him. "Are you perhaps sure that I can't ask Helga to fix you food, or a drink perhaps? Something to help you relax yourself, make you comfortable."

Nick shook his head again. "No, thank you, but I'd like to hear this if you think it's important, Sir. I don't want any sort of distractions."

"Once I tell it, dear boy, I won't stop. It'll go until the end. A story like no other you'll ever have heard, believe me on that one." Frewster smiled, the sorrow etched on his face. "This story might be the last little bit of entertainment within me."

Nick felt his heart kick with sorrow. He felt bad for the old man. Frewster gave the impression life had given him everything and now the end was approaching, he was embroiled in a great struggle with his own mortality.

"I'm sure you've got plenty of time left yet, Brennan," he said, more out of politeness than sincerity. Now he looked at him closely, he could see how thin Frewster was, how his limbs trembled with the rigours of age, and his eyes appeared red and tired. He'd been weeping, by Nick's guess.

Spectres of the past spared no man.

"You're a good liar," Frewster chuckled, his laughter turning into a cough, a hacking one that he swallowed down with great effort, his face taking on a blue tinge as he beat a withered hand to his chest. His hand shaking, he poured himself another firebrandy and drank it as rapidly as he had the first one. "I almost believed you. But now, you must believe me when I tell you that every word of this following story is true. I swear it on the life of everyone that you and I hold dear."

"Listen up lads and lasses, and make sure that you listen up well, for it's time for you to hear a story. Yes, I'll tell you a tale, a tale of hart and hale, from a book of courage and pluck, for those are the stories here on Frewster's Glories. The words are in my blood, the tales are in my soul, a sum of parts no greater than the whole. A story untold is a crime against culture and tonight, that mystery is unsolved before your very eyes!"

Opening monologue from Brennan Frewster's short lived but highly rated foray into children's entertainment, some twenty years ago.

"In order to tell you the full scope of my tale, (said Frewster) We must first go back a good number of years and I'll thank you not to interrupt me at any point through it. Back to the dawn of the five kingdoms and a particularly painfully memory from my past. We find ourselves, oh, must be forty-five years ago if it's a day now, in a simpler time. Everyone was happier back then. Unification was still fresh in their memories, we remembered when times were harder, and we thought we were going to be better together. We'd succeed as a union or we'd die as a union. The Senate wasn't yet floundering like it is now, they'd ridden out a few tough years governing the collective kingdoms and it felt like they were starting to get their act together. Crime was down. Spirit calling was on the rise, they'd just released the first prototype summoners and it was going to make everything easier. You know, that was the first joint developed project across the five kingdoms, they had scientists from all of them working on it despite language and cultural differences. I remember when they first displayed it, it almost blew my mind. I'd never seen anything like it before, never would again. That was the real turning point in my mind for the kingdoms. Once those things had been created, we'd never go back.

Before that, we could tame the wild beasts, but we couldn't truly claim them. Not into crystals like we do now. That was another genius move, you know. Perhaps even more so than the callers, but it's worth remembering that one cannot function without the other. A fitting metaphor for the kingdoms overall back then. We'd do what we could alone, but we'd always be less so than if we were together. It sounds trite today, I know but that was how we felt back then in the day. Pride in where you came from was pushed back for the good of the whole. It's different now, I've seen it. People don't want to belong to a whole these days, they think being part of a whole weakens you, that it means picking up someone else's slack. They want to consolidate and strengthen what they see around them, not give up what you could potentially have so that those a thousand miles away can be helped. It's an old-fashioned idea. Not necessarily a bad one.

Anyway, I was a younger man then, obviously. Not as jaded as I am now. I remember feeling the same optimism. We happy five had formed Unisco together under the guidance of the new Senate, it sounded a hard task but that doesn't even do it justice. Five agents for five kingdoms, we were each given one and ordered to build from the ground up, we'd recruit who we needed, build what we needed. Nicola Nochi, the first chancellor gave us the task, told us that the funds would be there should we need them. Security was always going to be the priority. When you have built it, you need to be able to defend it. An organisation that cannot protect itself cannot protect others. That has often been the sad way of life going back as far as history tells us. The moment something becomes weak, the end is all but assured. It's an undeniable pattern throughout, a constant in constants. Though it may survive, change is all but inevitable and change is another part of death.

We'd started with those that we trusted, people from not just the intelligence community who we'd worked with before, but those from our personal lives. Nwankwo put all but one of his family in civilian positions, set them about building the infrastructure of Unisco in Vazara. He always said that trust was a fleeting thing and even with family, it was a line of credit that would only extend so far. Most of them he trusted, they'd not done anything to deny that trust, so he returned the favour to them. Most of us tried to keep our family lives separate from what we had. That's been a tradition we kept up ever since, as you're probably aware. We stand apart. I wanted that to be the Unisco motto, but it never stuck. People thought that it gave the wrong impression about what we hoped to achieve. You can never be part of the solution when you make people think that you're too far disconnected to the problem. They accuse you of lacking perspective.

I think that's the one thing that Unisco has never lacked, if I'm honest. Sometimes I think the opposite is true. Too much perspective. We try to keep an eye on everything. We watch every little event where we can, just so that we can try to pre-empt whatever problem comes our way. We're scared to fail so we make unreasonable goals for success. We don't want to be blamed for what we could not possibly have prevented. Back then, perhaps it was easier. People didn't know what to expect from us. We were originally designed to keep the kingdoms safe, to supplement local police forces with highly trained and heavily armed response teams. Later we were given the responsibility of investigating and stopping those who misused spirits outside of the legalised competitions that were springing up around the kingdoms. You see why I think the introduction of the summoners changed things? Didn't necessarily mean it was for the better. Whenever the chance emerges, there's always the potential for someone to misuse it. And misuse became rife at the start, especially until we were given the mandate to deal with things. With the ghosts out of the bottle, we had to work fast. Maybe things were a little heavy-handed at the start. We did things that we wouldn't possibly get away with today.

Anyway, for me, I was set to work in Canterage, I had to build the Unisco departments up here. It was a massive challenge, I must say, perhaps the greatest I ever faced in my long life. There's been plenty but none like this. I was nominally the most prominent figure, but I quickly decided I didn't want that responsibility for longer than I had to. I didn't want to do it forever. I've seen how jobs like that wear people into the ground. Have you seen how bad Terry Arnholt looks since he got the job? I know it's a difficult circumstance, but he looks almost in his sixties these days. Divines alone know what the role would have done to Brendan, he'd probably be in his grave right now. I wanted to build it, but I wanted to have a life apart when the job was done. I suspect you know the feeling, Nicholas.

Ric Lazlo and Tom Walker, they wanted to be the main men, you know? They wanted to build a Unisco legacy with them at the top for a long time. It didn't work out that way, I remember when Tom was killed in the line of duty. Five became four. That's the unfortunate way of life. People come, and they go, then different ones step up. The problem with the way those two ran things, I had questions about the people they were choosing. Solid but unspectacular is probably the polite way to say it. I said it then, I'll say it now. It doesn't change anything these days. People who could make their results better, all while not necessarily challenging them in their lofty position.

Me? I just wanted the best people. The best I knew. I told them to talk to the best they knew. Best but trustworthy. I told them it all straight. I told them I wanted the organisation in Canterage to be the best it could be, I wanted it built to last. I told them that no doubt some of them might want my job one day. I was willing to step down once it was all built and there was some stability. I valued my family and my sanity above all else back then. Staying with Unisco would have damaged them both long-term. I didn't want that. Impress me while you're here and you'll have a chance to push for my job when I leave. If you want it, it's yours to take. I didn't want any sort of rivalries beyond the sort that encouraged everyone to be the best they could be.

Maybe I was a touch naïve, but I believed back then that it would work. If I want one thing written on my head stone, it's that I always tried to do what I felt was right at the time. Nothing more. Nothing less.

Personally though, I was in a bad place at the time. My first marriage had failed, I'd been caught unaware by her walking out on me. I didn't realise how bad it was at the time. Only looking back can we get perspective. I'd been spending most of my spare waking hours every day trying to get Unisco off the ground and well, once I'd gotten the Canterage division up and running, I also had a wife who didn't want to see me anymore and a son she was doing her damnedest to try and turn against me. She didn't quite succeed but she didn't fail either. That's the biting thing. Indifference is worse than hate, Nicholas, believe me on that.

Then there was my father. He was dying, I knew that. The doctors knew that, but they weren't ready to give up on him until they'd extracted every credit they could out of him and his family. You don't know the number of times I heard that they were close to a breakthrough, that with a little more time and credits they could not just save his life but prolong it for several more years.

Looking back with the blanket of a couple of decades, I'm not ashamed to admit that paying for that treatment over several more years was not an attractive option. He was on life support; his body could barely function without it. Crazenbergs syndrome was killing him by inches, his lungs were taking in oxygen but couldn't process it. You know they call it the long suffocation. He was in and out of hospital a lot, I went to see him as much as I could, but you can imagine it perhaps wasn't as much as I might have wanted to. If I couldn't make time for my wife, you might imagine how difficult it was to do it for my father.

Still, I found that the universe turns on a strange sort of synchronicity. The first time in a month I'd made it to the hospital and I was in quite a good mood for it, even if I do say so myself. I'd even brought him a present, some alcohol-free wine I thought we could share, his meds didn't allow intoxication for him, but I imagined this would be okay. I signed into the hospital as a guest and took the long walk towards his room, a dozen flights of stairs. I didn't have much truck with elevators back then. Stairs were a lot safer and I was young enough that the exertion wasn't going to kill me. I miss those days, Nicholas. I miss them so damn much, believe me on that

I remember that I got to his room, saw the door was shut and the blinds were drawn back. That was telling, I thought. He always liked to see what was going on in the world outside. He was nosey like that, my old man. Always felt other people's business was something he had a divine right to peep in on. Didn't make him popular at times but what can you do? You have to forgive some people their eccentricities, especially when they're related to you.

I stepped closer to the door, I remember I was humming at the time though I don't remember what song, I put my hand up ready to knock for I thought maybe he was being consulted by one of the doctors, when I heard a voice.

"Tell me," the voice said, it did not sound a friendly one in any sense of the word and I stiffened up at the sound of it. My hand went into my jacket for my service weapon. Back in the day, we'd chosen the brand new X1F as our sidearm. I look at some of the blasters you boys and girls get now and I'm impressed. Really. Ours was cutting edge technology back then but they look like antiques now. If that's not a metaphor for life itself, I don't know what is.

"Tell me," he repeated once again, and I heard little gasps and moans coming through the door. "Tell me where your son is."

That hastened me to action, I kicked the door in and stepped through it with my weapon drawn. I saw the ruffian right away, a skinny fellow with the face of a demon. It struck me as horrific at the time, even though I knew it to be a mask. He had my father up against the wall, almost had his bed overturned, his face going blue from lack of oxygen and I lost control.

He tried to fight me at first, sprang at me but I hit him with the butt of my blaster and he went down in a flurry of robes. I felt his hands scrabbling at my boots, it took a kick to the head to dissuade him from that course of action. I wasn't impressed, went to kick him again but I heard the gasp from my father and I stepped over the intruder to get to him. I'd seen father look better, he was clawing at his chest and his face had contorted in agony. I could hear him gulping harder and harder for breath, he was struggling, and I moved to get him connected back up to the machine. Out of bed and disconnected from his apparatus, he wouldn't last long. The long suffocation would be over in seconds, I knew. For all my thoughts about it being a cruel, painful end, I wanted him to hang in there even longer. I didn't want him to die.

I shouted and shouted, told him to hang on, screamed for help but none came. At least not at first. I didn't know why. I didn't know what to do, didn't know how the machine worked, only that it kept him alive. All I could hear was the increasingly desperate gasps for air, the rattle in his windpipe as the life slipped out of him. It was death by millimetres, I'd done everything I could, but it wasn't enough. Not even close

Eventually they came, more doctors and nurses than were needed but they managed to get him back into a stable position, made him comfortable in his bed and got his breathing back to normal. I never saw my father look like that before, there was something I saw in his eyes that I never wanted to see in another human being ever. Resignation. A sense of loss. The urge to keep on living just wasn't there. He didn't care if he lived because he wanted to die.

At the time, I didn't understand. These days I can sympathise. I know how he felt because lately I feel the same way. Waiting for death to take you is torture, Nicholas. Just the feeling of your body failing you, knowing that death's inching closer. He didn't last much longer. He died a few hours later, the shock killed him. He died alone and in pain, filled with terror. Nobody should go like that.

That's not important to the story at this moment. With him getting the best care immediately available to him, my own attention went to man who'd tried to kill him, I flashed my identification to the doctors and they were surprised for Unisco badges were uncommon by that point, but they didn't intervene as I dragged him to his feet and into the room next door. I'd seen it was empty on the way in.

I'm not proud of what happened next, it's not my finest moment, but I was furious, I wasn't thinking and although that isn't an excuse for my actions, I don't regret it. I'd snapped. I couldn't have done anything else. That room was empty, he tried to fight me as I threw him in it, I hit him. Divines know how much I hit him, just punched him and punched him until my knuckles bled. There was a chair in there, I'd put him in it. I think I'd been screaming, I didn't even entirely think I was going to get an answer, I just kept screaming "Why?!" over and over again at him.

I'd have killed him if cooler heads hadn't prevailed. Joseph Butcher, my number two at Unisco, they'd gotten in touch with him moment the screaming had started, and he'd hurried over. He knew what I was like, he knew I had a streak of anger within me that was tough to tame. He wanted to make sure I didn't do something I'd regret, all to make sure Unisco didn't suffer for my moment of anger. Now, I know you've had occasions like that. Everyone does. He managed to talk me down, I came to my senses and saw this bloody, broken mass in the chair in front of me, coughing up blood. I'd never felt so disgusted with myself.

He wanted me, Nicholas. He wanted to know where I was. Again, I wanted to ask why but I had a feeling I knew. Already the list of Unisco enemies was growing with every passing day. If that was to be the way it had to be, then so be it. That meant we were doing our job right if people were out to get us. Although it did bear witness to the fact that we did need means of concealing our identity going forward. The mufflers you use now, they came a lot later.

I was wrong though, you know. He didn't say much more but when I asked him, he mentioned my mother. That was a shock. Of all the words he could have said, those were not even close to the top of the list. My mother was an unremarkable woman and even though I loved her, it's very possible that I was her greatest achievement in a life cut short. Tragically, I might add. It was when I was young. I was heartbroken at the time, naturally. To have it dragged back up like this, it was unsettling, and I wanted to know why she was an issue here.

He mentioned two more words before passing out and I let Joe take him into custody. I wasn't going to get anything else from him. Two sole words, Nicholas. Do you know what they were? Forever and Cycle."

Frewster paused, looked across at Nick and smiled wearily. He got to his feet and strode over to the cabinet, pouring himself another glass of firebrandy. "This stuff is about the best for keeping out the aches and pains, you know. Numbs them until you can't feel anything else."

"I drank a few bottles of it after my fiancé died," Nick said. He remembered those days too well. "It didn't kill the pain. Just made it worse when it came back."

"Forget it, kill it, it's all the same as long as you don't suffer. Nobody wants to suffer unnecessarily. Divines put suffering in this world so that we could live the life we were ultimately capable of. If you got past those obstacles in front of you, you'd be better for it." He swallowed from his glass, made little lip-smacking sounds as he did. "I was very sorry to hear about Ms Arventino, Nicholas. I met her several times and she truly was a remarkable woman. You must hear that a lot."

Nick shrugged. "Not as much these days. People move on. Yesterday's news."

"I heard a rumour Coppinger killed her." There was a hint of question at the end of his sentence and Nick sighed.

"Not personally. That big lummox she has working for her did it, Harvey Rocastle. He was the one who pulled the trigger. More or less admitted it to me."

"I'm surprised he's still breathing."

"He got very lucky," Nick said. "Had I not had mercy on Carcaradis Island, he might very well not be."

"You showed mercy to the man who killed your woman?" Frewster sounded aghast. Nick only remembered the circumstances that had stopped him shooting Rocastle through the head when he'd had the chance. As much as he'd wanted to do it, he'd chosen a different play. He'd live with that choice.

"I didn't do it for him," he said.

Frewster smiled, didn't push the matter further and swallowed another gulp of his drink before sitting down. "Right, where was I?"

"I returned to my father's bedside after Butcher had taken the man away, I could tell his final minutes were approaching. Only then did I feel regret I'd not spent more time with him as he approached death. I took his hand, he felt small and withered and I told him that I was here for him and I wasn't going to move until he passed on.

That said, I did have to know, of course. I had to know why and with the assailant not giving anything away, there had to be a reason for it. I might never get the chance again. If he died, everything he knew died with him and I wanted it to have been for a reason that his end came early. So, I vocalised the question that had been troubling me.

"Father," I said. "Why? Why did he attack you? What did he want with me? And…" I needed to know. "What is the Forever Cycle?"

He could barely speak, remember that, he was in horrible pain and shaken up, I'm not going to insult his memory by doing an impression of his voice. But I remember the look in his eyes and this time it wasn't just that they lacked the will to keep on going. There was genuine terror in them, more than just that which came from a cowardly assault on a dying man.

I always remember my dad as a strong man, a vicious bastard but never to me unless I really deserved it. And oh yes, there were times when I deserved it. They'd probably have described us as hooligans these days. Back then, we were just having a laugh. We'd strike out at those who had more than us, just because. We never went for anyone worse off though. We had standards. That's more than can be said for them today. Some of them will go for anyone and everyone just for something to do. Seeing what I'd seen my father do through his life, that terror haunts me. Has ever since I saw it.

What he could say though, it left an indelible stain on me that no amount of alcohol has ever been able to scrub away. He grabbed at my shirt, pulled me close to him and I could smell the death on him. People say that and usually they're exaggerating but I'm not. I could smell it. I could smell the life leaking out of him.

"Son," he said. "Brennan. Don't chase the Forever Cycle. It will only bring you misery. Knowing who you are and who your mother was, it will hurt you. I never wanted you to know. I found out and it tears me apart every time I look at you." He let his head sink back to the pillow. "You're my son. You're not hers. Blood doesn't make family. She left. She's got no right to you. Don't chase it, son. Please. Vow to me. I'll be gone soon and you're my legacy. Promise me you won't push this any further. If it's the last thing you ever say to me, then swear it."

I couldn't really deny him that, so I had no choice to promise it to him. I didn't want him to die angry at me. I didn't want his last moments to be unnecessarily painful. So, I swore it to him, made a big show of vowing that I wouldn't go looking for trouble. I'd feel guilty after he died, and I went to investigate it regardless but that's not the point."

"Tell me," Nick said. "Your entire story here isn't just that, is it? That you feel bad about lying to your dad on his deathbed."

"My guilt was a fleeting thing," Frewster said. "But I wish I'd listened to him. He was right, you know. What I learned when I chased it down, it didn't bring me happiness. Far from it. I should have listened to him, I'd have had a happier life while doing it. But it is what it is."

Another long draw from his glass, draining the contents. He looked at the bottom of it, a little despondently. Nick got to his feet.

"I'll get you one," he said, moving to take the glass from him. "You look like you could use it."

"I've never told this story before, Nicholas. I've tried to avoid thinking about it for a long time. But these things come around. You can't hide from the past, you just hope that you'll die before it catches up with you. Because at least then you're out of it."

"I toyed with interrogating the man I'd apprehended further when I came back from the hospital, I decided against it for the time being. I didn't trust myself not to lose control again. My father had died at the age of sixty-eight, William Frewster was no more, and I was the patriarch of the name and a family that had long since faded into obscurity. My curiosity had been piqued, amidst all that, I still wanted to know why. Now that he was no longer here, I wanted to know that more than ever.

I knew a man who I had hoped to recruit to Unisco, yet I hadn't moved to do so in the knowledge that he was far happier where he was than wherever I could put him. I believe you know his son, a lad of some fifteen years by then already and I'd had his name up as a potential Unisco recruit. That man's name was Amadeus King and he was an expert on myths and legends, an interest that he passed on to young Brendan. We'd known each other for a long time, he even part-named his son for me, if you'll believe it. I was there when they asked

Gilgarus to bless his birth, I stood for Amadeus during his marriage. Our friendship had remained strong, if a little distant over the months with which Unisco had been formed. It wasn't my only neglect as I've already said but I felt it a justifiable one. It needed to be done.

I arrived at the home of Amadeus where his lovely wife greeted me, oh she did have a nice smile. The sort of smile that lit up a room. Age was being kind to her. Her laughter was like music. They welcomed me into their home and I ate at their table, an old friend coming back into their lives at long last, we ate the most succulent piece of beef I've ever had. Maybe it was the meat. Maybe it was the company. I don't know but we caught up and I felt peaceful, the troubles of the day melting away before my very eyes.

Eventually we retired to the study and I brought up my query to my good friend, pouring out everything that had happened over the course of the day I'd omitted to say over dinner. Amadeus was the sort of man who loved to listen, the rare kind of academic who didn't enjoy the sound of his own voice more than hearing others. He always used to say he'd learnt what he'd learned through his own research, but hearing what others knew that he didn't was worth its weight in gold.

He sat there, absorbed everything that I had to say and then said the one thing that I knew he'd have to say if he considered himself any sort of friend to me. He didn't disappoint me in that respect and for that, he will always have my love and my gratitude.

"Brennan," he said. "Your father told you to leave this well alone. Are you sure you're not going to heed his words, for what is learned cannot be unlearned. It may be a truth that makes you miserable, it may make you want to end your own life. Consider it at least before you ask me to go any further and I will help you if you still want it. If not, I'm willing to forget this conversation ever took place."

His words brought me to a halt, made me think things through in that moment. Their impact was enough to allow me the chance to pause and think on what had happened. Maybe I was traumatised. Maybe. We didn't really go in for that back then, we just tried to get on with it and all hells with the consequences. Maybe I'd seen what I'd seen, and I knew what I knew, and I was looking for an excuse to punish someone. If I'd gotten there a little sooner, maybe I could have prolonged the life of my father even if saving him may have been beyond me.

I'd made a promise to a dying man that I wouldn't investigate something he clearly didn't want me to. I considered that for a long moment. I'd made a promise. I'd always proclaimed my word to be my bond. If I promised something, I'd make attempts to do it. It was okay when it was stuff like swearing revenge, but I'd made an even more important one to someone I cared deeply for. If that wasn't worth something, then I really don't know what is.

You know what my greatest sin always will be, Nicholas? It's not the people who've died by my hand, they had it coming. It's not been some of the truly awful shows I presented, that was for the credits. No, it remains my curiosity. You cannot tell me not to search for the truth and expect me to do it. That is like asking a fish not to swim, a bird not to fly. It cannot be done, with the greatest will in the world, it is to deny a nature that seeks simply to be.

I looked Amadeus in the eye, I put a hand on the shoulder of my oldest friend in the world and I told him that I wanted to know the truth my father would deny me. I told him not to spare any detail about what he might know about the Forever Cycle. If he knew something, I wanted to hear it.

"Brennan," Amadeus said, I could hear the sorrow in his voice. It was then that I realised he did know something, and he was already feeling the heaviness in his heart at having to tell me. Perhaps I should have stopped him, should have guessed that if it was going to cause him as much pain to tell me something that was going to cause even greater hurt to me, it wasn't worth hearing. I am a prisoner to my own curiosity, it is simultaneously my greatest strength and my greatest weakness. It was part of the reason I'd made such an effective agent of Unisco. I believe that the truth is never what it appears to be at first.

"Brennan, if you truly desire it, then I will share it with you, though you must never repeat it to another human being. It is a legend, not a well-known one but one with a great deal of controversy attached to it, for reasons that will become obvious upon hearing it. Because of the nature of it, most respected theologists don't go near it. They don't want the stain of it anywhere near their credentials."

"Stop dancing around the subject, Amadeus," I said to him. "Tell me. I need to know. I want to know why he had to die, and I want to know what it had to do with me." I'd vocalised it now, there was no way he could deny me. I'd made it personal, revealed my interest in it was more than professional.

"I still say this knowledge will bring you despair and more questions than you might ever get the answers to," Amadeus said. He took off his spectacles and studied me with a curious intent. I'd always considered myself good at reading people, it felt strange to be at the other end of the examination. I knew exactly what he was doing. Amadeus always had been a good judge of character. Maybe not the most practical one, but a good one regardless. "But I see you have set your heart upon it. I cannot deny those who seek answers through the questions that people would rather not be asked."

"Now you sound like a theologist, my friend."

"I never wanted that, you know. I think a search where you're certain you already know the answers is pointless. If all you seek is proof, then what you see is always going to be coloured by what you desire. Some people seek to dissect the most natural beauty in things, others set out to just simply adore it. Neither way is right or wrong, it is simply a matter of choice."

I had nothing to say to that. Amadeus' opinions were his own.

"So, the Forever Cycle. As I've said, a controversial one. Not well known for that reason. Even those that do agree on it can't agree on a definitive version. The story starts based on the idea that once upon a time, the Divines were all human. They were humanity plus, they were the ones who had broken out of the mundanity and become exceptional. All of them in an ancient world had become renowned kings and warriors, queens and diplomats. These five kingdoms we inhabit today were largely formed during their era, they were the mould that shaped the clay that became the kingdoms. They came from across all the kingdoms, it is why some of them are worshipped more in some kingdoms than others. Of course, there are anomalies. The Vazarans, for example, are associated with Garvais and Incenderus but they tend to worship Kalqus and Temperus more. Because when you live in a desert, you don't want more earth and sand, but you will want more and more water and better conditions for growing your crops."

I studied Amadeus as he paused for breath. He took a gulp of water. My closest friend had always been a teetotaller and I respected his choice, though even then I enjoyed the firebrandy more than I should.

"Collectively, there have always been twenty-one divines, everyone knows this. We've attempted to categorise them as best we can but that would always be an errand of fools. We acknowledge Gilgarus as their undisputed king and Melarius as his wife and his queen. We acknowledge that they had their twin children, Dainal and Pellysria as well as Gilgarus' bastard daughter with Rochentus Skyrider, Griselle. We accept those five are probably the most powerful, Gilgarus at their peak for he simply must be to keep the rest of them in line. Gilgarus' power dwarfs the other twenty combined, so go some of the tales. A power he rarely used, as the tales go. He abashed shows of force in favour of negotiation and diplomacy. The tales go that even when he was human, those were the way. Of course, there is nobody alive to tell us differently. We just have writings to go on. Writings and images of a past we can't imagine."

At that point, my old friend paused to let it sink in. None of this was something I was unaware of. The stories of the Divines have been long told, we all know them in some form or another, even if we don't believe. I let him continue, for my curiosity had not yet been sated.

"The Forever Cycle is part of a theory that so much power upon the bodies of those that were once human is a strain and eventually, the time scale is disagreed upon for some say it is every century, others every millennium, but these Divines must cast themselves down from their eternal palace for a time to once again become human and siphon off some of that power."

"And how did they do that?" I inquired.

Amadeus smiled at me, shrugged his shoulders in calm ruefulness. "How does anyone pass on something? While they are human, it is their natural state to want to breed. They pass on any excess power they might have. They find a suitable mate, they consummate the relationship and a child is born. A child that for all intents, is human. They will not be immortal left to their own devices. They will live a normal life and die, though it has been said that some of them do inherit gifts from their immortal parent. There have been numerous such accounts of these children doing the spectacular, whether you attribute them to the divine or to their own skill is entirely up to you. It remains difficult to prove definitively and quantifiable, that much has always remained true."

I coughed, couldn't quite keep the sound down. That sounded utterly fantastical and not in a good way. Of course, I didn't entirely believe the stories of the Divines were anything more than just that. They might have been relevant once, but we were coming up to a world where their relevance was waning amongst the enlightened and the intellectually proficient. When you have seen the marvellous technologies and the wonders that science has come to perform, it is hard to place faith in that which you cannot see when there is so much that can be seen to be believed. It was a time when those who believed found their faith swayed, the unifications war had reopened a lot of eyes to the horrors of war always brings and with that horror comes a certain shattering of ideologies long thought to be stable.

"So, what does this have to do with my father?" I asked. More than that, I wanted to add, what does it have to do with me? There was one obvious conclusion, yet the idea was absurd. My mother had not been a Divine. I was not special in any way beyond the achievements I pulled through with my own two hands and my willpower. I was too stubborn to cede any fight, no matter how hopeless it might seem. It had saved my life on too many occasions during the war.

Amadeus looked as if he were arriving with the same conclusions, I saw him studying me with a frightful detachment, almost as if he were afraid suddenly of who I was and what I might do.

78

"There's a test, you know," he eventually said, his voice slow and languidly guarded. "One way of knowing for sure." His words were like daggers in my heart. I knew I couldn't be what he thought I was. It was ridiculous to even contemplate it. That one of my oldest and closest friends either couldn't see it or chose to want to believe it, I found it insulting. "I don't know exactly how, but…"

"Amadeus!" I said, unable to keep the anger out of my voice, it broke through the gap between us like a whip crack and I saw my friend recoil in fear. I wasn't used to seeing that on him where I was concerned. "Amadeus, this is madness, I beg you to rethink on what you say. My mother was not a Divine. I am certain of that. She was an unremarkable woman who, uh… did some waitressing or something before she met my father. I think they met in, uh…"

"You don't know, do you?" Amadeus said. "You know nothing about who she was before she met your father, I'd be willing to bet that he didn't either. That's always the rub with the Divines when they pull this crap. They appear, they have a hastily put together backstory that doesn't bear up when it's really pulled at. The universe folds around them, it doesn't break for them. It doesn't give them a free pass to run roughshod over it."

I opened my mouth, ready to chastise him for his foolishness further. I didn't get the chance, heard the clearing of a strange throat. My hand went to my blaster, I didn't know who'd just made that sound and I wasn't ready to take chances.

I'd never seen him before. Tall. Gaunt-looking. He looked sick, his hair blond and thinning, patchy in places. You ever hear the stories about the night man, Nicholas? That was what he looked like, dressed all in black from shoes to the cloak he wore about him.

Silence reigned through the room as the three of us stared at each other. I didn't know how he'd gotten in. Didn't know how he'd gotten past Amadeus' family. It was hard to sneak up on me, I'd made that a point of pride in my life. If you're never caught unawares, it's harder for someone to slip a knife in your back.

"Who are you?!" Amadeus demanded. "What are you doing in my house?!" He was furious, I couldn't blame him. I could see the angry terror on his face. He was worried for his family. Maureen and Brendan.

"I'm not here for you." His voice was like the whispers of the wind on the leaves, cracked but not broken. "I'm here for him. He is required."

"I'm not available," I immediately said. I wasn't going anywhere with this freak. He looked dangerous but more like a danger to himself than anyone else, you see. I could see it in his eyes, the fires of zealotry. Those people can't be trusted, everything they touch turns to fire.

"Mister Frewster," the stranger whispered. "I do not wish for violence to be exchanged here, I hope we can do this amicably."

"Me too," I said, before I drew my blaster and fired at him. It was perhaps unprovoked but at the same time, felt justifiable. Amadeus would back me up, that there'd been a dangerous intruder and I'd had no choice.

What happened next stayed with me for a long time. You never forget something like that. The blasts never came close to him for I saw something erupt out of his hands, he'd had something in them I'd not noticed before and that something was aflame with orange and blue. He batted my blasts aside with ease, his sword lighting up the room with its malice. I could feel the heat of it from where I stood."

Frewster paused, looked across the room at Nick. "We all saw weapons like that not long ago."

"I've used one," Nick said. "They're called…"

"Kjarnblades, I'm aware. There's more to the story. And we'll continue after some dinner perhaps, Helga makes the most delightful…"

His voice tailed away, Nick had already stopped listening and risen to his feet. They could both hear it. The familiar roar of engines in the distance, large engines, powerful long-distance ships for mass transport. Going to the window was stupid, no matter how curious he might be. He could see just fine from here, could see that a pair of aeroships incoming, they were flying low and heavily armed. One of them turned its rotary cannon down towards the speeder Nick had rented, sent a continuous flurry of blasts into it. Within seconds, it was molten slag, the fuel tank exploding in a radiant orange fireball under the assault.

"They've come," Frewster said. He sounded tired again, drew out his X7 and held it in a shaking hand. He looked like he'd aged years in minutes, the fatigue heavy on his face. "They want me, Nicholas. The cycle stays the same. They want me, they'll kill you and Helga to get to me."

He gave Nick a beseeching look. Nick tried to avoid looking at him. Privately he felt like this whole thing had been one giant setup that had now closed around him.

"Save me," Frewster said simply. He wasn't begging. It was a statement of fact, plain and simple. He had nothing else to say on the matter. "I'll explain all, just get me out of here!"

Son of a bitch, Nick thought. He shook his head in disgust, glanced about the room and then back towards the window. This didn't look good.

"I always find leading requires two things. One hand in their dreams and one hand on their balls. If you can achieve one of those things, you're halfway there. If you can manage both, they're yours for as long as you can keep that balance going."

Claudia Coppinger, speaking at a conference five years ago regarding unconventional management styles.

Claudia found herself restless.

She was these days, there was no denying it. Rather than bring about peace of mind, her journeys had perhaps done the opposite. These days, she was lucky if her head wasn't nearly split asunder by the furious migraines tearing through her brain, snarling at every nerve-ending, every synapse. Pure, unfiltered agony.

That was the price, she had to tell herself over and over. This is what it means to be no longer entirely human. You wanted to be something more and here you are. Brilliance does not come for free, there is always a cost to achieving what you set out to. This is your price for the moment. Pain. Constant pain. Unrelenting but ultimately endurable.

She would endure. She had no choice. To come this far and give up, it was anathema to her. She couldn't contemplate it. Giving up was not in her vocabulary. She'd never quit anything worthwhile in life up to this point and starting here would be the end. The humiliation alone might well kill her.

Her wrist ached. Had ever since she'd taken that trip into the first chamber. She could only remember bits of that trip, her mind foggy and useless when she tried to recall the exact details. She'd suspected that was for her own good, what little she could remember had been too fantastical to even try to explain to anyone who'd never experienced it. Human minds would struggle to comprehend it. Her mind was no longer human, it was something new and alien, hence the pain it seemed determined to inflict upon her.

She'd tried medication. She'd tried them all, sometimes mixing them together in an attempt to enhance their effect. Even that hadn't done a whole lot of good. Hota had examined her thoroughly, she'd insisted on it and he'd come up blank. Insisted in that awful lisping accent of his, that there was no medical reason why she should be suffering so. He'd been shocked when he'd seen her wrist. It always surprised her, no matter how much she should have gotten used to it by now. If the sight didn't surprise her, the pain did.

What didn't help was the knowledge that she could end it all if she wanted. All she had to do was yank it away. Of course, it would kill her. It was keeping her alive, she'd heard, and she had no reason to doubt. A second heart, a surrogate heart beating in time with her own. If she stared down at it long enough, she imagined she could see it beating, could see it twitch and pulse, pushing divine power around a body not strong enough to contain it. Part of her knew the name it beat to, the rest of her didn't want to acknowledge it.

Gil-Garus. Gil-Garus. Gil-Garus. Every beat, she could hear the thump of that name at the deepest core of her being. The Heart was a myth she'd chosen to believe in. More fool her for now it hung in her wrist, a part of her but its deepest mysteries remained unfamiliar. It wasn't giving them up any time soon.

Divinity. Desired but still denied to her. In the truest aspect of the world, she'd quickly found it wasn't all that had been expected. As wondrous as the Chamber of Fate, had been, her memories foggy and blurred of it, there had still been an element of smoke and mirrors about it. Like it was just a façade, a trick that would come tumbling down if the illusion was probed too heavily. She didn't want to pry. Better not to have her dreams shattered. Because the figure had been real. The figure in the cloak, cast in shadows but with a voice that shook her to her core.

She'd never forget that terrible voice for as long as she lived. That was a number of years by no means guaranteed to be a high one. Life had a way of surprising you. This whole situation was testament to that.

Claudia looked around the table, considered the figures that were looking to her for leadership. Not all of them were here in person, some of them all had places to be where they were more valuable. Only the ones she wanted to keep close remained aboard her command ship. Some, like Alaxaphal, were too valued to be left wandering free. Others, like Rocastle, she did not trust at all. She wanted them where she could keep watch on them. Rocastle had proven himself to be useful, it was the sole reason he was still here but there were still elements of his character that she could not rely on. His obsessions, for one. It was the reason she'd taken his leg when the opportunity had arisen, the limb shattered in a fight with Nicholas Roper. He was still acclimatising to the prosthetic, a top-end product but still no substitute for the real one by any means. She wondered if he knew about the transmitter inside. For as long as he wore that leg, she'd be able to locate him anywhere in the kingdoms. Not that he'd left the ship for months.

Since his humiliation and his mutilation, he'd been subdued. Content just to focus on his duties of training the young men and women he'd started to dub 'his Angels of Death'. She hated that name. It was far too melodramatically over the top. Just like Rocastle himself. Some of the worst aspects of his personality had been sanded away in the last months but she still didn't doubt him exceptionally vicious when the mood took him.

Domis was here as well, the one man she could trust beyond all doubt. A man whom she loved like a son, kept smiling inwardly as she studied him. He didn't sit, just stood behind her. Her bodyguard. Anyone wanted to get her, he'd rip their limbs off. He was capable of it, a physical miracle that nobody had ever been able to explain to her. His strength was beyond match, his metabolic ability off the charts. No wound could keep him down for long. She'd seen the footage of his fight with Nwakili, the crafty old bastard had nearly put him down, but nearly hadn't been enough. Quite crucially, Nwakili was no longer with them.

She cleared her throat, tried to avoid thinking of the hooded figure. That voice still echoed around her head, recalled with very little effort. It had all the subtlety of an air-siren and was just as loud.

CLAUDIA COPPINGER, it had said. She hadn't been sure of the gender. Maybe deep feminine or very high male. It wasn't dissimilar to the way Rocastle spoke sometimes with that creepy lilt to his voice. A mysterious all-powerful version of Rocastle. That didn't bear thinking about.

It didn't do to dwell too much on it now. The time would come when she had to face the figure again. This time, she would do it on a much more even footing. She would not be content with trinkets like the one that burned at her wrist.

"We have gathered here today," she said. "To discuss our progress. Because that is our aim, is it not? Progress. We have a set of kingdoms that have stagnated, atrophied even if you like, into something so much less than they could be. Once they were great. Now, what has the Senate done for them in recent years? Bickered and squabbled at the expense of the greater good. That was what I set out to do. Tear all that away. For years I worked in secret to ensure that when the moment came, I was ready.

She studied the faces again. Rocastle. Alaxaphal. Domis. Hota. Jake Costa, Alana Fuller and Dale Sinkins. Those present she couldn't afford to lose. The ship was currently on a course, none of them whom would be accompanying her. Except Domis, of course. He would walk wherever she walked. The only problem she had was that there was only one of him. All efforts to examine his genes and see what made him what he was had come to naught. The closest effort had been the Apex project, an approximate success but not entirely a desired result. They had an almost indestructible warrior, albeit one that could only be controlled partially. That was the name of progress, they were further along than they were yesterday and tomorrow they'd be further than they were today.

Maybe Sinkins as well. He was no Jeremiah Blut, but he was competent enough and she might need an opinion that only he on the ship was qualified to provide to her.

Present in holographic form were a reluctant-looking Wim Carson, her own personal Vedo and currently chasing something ill-defined in Serran, the new Premier of Vazara, Phillipe Mazoud with a suitably deferential look on his face and Subtractor. That was the name he'd given himself recently and he was a new presence at these meetings, her own personal mole high in the command of Unisco. He'd belonged to her for a long time, ever since she'd started this venture and he'd been willing to partner with her for a cut of the profits. She'd not done it for the credits, there was little financial gain in being a deity, but others were less motivated by doing good and rather by lining their pockets with credits. She respected it, in a way. At least he wasn't simply paying blind lip-service to what she was preaching. He was willing to call her out on what she said when he didn't agree with it, never in public for he wouldn't undermine her precious authority in that way, but his private opinion was something she valued. He was secure in doing that. He was the hardest one to replace, not impossible but difficult enough for her not to want to unless it was necessary.

He hadn't warned her about her treacherous brother though. That irked her. Collison or whatever he was calling himself these days under his new identity, he could have ruined everything. She'd sought to give him a place at her side, ideally her daughter would have stood there as well, the last three in the kingdoms to bear the Coppinger blood. It was difficult to get what you desired. Meredith was an ungrateful little bitch, their meeting before her wedding had proved that. If she was honest, it was no great loss. She should have terminated her before she was born, as horrific as it might have sounded. The presence of a child into a busy life would always lead to complications, how many and how quickly had been something she'd been unable to anticipate.

In short, although the moments of joy and affection had been there, they'd been fewer the longer time had gone by. Recent years had been a battle for supremacy, one she had no intention of losing. A spoilt teenager become sulky young woman couldn't hope to outmatch her.

She'd crushed better opponents than her daughter long before she'd turned her thoughts to divinity.

YOU! YOU HAVE COME TO SEEK WHAT ONCE WAS LOST TO ALL OF MORTAL MANKIND!

She shuddered. The voice rang through her ears, a booming echo that made her flinch. Domis put a hand on her shoulder, his concern touching. Rocastle blew on his nails. Mazoud kept his face impassive but she knew those eyes were searching for any sign of weakness in her. Weakness was abhorrent. She would not show it, not to her biggest supporters. These people all had their part to play in delivering the kingdoms to her and she had to keep them not just in awe of her but fearing her as well. The moment one of them stepped above their station, she'd smack them down.

"We're going to go around the room, you're going to enlighten the rest of us with how your project is going. We all have tasks after all. Left to right, from me. Mister Costa?"

Jake Costa, short of stature with his dark hair thick with grease, cleared his throat. He didn't stand up. Not that it would have made too much of a difference. Since she'd moved Rocastle to training, Costa was working the recruitment side of things. He was a natural organiser, he'd overseen many of the building projects she'd undertaken in the early days. He'd organised the building of her airborne base, it was a project that he'd live or die by and he'd absolutely thrived with the responsibility. He'd finished ahead of schedule and his rewards had been great. She could trust him more than most, of that she was certain. Trust was earned. That he'd done.

WHAT YOU SEEK WAS LOST FOR A REASON!

"I've put together a network," he said. "I think the previous organiser of this role…" He didn't look at Rocastle as he said it. She didn't like that the decision to make the change had been forced upon her. Rocastle couldn't be trusted to wander free these days. He'd used up all his chances in that respect. Once he gotten out from underneath her, where he thought she couldn't get him, he'd become too predictable in his unpredictability. He'd go do something stupid, it was just a trouble to work out what. It might well involve his biggest pet grudge but equally it might not. She couldn't keep someone on him day and night to make sure he toed the line.

"… Had the right idea in approaching those with a grudge against the current order. These people are the ones most easily persuaded to throw aside any lingering loyalties they may have had and take up a new cause. We know what you are selling, Mistress, nothing less than revolution and there will always be those eager to take a part in it. My network is building steam, I did my research and used the model they used to create Unisco. Irony, I think you'll find, is a beautiful thing sometimes."

She did agree with the irony, much as she'd never admit it, instead let him continue speaking.

"It started with me. I looked at the kingdoms we don't have a controlling interest in…" Mazoud bared his teeth at the comment, Costa either didn't notice or didn't care. "… I looked to Serran and Burykia, Canterage and Premesoir. I picked four names that I could trust, one for each kingdom. I explained what I wanted from them, what I was looking for and then I sent them off into the world. They were to spread their influence, they were to find people they could trust and implant them into each major city across the kingdoms, like a pyramid. If we can get enough people sympathetic to our cause, it will make the difference when it comes to taking the kingdoms with military might."

RETAKING IT FOR YOURSELF WILL TAKE YOU DOWN A PATH YOU WILL NOT EASILY BE ABLE TO BREAK FROM!

Another pause, he wetted his lips with his tongue. Underneath her clothes, she was sweating. Those memories felt all too vivid. "As for direct recruits, I ask them to keep the names of some of them aside, those that they think hold the most promise. Some can go into our private armies, some into Mister Rocastle's specialist forces, some into key positions we don't want to trust to clones."

A casual comment but one with spite running deep within it. She knew that some of her people thought that way. It wasn't much of a secret, they had their grudges. They'd worked for her and then along came the clones. That they were to be used mainly as cannon fodder and expendables was something that hadn't truly ever occurred to them. She'd overrun her opponents if it came to it, swarm them with body after body until they could fight no more. An inelegant way to win a battle but effectively simple. Alaxaphal had assured her that any victory was a good one.

YOU THINK THIS WILL BE EASY, A SIMPLE THING. SOMETHING THAT COULD BE DONE BY A CHILD. YOU. KNOW. NOTHING!

"Very good, Mister Costa," she said, keeping her face straight. The voice wasn't present. Only her memories of it. Those memories couldn't hurt her. Not if she stayed focused on the tasks at hand. That train of thought she'd been on took her nicely to the next speaker. "Grand Marshall Alaxaphal?"

Bernd Alaxaphal got to his feet with a smile and a swagger, his hands twitched at his sides, she could see he was trying to shake off the impulse of too many years of military service. He wanted to salute her, the way any serviceman would salute their commander-in-chief. His career had ended in ignominy, not the way that a true hero should be permitted to go out after years of dedicated service. Subtractor had pointed him out to her. The man had good instincts, she had to admit. Overtures to Alaxaphal had been made. He'd been drummed out of the Serranian military, had been acknowledged as a fine tactical mind. He'd never seen eye-to-eye with his superiors, Subtractor had told them. There'd been some incidences regarding the early skirmishes with her forces. Alaxaphal had wanted to do one thing, his superiors had demanded entirely another. He'd done his own thing, a risky move that had failed to pay off and hundreds of Serranian armed forces servicemen had been wiped out. It was the conflict that had led to the single greatest loss of life in her civil war so far.

Strange really that Alaxaphal should wind up on her side then. He'd been willing, she'd seen the bitterness in him. He'd jumped at the chance of taking charge of an entire army, the one man responsible for overseeing everything. She wanted a figurehead who could do the job and one battle in which he'd made bad choices should not tar him for life. Part of her wondered if the disagreement with his superiors had rattled him, forced him into decisions he might not normally have made. She'd promised him complete autonomy, only that he reported to her at times like this with progress.

"Thanks to the help of Premier Mazoud's forces in Vazara, that kingdom has been pacified," Alaxaphal said. With his iron grey hair and moustache, he held the perfect poise of authority that she wanted. When he stood up straight, you might never have guessed at the limp he carried when moving, the souvenir of an old battle he'd never had fixed. "There may be some stray pockets of resistance, but we are in control. One of the kingdoms is ours. I am currently in the process of formulating attack plans to take the other four. Based on proximity to Vazara, I suggest trying to annex Serran next. We have a solid platform from which to build, as well as a plentiful supply of reinforcements from Premier Mazoud's troops."

"I'm not removing my men from their positions to back up your invasion of Serran," Mazoud's hologram piped up. Claudia stiffened at that. "I need the Suns where they are. You mention these pockets of resistance but they're more than that. If my military presence is removed, I could end up with a full-scale rebellion and I don't need that right now. I'm in favour of invading Serran, they're the worst sort of offenders against my kingdom, but you surely have enough…"

"Phillipe, you'll do what you're told," she said. Divines, she'd enjoyed seeing the way the look went off his face as if she'd strode up to him and slapped him. "If we need your troops to take Serran, you'll move them to Serran. In the meantime, if you do have a problem with a rebellion, then you crush them like insects. If you're incapable, I'm sure we can find someone who isn't."

"Mistress," Mazoud said pointedly. She could hear the indignation in his voice. "It is not as simple as you think. These people are rats, they scurry into their bolt holes and their safe dens. It is a case of finding them before we can crush them."

SIMPLICITY IS GOING TO BE DENIED TO YOU. YOUR PATH IS A LONG ONE. ONE THAT WILL MAKE YOU OR BREAK YOU.

"You knew this could happen," she said, velvet creeping into her voice. "You said as much to me before when we discussed this. And what was it you also said to me? Don't worry, I can handle it. You've been in the job for a few weeks, Phillipe, you made me a promise and I suggest you handle it. It would be disastrous for the stability of your kingdom if you were to be removed from power already."

"I took this kingdom by right!" Mazoud snarled. "It is mine and…"

"And if you wish for it to remain that way, you won't try and dictate terms to me," she said. "Better men than you have tried. Men who had the right to think they could make the attempt. Remember your place, you're nothing but a mercenary who I raised above his station. I made you Premier. I can take it away again if I wish." He looked furious but held his tongue. She relaxed her scowl, let her lips curl into the alien gesture of a smile. Her teeth itched but iron wrapped in velvet made more of an impact than one or the other. "I don't want to. I think we can go on to do great things together, Phillipe. All of us are here because you chose to believe in what I promised you that we could do. I do not have any desire for the invasion of Serran to start any time soon. Too many more pieces have to fall in place. None of you will move to attack without my express permission."

She felt the twinge in her wrist, confirming her suspicions. They did believe. Some of them believed in her now more than ever. More of them feared her but fear was just another form of worship. Fear had a different taste to love, a taste so much more expressive. Fear and love, two sides of the same credit. Either way, they'd surrendered a part of themselves to her whim.

YOU HAVE MUCH CONFLICT IN YOUR HEART. A DESIRE TO DO WHAT YOU BELIEVE IS RIGHT.

"Since you seem so eager to talk, Phillipe," she said. "Tell me of your progress in Vazara, other than your latent inability to crush these rebels you talk about." Privately she doubted his words. Talk of rebellion felt like an excuse for failure.

Mazoud looked a little more mollified by her words, puffed his chest out like a majestic pigeon and cleared his throat. It sounded like a speeder choking smog out of its own emission pipe. She hid her disgust. "Since I took the throne, there have been constant attacks out in the outskirts, Nwakili supporters all of them, we believe. They don't like the way I became ruler. They said it was unlawful. These people are weak. They want to hide behind words rather than actions. They forget the old ways that Vazara practiced for years. We elect our leaders through blood. Not paper."

And how did that ultimately work out for you, she wanted to ask him. She'd savaged his ego enough for today. Pricking it further might lead to him wilfully disobeying her, taking his own initiative and that could be fatal. Vazara had always been a piss-hole of a kingdom, full of those with nothing being dictated to by those that had snatched everything. When you had everything, it tended to blind you to what mattered. Not her though. She knew what mattered. She would never have gotten this far without her fortune. It hadn't been a fortune when she'd acquired it though, oh no, building it up had been all her. It had been split between her and her brother after her parent's death, Collison had given it away and she'd been furious with him when he'd walked out of her life.

YOUR BELIEF WILL COST YOU MANY THINGS. YET WHAT MUST NEVER FAIL IS YOUR CONVICTION.

Mazoud continued, oblivious to her silent musings. "… Have since sought to educate more, I've passed a bill through the warlord council to see that a dozen new schools are built in each major city within two years. I've put someone ensuring that the Vazaran Suns are the premier enforcement organisation across the kingdom, splitting the organisation into branches, one domestically, one paramilitarily, one covertly, etc. We will need a mass of new recruits, specialists in chosen fields, I hope to create something that can serve as a counter to the Unisco model."

Subtractor laughed at that. "You don't have a hope, Mazoud." She saw him bristle at that. He didn't like being referred to solely by his last name. He'd had bad experiences with authority figures who did that. It was thankful for all involved that neither of them was physically present. "Dozens have tried to copy the Unisco model. It was set up in a different time by five remarkable individuals through willpower alone, it has adapted to still be relevant today. To be accepted, Unisco had to endure, to change where change was due. The model of fifty years ago wouldn't work today, today's model didn't just spring up overnight. It's fifty years of building and adaptability. You can't hope to replicate that in months."

YOUR CONVICTION WILL REND YOUR PATH
SMOOTHER. IF YOU DO NOT BELIEVE, THEN YOU WILL NOT
REACH YOUR DESTINATION.

"Says the traitor," Mazoud hissed. "You know what we do to traitors in Vazara?"

"The same as anywhere else," Subtractor said, his voice flippant with a lack of concern. "Death, I imagine? Am I close? Disgrace? Oh, that's a good one. Hmmm, how about stripping of all assets and personal property? I think you don't even need to be a traitor for that to happen in Vazara these days, if I'm correct? Am I right, anyone want to tell me otherwise? Still, all in progress, eh Premier?"

"It sounds…" she interjected. "… like you are doing something, at least, Phillipe. The same cannot be said for the majority of politicians these days. All they wish it to bicker and squabble, line their pockets. Those that do wish to do good are swallowed up amidst a cradle of corruption and venal self-interest. Your predecessor set out to do good things and what did he ultimately accomplish that will be remembered with any sort of fondness?"

"It is a challenge that I could not turn down," Mazoud said, not a hint of pride in his voice though she could tell he was bursting to let it out. She had the measure of the man and what his ego desired was recognition more than anything else. "If history remembers me as an illegitimate ruler, I care not one jot. If it remembers me as a great leader, then I have done my job. I have done my duty towards every true Vazaran, the ones who came back when I ordered them to. Any who remained nestled behind the lines of our enemies will be treated as pariahs when we take the kingdoms."

A DESTINATION AWAITS YOU. ONE OF PARADISE,
ONE OF DESPAIR. STEP TRUE FOR ONLY ONE IS YOUR
LEGACY.

It's we now, is it? After you initially refused to help with the invasion of Serran when it was put to you. She couldn't help but let the small smile spread across her lips at that realisation. Mazoud could be quite selective when he chose to be. He wanted the glory but none of the effort. He'd spent a lifetime using his mouth instead of his hands, he'd managed to manipulate the Suns into making him their leader, but she wasn't falling for it. He had his place and she meant to keep him in it.

"Mister Rocastle," she said. She'd heard enough from Mazoud for the time being. "Report."

Harvey Rocastle got to his feet uneasily, he didn't hold himself with the same swagger as he had before, she noted with private amusement. Losing a leg could do that to a man. He didn't have the same edge he'd possessed before, though she doubted it had left him completely. The hunk of metal perched out the end of his stump left him looking unbalanced, a tree swaying in the wind but never quite falling. He hadn't gotten used to it yet. Sometimes she imagined him confined to his quarters and weeping. He was the sort who would resort to that. He liked to think he was big and tough, but he was like glass. He'd shatter under pressure. He'd really let himself go, she saw, the disgust curling at her like smoke. He'd always been on the heavy side since she'd known him, now the buttons on his shirt were straining to contain him, sweat thick across his collar. It wasn't a warm room, but he looked like he was suffering.

EITHER PATH WILL TRIAL YOU COMPLETELY. SHAPE YOU ANEW. LEAD YOU TO YOUR TRUTH.

Discretely, she slipped her hand below the desk and fiddled with the room controls. She didn't have to look, her fingers found the appropriate knob and she twisted it two notches, three notches, four. The temperature was going to rise shortly, she enjoyed seeing him in discomfort. More than that, she wanted to see how he reacted under pressure. Maybe the lessons she'd bestowed on him had helped mould him into something better. The heat didn't bother her.

"Well, Mistress," he said. Always that simpering tone that made her want to slap him, offence to her ears that couldn't be blotted out. "My angels are proving their worth, I think you'll find. Already we have despatched them on several successful missions, I have to say. They're currently out in the field as we speak, at your request we deal with the old man." Another way in which Subtractor had come through for her, he'd pointed out Frewster as a person of interest based on some old documents he'd turned up. "Our numbers are at an all-time high. We have seventeen currently ready for active duty at any one time, we must presume that dear Reda is lost to us…"

"He's still alive," Subtractor said. "Though I cannot help you with that. He is the current property of Criffen. Wherever Criffen goes, Ulikku ultimately goes as well. Though how much anything they can pull off Ulikku is worth these days, I don't know."

"Yes, well…" Rocastle sounded annoyed, a hint of petulance in his voice at the interruption.

"You're welcome. I moved swiftly," Subtractor said. "You'd have lost a lab if not for my efforts. I managed to get into position, take one of the Ista Neroux and wipe out the team. They think it was a trap and they got caught up in it. They're not going to quickly trust anything Ulikku says again."

THE TRUTH AWAITS YOU. IT MAY NOT BE THE TRUTH YOU SEEK BUT A TRUTH REGARDLESS.

She tried to hide the hint of pride in the very centre of her being. Her faith in Subtractor was growing by the second. She hadn't sanctioned his mission, nor his use of the Ista Neroux. They were specialised spirits, the very best, the most powerful in all the kingdoms. They'd been engineered to be the strongest. Two had already been lost, one to Nicholas Roper in the Unialiv, a being that was supposed to all the Unisco invaders when they'd invaded her most personal sanctuary. The Sabuyak had been lost for months, at least until she'd recently seen it at the Quin-C final. It had always been regarded as the runt of the litter, one scheduled for termination. Currently in the care of a noted spirit caller, she'd made the choice to leave it there, curious if he could coax the best out of it.

"This was a defeat that cost them," Subtractor continued. "I took the Lazaridis and wiped them out." She approved. The golden-green serpent was a beast she took exceptional pride in. The camouflage alone was worth every effort they'd put into developing it. When it held still, it was almost undetectable by human senses. Add in the impervious skin and the poisonous jaws, she could almost pity the Unisco team. "One of their best teams and they're gone in a flash of blood. Nicholas Roper took a hell of a can for that. He's not going to be a problem for the time being. They want him out the way."

He looked over at Mazoud. "Incidentally, do you know a Unisco team entered Vazara recently to investigate your new-found fauna?"

Mazoud snorted. "Preposterous. I would know. Immigration checks are one of my top priorities. Anyone entered announcing themselves as Unisco agents would have been turned away at the border. And besides, what business do they have in examining a phenomenon like that?"

"Excuse me?!" Rocastle said. Again, that delicious petulance. "I believe I had the floor."

THE TRUTH OF ALL THINGS WILL COME TO YOU. LIFE. DEATH. GOOD. EVIL. THESE ARE JUST WORDS.

"Continue," she said, not letting her face betray any emotion as she glanced at him. "You did indeed. Do not interrupt the man until after he has finished enlightening us."

"You don't have to be like that," Rocastle murmured. She let it go. "Ulikku is lost to us. No great loss. He knew the risks. He was careless. I had high hopes, but he was never likely to succeed. I knew that early on. Unfortunately, some of his lifestyle choices left a lot to be desired where this venture was concerned. We have many more. We can move on. I currently have fifty in my class, fifty potentials marked up by Mister Costa over there. Early evaluations show that maybe half could be ready to be deployed at the end of the year. The rest may not pass muster." He shrugged, as if he were trying to read the inscrutable expression on her face. She'd kept it blank. Inside, she wasn't impressed by his predictions of numbers. She wanted better results than a guaranteed half. A lot better. Still, the days were early. Give it time, maybe the yield could be improved. "I only have so much time to bring about my personal brand of experience to their lives, I'm working day and night with some of them, but they still won't learn. They won't cast aside their empathy for their fellow human and it sickens me." He said empathy like it was a disgusting word, almost spat it out as if it left a foul taste on his tongue. "It must be cut out of them and I am the knife to do it. Leave them with me, Mistress. They'll do, or they'll die."

"Remember, a true teacher gets through to the unteachable. Not just those that want to learn," she said, not meaning it as an admonishment. Knowing him, he'd probably take it that way though. She wasn't pussyfooting around his emotions. She didn't have time. If she stroked his ego every time, she'd never get anything done.

"I'm curious as to what even qualifies you to do it." Fuller finally spoke up. Unlike Rocastle, her feelings towards Alana were cordial, warm even. The woman had proven herself countless times. She'd been her right hand at Reims. She'd kept Ritellia close during the Quin-C, at great personal humiliation to herself. Apart from Domis, Fuller remained the one she trusted the most. She'd earned it. If she were to baulk, she'd have done it before now.

NEVER SHALL YOU KNOW PEACE UNTIL YOU REACH THE END OF THE ROAD. IF YOU EVER REACH THIS PLACE AGAIN, IT WILL BE AS A SUCCESS.

"Dear Alana, the council whore," Rocastle said, his face contorted into the rictus of a grin, the curves at the corners of his mouth so wicked they might have been slashed in with a blade. "Remind me what you bring to this whole operation again? Other than fucking Ritellia to death, I don't think you've made one single…"

"Harvey!" she warned, stepping in. Fuller looked furious. Claudia knew she'd started to carry a blaster, there'd been threats against her life because of her tryst with Ritellia, and even though no harm would befall her here, she thought it might change the atmosphere of the meeting if she blasted Rocastle through the face with it. "Ms Fuller has my full backing. She has the most important role of you all. Because after all, without credits, everything grinds to a halt. Would you like to enlighten us, my dear?"

"As we all know, the Senate clamped down on Reims," Alana eventually said, patting her lips with her tongue to moisten them. "That was no great loss. All our Mistress' capital had already gone from it. About the only thing of value that was left with it was the name and that value was lost about the same time our efforts came into the open. I've been apportioned some of that fortune, my orders have been to ensure that we have a fresh stream of revenue coming in where we can get it. Reims made millions every day. Though the investments have not yet paid off anything like that, I believe it is only a matter of time before we can strike back from the financial shadows."

It had been the only job she would have trusted Alana with. The funds, while not exhausted yet, would soon be in danger if they didn't get some replenishment in. Hence Alana quietly buying up controlling interests in companies that looked like they'd be going places soon. Especially weapons and transport. The militaries were going to want better and better in both and that meant a boom was coming, one that had been steadily building ever since the start of this whole damn war. When the boom came, she'd profit from the other side. A genius effort on her part, she had to admit.

SHOULD YOU REACH THIS CHAMBER AGAIN, WE WILL DISCUSS MORE. YOU KNOW WHAT YOU MUST DO, EVEN IF YOU ARE NOT AWARE THAT YOU DO.

She didn't expect anything from Sinkins. Subtractor would say his piece shortly, in additions to the ones he'd already made amidst other's declarations. Hota stood up, cleared his throat. "Jutht a quick note," he said with his lisp. "Thubject Apex. Firtht trial was a thucceth. We thent her after the traitor Davith Teela. He hath been terminated. With prejudith. Hith part in Rebirth will not be mithed. Already I theek a replathement."

Betrayal sickened her. She was trying to change the kingdoms for the better and the idea that her people grow a conscience all of a sudden was unhelpful.

"Thank you, Doctor Hota," she said. Apex had been a gamble, one that looked certain to come good sooner rather than later. Rebirth was even more of a risk, but she had high hopes for it. Only she and Hota knew in this room. Not even Domis had been informed. "Most helpful."

He smiled at her, sat back in his seat. That only left…

"Master Carson," she said. "You've been quiet amidst all this."

The Vedo master raised his head and studied her. Her own personal Vedo, as tarnished and ruined as he might be. He owed her. That was what he believed. He'd made a deal and his own personal sense of honour compelled him to follow it to the end. He didn't like it though. She could tell that with minimal effort. For a man like him, sullying himself with the likes of her must be true torment. If he was conflicted, she didn't care. She'd helped him in his darkest hour and now he could help her through her most trying times. He'd had nothing, and she'd given him something back, a purpose he'd desired. He proclaimed to be a man of his word and he'd given his word that he'd help her. He could swallow down any conflict he might have within himself.

"I have been listening to what you all say, I truly find myself wondering if you have considered every possible ramification of what you set out to do. You speak and speak like this like the kingdoms are your enemy, you preach war as your own personal weapon, the people like enemy combatants. They are not. You're dragging them into something that none of them want to be a part of. You think they care, truly, whether you win or not? Most just want to live their lives."

"Your point, Master Carson?" she asked. If she'd had something in her hand, she'd have been tapping it listlessly against the table right now. "I'm assuming you're going to make one."

"People are going to die, that is the natural order of things of course. The old must die, the new must replace them. It has always been and always will. My point is that there's a right way to win and a wrong way."

"You know what I must say to that?" she said. "The victory is all that matters. We can move from there. If there's a cost to it, so be it."

YOUR CONVICTION WILL GUIDE YOU. FOLLOW YOUR HEART ALL THE WAY. YOUR INSTINCTS MAY MISLEAD YOU BUT FALTER YOU MUST NOT FOR FAIL YOU THEY CANNOT.

He shook his head. "A victory with a solid foundation will always trump one that was built on sand. If you slaughter half the population indiscriminately to achieve it, you'll be laying down the embers of your own destruction before you've even begun. Wipe out your enemy's army if you must but I hear stories of how fleeing civilians were gunned down."

"This is true," Mazoud said proudly. "They didn't welcome us as conquerors…"

"They saw you as invaders, you ass," Carson said. "Armed invaders shooting anything that moved. I'd run too. What did you expect them to do?"

"It is the nature of all true Vazarans to embrace what I did in ensuring that Nwakili was removed from power. I have given the kingdom its independence back."

"You've exposed it to attack," Carson said. "You have discontent now, you'll have insurrections tomorrow. A week from now, you'll have rebellions and give it a month, you'll have civil war if you carry on down this path."

"With the greatest of respect, Carson, I could care less of the word of some fraudulent shaman," Mazoud said. "Where are you, hiding down some hole in Serran? You…"

His eyes bulged, his words cut off with a choke. Wim Carson's holographic form studied him, one hand extended up in a pincer motion.

"Fraudulent, you say?" he asked. There was no mistaking the exaggerated politeness in his voice for anything other than a threat. "Because you cannot comprehend the intricacies of anything that is not spelled out for you in bright colours and one-syllable words, I feel the need to avoid explaining myself to you. We are all connected, Mazoud. It's the reason I can reach out and touch you from a kingdom away. I could kill you if I desired."

"Release him! Now!" Claudia said, though the temptation to allow him to continue was there. "If you kill him, I'll have to find another Premier for Vazara and I don't think he's outlived his usefulness just yet. Master Carson, you've made your point, let him go!"

This was the test, she thought. If Carson obeyed her, she'd be fine. If he defied her for a few moments longer or even failed to let up at all, the first cracks would have appeared in her domination.

For a second, she was left wondering. Carson lowered his hand and Mazoud dropped to all fours, gasping for air, his eyes bulging and tears streaming from them.

"You dare lay a hand on the Premier of Vazara!" he snarled. "I'll have you killed for this!"

"I think you'll find that I didn't touch you," Carson smiled. "Did anyone see me touch him? As I was saying before I was so rudely interrupted… Anyone else want to do that by the way?" He playfully waggled his fingers and she saw the light in his eyes, the spark of madness that would blow them all up given the chance. She wondered how in control he truly was of himself. "There's a right way to do it and a wrong way. For now, I look to other threats that might fall upon you beyond Unisco, Madam Coppinger. I look for weapons to combat them, I look for men and women beyond what you have. Because some things cannot be created or manipulated, they can only be forged amidst a fire."

He bowed his head. "I have nothing more to say."

Before she could say anything else to him, the comms beeped on her desk and she hit the button to reply. "Copy?"

"Mistress? We've arrived at your coordinates. We hope to locate the wreckage of the Aerius very shortly."

She cut the contact, smiled at the room. "This has been a productive use of our time. Now if you'll excuse me, I believe we have a pressing issue to deal with imminently. Let's split for the time being, we will meet again very soon. I think you've been kept apart long enough. If we are to succeed, we will do it together. Not as individuals. Thank you for your time, ladies and gentlemen. The best of luck on all your endeavours and may we meet again under more fortuitous circumstances."

"I'm putting you in charge of this program. I think you've got potential, Mister Rocastle. You recruited quite a bunch of these people involved in it, therefore I think it's only right you should have a part in what they become. They're your responsibility now. Let's see if you can impress me. I suggest you don't dwell on what will happen to you if you don't. It's good to avoid distractions. A busy mind does that. You're in charge of the Angel's program now. The conditioning will take care of itself. I want you to forge them into my sword and my spear. You're going to be far too busy to dwell on your obsession with... Well, you know who. I'm not going to say her name."

Claudia Coppinger to Harvey Rocastle, months ago on his promotion.

The holograms faded, and the Mistress was first out the door, Harvey Rocastle leaned back in his seat and stroked his silken chin with his unruined hand. He tried not to acknowledge the other one any longer, not more than he had to certainly. It disgusted him if he was truthful. He'd always had beautiful hands, big but not too big and a certain smoothness to them that hid what he'd used them for too many times. He was an artist and his hands were an extension of his soul, he always dreamed of the day when he'd wrap them around some poor little bitch's throat and squeeze and squeeze until he felt her slut body go limp under his touch.

Those days had been too few and too far between. He'd always held himself back, too scared of the consequences of getting caught. He knew that if he started, he'd never stop, he was lucky that he'd gotten away with it as long as he had before they'd started to know his name. Anonymity was one thing he'd never wanted but at the same time, he'd known that it had its perks. When nobody knew your name, nobody looked for you. Nobody wanted to find you. Nobody wanted to look for you. Nobody wanted you dead.

There were too many who wanted him dead in these times. He had a feeling that the Mistress only kept him alive out of loyalty and the moment he betrayed her, she'd put him down. Worse, she'd probably have that big goon, Domis, do it. There was no fighting someone like him. Harvey didn't know who or what Domis really was, but he couldn't be human, not entirely. He'd suspected he might be a Vedo or have some element of that power but as time went by, it appeared increasingly unlikely. He'd even asked Carson about it, that smug self-proclaimed expert and he'd come up empty in answers.

Typical. Couldn't rely on anyone except himself.

His stump ached, he glanced down at his leg, tried to avoid thinking about it. He could remember it being broken, could recall the snap as it had shattered. Still suffered from the memories of the way the bone had torn through his skin. Nicholas fucking Roper. When he thought of the beating he'd been given, he felt the stabs of anger rushing through him. He was glad that he'd killed his bitch fiancé. His only regrets were that he hadn't dragged it out longer, that she hadn't suffered more, that he hadn't taken that fancy laser sword of hers and cut her skin off inch by inch, maimed and mutilated her until she was unrecognisable.

Roper might have broken it. The Mistress had taken it though. She'd ordered Hota to amputate while he was unconscious, passed out before he'd been broken by the pain. Hota, being the good little endroid, hadn't hesitated. Harvey had to give the doctor credit though, he'd helped him through the physiotherapy that had followed. Those first steps with his new leg had been hard, it had just felt so alien, so different to what he'd been used to. He felt clumsy and ungainly, he wept for the grace he'd had before and lost now. Light footsteps were always going to be replaced with the ugly clump the foot made when it came down on the ground. There'd been nights when he'd lain with the sheets at the base of the bed, silent tears streaming down his face as he stared at his stump.

The wounds to his hand hadn't affected him as badly as this. He'd lost a few fingers to that little bitch they'd kept locked up, the one that they'd found on the mountain, but that had been down to his own carelessness. Finger prosthetics weren't as bad once you got used to them. After six months, the false skin had become barely indistinguishable from his own, taken on the same colour, the same texture worn down by hours of activity. Should they cease working, it didn't impede movement. When his cybernetic leg had once ceased working, he'd fallen over right in front of his class and their silent laughter had rung through his ears as they took in his moment of humiliation. There'd been no sound, any of them who had shown audible mirth would have been punished. He'd have seen to that if it was the last thing he'd ever done. It wouldn't have been a swift punishment either, death by inches. He'd seen it in some of their faces as his trousers had ripped, the lower half of his leg left stood at the front of the classroom while he was flat on his face.

He'd made all of them run twenty laps around the ship following that, had been pleased when none of them had made it past fifteen. It was a gruelling run, he'd had someone count it out at the start. Each lap had to be a couple of miles long. Those last few to collapse, they'd run until they couldn't run any longer, they'd crawled the last few feet. Just like he'd crawled back to his leg. They'd not been laughing then.

He was unsettled these days. The Mistress had changed over the last six months. He'd never liked her, not really. She'd always been cold. Normally he couldn't care one jot for the approval of women. There was only one that he cared about, the only reason that he did anything. There was one other that he could just about tolerate. They were blood after all. He'd not seen Lola for months, they weren't encouraged to contact the world outside this ship, except with the express permission of both the Mistress and the captain. He'd last spoken to her weeks ago, seen how the burden was going. Even then, she was playing hard to get. She didn't want to talk to him, even before he'd gotten himself in this situation.

The moment she died, he'd told himself, he'd get out of this. Once she died, the burden was over, and he could go back to his life. He'd told himself that story so many times, he'd started believing it. Except he couldn't. Not now. The Mistress had caged him for all purposes. His life was over. Every law enforcement officer in the kingdoms was looking for him. If they caught him, he might not even reach trial. Rumour had it that any Unisco agent who captured him was under orders to execute him for what he'd done to their director's daughter. The sheer injustice of that hurt him. He hadn't known that was who Mia Arnholt was. He wanted her dead or suffering for a whole bunch of other reasons. Her father had never come into it. How arrogant was Terrence Arnholt if he thought that he was the only reason that someone might want to harm his daughter?

No, he was trapped. He'd live or die with Coppinger. She was his only chance at being able to resume a life that now felt so alien to him. Everything did these days. At least he was enjoying what he did. That was a blessing.

He'd needed the credits back then. Lots of them and fast. The burden had only grown, reached the point where she needed around the clock medical care and attention, not the sort that could be found cheaply either. The sort that bankrupted families and wiped out inheritances. That he resented. All these years of being the sort of dutiful son that deserved a reward at the end of it and it had been snuffed out in one continuous heartbeat, a heart that continued to beat when by rights, it should not.

By rights, he should have placed a pillow over her face. Held it there and watched her twitch, feel her struggle as she gasped for the last few breaths of sweet air. He'd probably have been denied even that. She'd never been the most helpful sort of woman. Even when he'd been just a little boy, her affections had been saved for his sister. It had been all 'oh Lola, you are marvellous' and 'why are you still here, Harvey?' She'd never really appreciated him. He was the one who'd gone out and made something of himself. What had Lola ever done in the end? She'd had talents, she'd chosen not to use them, although being a tattling little bitch who couldn't keep her nose out of stuff wasn't really something that ever translated to success.

He laughed, the bitterness in his voice an old friend come to visit again, balled up his fist and beat it against the wall. Heard the clang of his prosthetic fingers against the metal. A whole false hand, he might be able to leave a dent in it. As it were, all he'd do was mangle his real digits. Pain stabbed up through them, he grimaced and let himself lean against the wall.

He'd been a spirit dancer. He'd been excellent at it too, truly reaching the prime of the art. He could out-do anyone, could step onto the stage and own it. He had the soul of an artist, the heart of a musician and the mind of a calculating son of a bitch. All three had served him well. He knew what he had to do. He knew how he needed to do it. Whatever it takes as quickly as it takes to do it. If there was someone he needed to step over, he stepped over them. Sometimes he left the boot in if he needed to, left a metaphorical footprint on their face to remember him by. He'd always figured that a swift and brutal dismantling of their hopes and dreams was the fastest way to get to the top. If he managed to intimidate opponents into their shell whenever they tried to face him, that was just gravy. He'd built an aura before long, had stepped out onto every stage like he owned it. He'd wanted it all and he'd gotten so close.

He'd taught himself. He knew what it was like to come from nothing, to be entirely sufficient. He'd taught himself how to survive. After that, spirit dancing was easy. He'd buggered off away from home as soon as he could, wanted that bitch to be out of his life forever. He wasn't her son. She didn't acknowledge him as such. She'd always said he was like a parasite; had been ever since the day he'd been ripped out of her. Words like worthless and pathetic had been the lullabies he'd been soothed to sleep with. Lola had gotten the praise. Lola was the wonderful one. The dutiful daughter who'd never left home. Lola was the one she'd loved. Lovely Lola. Perfect Lola. Princess Lola.

He'd never known adoration until the first time he'd stepped onto the stage and felt the roar of the crowd at his back. He'd tried the calling side of the performance, he'd found it too insufficient for his needs. They wanted blood when he wanted to give a performance. They wanted savagery when he wanted to give them art. War and art were mutual opposites, never to collide. That was an immutable truth where he was concerned. They were contrasting pages in the book of life. Nothing good came out of pain and death for the sake of it.

In spirit dancing, he'd found that. A place where he could belong. The community had welcomed him at first as they'd welcomed all new initiates into their group back then, they might be rivals but, in a world, where theirs was of a lesser interest to the amateur butchery of spirit calling, everyone had each other's backs. They'd do for another, they'd die for another though obviously most of them didn't have the spine to hope it came to that. Most of them would sell out their principles and their fellow dancers for a chance at a bigger purse come the next competition.

His first few dances had been, well he'd never experienced anything like it. Cacalti, his troll and a gift from his mother... That memory rankled. An ugly little shit, she'd said as she gave him the crystal. Just like you. May it serve you better than you ever did me. Because life's full of disappointments, son. It's a shithouse you can't escape, you just hope that you get dealt a better hand next time.

That had been one of the more pleasant exchanges the two of them had ever had, as painful as it had sounded. He wanted to take the positives from it, that she'd handed him a potentially powerful spirit that he could use as a keystone to make his way in life. All until Lola had been given a unicorn. One of the rarest beasts of the lot of them. And what had she done with it?

Nothing! Nothing, nothing and a whole lot more of nothing. She'd kept it to herself, not let anyone else have the chance to appreciate its beauty and poise. It was still little more than a wild beast, she'd never put in the effort to bend it to her will. What a fucking waste.

When he and Cacalti had entered the stage, he a little overweight and shy, Cacalti a troll in an arena usually dominated by sylphs and slight spirits, they'd drawn glances. Amidst the cheers, there'd been jeers and boos, people had wanted them to fail. More than that, they needed them to fail. He'd been all too aware of what people had said outside the arena. They'd said it wasn't a competition for the likes of them. They seemed only to want beautiful people and the two of them, him and Cacalti, didn't pass up to the muster of their expectations. It was easier to support the pretty people when it came to the heat of competition.

What he and Cacalti might lack in looks, they made up for in other areas. Neither of them knew the meaning of the words 'give' and 'up'. Neither of them would want to stop until the job was done. It was the sort of quality, he'd had to admit in some of his more reflective moments, that might well have made him a top spirit caller if he hadn't found the whole notion to be so ridiculous. That said, he had learned how to fight. Dearest Reda had gone that way, learned the often-disregarded ways of the battle dancer. The two of them had sparred together more than once, Harvey had been overjoyed when Reda Ulikku had come into the program. He hadn't been overseeing things then, had missed out most of the rush job of training to be thrust on Ulikku. No wonder he'd been taken down. The Angels of these days wouldn't be so easy to beat. They'd engaged in months of intensive training that could put them on a par with hardened Unisco agents.

Still, he wasn't convinced yet. Sure, the killer instinct was there, he'd done his best to bully and kick most the compassion out of them. The training was there. All they lacked was experience beyond a few missions he and Hota and Fuller could probably have accomplished between them. And look at the three of them. Him, crippled. Hota, useless in a fight. Fuller, female.

He had to admit that some of his best Angels were girls, that didn't mean anything. He'd reluctantly given command to one of them. Maybe he needed to encourage their male counterparts to try harder. They weren't working hard enough. Their failure reflected badly on the program overall and especially on him.

Thinking back to how easily he'd cowed the room at first and how any of them could kill him with ease now brought about sobering thoughts, made him feel like all his life choices to this point had been dubiously interesting ones he had the potential to regret.

His prime method of spirit dancing had been to needle and intimidate where he could, undermine and criticise with the best of them. He'd gotten good at it, he'd learned how to read people. Of course, there were always those that just wouldn't fall for intimidation. He could remember his dance-offs against Jesseka Blake, that fiery haired little bitch. She bore her marks of ruin, she did her best to hide them. Maybe she was as ugly on the inside as she was on the outside, a hot-tempered little minx who did her best to hide it. Couldn't trust women like her. She'd never fallen for his intimidation, had instead sought out to beat him down harder for it. That made her predictable, he had to prick at her anger, coax any sort of sense out of her and she would be his for the taking. Sometimes it was about playing the opponent, sometimes it was about playing the crowd and sometimes it was about both to the best of your ability.

The only one who never fell for it ever, was Selena Stanton. She'd been the first dancer he'd ever met, not quite a champion then but well on the way. She'd taken him under her wing, she'd smoothed out a few of his rough edges and he'd been better for the criticism she'd given him as much as he'd hated it at the time. Begrudgingly, he'd come to respect her, had found a burning desire to beat her. It had never come. She'd been just too canny, more experienced than him and she'd always used it well. She was to spirit dancing what Sharon Arventino had been to spirit calling. Both had been filled with the grace of champions, they'd risen to the top and stayed there for quite some years, neither of them had let it change who they were as a person. Both considered beautiful. Pioneers of women as ultimate competitors. Both had had their lives ended by him in devastating fashion.

Sometimes he thought about that day on Carcaradis Island when he'd killed Sharon Arventino. He'd had a kinetic disperser in his hand, she'd had one of those laser swords he wanted so much, she'd been distracted and fighting Wim Carson who wanted to take her alive. He wanted her, he didn't know what for, but it couldn't have been anything fit for purpose. He was old and broken, she was young and vibrant, every inch the professional even in death. He'd fired, she'd taken the blast in the back of the head and fallen on the sword. She'd been dead before she hit the ground, a life snuffed out in an instant.

Just as often, he thought about what he'd felt during that moment, the instant when his finger had closed under the trigger guard, curled around the trigger and he'd felt the kick of the huge weapon explode out, saw the first fragments of bone and blood hit the wall behind him. One fleck of blood had hit him on the cheek, he could still remember feeling that warm trickle run down his face. He'd stuck his tongue out, licked it up from the corner of his lips.

He'd felt nothing. Not sorrow, not regret, certainly not joy. He didn't have any sort of beef with Arventino, he'd never really met her in person. They walked different paths. He might have seen her at the Belderhampton carnival a year ago if he thought about it, but he couldn't be sure. No, most of his enjoyable moments came at the expense of those that he knew. What had happened with Stanton, that was a feeling he'd never replicated. The betrayal there had been delicious, he'd watched her eyes close and down below, he'd felt a few droplets escape into the silk boxers he always wore. They'd stuck to his skin for the rest of the night, but that discomfort was a small price to pay for feeling on top of the world.

And then there was Mia. He imagined that dealing with her would be better than what had happened with Selena Stanton, by miles. No way it wouldn't be. It could be argued that most of his troubles had started when he'd made the choice to try and lure her from the land of the living into the sweet embrace of death. He'd been so careful, had cornered her on that damn island and set his own personal investigator after her.

Maxie Brudel. He had fond memories of the boy, he'd been sweet in a way that had left him imagining how he tasted. Harvey always imagined that he'd taste of bananas, sweet and chewy with just a little hint of exotica. Not that it made much difference. Brudel had died long ago. Harvey had drowned him. That had been the first part of his downfall, he'd been informed that that death had left people looking for him. He'd cornered Mia, was about to shove her off a roof... oh no! What a tragic accident, the poor dear cut down in the prime of life while her greatest friend was helpless to stop her... when Wade Wallerington had shown up. What they knew about him now, it made sense in a way. Then there'd been Roper on that last day and Harvey remembered painfully how that turned out. He wasn't ever going to forget it.

Mia Arnholt, the bane of his fucking life. One day. One day, he'd get her. He'd have her in his grip and he'd tighten it until he felt her slacken. He'd break that pretty neck, ruin that face that she valued so much. Maybe he'd take a knife and ruin that body she'd work so hard to build. Wouldn't be the first time. Amateur vivisection was a little hobby of his, one he'd never had opportunity to indulge in frequently. His dirt little treat.

The things he'd like to do to her, thinking about them kept him warm during the cold nights on the ship. She'd been fortunate enough to escape him three times now. Her luck would not save her forever. Soon, he had to enjoy some luck himself and when he did, her time would run out. She'd run out of people to save her, she wouldn't be able to save herself. Not that he believed that was something she was capable of. She'd always been a little parasite, worming her way around those with so much more. First her father. Then Selena. Then her first boyfriend, Andrew Donohue. Harvey had always liked him. He should have done better than that little whore. He'd always considered Donny, if not a friend, then something like one. Someone whom he'd have liked to be closer to. Andy Donny had got him. Donny understood where he was coming from. Sometimes he'd have been voicing his thoughts, going dangerously close to showing his true self and Donny and always been there, nodding and smiling as if he understood. He wondered what Donny would think of him now, if he could see him. A future lord of the new world order. Maybe even one day he'd rule it all. The Mistress had no heirs since her bitch daughter had disowned her. He knew Meredith Coppinger from the circuit as well, never as talented as the cunt-licker she'd hooked up with Lydia Dupree had something about her, not a lot but something there. He might end up with it all one day. Coppinger's empire. Perhaps. Unlikely but not impossible.

And to think, all of it had stemmed from that one fateful meeting.

Back then, the diagnosis had been like a thunderclap. The call from his sister, he'd heard it in the changing room before the finale of the Kenzaris Invitational. Premesoir was lovely that time of year, especially down in the warm south-west. He'd had a chance to peruse the promenades, enjoy the sights of the shirtless out enjoying the sun shimmering down on well-toned bodies. The sand and the sea and the hints of sex. All so subtle but throw them together and it might as well become the chance of an orgy. That would be sweet. His loins ached, had been too long since he'd had something bad for him. Maybe he'd find some nice young man, a fan, nervous perhaps, it's his first time and he's oh so shy as he has his clothes ripped off…

The news hadn't been great. Four words. Lola had told him in four words and then she'd cancelled the call, leaving him with that bombshell. Four words and his life had changed forever. That was it, the turning point. Looking back, he could see it now, the start of a path he'd never intended to walk. The path that had cost him his leg and his fingers, and the pain that persisted in his wrist where Wade Wallerington had broken it months earlier. More than that, it had cost him his freedom, his ability to walk the streets unhindered.

"Our mother is sick."

Four words that changed everything. He'd called her back. Repeatedly. There'd been times when he thought he wouldn't get through to her, but he'd persisted. He'd not given up. He couldn't. He wouldn't.

Because he was a better human being than she ever would be, even after everything she'd done to him, he wasn't going to give up on her. That was the decision he'd made there and then. He'd devote his life to ensuring that she lived as long as was possible. Even after how crappy she'd treated him. That'd show her. She'd regret it when she realised that she wouldn't still be alive without his efforts.

He'd gone into the final that evening with renewed vigour, pulled out every stop he could think of. Cacalti was magnificent, even by the high standards the two of them had built before. Every spin, every pirouette, every successful move, it had been the greatest rush he could imagine. Everything had been inch-perfect and when the points had gone to him, when the crowds had burst into ecstatic applause as the judges had named him their winner, he'd run onto the stage and chest bumped Cacalti. He wished he could bottle the feeling to sup over and over in times of crisis.

107

That had played well with those watching at home. His approval ratings had gone up. It didn't mean a damn thing really, not in any real physical way. It didn't impact how good you were at the art or how many credits you made. Yet some did use that to judge how successful you were. If people liked you, they were more likely to watch your performances. If they watched your performances, the more views the broadcasters got. The more they got, the more credits they put up to get the right to show it. The more credits, the bigger the purse. The bigger the purse, the bigger the cut. The bigger the cut, the more credits in the hand of the winner. Simple mathematics really.

"I guess, just wow, how super honoured am I to win such a fab tournament." That had been the first line of his victory speech and despite the serious news he'd been dealt earlier, he hadn't been able to entirely stop grinning at the way the people were chanting his name, Har-vey, Har-vey, Har-vey! Hearing it over and over again made him feel like the most popular man in the kingdoms. His face had taken on a serious note as he studied the thick black eye with something he hoped approached detachment. "This would have been one of the greatest days of my life. It would have been, I mean it. But…" He'd let a note of sorrow slip into his voice, his face turning almost to tears. Screwing his eyes up hurt, he could just about see the blinking red light letting him know that all this was going out live to everyone watching. "But, it comes on a day of bad news for me, the worst I've ever had."

The crowd went silent at that and he had to smile inwardly as he looked back on that memory, months later. Suckers. Get them on your side, it's like herding cats at first but it's twice as rewarding when everything lines up and you reap your rewards for it.

"I just heard this morning…" He'd paused, looked up and around, threatened to blink back tears that weren't quite coming. He dug his nails into the palm of his hand, hoped that made him look suitably pained enough to make the point. Didn't quite cry. Didn't quite draw blood either. It'd have to do. He let a little cough slip into his voice, a choke that could have been mistaken for a sob. He'd always thought his acting talents mediocre at best, but people always seemed to want to fall for it. Maybe he was better than he realised.

Or maybe people were just stupid sheep looking for a flock to follow. They'd follow anyone willing to stick their head above the parapet and call themselves a shepherd. Maybe they were that fucking stupid!

"I just heard this morning…" Another dramatic choke. A hand to the eye. A sniffle and he managed to force the next words out. "Oh Divines, I just heard this morning that my mother, my dearest, sweetest mother has maybe months to live. My mother who never had one harsh word for me..."

Not technically a lie. Her insults had always come in strings of three or more. Appearance, attitude and sexuality were always her favourites to bring up. She was lucky really, she'd reached the point where a horrible disease was going to kill her. His control was absolute. He'd wanted to kill for less. Yet he'd never thought about laying a hand on her, much to his horror as that realisation had dawned on him. She'd probably call him chickenshit for it. Not even the bollocks to put someone out of their misery. He could hear it now and it made him want to put his eardrums out in defence of his sanity.

"... I can't do this right now!" He put both hands to his eyes, let his shoulders shake. Some people in the crowd were muttering, he couldn't hear any sobs but that was to be expected. At least they were still silent, they hadn't started to jeer so they didn't think he was making it up. That was good. Moments like this when dancers had emotional breakdowns could go either way with a crowd. If they believed it, there was sympathy. If they didn't, it got ugly. If they believed it and it turned out to be a lie, things got even uglier when it came to light.

"This cheque will go a way to helping her but it's not enough. Right now, it feels like whatever I do, it won't be enough. I want to be by her side, I want to be here in front of you all making the credits to pay for treatment. What do I do? I don't know." His voice had gone low, he was horrified to find he actually meant some of the words. Sympathy bloomed like a fire flower in his stomach, sweet but sickly in its sudden drip through his system. What the fuck was wrong with him? He hated the bitch, wouldn't piss on her if she was on fire. Why was he feeling like this? It wasn't natural.

The tears had come, this time for real, he'd taken the cheque and beat a hasty retreat off the stage, slipping back towards the locker room. The first beats of applause had come as he stepped off the stage. There were no cheers, no shots of his name or screams of adulation. He would have liked that but instead the applause was heavy with respect, fifty thousand men, women and children thundering their approval towards his situation. His arms were shaking, threatening to drop his giant prize and he was silently urging himself not to do it. It wouldn't look great. Or maybe it'd make it look that little more real. Appearances were everything after all. If people believed that what they saw was what they got, they went home happy. They didn't question things.

No doubt he'd suffer for this little stunt. If Lola had seen it, she'd probably refute it just to spite him, just to make him pay for some past slight. There were plenty of them, he knew that. He and his sister had been like a pair of wildcats back in the day, feral and furious in their competition with each other. She'd do something to him, he'd do something back to her, meaner and nastier. Slowly it became a game of escalation and it would end in tears. Sometimes him, usually her.

All siblings fought but their games had a nasty edge to them that nobody could ever quite predict the outcome to. He'd nearly stabbed her once, had been locked in the cellar for three weeks as punishment after his sister had been permitted to beat him with a steel rod as reparation while his hands and legs had been held down. She'd hit him so many times in the stomach and the groin he'd pissed blood for the first of those three weeks.

In later months, when he took to approaching callers and dancers to recruit to Coppinger's private army, he could appreciate the way that his future had taken shape by the way he found the figure stood waiting for him in the locker room. Harvey had never seen him before, although he had to concede that he was one cute bastard. He had the sort of tanned good looks about him that Harvey had always envied. He was short though, Harvey towered over him and his hair could have powered a speeder for a good few minutes, such was the quantity of oil pressed within it. One minute, he hadn't been expecting him and the next, he was there, a presence in his life.

"That was an outstanding little speech you just gave," the short man said. "I have to say." He had to be from Serran with an accent like that, somewhere towards the southern peninsulas, Harvey would have guessed. Where the days were warm, and the fruits were thick with sweet juice that exploded all over your chin when you bit into it.

"You are, Sweetums?" Harvey asked. He waved a finger at him. Some of his old bravado felt like it was coming back to him following his little emotional outburst out there. He felt himself again, the shaking had ceased, and he no longer felt the urge to weep. Instead, that sorrow had been replaced with disgust, not just with himself but that this stranger had gotten in here without so much as an invite. Not that he wouldn't have invited him in, but that wasn't the point. It wasn't the point at all. Principles beat points any day. "You shouldn't be in here. Competitors only, my dear."

"Cut the crap, Mister Rocastle. You make this big friendly face to people, mix the threats in with the flamboyance and people don't realise it."

"I don't make threats, dearie. I don't need to." Big smile as he said it, then he swallowed it down in bemusement. Did he really do that? Was he that easy to read? If he was, then how come nobody else had managed it beyond this strange man? "After all, what threat could little old me provide to someone?"

The man didn't laugh, though he looked like he might well want to. Instead, he straightened out his lapels. "You had people believing you, you know?"

"What's to believe?" Harvey had said. "It's true. My sister called me earlier." The bitch, he wanted to add, but restrained himself. It wouldn't be good to expose his true feelings in front of this stranger. He could be a journalist out to make a quick credit off him and that wouldn't do. Exposing himself in the dirty glare of the media would be a fool's task.

"What disease?" It sounded like he cared for a moment, the short man closed his eyes and took a deep breath. "Sorry, that's none of my business, I'll understand if you don't want to share."

"I don't. Besides, she didn't tell me." It felt shameful even admitting that silently to himself, never mind out loud. He wanted to tell someone though. Wanted to get it off his chest, hells maybe he just wanted some sympathy. He'd gotten fuck-all of it in his life to this point, it might be nice for a change. "Four words, then she hung up."

The short man whistled. "What a cunt."

Harvey's eyes twitched at that, he almost burst out laughing. It was a little juvenile to find it funny, a bad word, time to split my sides. It felt apt though. He'd had those feelings about Lola himself at one time or another, more than once, many, many times more than once. Screw it, he did let go with a giggle that echoed eerily in the enclosed space of the locker room.

"Harsh," he said, eventually. "That's my sister. I'm the only one who gets to describe her thus." He stuck out a hand. "So, what do I call you, handsome?"

If he was unsettled or offended, he didn't show it. He took the hand, gripped it firmly and shook with a warm smile on his face. He had the sort of hand Harvey liked. Masculine. Rough. Warm. Not a hint of sweat. "My name's Joaquin Costa. Not that people ever call me that. They call me Jake. Makes it easier to get a foot in the door some places, you know what I mean? They think you're something you're not... I probably don't have to tell you, do I?"

"Nice to meet you, Jake," Harvey said. "Or Joaquin... I could get used to calling a man that. Lovely name. Feels great in my mouth." He gave him a wicked grin. Not that Jake showed even any sort of recognition to it. Harvey felt the corners of his mouth curl up in delight. Teasing little bastard. Playing hard to hump. "But I've got to ask what you want from me. You show up... Did someone pay you to be here? A little congratulatory gift for winning here... Is Selena watching with a recorder?" He glanced around the room, made a playful show of doing it.

"As I was saying, you had people believing your story. Didn't matter if it was true or not, you put it out there and they wanted to believe that what you said was the truth. You showed them an exposed part of yourself and they took you to their hearts. I was in here. I've never heard a reaction like that. Ever. It was spooky. Just pure sadness. You did a great bit of manipulation there, though I can't work out what your plan was going to be."

"Who said I have a plan, Sweetums?" Harvey asked, mock-innocence in his voice. He layered it on thick, put on a puzzled expression to accompany it. He tried to ignore the surprise at how natural it felt "Just hurting. Just wanted to..."

"Don't start crying again." No hint of begging, just hard words. "I didn't buy it the first time, I'm not going to a second either. You want to know what I think?"

Harvey shrugged, started to undo the taut buttons across his great belly. The strain at the front of his belly was immense, the seams of his jacket sighed with relief as the buttons were permitted a respite from their thankless task. "I think I'm going to get changed, then find somewhere to take my giant cheque to transform it into credits. When I walk out of here, I'm going to forget what you've said but probably not your face, darling. I'm sure I'll see that every time I close my eyes and slip a hand down beneath the cover for some fun." He bared his teeth in a grin. "Anyone ever wanked themselves off over you, Jake?"

"I couldn't possibly comment on that," Jake said. That sense of self-control was starting to irritate now. He looked like he had it all together and that fucked Harvey right off. He wanted people to have a part of them that was a hot mess. They needed to be as fucked up as him, there had to be a small side to them that was just broken beyond repair. Everyone had the potential for it. "But I do know how you can make enough credits for your mother to enjoy her last days in peace, however many days she may or may not have left."

That had caught his attention. And the rest was history.

He liked this room on the ship. His nerve centre for what he did. He had inherited it from the previous director of the Angels program, had very quickly set about putting his own stamp on things. He'd never met the previous director, but he'd read the meagre notes left behind. The Mistress might have done many things right but her initial choice for the role had been a poor one. He'd not had the stomach for it that Harvey knew he had. He'd just been a scout initially, see what he could scrape up out of the dregs of the Quin-C and he'd taken those names, he'd vetted them, and they'd wound up in the program. All to be the best that they could be for a woman who'd taken them in when a kingdom no longer cared for or wanted them.

Things had changed and him with them. The previous director had gotten into a disagreement with Domis, thought himself tougher than he really was, and the injuries had killed him. Hota had told Harvey in a moment of melancholy that it was like he'd fallen into farming machinery. There was an object lesson in that. Don't fuck with Domis. Even before he'd gotten his injuries, he'd fancied himself as a tough guy. He was big, and he could throw a punch, but he would rather go another few rounds with Roper, before he took a crack at the Mistress' right hand. Considering Roper had nearly killed him, that said it all, for him. Domis didn't even look human sometimes. Like he was violence and death personified.

Harvey pressed a few buttons, entered his passcode. He'd been overjoyed when he'd been given this office to direct operations from. He'd never expected it, the technology the role brought him into contact with was beyond his wildest dreams. He'd always enjoyed the way stuff advanced, he always had to get the newest gear despite the biggest difference often being in the price. The screens burst into life, he picked up a headset and slipped it over his head. The console was top of the line, the best that the Mistress' credits could buy. Everything on this ship was bleeding edge, why should this stuff be any different? The Mistress wasn't so stupid as to skimp on areas like this. It would be suicide. There were more monitors than he could count and if that wasn't a good thing, he didn't know what was. Each of them served a purpose, he couldn't possibly look at them all at the same time but having the information available to him live and updated and easily accessed wasn't something to complain about.

"This is Angel One," he said, taking in the pictures, the eclectic-looking mansion, a dozen real-time feeds coming in from the headsets that his angels all wore. He wanted to be able to see everything they saw, wanted to be able to play it back for them if there was a fault in what they did. They would learn, or they would die. Preferably the former but he could live with the latter if it had value. "The Mistress wants Frewster. Alive. Kill anyone else in that building." He studied the speeder at the base of the driveway, made his choice. "Cut off any sort of escape route they might use."

His command was obeyed in a heartbeat, the rotary cannons on the air assault ship spinning into life and he saw the rain of scarlet light up the solitary speeder, the explosion beautiful in the afternoon light. The cannon fire died away, he stroked his chin. "Excellent.

113

Commander Saarth, you have your orders. Ensure that they are carried out. I'll await your report."

"Sir!" Weronika Saarth's voice filled his headset. "We have reports that the Unisco agent Nicholas Roper is on site and engaged with the target."

Harvey stiffened up at that. The mention of the name was enough to bring up the hairs on the back of his neck. What was he doing here?! He should have asked that man Subtractor while he'd had the chance. Of course, that would have required the services of a fortune teller and if they had one of those, things would have been different. Very different.

"Commander Saarth," he said, trying to keep as little emotion out of his voice as possible. They weren't the only ones who were being recorded. "You have your orders to eliminate anyone who gets in your way. He undoubtedly will try."

Inside, Harvey was smiling. He could play these games with the best of them. All a matter of knowing which move you needed to make. He couldn't be accused of making it personal if he didn't treat it like it was. "Saarth," he said, making sure to leave her rank out of it this time. Weronika Saarth had been a late addition to the program but one of the more disturbingly capable out of the lot of them. She'd been put in command of this missions. It had been jointly decided she had what they both wanted, and more crucially, what they needed. "Kill him, dearie! Permission to engage, right now."

"Understood, Angel One. Your will shall be done."

He settled back in his seat, wished that he'd gotten some popcorn to bring to the observation room with him. Watching this would be very interesting indeed. He hoped Roper's death would be slow and painful.

"What, Withdean? Yes, yes, dear boy, I designed it all myself. Architecture has often been a hobby of mine. I like the mechanics of it. I laid the first brick down in the foundations, though not the rest of them admittedly. Withdean, it's named for an old friend of mine. Dean Saunders. Cracking chap. Complex. Layered. I made my house that way in his memory. Died a long time ago, back in the war. Unity has its price unfortunately. You know what they say about the good and when they go. The arseholes live forever unfortunately, if you know what I'm saying. The older I get, the more I think we should have a war every decade or two, just to cut some of the chaff from society. It's a terrible thing, I'll admit that. But I don't necessarily think it's a terrible idea. Forgive me, my mind wanders sometimes. What was the question again?"

Brennan Frewster in an interview five years ago.

Typical!

Nick swore under his breath, hand went for his blaster. He had the X9S in hand already as he looked across at Frewster. Part of him wondered if the old man had set this up, the rest of him quashed it down. There'd be time to wonder about that later. Right now. Survival. That was the aim. Best to quickly realise that before the violence started. Split focus served no master.

A distant explosion rocked the house, and he struggled to hide the wince. That sounded like the speeder he'd hired. A glance out the window and he saw the plumes of smoke dancing above the flames, reaching towards the sky. He'd like that speeder as well. Some part of him felt annoyed at the notion he'd just lost his security deposit.

"They're taking out any chance of an easy exit," he said. "Tell me you have some other way to make a break for it."

"Dear boy," Frewster said, managing to raise an irate eyebrow. "We currently have two speeders in the garage. We will not make it out of here with that ship in the air. It cut yours into pieces with little effort. I simply dread to think what it'll do to mine."

"You have surface to air defences?" Nick knew it was likely a stupid question. He'd be surprised if Frewster replied with anything other than a withering look. Duly, he was obliged. The old man gave him the sort of look that said, 'don't be so fucking stupid'. "I didn't think so. I can't take that thing down with a blaster. Not…"

He didn't get the chance to finish saying what he couldn't do, he heard the crash of glass shattering behind him and he turned on the spot, blaster raised. His finger was on the trigger, would have pulled it had the figure not been inside his reach before he could get the shot away. An elbow crashed into his wrist, fingers opened, and the blaster bounced away across the floor. He let out a gasp as a palm hit him in the chest, the breath driven from him as another fist came towards his face, he managed to get a forearm up to block it, sucking in grateful gasps of air. It hadn't been a hard blow, he'd taken stronger.

The features of his attacker barely registered, the jumpsuit black with pink stripes on the shoulder, not a design he'd ever seen before. It didn't matter. Going for his other weapon wasn't an option, she didn't look like she had a weapon, at least not one that he could see. Her hands were empty, already her other one was coming at him. He blocked it, grunted with the effort. She might not be the biggest, but the little bitch had one hells of a swing behind her. He'd fought men twice her size who didn't hit like her. Disciplined as well, he had to note. Perfect form. That didn't bode well. There were Unisco graduates who didn't fight as naturally as her.

Time to test her, see how good she was. He slid into a fighting stance, not moving to attack, just keeping a wary eye on her. She circled, studied him like a cobra perusing a tasty-looking mouse. She was good, he almost didn't see the attack coming until it was on him and then he moved, ducking the blow and hitting her midriff with a shoulder. She was good, she wasn't terrific. He recognised it now. She knew how to fight, but it was how she'd been taught, she hadn't become a master through experiencing it for herself. She'd been taught the moves, it was all well and good until it came to face another opponent.

Fist fights were chaos, you could know all the moves you wanted, but it didn't mean you'd get the chance to unleash them all one after another in flawless motion. Especially not against an opponent with years of experience earned fighting for his life. You often had to work with what you got. She doubled, just slightly, he brought a fist up towards her chin and her head snapped back under his blow. He hadn't expected her neck to break.

At the same time, he hadn't expected her reaction, a casual tilt to the side and a smile. He caught the expression in her eyes and his blood ran cold. Pure, unadulterated hatred, anger and fury, a marriage of emotion blazed across her face. Either she'd entered the fight mad or he'd really pissed her off since the punches had started being thrown. Maybe both, Nick thought, he'd been known to have that effect on people. Her eyes were grey, almost colourless while she looked like she hadn't seen the sun in weeks. Her hair was shorn almost to the scalp barring a thin length down the middle, eyebrows ripped away.

Something about her looked familiar, he couldn't place the face. Not that this was the time to do it.

She came at him again, crashed the full weight of her slender body onto him and he tried to duck back, almost tripped over the coffee table. She took him down hard, he felt the pain jar through him as he landed, her nails going to claw at his eyes. Panicked, he flailed out, searching for anything that he could use. Nothing.

Come on!

His fingers scrabbled around empty air, nails scraping against the glossed wood. Had to be something. His face was starting to bleed, he could feel the cuts, she'd started at his cheeks and was moving upwards. He brought his head forward, smashed the bridge of his skull into her nose, heard her shriek in pain as the cartilage gave way under the force of the blow. Dull pain thudded through his skull, he bellowed himself, trying not to let the feeling get to him as he brought it back again and again. He'd drive that cartilage back up into her brain if he had to, kill her that way. Her hands were away from his eyes, slender fingers locked around his throat and starting to squeeze. The way they'd locked together, he couldn't move his neck, the breath cut from him.

He swept his eyes back and forth, anything, come on, anything. Asphyxiation was a horrible way to die, he'd heard. Painful. Just a little humiliating. The glint of the light off something caught his gaze, he reached out, stretched the sinews in his arm. The agony swept through him, a thousand burning needles tearing at his straining muscle. If he survived, he'd deal with it then. It was heavy, all too solid and it took him a second attempt to close his fingers around it. As he pulled it towards him, he heard the swirl of liquid inside it, the most beautiful sound he'd heard in a while.

It took a supreme effort, he tugged it into his hand, and smashed the heavy glass straight into the side of her face, a dozen sharp pains digging into his hands as it shattered under the blow. She screamed again, he couldn't tell where his blood ended and hers began. One chunk of glass had embedded in her eye, suddenly he could breathe again, and he brought back a foot to kick her off him, drove it hard into her chest and kicked her to her feet, his body crying out in relief.

A miniature explosion rocked the room above him, and she hurled forward as if she'd leaped from a spring board, head smashing into the wall before she slid into an untidy heap against the skirting board. He could almost see the floor beneath her through the hole in her back, blood already starting to gather underneath her in a sticky pool of claret.

117

Frewster swore, slid the pump of his kinetic disperser and broke the empty cartridge out of it, it hit the carpet with a tiny thud. "My best bloody carpet," he said. There wasn't any mistake as to the outrage in his voice. "Hells."

He didn't want to know where the old man had got the weapon from, it was a question that didn't have a good answer. Kinetic dispersers were brutal weapons, loaded with shells filled with highly pressurised ionic energy, the blast something nobody in their right mind would want to get hit by. Normally they were used against foes who'd coated themselves in personal shields for defending themselves. Even a shield wouldn't prevent the side effects. He'd seen them employed to devastating effect, hurling the targets several feet back through the air at rapid speeds, fast enough to hurt when they inevitably hit something.

"Thanks for the rescue," he muttered. Gratitude hurt here. He'd just been saved by someone three times his age. It took him a moment to spin it as three times the experience, that did a wonder for his bruised ego. With that in mind, Nick glanced back at the body. Shit. What a mess! He shook his head, tried to clear the fog that had filled his head. Deep breaths, he had to still have some composure somewhere. He closed his eyes, tried to focus on his heart and the consistency of its beat. He needed to be sharp. Anything to get his mind back in the game. His eyes swept back and forth, fell on his dropped blaster.

Somewhere else in the mansion, he heard more booms of disperser shots followed by the higher chatter of a blaster rifle retorting. He picked up his blaster, checked everything was still in working order. Nick glanced back to Frewster, saw the colour had drained from his face.

"Helga," he said. He could hear the terror in the old man's voice, almost quavering with the fear. "They're hunting her."

"They're after something," Nick said. He inclined his head towards the weapon. "You got another one of those."

The old man shook his head, cradled it even closer to his body. "Just the one in here. The one downstairs. Helga probably has it now. That was her order. Get it and shoot anything that moves if this happens."

That didn't bode well. Nick fought the urge to shake his head. "Terrible. You think we'll be able to get close to her?"

"Helga has all manner of training in proficient use of the deadly arts, Nicholas," Frewster said. "I pity those who cross her path."

"Your butler was trained in the deadly arts?" Nick asked. He didn't even want to know how that had come up. "That's one way to ensure nobody steals the silverware."

118

"I don't appreciate your flippancy," Frewster said, one eye on the window. It wasn't out of the question someone else could come through it. Nick had been mentally preparing himself for that eventuality ever since the intruder had gone down. Next one who came through would get the greeting of a laser blast to the face. Fuck screwing around with hand-to-hand combat. They might not be the toughest one-on-one but two or three would be tricky, even before factoring in their resistance to pain. "It was long before I met her, if you must know."

"Uh huh?" Nick didn't care. He could still see the outline of the aeroship hovering outside, cutting off any easy escape route. "We need to move, you know that. Get out of here, get to the garage, take a speeder and head for the nearest Unisco office."

"That would appear to be a plan. However, I do see several flaws in your thought process," Frewster said. Nick tried to ignore the sarcasm in his voice. "We cannot escape. Not while that ship is out there."

"I've got a plan," Nick said. "Sort of. We need to go though. This room is compromised." He jerked his head towards the window. "Too easy for them to gain access. Sooner or later we'll be overrun if they take that route." He looked at the video feeds on the screens in front of them, tried to formulate a plan.

Shit!

Too many to count, he could see them on every screen, all of them different shapes and sizes, maybe about twenty if he had to make a guess. One screen showed Helga with the disperser in hand, fury etched on her features as she fired, cycled, fired again. Frewster shook his head as he studied that one. A line of bodies led away from her, all of them looking like they'd suffered horribly. Limbs had been torn away, torsos crushed under incredible force, heads blunted back into unrecognisable shapes. She knew what she was doing, he had to give her that. Woman was a surgeon with the weapon

The crunching of glass gave them away, another two trying to get through the shattered windows behind them, he turned and put three shots through the first one before Frewster could even point his weapon at them. The first intruder gave way, staggered backwards through the window and took the woman behind him with him. The scream followed them all the way to the ground.

"Told you," he said. "Compromised." He jerked his head towards the door. "Come on, Brennan. We need to get the hells out of here as quickly as possible. I'll take point. Follow my lead. Anyone who comes up behind us, blast them. I'll deal with anyone who comes towards us. You good to do that?"

"Agent Roper, I was doing this long before you were born."
There was more than a hint of indignation in the old man's voice at the
way he'd asked the question. That was good. Nick wanted fire in
Frewster's heart. He wanted him pissed off, he wanted him alert. That
might be the difference between surviving or dying and he'd take every
slim advantage he could get. The slim margins were the decisive ones.
"I just hope you can keep up with me. That one gave you some
trouble." He pointed the weapon to the one he'd already killed.

"Took me by surprise," Nick admitted, already making for the
door. "Not going to happen again. Someone trained them well. I'd
think you'd be able to appreciate that, Brennan."

"Training is good," Frewster said. "There's no substitute for
experience though, I think you'd know that by now."

"Oh, I do," Nick said. He put a hand on the door knob, deep
breath and twist. It slid open with practiced ease, just a fraction and he
put his eye to it. Nothing in the immediate vicinity. He pushed it open
further, led with the X9S. Just in case. This house was hostile territory
right now, he'd treat it as such. He didn't want to think about the
consequences of doing anything else. He managed to step out of the
room, swept the corridor with his weapon. Only one direction. That
was good. Meant they couldn't be flanked. Getting caught between two
forces with only a single blaster was a recipe for disaster. "Clear!"

Ideally, he should have taken the weapon from Frewster. A
disperser would clear out any opposition with a lot more ease than his
blaster pistol. He wasn't surrendering his weapon to Frewster. Nor was
he going to leave him defenceless. There wasn't much of a choice to be
made. The old man knew what he was doing. He'd called it right, he'd
been doing this before Nick had been born. Who better to have his
back? The killer instinct was still there inside Frewster, something
hard-earned, even harder to lose. In the circumstances, he was glad to
have him watching his back. Ideally, Frewster would have led the way.
He knew this house better than any of the intruders. Not a chance he
could let him go first.

"We'll get there," Frewster huffed. "Doesn't matter how long it
takes."

"You might be right there," Nick said. He'd seen the artillery
they'd brought in to stop them leaving. That aeroship was bad news. It
had taken out his speeder with little effort. "We might have time on our
side."

"What do you mean, lad?"

"If they wanted to kill us, they could level the house without too
much sweat. No, they want someone alive. Might be me. Might be

you." Nick shrugged. "They could have taken me on the road here if they really wanted to. So… Like you say. They've come for you."

"Excellent deduction, Nicholas. Is it really relevant now?"

They reached the T-shaped junction at the bottom of the corridor, Nick looked at the old man. "Which way to the garages?"

"Left. Down the stairs. Through the dining room, there's a room at the back that leads to a corridor. One door in there leads to the kitchen. One to the garages. Servant's route. I've not been there for years. Helga always picks me up out the front. Nicholas?" He paused behind him, came to a sudden halt. Stubbornness etched his genial features. "I've made my choice. I'm not leaving without her."

The strange thing was, he could appreciate the sentiment. People got attached to each other. There was clearly some strange sort of relationship there. Maybe Frewster was a deviant and Helga hit him about a bit to get him off. Exceptional loyalty, he'd seen that in her demeanour. A mystery he could ponder all day.

"We need her anyway," he said. "Plan takes three people. We'll see if we can find her. You know where she was? From the monitors."

Frewster nodded. "Other wing. Looks like she made straight for the armoury."

Of course, she bloody would be. Nick bit down a curse, looked at his weapon. "Okay," he said. "Change of plan. We go for the garage. That's the obvious escape route. If it was me, I'd have most of my forces concentrated there. Try and overwhelm us as we make a run for it. If we got out the front door, that aeroship will corner us. Our options aren't fantastic."

Frewster nodded. "There are options though. They might be terrible, dear boy, but there are always options. We could surrender, for example."

Their eyes met for a moment before both burst out laughing. Unisco had been built on a foundation of never surrendering. To start now would be anathema for them. Laughing felt good, perhaps not the most appropriate time for it but truly appreciated.

"We'll go for Helga first," Nick said. "Get her with us. Three has more chance than two. It's still half a chance but it's better than nothing."

"That's the only sort of chance that we ask for. A slim one can work wonders for a sense of motivation to make the best of a bad situation."

"No arguing there, Brennan," he said. "Okay. Armoury. Let's get there. Hopefully she hasn't gone too far."

"Helga's a sensible woman," Frewster said. "She can survive a siege in that armoury. There are weapons in there. Old, but still serviceable. The old ones are those that pack the biggest surprise."

Egotistical old bastard. Nick wasn't entirely sure he was talking about blasters any longer. Not with that smile on his face.

They'd run into resistance twice on their way to the armoury, the first instance being a pair of sentries who'd allowed themselves to relax at an inopportune moment. Nick had shot them both through the head at short range, one after the other they'd hit the ground. Recognising them was going to be a challenge for whomever was paid to care about it. He didn't know who they were, just that Coppinger likely had something to do with it.

The uniforms, he'd never seen anything like them before. When she'd made her assault at Carcaradis Island, her troops had worn black uniforms with body armour. They'd made no show of attempting to hide their faces. Given what they'd since found out about her troops being supplemented with clones, it made sense. They wouldn't be in any sort of database; therefore, they had no need to hide.

Then there'd been the people like Ulikku. Those who Caldwell had told them about. The conscripts. The ones that Rocastle had been put in charge of turning into an army of the outcasts. An army of people just like him. The freaks and the deviants, the weird and the social misfits. The ridiculed becoming the rulers. An unsettling idea. They went through the same training as the clones, years of training condensed into weeks and months. It made sense.

Didn't matter right now. They were dead, and they weren't getting back up. He considered taking their weapons, decided against it. Wouldn't have put it past someone on Coppinger's side to booby trap the weapons, just in case they were ever turned against them. He didn't want a hand getting blown off because the weapon backfired and exploded. Or a paralysing shock because someone had a sick sense of humour.

Sick sense of humour was probably a job requirement if Rocastle oversaw training them. It'd probably be their only way to get through the day. Nick remembered fighting him, he'd have to be doing a better job with them than he had in his own efforts at fighting. He'd nearly concussed himself in that fight and he'd still done little more than toy with him.

The second lot had been tougher, they'd been spread out and the three of them had been on him and Frewster before they'd been able to ready a defence. Nick had hit the ground, felt the shots go high above his head. Frewster had yelled in pain, the boom of his kinetic disperser had taken one of them down, their arm blasted away from the rest of their body. Blood stained the carpet, the soldier's face twisted in pain. He wasn't going to be fighting back, the colour draining from his face. Already he was going into shock, he wouldn't last long.

Two of them left to disable. He was younger than Frewster, best that he be the one to deal with them. Nick sprang to his feet, weapon came up. His blaster spat energy towards the closest, they dropped into a crouch, he covered the distance and drove a kick into their face. They reacted just a little too late. The impact that jarred up his leg was satisfying, they crumpled under the blow and he turned to face the other. This time, he wasn't underestimating any of them. That one woman had nearly done for him. How good they might be, it was time to remind them that he was better. The other soldier facing him was female, something vaguely familiar about her. Maybe he'd seen her at the Quin-C. Maybe. Either way, it wasn't something that meant he was going to hold back. She pointed her weapon at him, he lunged forward, dropped and rolled under the blast as it screamed above his head. Before she could readjust her aim, he hit her in the stomach with a shoulder. Nick felt her crumple, a knee came up, caught him in the cheek. Stars exploded across his vision, the grunt of pain escaped him. The side of his face was on fire, it had been a whiplash blow, thrown with power rather than accuracy. She brought down both fists onto his back, he pushed through the pain, rose to his full height. She'd tried to block the punch he'd thrown, only partially successful in her effort, and he'd tagged her with his left hand. Anger creased her features, she threw herself at him, he twisted out the way and watched her sail past. He'd even helped her, thrown a kick at her spine as she stumbled, saw her fall flat on her face.

He couldn't help but wince at the crack that ruptured through the room as he brought his foot down on her neck. She wouldn't be getting up again. Ever. Once more, he retrieved his blaster. Frewster shook his head at him, the sleeve of his jacket ripped and smoke gushing from it. Underneath it, he could see the skin was red and blistered.

"Little bitch winged me," Frewster said. "You lose your weapon a lot in a fight, Nicholas, do you know that? Unarmed combat can only take you so far."

"I'm three for three, you know that?" Nick replied. The other invader hadn't gotten back up, he wouldn't for a while Nick guessed. The kick had been well placed, driven right into his nose. Might not even get up at all. "These guys aren't messing around."

"Of course, they aren't, whoever thought of an invader who did play games," Frewster chuckled. "I merely advise you that proceeding with caution might well be the more prudent approach. You know that in your profession, a blaster is just as important as a hand or a foot."

Nick had heard that comment before, he hadn't bought into it then, he wasn't buying into it now. If you didn't have hands or feet, you wouldn't be working in the field for Unisco.

"You're more than welcome to put them down," he said. "You're not doing too bad with that thing." He nodded to the weapon in Frewster's arms, the disperser cradled lovingly like a favoured child.

"Dear boy, I was a surgeon with this weapon in my younger days. We have a long acquaintance that I did not think I was ever going to get the chance to renew."

"I'm glad you're having fun." Nick found it hard to keep the sarcasm out of his voice. If Frewster was bothered by it, he didn't show it. "Anyway, cut the chatter. We need to find your housekeeper and get out of here."

"My dear boy, Helga is so much more than that."

The time came that Nick thought he might have to agree on that. Frewster had gestured to the armoury, he'd prepared to lead the way in when the doors had shattered through, one broken body hitting the ground in front of them. Still clad in her uniform, Helga strode out like a hardened combat veteran, a blaster in hand. Nick could see that despite the grievous injuries, the figure on the ground still twitched, some part of them still alive. Helga saw it too, one long step, one slight adjustment of her aim as she pointed the weapon at the fallen man.

The sound echoed through the hallways, Nick saw the head snap back and he hadn't realised he'd been holding his breath. One long exhalation. Cold. That was cold blooded. It made tactical sense. Finishing them off when they were badly injured stopped them from taking revenge later. It just took a special sort of human to be able to pull the trigger when their enemy was like that.

Throughout his career working at Unisco, there'd been a handful of incidents when he'd killed in cold blood. Jeremiah Blut had been unarmed, but he'd needed to die. Lucas Hobb had been helpless but no less a threat when Nick had suffocated him. They bore unpleasant memories he was never quite happy to repeat. They stained him far more than those where the killing had been justified. There was no honour in killing someone who couldn't fight back, even if it made sense from an operational point of view.

"Helga," Frewster said, his voice jovial. He strode over, embraced her. "We have to leave now."

She didn't look impressed. Nick didn't care. To hells with what the help thought. If they stayed here, they'd die, there was no other way

124

of looking at it. He didn't care if Helga stayed or went. That was a lie, he realised quickly. They had a better chance with her on their side. There was something about her. She knew her way around a fight. Plus, her name sounded familiar, it struck a chord he couldn't ignore.

"Here's the plan," he said. Someone had to take charge of this sorry shower of shit and it might as well be him. He had no delusions of grandeur over his own importance, just that they needed a plan. If they didn't stick to it, they'd be dead. "We get to the garage, kill anyone in our path, get a speeder and leave. I've got a plan to deal with the aeroship out there but..."

"Are you concealing anti-aircraft weaponry in your pockets?" Helga inquired. Nick ignored her. She didn't look like she was going to let it go. "Explosives up your sleeve?"

"Something like that," he said, deciding to keep it cryptic. The less she knew, the better. He didn't want to keep them in the dark, but at the same time, her attitude annoyed him. "That's need-to-know." Normally, he hated those words. Now, he appreciated them like no other. "Just trust in me. This isn't my first siege."

"It's true," Frewster said sagely. "They do teach you about siege-craft at the academy. Never know when it'll come in handy."

"They do like their contingency plans," Nick said. "Any situation they can think of."

"Nice to see that some of my legacy remains then," Frewster replied. "That was all me, dear boy. I instigated that too many moons ago myself."

Not that anyone remains alive to dispute it, Nick thought. He held his tongue. Calling Frewster on some of his statements wasn't going to get them out of here. Instead, he glanced past Helga, into the armoury. He'd seen war dramas that had less bodies in than that room, he wasn't squeamish but some of them no longer looked entirely human. They'd suffered. That much was clear. "Any weapons we can use in there? Few blaster rifles, maybe?"

Frewster hadn't been kidding when he said some of the stuff in there was old. Most of them were projectile weapons, gone out of fashion years ago. An old Femble snipers rifle lay at the back of the room, the barrel bent out of shape. He had some personal experience with that weapon, none of it pleasant.

"Sorry," Helga said. "I had to make do with what was in there. Empty now." No hint of emotion in her voice, just certain statement. She'd done a job, she almost sounded proud of it. Nick said nothing. He held up his blaster, ejected the power pack and examined it. He had a spare in his pocket, three quarters of a charge here. Thirty-five shots.

He'd have to make them do. If it came to need more than that, they were screwed. It was indisputable.

"Let's do this," he said. "I'll take point. Helga, take the rear."

She looked like she wanted to argue, he stood his ground and kept his eyes locked on hers. If she wanted to argue, he wasn't backing down. "I know I've got no authority to order you around, I'm thinking of him." He jerked a thumb towards Frewster. "We need to get him out of here. If he's between us, he's got more of a chance of getting out unscathed."

Helga didn't blink. "I'll take point," she said. "I know this house better than you do. You bring up the rear." She dropped the pack of her blaster rifle, inserted a fresh one, locked it into place with a brisk slap of her palm against the metal. The thud sounded like a challenge in the silence of the hallway.

"You're a civilian," Nick said. It sounded half-hearted, he couldn't muster much more of a defence. If she wanted to lead, she could. He didn't care either way. Long as someone took point, someone kept an eye on their rear, kept Frewster safe, it'd be golden. "You sure you know what you're doing."

She smiled for the first time. It might just have been the single scariest expression he'd seen on any human ever. "Do you? These people invaded my home. Killing them all is the very least I can do. It sends a message to the others about not repeating the insult."

"She's exceptionally loyal," Frewster said. "I couldn't ask for a better companion. Believe me, Nicholas, she's qualified."

"You teach her some of your old tricks?"

"I didn't need to," Frewster said solemnly.

They'd run into resistance once again on their way to the garage, if it could be called that, resistance that had barely had the chance to put up much of a fight. For an invading force, their attention wasn't what Nick would have expected. They'd been caught by surprise far too often. If these were Coppinger's elite forces, then he'd have been amazed. There was always going to be a certain amount of wheat and a certain amount of chaff but not like this. Individually they were good, as a team they had something lacking.

That was what made him think that maybe they just might get through this after all. A well organised smaller force trumped a disorganised large one every time, given the right strategy. Between the three of them, their kills had to number double figures now. Helga had opened fire the instant she'd seen them, her weapon dancing in her arms. Nick brought his own blaster up, hadn't fired, just watched her. She was good, he realised that very quickly. She didn't waste shots, others with a weapon like that might have gone fully automatic and laid waste to the entire room. She showed discipline, fired in bursts of twos and threes that found their targets more often than they didn't.

Finally, he fired, drew a bead on the one target left standing, pulled the trigger and watched the head bounce back. He went down, and Nick blew the smoke away from the barrel of his blaster. Five more bodies to add to the kill count.

"Terrible," he muttered.

Frewster looked at him. "You can't have sympathy for them, surely?"

He shook his head. "Just waiting for the other shoe to fall. This is too easy." Frewster grunted at that comment. "I'd have expected more resistance," Nick added.

"Don't question it. Enjoy it while it lasts," Helga said. "We don't have much further to go."

He'd never seen a garage quite like this, two speeders as promised. Neither of them looked desirable, built far more for luxury and status rather than speed. That wasn't good. Swiftness was what they needed to get away, a far more useful quality than looking fancy while they were killed.

There were more of them here, the realisation hit him a damn sight faster than it might have done, and it undoubtedly saved his life. Five, six, seven, eight of them at least. They'd been waiting, the group had already moved to set up an effective firing line. Helga fired into them, weapons burst to life and Nick pulled Frewster down with him to avoid their blast, the old man cursing and moaning as he hit the floor. Tough old bastard as he might be, the indignity had to hurt. "Damnit all to hells," Frewster spat. "Leaping around like this is a younger man's game!"

"Getting shot is a dead man's game," Nick retorted. It wasn't helpful, it took the bite out of the situation. "You're welcome." He rose, pointed his blaster over cover, fired again and again. Somewhere, he heard a yell and a thud. He still had it. Across the room, Helga had dropped, sliding a fresh power pack into her weapon. He didn't know where she was getting them from, she looked like she had enough to repel an entire army. Maybe she did, it'd be helpful, but he doubted she had much left. Frewster's kinetic disperser boomed again and again, Nick reached out and snatched it from him before the weapon's charge cells went dry. "I'll need one shot, Brennan. Save it. Trust me. I've got this."

He looked at the old man. "On the count of three, I need you to get to the closest speeder. Fire up the engines. We'll cover you." Nick looked across at Helga, saw her listening to them, even above the roar of blaster fire. They were hitting everything, bar their targets. Above them, the walls had been torn to shreds, thick blasts of laser fire ripping gouges into them. "Cover!"

Helga nodded, raised her weapon. Deft fingers ran across the slide, she ratcheted it back and grinned at him. Still a scary expression.

"One."

The fire lulled to a silence, Nick shot a glance at Helga. She shrugged, kept an even tighter grip on her weapon. If she wasn't being fooled, neither was he.

"Two," he muttered. Frewster gave him a thumbs-up. A dozen feet to the closest speeder. He didn't want to think about how quickly a blaster bolt would cover the distance. Maybe he should go himself. Have Helga cover him. She looked like she knew what she was doing.

"Three," Frewster said, finishing the count for him. The old man was gone, he might have been shoving ninety, but he didn't look it with the way he shuffled across the floor. It wasn't the swiftest of runs, not entirely surprising, but he could hustle with the best of them. Nick rose, his blaster dancing in his hands, shots finding targets. The low roar of his weapon beat a nice concerto with the high chattering of Helga's rifle. A shot caught her in the side, Nick saw the acid green blast rip through the air and she staggered, a barrage of shots from her own weapon peppering the ground in front of her as her aim went wild.

"Go!" she shouted, her voice barely audible. She sounded in pain, a croak of agony layering her voice. Concentration etched her face as she dropped to one knee, brought the weapon back up. "Get Brennan out of here. Protect him!" Anything else she might have said was lost behind the blast of rifle fire.

To hells with that, Nick thought. He dropped, let his empty power pack spin away out of his blaster and he slammed the replacement in. He had Frewster's weapon, he had his ace in the hole. It needed to be good.

More of them were coming, he could see that. They were filtering in at the back of the garage, coming in through the sliding doors. At least they had an escape route. Frewster had the door of a speeder open, had fallen into it. One of the windows blew out above him and Nick heard him bellow as glass cascaded down onto him.

"Go!" Helga repeated. Crimson stained her clothes where she'd been shot, a ragged hole that caused him to wince as he looked at it. He wasn't a stranger to injuries on the battlefield, it never got any more pleasant though when you had any experience of them. He'd had a hole like that himself before and he was still kicking. Nick glanced about the area, saw a pile of cleaning rags above him that looked sterile enough.

He grabbed a handful of them, shoved them into his jacket, rammed them hard into a pocket.

"Not yet," he called back. "Helga, go get to him. I'll cover you. We make it out together or…"

"No!" she roared, her voice almost incandescent. "You need to get him out. I vowed to protect him…"

"One of you get the fuck over here and hurry!" Frewster shouted. "Quit bloody talking about it!"

"Ladies first," Nick said, tossing her a wink. "Come on, Carlow, bloody get to that speeder before I have to drag you there!"

He pointed his blaster at the closest invader, a dark-skinned Vazaran and pulled the trigger, the shot took him in the chest, the force of the blast took him down. "I'm running out of shots! It's now or never."

"Helga, hurry!" Frewster shouted. He was probably in the best place, they were doing their best not to hit the speeder. It brought weight to his theory that they'd come here to get Frewster and not either him or Helga. "I order you not to bloody die here now quit being a fucking martyr. You don't get out of it that easily."

She didn't look happy as she glanced first to him, then to the readout on her weapon, all blaster rifles had them to count the number of remaining shots. Her mood looked like it had darkened, it wasn't good news, that was for sure.

"Three," she said. "We go on three."

"You go on two," Nick said. "I'll cover you, I'll go on four, you lay down fire for me!" He nodded at her. "Leave nothing behind. This is all or nothing!"

Begrudgingly, she returned the nod, already had her weapon up as he counted out one, and then two. She was on her feet and charging for the speeder, limping as she clutched at her side while firing one handed into the army. Nick's blaster reported again and again, scattering those who'd avoided taking cover under Helga's initial assault, he counted out two more beats in his head and then ran himself for the speeder. Frewster had a key in the ignition, the engines roaring to life as he hurled himself into the backseats and then it kicked forward like a mule. A couple of dull thuds and a scream, he saw a couple of bodies laid out by the bumper, someone who hadn't gotten out the way fast enough. The speeder was moving, slowly kicking into life but it was going. He saw Helga leaning out the shotgun window, emptying her last power pack into anything that came close, her face screwed up in concentration. Her weapon clicked empty and she tossed it away, let it drop where she'd held it. Shots peppered the rear of the speeder, took out the window. Nick buried his face into the seat, shards of glass slashed at his neck and ears, he rolled onto his back and felt them bounce away.

More and more shots were missing now. They were almost clear of the garage, almost outside.

Almost.

He looked up and he could see the command aeroship above them, moving into an attack position. He tried not to think about what would happen if it opened fire on them, they wouldn't stand a chance. Maybe a skilled pilot in a faster speeder could evade it indefinitely. An aged man in this heap of expensive crap wouldn't stand a chance. In the front seat, Helga was writhing in pain as Frewster slalomed the speeder about the fields, trying to make the line of fire unclear as possible. He doubted it'd be anywhere near enough, but the efforts were appreciated. He didn't want to die like this after all.

Nick reached into his coat, tossed the rags to her. "Try and staunch it as best you can," he said. He gave her an apologetic look, one that told her he knew it wasn't much, but it was better than nothing. She smiled, jerked her head towards the ship. It was a look that said, if you're going to do something.

He sat up, punched open the roof window and pointed his X9S at the aeroship. He heard Helga give out a pained chuckle. Frewster coughed. "Dear boy, you can't possibly bring down one of those with that little blaster."

Nick ignored him, pulled the trigger, emptied the weapon in the direction of the aeroship. The prediction was a good one, if the pilot showed any awareness of being hit, it didn't bother them. If anything, it drove them into an attack position, the afterburners kicked up a gear and, in a heartbeat, they were almost on top of them. Nothing like the threat of an attack to bring the predators into a sense of ruthless overconfidence.

"Nice plan," Helga said. "I thought you had something better. What next? You going to throw rocks at it?"

Nick winked at her, dropped a hand to her shoulder as he slid back into the speeder. He found the disperser, fumbled into his pocket, rooted around for what he was looking for. "Oh, I saved the best surprise until last. When all else fails, throw credits at the problem."

"If you're going to do something, then hurry," Frewster said. "We can't dodge forever."

"I think we should stop," Nick said. "I need a clear shot at it, I need it to be as close as possible for it to work. The moment I say so, Brennan, I need you to hit that accelerator as fast as you can. We do not want to hang around here or we'll die. End of story."

He found what he needed, slid the credit into the palm of hand. Either this would work, or it wouldn't. He prayed it would. Alvin Noorland had done good work, he'd assured everyone that there was no mechanical reason why it wouldn't. He could still remember that lecture even now, could recall Noorland's voice as he'd urged them not to do it unless they absolutely had to though. 'Because,' he'd said in that rough voice of his. 'It is hands down, the dumbest thing you could do.'

If Alvin Noorland was watching him in the afterlife, he hoped he was smiling on them all. He needed all the help they could give him. Helga glanced back, a handful of rags pressed against her side. She cocked her head to the side, a bemused look.

"What is that?" she asked.

"Al Noorland's last gift," Nick said as the speeder came to a halt. Frewster kept his engines running, one hand hovering above the accelerator stick. "Saving lives even though he isn't with us anymore."

They were coming, the ship was swooping in, he could see them getting closer. If he concentrated, he might be able to count the enemy forces sat in the back. He stood up, brought the disperser to his shoulder and aimed down the sight. Centre mass. Control your breathing, he could almost hear his old shooting instructor saying.

Closer.

They were hovering above them, a good thirty feet up and twenty away. Still not close enough to be effective. They might sense a surrender, but they weren't treating it as a certainty yet. They were wary.

Closer!

"Nicholas," Frewster said. "Whatever happens, it's been an honour. Nice to know that Unisco didn't squander my legacy."

Closer, damnit! He watched. Twenty feet up, ten away. He could make out the details on the pilot's face. Behind them, a crimson haired figure, barely taller than the seats in front of her from this angle. She was gesturing, telling them to lower the weapon. She suspected something. Nick smiled.

"Boom," he said. "Make me!" He stood up straighter, kept one hand on the weapon to keep it steady, gave them the middle finger with the other. "Fucking make me, you bitch!"

They moved closer, the magical range. Studies had shown that kinetic dispersers were truly effective over ten feet, less reliable over twenty and truly useless over thirty. He only needed an element of reliability. Closer still. He'd riled them, he could see the fury on their commander's face. Even if she'd not heard the words, she'd gotten the gist of them. She wasn't stupid enough to miss them, though he hoped she was dumb enough to fall into the trap.

He glanced at the credit coin, a white colour and worth five hundred credits, smiled and pushed down on the centre of it. He dropped it into the barrel of the disperser, saw them oncoming and pulled the trigger.

Nick felt the kick of the weapon blast back into his shoulder, some part of him was screaming for Frewster to go, go, go and the speeder kicked off into action, already on the move. The blast itself hadn't done anything, the force dispersed before it even came close to damaging the aeroship. The credit though had carried on going, driven on by the momentum of the shot until it lodged deep in the windshield. Nick saw the look of surprise on the pilot's face, only for a moment but it was enough.

The last moment anyone aboard would ever have. He had to shield his eyes, covered them with his arm as the giant fireball ripped through the aeroship, tossing it onto its side and driving it towards the ground. It was on its death throes, any idiot could see that, Nick watched as it became little more than a speck in the distance, further and further away. By the time it hit the ground and the explosion engulfed the wreckage completely, they were too far away to do little more than hear it.

"You're welcome," Nick said, dropping back down into his seat. "Now fly. Let's get as far away from here as possible."

"The pride of the skies, the greatest wonder of the kingdoms you'll see in this life or the next. She'll fly you from one edge of the civilised world to the other and she'll do it in so much style you'll want to do it again and again. Come ride the Aerius, you'll never feel more like a Divine. One day, you'll tell your grandchildren you were amongst the first to ride it."

Promotional advert from the days when the Aerius was about to take her maiden voyage.

Nobody quite knew why the Aerius had crashed when it did. Nobody had ever been able to find the wreckage, hence the confusion. Without any sort of quantifiable evidence to support a theory, it was doomed to fail before it had gotten off the ground. The only sort of supposition was conspiratorial at best, with none of it concrete. She'd heard them all, the Aerius had always been a pet interest of hers. Not knowing was something that she'd hated. If you didn't know, you were at a disadvantage.

One theory was that it had been hijacked, not very expertly and they'd brought it crashing down. One that it had been carrying cargo that had vaporised the entire ship. That explained why nobody had been able to find it until now. Hard to find something when it had apparently been broken down into little more than trace atoms. That theory had been proved false. When she'd been in the Chamber of Fate, she'd seen it all. Everything that ever was, everything that ever could be. She'd seen it all and she'd wept, so much suffering and so much death. Little interspersions of joy didn't make up for that. Triumph didn't cover tragedy, not when there was so little against so much. It had filled her with despair, she'd seen the world the way it truly was and not the way people believed it to be.

Not many of the memories remained. For a few moments, they'd burned brightly into her brain, searing her grey matter. She couldn't see anything but them. With time, they'd faded. The old man who wasn't a man had told her that. He'd worn the face of her grandfather, but he'd been anything but. There'd been something worse than malice in his demeanour.

Indifference. He hadn't cared what she did with the knowledge, just that she wouldn't be able to take most of it with her.

That, she suspected, was the test. What you did with what you took. He'd explained it to her, thus. Three questions. The answers would remain with her. Knowledge she would not be able to forget.

"So many," he'd said with a smile. "Come here and ask the wrong questions. They ask what they think they need to know rather than what they truly need to. Panic. Pressure. It gets to them. That is why they fail. The coolest head inevitably prevails. What sort of person are you?"

She'd asked her first question. "Why can't I take everything I know now from here with me?" An impertinent question, but not an unimportant one. To understand things, you needed context, she'd always found. The answer to her first question would tell her a lot about the way to move forward.

"Because all knowledge costs something. To remove the knowledge of everything, the price would be tremendous. To take away the knowledge of everything that has been and could be, it is not meant for the minds of man or woman. It would destroy you to walk in the mortal world with that knowledge. Why do you think seers go mad eventually?"

"I assumed that they were sick to start with," she said. "A long time ago, I thought that. I've recently started to believe that may not be the case."

"One does not simply start to believe. One always believes. It's merely a matter of acknowledging it or not. A denier always wants an excuse to deny. A believer will always find a reason to believe."

She couldn't argue with that. Even as far back as she could remember, now she thought about it, there'd always been that fascination. That key on the mountain had been the prime example, when she'd pushed that old man to his death. Here in the Chamber, his face was as clear as the day, a memory she couldn't ignore.

"Yes," her host said. "Every memory, good or bad." His face faded, replaced with the old man from the mountains. "Ye 'member me, do ya, little missy?"

"Do you do other impressions?" She wasn't impressed. "Or just dead old men?"

"Is that ye secon' question, missy?"

"It is not," she said. "My second question is, how does one acquire this knowledge and take it back without it consuming you? I do not wish to be destroyed by it."

The old man chuckled, a sound not unlike bricks smashing through a window. His lungs sounded ruined. A thin stream of crimson trickled from his eyeball. "Ain' never that easy, little missy. Death is all part of' been human an' ye can' change that, no ye can'."

"I didn't ask you why it can't be done. I asked you how it would be done."

"That ye did. That ye did." His lips peeled apart, a crack of a grin

134

appearing. "The reason we can all hold that knowledge, do ye know, is because we're differen'. Ye get? We're not like ye. We have that spark of div'nity in us."

He gestured to her wrist, her eyes had fallen, and she'd reacted with a start at the gem there. For a moment, she thought he'd slipped a bracelet on her. "Ye know what that is? That be a gem from old Gil himself. Contains just a weesiest of his power. Enough t'get ye started I think. Bet ye expect more from his heart, yeah?"

No bracelet. She realised that now she looked closer. It was a lovely piece, all the colours she could ever imagine and at the same time, none of them. Effervescent water. That's what it reminded her off. Oil on an ocean surface, bathed in sunlight. One made the other. The presence and the void. She could see the gentle pressure point where it rested against the skin of her wrist, could feel the tip digging gently into the vein.

"Div'nity can' never be bought. Only taken through blood 'n' death. That be the only way you can do it. Mebbe ye unite the seven but ye don' want to do that."

"Divine blood," she said thoughtfully. The pressure on her wrist increased. The crimson broke down her skin like a stream of tiny red ants. "I have one question left." Not a question. She'd made sure of that. A statement. At this point, the mystery man could have taken anything she said any way he liked. He'd made that point earlier enough, he'd let her off when she'd asked him about his impressions.

The face shifted again, swirled about like a whorl of spilled puddling, the body going with it. Her breath caught in her throat, flushed her face as she saw the familiar white bridal gown. She'd paid for it for Meredith after all. Meredith whose face looked the way it had on her aborted big day. Petulant but happy. She was lucky she'd gotten a wedding at all.

"You do have one more," she said, with Meredith's voice. "I'd say you should pick it wisely, you know."

"You don't sound like her," she said. "You're not a good impression of my daughter."

"I haven't had to put up with you like she has," the figure said, more than a little spitefully. There was no need for that, surely. "That old man, your grandfather, they've both been with me for a long time now. Your daughter still lives."

Her face pulled up into a scowl. "Yes. As to whether that is a good thing or not, I'm afraid that we may yet disagree."

"You dislike her?"

"I don't care much for her attitude. I tried to do my best by her." She meant it as well. If you were going to deny something, there was little benefit in doing it to a being like this. "She did not grow up the way I would have liked. I would like to have done a little better. I would have wished she'd done a lot more with what she had rather than picking the easy life."

"You have a third question," Meredith-who-wasn't-Meredith said. "Ask now and take your knowledge as reward for reaching this place. Few before you have. Already you are exceptional in that regard. None have ever gone all the way."

She said nothing, stood back and thought through everything she knew that would stay with her. Her thoughts, not the knowledge that now slid through her unrestrained. It felt hard to tell where one began, and others started, yet she persevered. To give up was not in her nature. With that knowledge split from her own experiences, she started to go through every bit of information related to what had just been said to her. Knowing that all this would be lost to her the moment she left was infuriating, she felt her skin crawling with anger at the very thought of it, but it was what it was, and better this than being left a vegetable by unrestricted access to it all.

"There are two types of people in these kingdoms," she said. "Those who complain about what their circumstances are, and those that get on with it."

"A point of pertinence." That was a bigger word than she'd ever heard Meredith use. It truly wasn't a good impression of her. "Do you know what you wish to ask?"

"Quiet! I'm thinking."

Everything. What could she do with everything? She could break the world, she could put it back together. She considered her options, left her foot tapping against the ground. Seeing every possible future, every truth and lie, knowing what could happen, it was truly humbling. The strangest thing of it all was that even seeing the most likely future didn't leave her wishing to abort. If anything, it only strengthened her resolve, realising that things weren't as they seemed.

"Clever," Meredith said. "Most people say the first thing that enters their head. It is usually the most important question they could ask, and yet they fail to rise beyond the mediocre."

She ignored her. She'd had plenty of practice at tuning out anything Meredith had to say. It wasn't much of a stretch for her talents. If the vacuous little bitch ever said anything worth listening to, it would have been different.

"Okay," she said. She was as confident as she ever would be that the answer was right there in front of her. She saw what she needed, she knew what she needed to ask to ensure that the memories stayed with her. This was good, she felt the elation flooding through her, like sucking honey straight from the hive. "My third question. Here it comes. What are the exact coordinates of the location of the Aerius?"

Meredith blew out through her lips, looked up at her with that oh-so-familiar expression she'd often felt the urge to wipe off her daughter's face with a few well-chosen words. Failing that, a slap would achieve the same effect. It didn't suit Meredith, looking smug. She had nothing to be proud about.

"Clever," she said again. "The Aerius contains all the answers you need, as well as the tools. Knowing how to work the ritual wouldn't do you any good if you do not have the equipment. A sound stratagem. The knowledge is a gift from the Divines, three questions answered truly, knowledge as much a part of you now as if you experienced it first-hand." Meredith laughed, something disturbingly familiar in the way she did. Another breath caught in her throat, she felt the coordinates emblazon themselves across the forefront of her mind. She couldn't have forgotten them if she'd wanted to. "I've never seen it done that way before, you know. Everyone wants to know the fastest way to achieve power when they get here. They never think about the logistics of it. Power which cannot be reached does nobody any good."

"Exactly," Claudia said. As much as she tried to keep the excitement out of her voice, it threatened to be a losing battle. "It's only good to you if you can make it work for you. Everything I need is on the Aerius. And now I know where to find the Aerius." She buffed her nails against her jacket, gave the thing that looked like her daughter a smile. "This has been a productive trip."

Her smile faded, lost amid the sharp rip rushing up her arm, the gem sliding in. Her skin proved no opposition to it, neither did the muscle below. She ground her teeth together, refused to scream. Only when it came to the bone did it halt its incursion, the tip grinding hard into her. If it hadn't, she would have broken. She could feel the force behind it, had gone deadly still as if the slightest movement would sever her hand.

"Pain is sometimes its own price," Meredith said. The way she cocked her head, that simpering vapid smile. She regretted saying that this thing couldn't act like her daughter. Right now, it could out-Meredith Meredith. "Consider that little jewel a gift from me. I took it from Old Gil himself, you know. A long time ago in a different world. Stole it right off his shackles. One of seven little trinkets that could change the world. Little piece of him to take with you. More divinity in that one little jewel than there is in your world combined. Why you think he hid it here and not out there with the rest of them? It doesn't make you what you want to be though."

"A gift?" She studied her wrist, looked at the way the skin had fused around the stone without even a hint it had never belonged there. Tentatively, she touched it, prodded and probed with a fingertip. Not pain. Not pain as she recognised it. Something alien, an emotion she'd never experienced before. All she knew was she didn't like it.

"I want it back one day. Nothing lasts forever. That will though. It'll outlast you, I'm afraid. When you're nothing but dust and decay, that stone shall look the same. I'll reclaim it then." Meredith smiled, her face shifted back into that of the old man who looked like the pictures she'd seen of her grandfather. She'd never met the man, at least not that she could remember.

"I'll probably not need it then," she said. "It shouldn't be an issue."

"It won't. Never mind shouldn't." She saw the annoyance flicker across his face. "You can be certain of that, I assure you."

"Who are you?" she asked. "What's your name and why are you helping me."

The old man cackled, clucked his tongue in glee. "Oh, my dear, if you wished to know that, you should have asked before. Everyone has their reasons, I will say that. It's hard not to toy with mortals. You're just so delightfully self-destructive. You know you shouldn't do something, and yet..."

He raised his hand, let it fall as a whistle slipped from his lips. "You'll always find a way to jump when you should be backing away from the edge."

"We'll see who jumps," she said. "I'll be back here soon." "Maybe. Maybe not. Divinity has its pitfalls. Even with the help from that little trinket in your wrist, there's no guarantees. Games are so much more fun when you know the outcome."

She opened her mouth to say more, yet no sound emerged, silence followed every twitch of her oral muscles. Her feet slipped, the ground was no longer solid beneath her and suddenly nothing was rushing up to greet her, nothing but unending blackness as far as she could see...

That had been months ago. She'd been busy. Not knowing now what she had back then about the Aerius, she'd set about the research, putting Sinkins on it. He did so love to hit the records, dig through those mysteries of the past. Besides, there was a war to wage and she couldn't chase her own fantasies half cocked. Now. Now was the time. And only now had she succeeded.

A smile played over her lips as she stared out the window at the view below. "Perfect," she said to herself, knowing nobody was around to hear it.

The Aerius had been a magnificent ship in her day, her maiden voyage nearly fifty years ago had been to explore the newly minted five kingdoms. She'd been a joint project, a vision for the future using the labours of the past. Over two thousand feet long and half as high, massive for the time and still a record for the largest non-military vessel ever built. She'd always been fascinated by the mystery. How did something so large and constructed so perfectly just vanish from sight without even a hint as to where it had gone. People had searched for it ever since. If it had been at sea, that might have been explained. There was a lot of unexplored ocean out there. It was hard to chart every inch of the sea floor, not to mention a wasted expense. The Aerius had crashed on land. It had been over Premesoir when it had, somewhere amidst the mountains. That explained much.

Even now she knew where to look, it was still a challenge to see it. Over time, stones and shale had covered the hull, already colours on a par with each other. There'd been bronze in these mountains once, patches of discoloured earth remained where the metal had once resided, stagnant deposits too worthless to dig out. Those patches mingled with the layers of rust spattering the hull, making the task even more challenging.

They'd left the Eye in a smaller ship, to bring her stronghold down this close to the ground would have invited catastrophe. It might be shielded against radar, but they'd already found out that it could still be seen by the naked eye. The last thing she wanted was another attack. The first one had cost them too much. They'd had to jettison half the station. Too many resources lost. Some of them had never been recovered. Rocastle had made the choice, and she hadn't blamed him. She couldn't, not when it would have been her decision to do the same thing. Things could be reclaimed if one was in position to do so. If the entire thing had been destroyed, her efforts would be futile.

She glanced back across the hold behind her, studying the armed force that she'd brought with her. She didn't anticipate trouble, anyone aboard had to be long dead. Yet it didn't pay to take risks. Claudia shot a glance at the gem in her wrist, the Gilgarus Heart. Since she'd gotten it, she'd survived two assassination attempts, being shot and stabbed no longer appeared to bother her as much as it once might. A fantastic situation yet those words about pitfalls echoed too deep in her ears. She couldn't shake the feeling that when the moment came, and she might need it, the feeling of invincibility might fail her. She didn't know where it came from. Maybe some lost remnant of omniscience that hung back from her time in the Chamber. Maybe. The Chamber had been a means to an end. Trinkets and artefacts of an earlier age were one thing. This stone was pretty, it had its uses. There were items of true power out there, the things that the Divines themselves would kill to hold onto.

Too many words had been spoken about the stone in her wrist, the Gilgarus Heart and why it had been created and by whom. She'd heard the stories too many times. Jeremiah Blut had believed in them, had fanned the fires in her soul and though Sinkins proclaimed a denial of belief, there was still something in his eyes that spoke of the wonder. He looked like he'd tried to suppress it, yet the anticipation had only grown. Belief was a powerful thing and seeing it in front of you tended to strip away doubts.

That was where the stunt at the final had come into play. She wanted a show of force. She wanted people to fear her. That was how the Divines had started out. They'd come, they'd conquered, they'd won the respect of their people and the enmity of their enemies. People loved them. They feared them. Over time, that belief had only grown. The more they'd believed, the more powerful they became, thriving on it. She'd heard Carson voice the theory that they'd been powerful precursors to the Vedo, they'd drawn the power from the Kjarn in ways that people today could not even start to understand. She didn't think so. She suspected it might be more than that. Carson knew things that she couldn't. He wasn't all knowing. Not at all. He was fallible, he wouldn't have fallen as far as he had if he wasn't.

Alaxaphal had insisted on sending a squad of his finest with her. Twenty of the best soldiers trained up under the programs. They were overkill, she thought. She didn't need them. Not when Domis sat next to her. He was worth fifty of them. More. One hundred. He was worth a hundred other men and she'd say that to anyone who argued. Sinkins had wanted to come, she'd left him on the Eye. He was needed there. She wanted everything and anything he could come up with that might give them an edge as they moved through the Aerius. His was the mind that might unlock this mystery, better suited there than it was down here.

"What are you thinking, Mistress?" Domis asked, his voice soft amidst the sounds of the engines. The men in the back were silent. Just the way that she liked. They were too well-trained to allow idle chatter to filter into their wait. A mix of clones and recruits. The best sort of blend. She didn't like groups that were too much of one or the other. The clones could learn something from the recruits. The recruits could learn something from the clones. Subtractor had pointed it out that it was ironic that those qualities desired to be suppressed in the clones,

140

the ability to creatively solve problems using unconventional methods, to follow initiative as well as orders, they were the ones they sought after in their recruits. They'd recruited heavily in Vazara in recent weeks, sought to augment their armed forces using volunteers for the cause.

Mazoud had spoken big about making Vazara better, but they were just words. The reality of it all was that they had no desire to do so. The worse things got over there, the more likely the disaffected would be to join up. If they joined, her armies would be stronger. More men, plus the dozens of clones they turned out daily would swell her numbers and the more they had, the more her enemies would have to kill.

She couldn't fail to win this war. Not if she avoided the sort of carelessness that would be fatal. Complacency was a bigger enemy than Unisco, a greater foe than the Senate. She couldn't afford it. Not now. Not ever.

"I'm thinking," she said. "I'm thinking that I want this whole sorry mess to come to an end as quickly as possible. I'm thinking that hoping they would accept my mercy was a grave mistake."

"Mercy is always a mistake," Domis said. There was no missing the scorn in his voice. She knew what he thought of mercy. It didn't take much to see that he thought of it as weakness and oh how he despised weakness of any form. His secret that wasn't a secret. She still remembered the day she'd found him. She wondered how much of it he recalled and how many horrors still lingered locked away in that inscrutable mind. "It's just weakness that has yet to strike back and cripple you."

"Perhaps. I think mercy used correctly can be a more potent weapon than all the soldiers in the kingdoms. It's about knowing when to release your boot or when to clamp down. Give them your hand in friendship or offer them a knife in the belly. One or the other. No middle ground."

"Yes Mistress." Either he didn't understand, or he didn't agree. One or the other. She turned her attention back to the controls. They were on approaching, scheduled to land in minutes. She was putting down amidst the snow, she'd dressed for the weather in weatherproof skins. All of them had. One didn't come to a place like this and not prepare. It was suicide of the highest order and she didn't intend to die in a place like this. Should all go to plan, she might never need die at all. At least not in the traditional sense. As long as people remembered her name, she would live forever.

"Domis?"

"Yes, Mistress?" He was alert immediately, looking at her the way a particularly devoted puppy greets a departed owner. He was a murderer, but he was a sweetheart in his own way. More than that, he was her murderer.

"Give the men a few words. Tell them what we're to expect down here and what I need them all to do. Leave them under no impressions that this is going to be an easy mission." She smiled at him, patted his hand. "Motivate them."

He could be quite motivating when he wanted to be. Only a fool would fail to heed his instructions. He rose from the co-pilot seat, straightened his huge coat and looked out to the hold. His face split into a mean grin, meaty knuckles cracked together. She wouldn't want to be the one to argue with him.

"Right!" he said, his voice breaking the silence. All eyes were on him. "You know we're here on an exploration mission. That means you touch nothing you don't have to, you don't break anything either. The Mistress' grand plan continues here. Should you be the one to derail it…" He let the sentence hang, his grin growing wider and wider. "Ah, you're not going to be the ones who derail it. You were picked because you're the best of the best and when our Mistress moves, she wants the best around her. Consider yourselves to be her honour guard, a beacon to be looked up to by those left behind. Remember your training and our mission will be a success."

She brought the landing gears into play, felt the runners kiss the snow and she settled her head back. The engines died as silence overcame them.

"You're all going to be fine," she said, shooting a grin back at them. The rictus on her face was uncomfortable, but her words sounded more reassuring than Domis' had. "Now let's move out."

Divines, it was cold. She'd bunched her coat up around her neck and ears to try and shut some of it out, yet still it threatened to chill her to the bones. She could see her breath in front of her, her hands frozen in her gloves. When she tried to move her fingers, the simplest motion brought tears to her eyes, smearing the goggles. They'd all worn the goggles. Not the most fashionably flattering of items but without them, she shuddered to think of how devastating this would be.

Domis bore it without complaint or protective gear, just strode off into the storm without a care for his own safety. She worried for him. Just because he hadn't found anything that could kill him yet did not mean that that day might not come. Without him, things would grow harder. He had done his part in killing Nwakili, though that fight had almost brought him down. A cunning opponent could work around him, despite that fantastic healing ability that had brought Domis back from the brink so many times and that uncanny strength that she'd seen him display.

"Be safe, my black scoundrel," she said under her breath. She didn't want the grunts to hear her. She didn't want Domis to know she worried about him.

More than once, she'd wondered about his origins. When she'd found him, she'd known she was in the company of someone who had the potential to be truly special. He'd practically been raised by her, a proto-son to go with her ungrateful bitch of a daughter. If only their better qualities had rubbed off on each other, Domis getting some of Meredith's composure and restraint, Meredith getting any of Domis' anything would have suited her. It was a mystery yet to be denied to her. Maybe she'd found out when she'd been in the Chamber of Fate. Maybe the answer would have shocked her. Now though, she couldn't say. It would come back to her. Soon.

The answers were here. She knew that for certain. Something about this ship called to her, its very presence screaming out at her to come enter it, a dull wail under the fine webs of her soul. It made her head ache just listening to it.

They'd enter soon. Already two of her men were starting to fire up a thermal lance, they'd cut in through the hold and make their way up towards the passenger cabins. At least the heat from the lance made the task somewhat bearable.

"Good job," she said, taking a step back to watch them. She stopped, looked around at the Aerius. It had landed on its belly and skidded across the dirt by the looks of it, though any groove in the ground had long since been covered by the elements. Claudia glanced back and forth, she'd noticed some impact damage as she'd brought the little shuttle in and it didn't look better from the ground.

"Now what happened here?" she mused to herself. "What brought you down?"

She could feel Domis next to her, silent and unmoving.

"We're the first people to see this in a long time," she said, looking up at him. "Exciting, isn't it?"

Sinkins was the man with the plan, he'd managed to get his hands on the floor plans of the Aerius, the picture boxes and videocams on the outside of the shuttle had scanned the entire area, recorded it all for their entry into the unknown. Right now, as the snowflakes slapped at her, she knew they had to wait.

Domis smiled at her. He inclined his head and bowed, even as his own skin was chapped pink by the air. His eyes looked shocking, the water running down his cheeks threatening to freeze as he stood there. He brought back an arm, wiped them clear and bowed again. The moment was broken, the sound of hot flame meeting aged metal, ripping through it with the hiss of arrogance.

It might have been old, but things back then had been made to last, some parts of the hull further away had torn into high-rising rocks and they'd come off worse by the looks of the landscape. No expense had been spared in putting this ship together, yet something had gone badly wrong when it was in the air, the same something that had brought it down mostly unharmed. The lance beat a slow path through the metal, the flame burning brighter and brighter as it laboured its way onward.

It might only have been mere minutes, but that time out here was worse than hours spent elsewhere. She was too grateful to hurry through the rough gap, free from the assault of the elements. Ahead of her, the two point-men led the way, blaster rifles up and ready. She doubted they would be needed but being careful wasn't a sin. Anyone up here would have been dead for years, if not from the elements then from starvation. Any length of time here was a death sentence. Domis followed her through, having finished directing the remaining men. He was good at that, she'd noticed it early on. A natural organiser. He'd left three troops with the shuttle, two at the entrance. That cut their party number to seventeen. An interesting move, she had to admit. If the shuttle was sabotaged, they were doomed to fail, for death wouldn't be far behind. Leaving someone at the entrance was a wise choice.

"Remember," she said. "You know what we're looking for. Anything vaguely mystical. There's something here that will help our conquest." Our conquest, not hers. Anything to throw them a bone, make them feel more valued.

The truth was, she didn't know what she was looking for, truly. Just that there was something on the ship that would help her achieve her goal. The ritual. The Forever Cycle. A tacky name, she thought. It promised so much and likely would deliver little. She could only hope that the name was deceptive, that its power hadn't lain solely in the imagination of those who named it with such disregard.

It could be anything, she thought. Only the vaguest hint of memory lurked within the recesses of her mind, nothing concrete, nothing certain. She knew it was important, she knew that the memories she had been permitted to bring back from the Chamber of Fate told her that. Knowledge was never wasted, just too often misused in her experience. That was just what people did. They didn't focus on what was important, they sought to bundle themselves down in minor details until the fear of inaction brought them to a halt. She despised people like that.

"Okay, can you hear me now Mistress?" Sinkins asked, his voice coming through loud and clear. She tapped a finger to her earpiece, cleared her throat. "Sorry for the delay there, weather conditions outside are less than ideal. Plus, we don't want the Premesoir authorities to know we're here. We don't have any friends in the Oval House any more, do we?"

They didn't. Their one foothold in Premesoir had been lost in that respect, with the arrest of Thomas Rogan months ago. If you wanted someone in your pocket ready to usher in a new regime, a vice-president was a good card to have. She'd looked at Joseph McCoy, the current president and decided he wouldn't be sympathetic to her. He had too much allegiance to the way things were. The Senate had done much for him to get him into power, Premesoir traditionally held the title of 'Most Powerful' in the five kingdoms and the Senate preferred that it was submissive to them in as many matters possible. McCoy would have to be dealt with and Rogan would have been the one to replace him. Now though, that plan had been discarded for the immediate future.

"I can hear you, Doctor," she said. "Where are we going here?" Two of the men were already placing sensors on the wall. They'd been Sinkins' idea. Archaeologists used them to map out ruins, use their readings to formulate an approach to whatever they were searching for. She'd not been sure about Sinkins at first, but his approach had been refreshing. When one had dealt with the fanaticism of his predecessor for as long as she had, Sinkins had been a welcome change.

"Sensor readings are already transmitting, I'm comparing them up with the maps we already have to get a read on your position."

"I want half of our number to go to the passenger cabins and search each and every one of them thoroughly, I want Domis to go to the captain's cabin and check the safe, I want the other half to move to the cargo hold. It may be any of those places."

"It might help if we knew what we were looking for," one of the soldiers muttered. She glanced back at him.

"It might," she said. "Anything that looks out of the ordinary. That's your only brief. Use your judgement. You find anything, you report it to me or Domis immediately. You remember where it is, you secure it, you move along. I want to stay here for as little time as possible, but I want it done right."

She rose to her full height, about level with Domis' elbow. "A reward to the man that finds it." She ran her eyes across the insignias on their uniforms, found the man with the lieutenant's bars. Nodded at him. "Promotion awaits. I reward well those who do not fail me."

The less said about those who did fail her, the better. She'd never tolerated it before. She wasn't about to start now. She'd considered putting a rank to the offer. Whoever finds it gets made a captain. The thought had briefly flirted with her mind, before she'd come to her senses. Better to leave it open to interpretation. Better for those more qualified to judge where skills lay, rather than have someone promoted who was painfully unqualified for it.

They'd reached the point where the corridors of the Aerius intersected and they'd gone their separate ways. Half the men had gone towards the cargo hold, she'd watched them leave with resignation in her heart. She wanted to trust them to find what she was looking for, yet she couldn't shake the ache inside that she'd have to make the pilgrimage herself down there to check.

She didn't delegate well. Not with matters of this importance. Not with the pitiful intelligence that they had. Vague memories from a man that wasn't a man. Her say-so. She was lucky they were following her at all. Credits only bought loyalty for so long. They probably thought she was a madwoman. They could think what they liked. She'd be vindicated in the end. Back when she'd been the CEO of Reims, she'd never had issues like this. She'd always felt so confident, that feeling had flooded through her veins like so many designer drugs, never threatening to overwhelm her but a feeling she'd never forget.

Like most highs, it had faded with time. That feeling was something that no longer excited her. The only way to go was for higher stakes. Different rules. Larger rewards. Scratch that, the greatest rewards of the lot.

The air was warmer in here, not that that would be hard given the freezing temperatures outside. She could breathe again, though every inhalation brought something stale to her nasal passages. Stale, musty and pungent, not a scent she could place. It was time, she guessed. Time and air, sealed in, locked down here for decades.

Domis broke away from them, she heard Sinkins giving him directions and he made for the captain's cabin. She watched his huge profile stride away into the shadows. Jewel in her wrist or not, she felt exposed without him. He was very comforting, like a loyal gorilla that didn't know it wore a leash. Her soldiers were trained, she had their loyalty for the time being, but they weren't the same.

"Right, Mistress," Sinkins said. "I've been looking over the passenger manifestos from the Aerius, at least the ones that we could find and trying to find possible matches for whomever might have brought onboard the thing that we were looking for. Given the lack of intelligence, other than the description of 'some sort of artefact,' it's tricky. The Aerius flew out of Canterage on her maiden voyage, was going to head over Premesoir and onto Serran. Quite a long round-trip really, but looking back then, there weren't many options. Not like there is now. Cross-kingdom travel…"

"Really kicked off in the last few decades, I know," she said, frowning in the darkness. She didn't need Sinkins giving her a history lesson. She'd owned a few airlines in her time, she knew how the boom had affected travel. "What do you have?"

"Well, it landed in Blasington, then set off towards Serran. Only one stop here, the capital. If the people were still onboard with the item, we can discount anyone who got on in Blasington and anyone who got off there. That still leaves well over four hundred suspects."

She said nothing. They couldn't search that many cabins. Not before someone realised they were up here. The Eye had flown low to await their return, someone would spot it sooner or later. This area of Premesoir was notorious well-patrolled by their air force. They conducted training exercises across the nearby flat snow lands to test their skills in less than ideal conditions.

"But, I have examined those four hundred further and cut some more names out. Anyone who booked the trip well in advance has been pushed towards the bottom. Some sort of artefact. That could cover anything. But given the rarity of said artefact, I've moved last minute arrivals to the top of the search list."

"Why?" she asked. Something about it made sense, yet she couldn't place why. Sinkins sounded confident enough with his logic, she was curious as to his reasoning.

"Mistress, I've been in the position. Before I came to work for you, I handled artefacts. Some of them were legal. Some of them were not. Given there was no record in previous days to the first flight of the Aerius, of any item classed as expensive or religiously significant being stolen, or bought for that matter, it is more prudent to presume that it may not have been a legal transaction. When you have something less than legal, it is quicker to move it on as fast as you can. Leaving the kingdom is a good start. I did notice something else as well when considering the past records."

"Go on?"

"There was a big bloodbath a few miles away from the aeroport where the Aerius departed. A large group killed, without any hint of the attacker left behind. Some had been shot, some had been dismembered. The files are closed, I can't access them, Unisco sealed them, until your Mister Subtractor opened them up to us. Local law enforcement suspected something had been removed from the scene. We don't know what it was, but the agent was Brennan Frewster. Make of that what you will. So, the Aerius link hints at a speedy getaway. It's only a theory but I think there's enough circumstantial evidence to support it."

She said nothing. Ideally, she'd have had Frewster in her custody by now. Rocastle had been left in charge of the operation to retrieve him. So far, he'd been quiet on the subject. That didn't fill her with confidence. Unlike most of the kingdoms in this matter, Frewster actually appeared to know something in relation to this matter. It had been a gamble to try and grab him but if he knew something, it was one worth taking.

His name had come up just one too many times. She'd met him before, quite a few times and the notion she could have asked him already was aggravating. The perils of hindsight.

"Besides, we don't have much else to go on. Might as well examine the rooms of the most recent arrivals first. Work our way down the list. It's as sound a strategy as any under the circumstances."

Claudia scowled. She couldn't argue with his reasoning. This whole thing was frustrating. She just wished that she could remember more about why they were here. The Aerius holds the Forever Cycle. She could remember that. She could remember why all that knowledge and power she'd accessed couldn't come back with her. She could remember that the Forever Cycle helped with that. Not how though. Nor what it exactly was. Just that it was here.

She cursed silently. Part of her hoped the Divines heard her. It was all their fault. They'd left this tempting little boon here and now they were waving her own powerlessness in front of her. Sinkins had come up blank when she'd mentioned the Forever Cycle to him. Said he'd never heard of it, though she wasn't sure if she believed him or not. His body language hadn't entirely spoken of innocence, she'd seen something in his eyes.

For the time being, she needed him. She couldn't afford to accuse him of duplicitousness, but that seed of suspicion had taken route. Claudia didn't know if she'd ever be able to trust Dale Sinkins ever again.

"Okay," she said. "Point the way and we'll take it from here."

"At once, Mistress. Your wish. My command."

"Nature cannot be denied. It can be cheated but not forever. You can pull someone back from the brink of death, but it does not mean they'll be the same. If death is ready for them, it will take them sooner or later. With this, it is merely a case of prolonging the inevitable, a moment of dying stretched out across days rather than seconds. Horrific, but a necessary invention. Sometimes, our people will die, yet that need not be their ultimate end. With this, they can have one last hurrah in your name, Mistress. It's not even close to being ethical, no organisation in the kingdoms would sign off on it. I imagine that doesn't trouble you though."

Doctor Hota to Claudia Coppinger regarding the development of a new treatment.

Her entire body hurt, every iota of muscle and bone in searing agony. She remembered too much, her eyes couldn't see but the memory of fire and death was there. The target had done this to her. He'd fired something at her, something she'd thought insignificant, but it had done so much damage. She didn't know how she'd survived. Maybe she hadn't. Maybe this was death and she was in the hells awaiting her judgement.

She tried to move her lips, let out a scream. Every movement sent fresh waves of pain wracking her body. She wasn't an enemy with pain but here it scared her, she'd never felt it so close and so strong. Death was close, she could smell it, just as she could smell her own cooked flesh and boiled blood. She should have already succumbed.

She hadn't. She wasn't dead yet. And like any good gambler, she still had one card left to play. Rocastle had insisted on a contingency for all of them, him and Doctor Hota had worked something out. She remembered the class all too well.

"Now, possum-babies," Rocastle had said, his face swimming in the vision of her memory. He wasn't so thin or as ugly in real life as she saw him now. Her memory had to be going. Breath broke out of her in shallow gasps, she coughed and tasted the blood in her mouth. That wasn't good. Maybe one of her ribs had punctured a lung.

Short answer. Not a lot of time left. Right now, she wanted relief. She wanted to die, she wanted it all to be over. If she lay her head back and closed her eyes, it'd come. She knew that. All she had to do was give up. She could do that, couldn't she? Just lay her weary head to rest, don't cry no more.

No. She couldn't. The tears had sprung to her eyes, the salt stung her ruined cheeks, the harsh pain snapped her into action. Her body was ruined. Broken. Nobody in their right mind would consider her a candidate for living a good long life right now. But there was a way.

"Chances are some of you are going to get hurt in the line of duty. You might find yourselves inches from death. If you give up, you've brought shame on yourselves and the Mistress. That's why we've put this in one of your back teeth." He'd held up a tiny capsule, the size of one little fingernail. She'd suspected, had woken with a pain in her mouth one morning and a fleeting memory of the previous night involving the sound of drills reverberating through her head. Not a pleasant sound, the memory had made her brain ache. She was glad most it was lost to her. She might never get it back and she could easily live with that.

"A last resort solution for when you're on your way out. Dying does not have to be the end. Granted, there are dire side-effects…" The grin he'd given them all as he'd said that had been horrific, like a shark with a pain in its rear end. "So yeah. Last resort. When the only other option is failing your mission, you break your tooth and you take it. Understand me?"

She did understand. He'd never gone into details about what the side effects were. Nobody had wanted to ask. Nobody had thought that they'd reach the point where death was so close. She knew she hadn't. All of this had spiralled out of control for her. It had never meant to be like this, Rocastle had never really told her what was going to happen, only that they wanted those who were pissed off with the system. She had been pissed, annoyed enough to listen, angry enough after talking to him to take him up on it. He'd been in a bad way, hopped up on painkillers and his hand bandaged up but he'd spoken a lot of sense, told her words that she wanted to hear about smashing the system up and starting anew. By the time he'd finished, she was ready to sign up on the spot and to hells with the consequences.

People had gotten away with things for too long. Ritellia was a corrupt man, he'd do anything to line his own pockets with credits and he'd long stopped caring about the sport. She hadn't been present when he'd died but she'd had mixed feelings. Not that she cared one way or another if he lived, but to hear that the Mistress had snuffed him out was intriguing. She wasn't messing about with what she did. It was going to be her way or the void.

It was also too late to back out of it by that point. The indoctrination had started. The first moments she'd heard that soothing voice in her head, the Mistress speaking to her, she'd been hooked. She'd listened. She'd agreed. Looking back now on what she'd done compared to who she'd been, it felt like a different person. She'd had to have been changed somehow. Because if she hadn't, then what did that make her?

Monster. Evil. Cruel. Uncaring. Vile.

All of it and more, she knew to be true. She'd been a nice girl, a good girl, one hint of adversity and she'd sold her soul to the first one to offer her anything for it. That she should end up in this predicament was not only fair but something she should have expected. Life throws obstacles at you and how you react to them determines where you end up.

She also wanted to live more than anything, any price to pay for a few more gasps of precious air into unbroken lungs, to walk on restored limbs, to taste and to see and to hear anything beyond the silence.

She bit down, felt the bitter taste flood through her mouth, couldn't muster the strength to swallow. It ran down her tongue, hit the back of her throat and she felt the burn, fought the urge to cough. If she choked to death, that'd be just about the topping on the truly shitty day she'd had.

They'd hit a stadium, Nick could see the crowds entering it from a distance and he remembered that the professional leagues had resumed under the command of Adam Evans, he'd proclaimed that Coppinger wouldn't intimidate the sport into silence. They would go again, and the competition would be fiercer than ever it had been before. Strong words, he was trying to distance himself from the weakness Ritellia had frequently shown when it came to make important decisions that didn't directly affect his pockets. Nick lowered his speed to almost a crawl, not letting the engines die away but neither moving to tear away. He could have slowed down miles back, he wasn't worried about more Coppinger forces. Not after they'd routed them.

There wasn't another way of putting it. So many of them and they'd been kicked back by him, Frewster and Helga in record time. Frewster was unscathed, Nick himself had come out of it with nothing beyond a few scratches. Helga though…

Not good. She'd gone pale, her skin grey and clammy, he could hear the shallow breaths rippling out of her. She was struggling, she needed medical attention. Frewster had clamped his jacket to her, trying to keep her warm. He'd closed the windows, turned the heating up to max but he could hear her teeth chattering together as she shivered.

"It's okay, Helga," Frewster said. "You'll be fine. We'll get to a hospital, we'll get you patched up and you'll be better than new. A new woman." He didn't sound confident. Nick couldn't entirely blame him. A bad situation, to be sure. "Because nothing but the best for my favourite." At least he was convincing, he'd give him that. The words were strong, laced with compassion as he lay an arm around her shoulders. "You're my favourite, you know? Always were. People came, and they went. You were always the best, you always stayed."

She laughed, it came out as a cough. Blood ran down her lips. "Where else would I go, huh?" Another laugh, this time they turned into wet hacks, her breathing little more than choked gasps.

"She's not going to make it," Nick said, glancing back. "The time we get to the nearest hospital, it'll be too late." He looked out front through the windshield, towards the stadium, mentally running through his options. Most stadiums had excellent, if rudimentary medical facilities. Given the right sort of attention, she might at least be stabilised, give them a chance for an emergency response team to get to them. As classic as Frewster's speeder might be, it didn't live up to the name. It was a more sedate ride for a calmer time.

"She'll make it," Frewster said. "She's a fighter."

"Can't fight death, Brennan," Helga said. "Nobody's ever won that fight. Everything dies in the end."

He pushed her hair out of her eyes, smiled at her like a father surveying a child. "Doesn't mean you can't hold it off though. Damnit, Helga, just hold the hells on. We will get you out of here. You'll be up and about again soon. How am I going to last the rest of my life without my best gal?"

Bitterness laced her laugh. "Your life expectancy and mine might not be that different right now, Bren. We're both running out of it."

At least she wasn't losing a flair for the dramatic in her suffering, Nick thought. He made his choice, swung into the parking area for the stadium. Two pairs of eyes moved to him, he tried to ignore them. They weren't important. "What are you doing?!" Frewster demanded. "The hospital…"

"Is too damn far away," Nick said. "We get her in here, we get her stabilised, try and find a doctor. There's got to be one in the crowd. He can keep her alive until we get a better solution."

"I like it," Helga said.

"I don't," Frewster said, more than a little obstinate. He glanced back and forth. "Too many people."

"That's good," Nick said. "We'll stand out less."

"There's also more chance of collateral damage," Frewster said. "Plus, Agent Roper, I don't see how we can fail to stand out. You're recognisable, I'm recognisable and we're carrying a badly bleeding woman between us. Inconspicuousness isn't something we are going to manage, I'm afraid to say."

Nick said nothing. He knew Frewster had a point there. All it took was one person with a summoner to get a picture or some video of them and it'd be out there. If Coppinger forces were still out to get them, which he had no reason to doubt they weren't, it'd be a short escape. They'd be down in force. The collateral damage could be immense.

Helga would die if he didn't. A tough choice, he knew that. Frewster cared for her, but by telling him to move along, he'd already made that choice. The least he could do was respect it. People were always the same when it came down to it, he should have learned that a long time ago. No matter how much he might profess to care for Helga, she was still his servant and he doubtless relished his own life too much to throw it away for her.

People were like that. They didn't change too much. You came into the world alone and you left it that way. Self-reliance did you a mass of favours in Nick's experience. Frewster had survived this long, he clearly was an expert at it. Sucked for Helga but she wasn't the purpose of the mission here, Frewster was the important one. It was all about him. Screw Helga. Screw the people who cared about her. There had to be someone. Anyone. Someone who would miss her when she died in service of a man who'd been too scared of what might happen to himself to lift a finger to help her. She'd taken a blast meant for him. The least he could do was make sure she had the best chance.

That made his choice for him. He fired up the engines, headed for the stadium, the main entrance looming above them. He'd seen caverns that were more welcoming, people shifted ou the way to let them past. He saw more than a few disgruntled faces, anger in the expression of everyone they passed. He'd have smashed his foot straight to the ground if they weren't here, hit that entrance and had her out of the speeder in no time.

"You're making a mistake, Roper." Frewster's voice had lost most of its charm, rough with patient agitation. "You're painting a big bullseye on this stadium."

"That was always going to happen anyway," Nick said. He didn't try to look the older man in the eyes as he said it. "They'll already know we're here. They're probably already on their way." He leaned back in his seat, kept one hand on the controls. "Probably been tracking us ever since we left Withdean."

He didn't add what truly troubled him, the notion that the attack had been immediate and without warning. There'd been no hint of any sort of trouble directed towards Frewster, even the information he proclaimed to have was, in his own words 'not entirely related to that dreadful Coppinger woman, but it could be useful for you." He'd heard half the story, wasn't entirely convinced that there was any sort of point to it just yet. He'd guess that if it was going to come from anywhere, it'd be in the second part of it. When that tale got told would be anyone's guess. It was certainly the furthest thing from important right now.

"You can't know that for sure."

"I can suspect the worst. That would be one of the possible situations we might have to deal with going forward. This's already gone on long enough to prove that underestimating them is a dumb thing to do."

Frewster gave him a look, resigned and smug, the face of a beaten man not caring. "You're the one who has to live with the consequences of your mistakes, young man."

He bit back the retort, cleared his throat. "I need you to find a doctor, Brennan." He pointed to the door. "Get out there, rustle on up and we'll get her patched up. We can spare fifteen minutes, surely?"

"I admire your optimism," Frewster said, opening his door. "Okay. I'll do that. Good luck, Nicholas. Get her there! I'll meet you in the medical room."

They'd tried to stop him parking, he'd pulled his ID and almost squashed it against the face of the guard, giving him his absolute best 'don't-fuck-with-me' face, the glare and the badge combining to force him back. Nick paid him no other attention, pulled the rear door open and scooped Helga up into his arms. She wasn't a big woman, she felt waif-like and tiny in his arms, fresh blood bubbling from her as he cradled her close to him. Her eyes fluttered open, she fixated on him.

"Why you help?" she groaned out, her voice sounding like she hadn't drunk for weeks. "You can't win. Bren is right, you know. Everyone dies."

"Not today," he said. "I don't know you, but I'm not giving up, I'm not letting anyone else die because of Coppinger if I can help it."

"Dear boy," she smiled, sounded all too like Frewster as the words slipped her. "Sometimes you can't help it. Thought you would have worked that out…"

She tailed off, lapsed into unconsciousness. Her head fell into the crook in his neck and he picked up his speed, darted through the open door and picked up his pace. Running while carrying someone was a dumb idea at the best of times, he needed to resist the temptation. They both tripped, it'd do neither of them any good.

154

The medical room wasn't unlocked, he hit it with his shoulder and the door burst open, he laid Helga down on the bed and unfolded a blanket, laying it over her. "You'll be okay, Ms Carlow," he said. "Lay your weary head to rest right now."

She didn't respond. Barely even moved. He tucked the blanket over her, made sure she was wrapped up warm. Now, he just needed Frewster to show up with someone more capable of helping her than he was.

Every footstep hurt. Her breathing was back to normal, but the memories of pain hadn't left her just yet. Her limbs had repaired, her skin had regrown and her vision had returned but none of it felt right. None of it felt like it was her. Not truly. Two separate beings, who she was before and who she was now. Neither of them was who she wanted to be. Not really. She'd always been better than this. Risen above her emotions, no matter how much she might want to do otherwise. One little outburst and her life had changed forever and not necessarily for the better.

Her gaze dropped to her hands. They'd stopped shaking now. That had been the main thing she'd noticed when the serum had taken its full effect and she'd sat up for the first time since the explosion had set her on fire. Her entire body hadn't been able to stop trembling, given the damage to her nerve endings, it perhaps wasn't a surprise. She'd still felt the twinges of fear when she'd shook so hard that she thought her remaining teeth were going to crack from the efforts of chattering against each other.

Weronika Saarth. She said the name over and over in her head as she looked in the mirror. Her face had healed but her hair and eyebrows hadn't grown back. Her glasses had been lost somewhere. She'd gotten so used to seeing herself with them that they were more of a debilitating factor in her failing to recognise herself than the lack of hair. Not that she felt like she needed them. She just missed the hearts around her eyes. They framed her face, made sure that she caught the eye. Without them, she might as well not be there. She'd always tried to turn negatives into positives. That had been the sort of girl she'd been, the sort of woman she'd become. Yes, her eyes were bad. Yes, she wasn't the sort of person people tended to notice straightaway. Enter the glasses. They were distinctive, a double advantage.

"My name is Weronika Saarth," she said. Her voice sounded different, lower, harsher. Her throat might have been damaged by the smoke. The serum might have fixed her body, but not entirely it would appear. "My name IS Weronika Saarth." She raised the section of her face where her eyebrow has once been. "Saarth. Weronika Saarth. Ronnie?" A smile. Her mouth hurt. "Ronnie Saarth."

Her clothes had burned. Her weapons lost. Her summoner destroyed. Her container crystals were about the only thing she'd had left. The speeder had pulled over for her, she'd seen the looks of concern and she'd smiled. If they'd had any sense, they would have put their foot to the floor and sped off right there, leaving her behind. Some people were too dumb to be allowed to keep nice things. The man she'd taken out first, smashed his head into the door and flipped him out, drove her toes into his throat. He wouldn't be getting up anytime soon, if ever. The woman with him had started to scream and scream, the shrill cries hurting her ears and she'd flung herself at her. Up on the seat next to her, the screams had silenced as if she expected death to come.

"Your clothes," she'd growled. "Give them to me."

She still had a mission to fulfil. She didn't want to let the Mistress down. The memory of her radiance flooded through her mind, the snarl was replaced with a smile that felt dopey even as she saw the fear intensity on the woman's face. This might work. She'd already run the numbers. They were about the same height, she'd guess. Didn't look a scrap alike, especially not now. Maybe she was a little bigger about the chest, but she could live with that.

While she'd stripped off, Saarth had dropped out the cab and retrieved the summoner from the man she'd maimed, taking the belt as well. His crystals she tipped out into a pile across his back. He wouldn't be needing them right now.

She let the woman keep her underwear. She wasn't feeling completely heartless, allowing her to keep her modesty for when someone eventually picked them up. A small gesture. After all, who would associate the psychotic-looking bald girl with former Quin-C contender Weronika Saarth? It was about the only reason she'd left the woman alive.

Alive but not comfortable. She'd kicked her legs out from underneath her, driven her face into the side of the speeder and heard her nose break. Blood spurted out, stained the door with claret. She'd dressed in her clothes, sweater and jeans and leather jacket. Badass, she had to admit. Very badass. If she was ready to prove a point, she was dressed for it. She tied the belt around her waist, plucked up the summoner and started to scroll through the CallerNet. There had to be something out there for her to see, some sighting of them. Some pages existed solely to track spirit callers on their journey, some did the same for celebrities. If anyone had seen Frewster and Roper together, it'd show up sooner rather than later.

All she needed was to ignore the pain. Soon she could rest. For now, she had one last task. She started to dial a number on the summoner. One last task for the Mistress and then she'd close her eyes.

Frewster had returned and with him, he'd found a doctor, a young fellow with balding brown hair he'd swept back with gel. He didn't look like a doctor, he looked like someone on their day off and for that Nick couldn't be surprised. He hadn't come here expecting to have to do this. Still, they'd made an oath they couldn't deny, just like he had when he'd become a fully-fledged Unisco agent. Shit happened.

"Doctor Aaron Ramsey," Frewster said by way of introduction. "Best I could find." He folded his arms, hugged himself as he did. "Nothing but the best for Helga, I think."

"She'll be fine," Nick said. "I'm sure she's in good hands."

"The best," Ramsey said. "Trust me on that. Dear Divines, what have they done to you, my dear?"

Nick left him to it, gestured for Frewster to follow him. They made their way out the room, stood in the corridor. Above them, they could hear the stadium coming to life, people making their way to their seats, pre-match entertainment stoking the atmosphere. Too many had missed out on spirit calling for too long and they were ready to see it start again.

"We need to leave," he said. "Call her some evacuation and get the hells out of here. You saw how many summoners were out there recording our appearance. We're probably all over the CallerNet right now."

Frewster shrugged. "You're probably right. We're running out of time." He would have turned to leave had Nick not grabbed his arm.

"Why do they want you, Frewster? Talk to me. If I know, it helps." He meant it as well, not that he was entirely surprised as Frewster wagged his finger at him.

"Not a chance I'm telling you, dear boy. I do, you'll cut and run. I might be doing you a disservice, but I can't allow myself to take that chance. I've not lived this long by taking unnecessary risks with my life and I'm not starting now."

He could appreciate that. He didn't like it, but he could appreciate where Frewster was coming from. If he had a card to play, he might well have found himself in the same position of keeping it as close to his chest for as long as possible.

"Does it tie into your story?"

"I was getting there," Frewster said. "Before we were so rudely interrupted."

"You could have just gotten to the point faster."

"I think you'll find that you need context to fully understand everything I wished to tell you. Without it, I'm just wasting my time answering your questions afterwards." He'd never quite heard so much arrogance laced into one sentence.

"Must be one hells of a story for something that happened fifty years ago to lead to them trying to capture you today."

"Sure is, Agent Roper. I think you'll find it is well worth the wait."

"I want to hear it the minute we're out of danger." He did his best to keep the bitterness out of his voice. As days went, this felt like it had been a bust. Fighting for your life gave you that impression, especially when it had supposed to have been an easy mission.

It felt good to get back out among it though, get his fists bruised and his danger reflex kicked up several notches. He'd not realised how much he'd missed it. The last months, being kept away from the action had left a hole in him he'd never realised truly was there until it came to fill it.

"I want to hear what happens to Helga first, her chances. Then we'll leave. Steal a different speeder…"

"I think you'll find that's a crime. The word you were looking for is commandeer," Nick said.

"That badge unlocks many doors, Nicholas, it justifies a great many actions that wouldn't be acceptable at most other times."

"Okay," Nick said. He didn't have a problem with the act, just felt like knocking at Frewster for implying he might leave him in the lurch when he was no longer valuable. If he was going to do that, he'd have let Helga die and they'd already have been back at a Unisco building. He'd said no more, and he'd meant it. "Go talk to Ramsey and we'll get out of here. Leave her in his care, we'll try and retrieve her later."

"Agent Roper?"

"Yeah?"

"Thank you," Frewster said. He held out a hand. "You know you're right. She would have been dead by now if we'd carried on. I didn't want that to happen, but I don't want my own life to end this way either. Running in fear, hiding."

Above them, the stadium had gone silent. Nick didn't notice. "You know, I lost someone, right? Back when all this started. I still remember that. Haunts me. I remember that moment when I found she'd died, I can't bear thinking about it sometimes. Someone somewhere cares for Helga…"

"Me," Frewster said. "I'm all she's got. No family. Nobody else."

"… And if she'd died, then you'd miss her. I'd have given anything for someone to have done their best to try and save Sharon when all looked lost. I can't let someone else die when I had that chance to help them."

"You're a very strange Unisco agent, you know."

"That's been said," Nick said. "I've done a lot of bad things in the name of the kingdoms. I just wanted to do some good for someone, you know?"

"Your bosses won't hear it from me, Nicholas. I'll tell them that you did absolutely everything by the book. They'll believe me on that, trust me. I wrote the damn book."

Nick smirked, heard the scream and the expression vanished. He raised his eyes towards the nearest viewing screen. All stadiums had them in their tunnels, unrestricted views of the battlefield.

"Oh crap!"

All eyes were on her as she'd flown down astride the back of her magnificent eagle, Geraint, great wings casting larger shadows across the ground. She could feel the adrenaline roaring through her veins, louder than the silence that threatened to engulf the two of them as the shadow shrank progressively the closer they came to land.

She was following in the Mistress' footsteps. She'd been here on that fateful day, she'd descended from the skies like this and the kingdoms had changed forever following that act. Any doubts she might have had about her course of action, they were lost amidst the mess of fuzzy feelings flooding her mind. This was right. This was just. The Mistress had done this, it was the single greatest act of imitation she could manage in her mission to ensure that her will be done.

Everything she did, she did for the Mistress. To do anything else was to deny her that acclaim. The Angels had been intended for this purpose, despite the stupid name Rocastle had festooned on them. Angels of Death. He'd tried to sound dramatic, he'd come off a bit of an idiot, but the name had stuck. Who was laughing now?

Her summoner activated, the second crystal firing into action. This one was special, she'd been given one of the Ista Neroux by the Mistress herself to carry out her duties. A special gift for one recognised, she'd said. A credit to the name Coppinger and a loyal soldier until the end. Very few had ever seen the creature that emerged onto the battlefield, landing gracefully despite its size.

It might have been a leopard once, if leopards grew to the size of houses, legs thicker than tree trunks and covered in onyx-black fur that she was sure shimmered in the sunlight. Its ears stood so prominent, they could have been mistaken for horns, the claws were the length of

159

Saarth's arm, sharp enough to cut through steel. She'd seen it happen. Nobody faced the Ista Neroux and lived if they weren't meant to.

The Mistress had made a brilliant choice in her wisdom, she'd wanted to be revered as a Divine, she'd seen how they'd been depicted in folklore and literature and she'd also seen how the people of the kingdoms worshipped spirit callers with their fantastic beasts. The two had been combined. Ista Neroux. New Divines. Icons. Win their hearts and you'll take their minds in short order. That sort of brilliance was why they would win the war. Nobody the enemy had could shine a light to her radiance.

Mykeltros bared its teeth, breath huffed out of its nostrils. She took care not to breathe it in, the stuff was toxic after all. A few people in the front seats of the crowd started to vomit. Her lips curled into a smile.

"People of…" What the hells was this town called? She didn't know. Saarth blinked several times. It'd come to her. "… Here. My quarrel is not with you. I seek someone within your midst!" How had the Mistress done this? Her voice felt too quiet, a faint echo amidst a great space. She should have stolen a microphone, commandeered the tannoy. "Give me Brennan Frewster and I will spare you all a poisonous death."

She gave the command, Mykeltros belched a thick cloud of gas towards a different section of the crowd, dozens of people started to vomit up blood instantly, their screams of pain and terror a music to her ears.

"Or maybe the old man wants to come out himself, save a lot of pain and suffering caught in his name. That would be the honourable thing to do in front of the eyes of the kingdoms, would it not? Maybe he's a coward. That's about right for someone like him. They talk a good game, they talk about honour and the right way to do things, but they'll soon take a short cut if it's in their benefit."

Maybe she wasn't entirely talking solely about Frewster. Some wounds faded hard. She was still annoyed about the way she'd gone out of the Quin-C. As much as she knew it ultimately didn't matter now, the memories lingered. They defined her. They were a final scrape of indignation against a mind that had tried to move on. She wanted someone to challenge her. She wanted to make an example of them. More than that, she wanted Frewster to do something. Anything. If he made a move, she'd gotten to him. Rocastle's training had covered psychology. Any advantage you could get was a good one.

A figure appeared at the tunnel entrance to the battlefield, didn't run but sauntered, hands in pockets and like he didn't have a care in the world. It wasn't Frewster, she could see that much. Too well-built, far too young. His face came into view, she couldn't help but feel pleasantly surprised. It wasn't Frewster, but he would do as an acceptable substitute.

Nicholas Roper. The man who'd damn near killed her when he'd shot that grenade into her aeroship. Revenge would be undeniably sweet. He'd tied a rag over his face, covering his nose and his mouth. He'd seen the poison, he'd taken precautions. They might not save him if she turned Mykeltros on him, but she wasn't ready to test that theory yet.

"I asked for Frewster!" she said. "Where is he?"

Nick shrugged. "Somewhere around here. Not entirely sure."

Her face contorted into a snarl, she balled her hands into tiny fists. "I want him!"

"Sweetheart, life's full of things that we want and not going to get. Now take your giant bloody cat and fuck right off before I kick your arse up between your eyeballs and handcuff what's left untangled."

He had a blaster tucked into the waist of his trousers, hadn't gone for it yet. Maybe he didn't want to murder someone live on television. Or maybe he didn't want to have to fight Mykeltros off if he killed her and the spirit went for him in a final act of defiance.

"I'd like to see you try," she said, her voice cold. She'd never heard herself sound like that before and it worried her.

"Trying implies that there's a chance of failure." He shot her a grin. "I think you tried at the Quin-C, didn't get you very far, did it?"

He knew who she was. He'd recognised her, even with the change of appearance and demeanour. She knew she didn't act like the person she was before. The old Weronika Saarth would never have done anything like this. She'd have been one of the terrified ones in the stadium, too scared to move or think, cowering under her seat like some sort of terrible coward.

"You didn't do too good yourself," she shot back, painfully aware of how inadequate it was as a response. If he thought it was bitingly witty, he didn't show it, just grinned.

"My promise still stands," he said. "Leave Frewster alone, leave this place and you won't get shown up again. I mean, it's only the first professional Canterage bout in ages, how many people tuned in to watch this around the kingdoms? Couple of million? Ten million? Twenty? Fifty? Fifty million people watching you fail."

"They won't," she muttered, loud enough for him to hear. "I will not fail her!"

"Ah yes, Claudia Coppinger." His voice turned mocking. "The nutcase with what we can only assume is some sort of masterplan."

Her heart pounded in her ears, blood dripped from her palms where she'd dug in her nails, old scars torn open. How dare he insult her! The Mistress was sacred, a target above all petty comments. She was trying to bring the light and men like him were forcing everyone to stay in the dark.

"You will regret taking her name in vain!" she snarled. Geraint vanished beneath her feet, dispelled back to the container crystal and she slotted another in. Sarge erupted out, the surang ape beat both fists against his chest and tore across the ground towards Roper with lumbering footsteps.

"If you go looking for a fight, it will inevitably find you. The righteous man who seeks to avoid violence may have it visited upon him, but never will he walk unwillingly into it. In this life, we all find the fruits of our labours to be exactly what we seek. Hard workers see reward, lazy workers see little. It's the same with men of violence and peace. Now I've never found those two notions mutually exclusive. You cannot have one without the other."

Zent Barkhuizen, noted Serranian holy man in speech to his congregation.

Nick had been prepared for this, ever since he'd stepped into the arena. He'd had his own summoner in his hands ready. If it hadn't been for that big black cat stood above her, he'd have shot her in the head already and had done with it. The number of shots left in the blaster weren't many, but they'd do. Better to wear her down gradually, make her angry or overconfident. He'd seen her fight before. She'd had Scott Taylor on the ropes at one point, no mean feat given how far he'd gotten at last summer's tournament. She'd thought she'd won, she'd gotten cocky with her imminent victory and Taylor had pulled it out via a method she hadn't liked, not that she'd been quiet about saying so either.

The complaints had come, those protests of unfair behaviour and cheating had gotten her the attention of Coppinger and her ensemble. Collison had confirmed as much to them when they'd pulled him out, told them how the whole thing worked. They already had Ulikku. Saarth was there in front of him. There were plenty more out there, though given what had already happened today, he had to believe there were less now than at the start of the day.

They didn't matter right now, not with the ape coming for him. He pushed a button on his summoner, Bish the garj appeared between him and the oncoming surang, simian bulk dwarfing elegant grace. It didn't matter. He had a plan. Fools rushed in. He didn't intend to turn it into a slugging match he couldn't win.

Bish leaped at the surang, sprang up into the air and planted one hand into its shoulders, leaping over its back with ease. The ape hesitated, almost stumbled and swiped at Bish just a little too late. Meaty fists closed around empty air and Bish thrust down, driving both elbow blades down into the opponent's back. The bellow that broke from its lungs was something truly to hear as it went berserk, tried to reach around behind and throw Bish off. Thick fingers scrabbled impotently at rough fur, muscles bent back at almost unnatural angles

163

but Bish had leaped clear. The surang rounded on his direction, feet scrabbling wildly in the dust, flung out a fist that didn't even come close to landing. As the blow struck empty air, Bish charged himself, took off at a sprint and was on the ape before it could react. Blades whistled through the air, struck Sarge's stomach in an X shape. Blood gushed out, spattered across the snow-white fur that made up Bish's face like an ugly tattoo. Sarge howled, threw out both fists towards Bish who danced backwards, evading the blows with dancer-like movements. Not content with powerhouse blows, the surang continued to swing out, throwing sledgehammer-like punches through the air. None came close, the ape looked cumbersome and slow next to Bish's speed. All power and no finesse.

He wasn't falling for it. Nobody had done as well as Saarth had to get to a Quin-C latter round without some sort of extra trick in her pouch. Brute force was okay, but it only took a caller so far. Couldn't depend on it, not against a better opponent.

Nick made the choice in that moment to show her why that was the case. He gave Bish the mental command to hang back, let the ape close in. Close in it did, bearing down on the garj, fist brought back ready to swing. He tried not to think about what might happen if Bish caught the blow. It wouldn't be pretty. The garj was fast but not the hardiest of creatures. Nobody would call them delicate, but they lacked for natural defences against creatures capable of snapping them into two pieces should the mood take them. Best form of defence was not getting hit in the first place.

Sarge swept in on the stationary garj, ready to crush him between those two huge arms, crush, smash, beat into a fine mist. Not going to happen, not while Nick had any command in the matter. One moment Bish was there, the next he was gone in a flicker of light, a distortion in the air all that remained. Sarge stumbled, suddenly trying to grab something that couldn't be held. The surang ape fell, landed flat on its giant face and Nick saw Bish reappear behind the simian opponent. The blades swung down in a scissoring motion, severing head from shoulders in a swift movement.

Saarth looked furious, exactly the sort of outcome he'd hoped for. She didn't like it when people looked like they were toying with her. His guess was she had a real chip on her shoulder about being taken seriously. When Collison had offered up his insights into the callers Coppinger had recruited into the Angels, Unisco psychologists had tried to build up psych profiles on everyone they knew had been recruited for sure. That was what they'd said about Saarth. Tiny woman. High voice. Cute-ish. Not very physically imposing. Easy to underestimate. That might have been then, he thought as he watched her. She might be small, but there were hidden depths to her. Beneath clothes that were too big for her, he could see the outline of muscle. Six months of training. It wouldn't be foolish to assume they'd had her on some sort of program.

She dispelled the dead ape into nothing, gestured furiously at him and Bish. The huge leopard bared its teeth hungrily. Nick clenched his fists. He'd seen something like this before. One of Claudia Coppinger's modified spirits. This wouldn't be easy. He doubted Bish could take it. He'd faced one before, it had wiped out an entire Unisco team and their spirits, as well as four of his before he'd gotten a handle on it.

No, this he'd have to play carefully. Nick glanced back towards the tunnel. He just hoped Frewster was following the plan.

When the woman had appeared with her eagle, Roper had sprung into action. He might be a strange one, Frewster had noticed, but he didn't lack for decisiveness. It was a trait missing all too often in the younger generations. Roper had seen a problem and he'd moved to address it. Not that he'd taken much encouragement to storm out onto the battlefield and distract the young lady with the drastic hairstyle. Frewster had seen them all, from beehives to mohawks and baldness wasn't unique, but he'd never seen it carried out with quite so severe an effect. She didn't look well, her skin pallid and her eyes rimmed with black.

Helga was okay, he'd checked in. Ramsey was still treating her, bless his heart. He'd glanced back, gestured with his head for Frewster to give him some space and he'd been all too happy to oblige. He had his part to play in all this. If Roper was distracting, Frewster needed to play his own part.

He'd made his way to the commentary booth, panting a little with the effort. He was in good shape for his golden years, but the day had been a trying one and even with the best will in the world, his flesh was weak. His heart pounded hard in his chest, he felt his vision swim at the top of the stairs as he gasped for breath. His legs felt like rubber beneath him, shaking wildly with the strenuousness of his efforts. He shouldn't be pulling stunts like this at his age.

The commentary booth had already been abandoned, the safest position in the stadium and the figure who would have been expected to be here had fled. Frewster clucked his tongue, refrained from vocalising his anger. Still, the job had to be done. The equipment might be modern, but some things never truly changed. He found the microphone, checked that it was connected to the console and hit the transmit button, clearing his throat as he did.

"Attention, all. This is a public safety announcement. Please exit the stadium in an orderly manner while the bad woman is currently trying to kill the good guy. Thank you, ladies and gentlemen. Quickly but calmly, chop, chop."

He laughed to himself, shook his head. It wasn't a laughing matter; the absurdity of the situation was getting to him. To be amid a situation like this, it was preposterous to say the least.

Too old. Too tired. Shouldn't be doing stuff like this.

He dropped to the chair, all the energy sapped from his limbs. Carry on like this, he wouldn't have much time left. The world was a dangerous place right now. He glanced down to the battlefield, saw the leopard circling. It had already downed Roper's garj and now the giant penguin was out.

The world had moved on. It had left him behind. It was no longer one that he recognised, or even one that he'd care to. Frewster knew to himself that he'd had a good run at it, he'd lived far longer than he ever could have dreamed of.

He had one task left. That could well be the end of it all and he'd die happy. Frewster leaned forward, pulled over the recording equipment and started to run his hands over the machinery.

He needed to do this and fast, yet it wasn't the sort of thing that one could rush. This would be his final testament to the kingdoms and he needed to do it with a clear head. Just in case.

Empson squawked in pride, bent his body forward and snapped the beak open, a torrential blast of water erupting from within him. It hit the leopard full on in the face, didn't faze it at all beyond forcing it back. Angry feline eyes glared at him and the penguin and it leaped, springing forward with preternatural agility, a dozen feet from a standing start. Those claws looked sharp, Empson brought up a steel-lined wing to parry them away, the sound of them scraping against each other made Nick wince. He felt like his ears were about to start bleeding.

They broke apart, the leopard roared angrily, Empson pumped up his chest to try and appear bigger. Didn't even flinch amidst the onslaught of sound being forced upon him. As the sound died away and the jaws closed, the penguin leaped forward, head bobbing forward to jab-jab-jab his beak into the giant cat's face. Fur went flying, blood spattered across Empson's face. Another few inches, it might have hit one of the yellowed eyes. Might still have done so had a huge paw not swept out, batted the penguin back across the arena. Empson hit the hoardings, bounced off and landed beak first in the dirt.

Nick's expression didn't change, kept it neutral. He'd already sent Empson in to feel out the creature, try and get some sort of gauge as to its power. So far, he'd worked out that it hit like a wrecking ball and it could move when the mood took it. Saarth had a creature of atrocious power there in front of her. He'd already worked out its breath was poisonous. He'd seen it when it had unleashed the effect onto the crowd, made them sick. At least they were out of the picture. Frewster's announcement had pulled them out, they'd started to run despite his best attempts in pleading them not to. Saarth had reacted, he'd thrown Empson in to keep her attention away from those that were running.

The penguin rose, puffed up his chest, Nick winced as he realised that it only emphasised the streams of blood pouring down his feathers.

"You can't win this fight, you know that?" Saarth said, her voice emotionless. "You won't win. You can't stand against Mykeltros."

"You name that bloody thing yourself?" Nick asked. He glanced around the stadium. Most of the lower levels were clear. Some stragglers remained, those that had been poisoned in the initial wav struggled across towards the steps and then fell, one after the other. He forced himself not to look. It wouldn't do anyone any good. He needed to deal with Saarth and her damn leopard before things got out of hand. The upper levels were still evacuating, but they'd be out of reach of any possible reprisals. Hopefully.

"All names come from the glory of the Mistress in her vision for the future."

"So, no, you didn't then?" He grinned to himself, then to Empson, before pushing the button on his summoner. The penguin vanished. "Didn't think you had the imagination for it, personally."

"You don't know me, Mister Roper." Not Agent. That was interesting, to say the least. Maybe she hadn't made the connection. There'd been a few that had, following his antics on Carcaradis Island the last time he'd been involved in a situation like this. "I've had enough of this world and if I can help her tear it down and build something better…"

"The only thing you'll be helping in building is an unmarked grave!" Mentally he punched the air. That was fighting talk. That'd do it. He worked the special crystal into his summoner, tried not to think about whom it had belonged to before coming into his possession. It had been in Sharon's kjarnblade, he'd driven the weapon through the creature's chest and it had shattered in his hand, the creature contained within the crystal and unable to break free.

Uni appeared in front of him. To fight one of Coppinger's special creatures, what better to turn to than one of them? The unialiv was his only previous personal experience of combat with these things, he'd claimed it, yet didn't want to advertise the fact that he had it. Coppinger had unleashed it on her airbase, sent it to kill the invading Unisco agents. Better she thought it lost than to actively start chasing it. The lengths some would go to in effort to try and reclaim what they considered theirs, he didn't like to think about.

By the look on Saarth's face, she recognised it. The shock told him that much and it bore more satisfaction than he ever could have imagined. Furless flesh glistened in the sunlight, red-blue muscle tight as Uni stretched out its arms. There was something distinctly ape-like about it, though it and the surang could never be mistaken for close evolutionary cousins.

"You shouldn't have that!" she said, outrage heavy in her voice. "You shouldn't! It doesn't belong to you!"

"Beg to disagree," Nick said softly. He shrugged his shoulders in dismissal. "You know the laws about possession? Finders keepers, I think you'll find. My crystal…" Okay, Sharon's, but whatever. She wasn't using it. He tried to ignore the pang of pain pushing potently at the pit of his being. "Makes it my spirit. That's how this works, after all."

"I'm going to take it back from you! The Mistress will be pleased when I do, maybe she'll elevate me to her inner circle."

He tried to keep the weariness out of his smile. So much fighting talk and very little to back it up with. She couldn't win this, she had to know that. She might have the Mykeltros or whatever it was called, but she was one woman in a stadium, alone with no backup, no reinforcements…

Shit!

He'd seen the videocams up around the stadium. Only now did he find the full realisation starting to dawn on him. He'd known they'd be recording, beaming the pictures out around the kingdoms. Maybe that had been her plan. Stall him and Frewster here long enough until Coppinger reinforcements could arrive. The other side to that was Unisco surely had to have seen it and be on their way.

Either way, all he could do was hold out. He had to. Whatever happened, he needed to deal with it. His was the only performance he could affect.

"You want it?" he asked. "Come and get it."

The leopard tensed its legs, he saw it getting ready to move, he made his choices. He had the advantage in that nobody really knew what Uni could do, only that the creature was off-putting with its three slit-like eyes, four ear-antenna and lack of mouth.

Mykeltros came, charged across the ground, paws tearing into the dirt. Uni didn't hesitate, brought back a fist and drove it hard into the leopard's face, a bellow breaking up over the sound of bone smashing. He gave the order not to let up, the unialiv brought a spine-covered leg up into the ruined face, spikes tearing through fur and flesh. The maw opened, giant teeth came tearing towards Uni, ready to bite down.

They didn't come close to landing, Uni's eyes started to glow at Nick's behest, the fangs coming to a halt inches from Uni's body. Telekinetic powers, Nick thought with a grin. Had to love them. Better that something like this was in his possession rather than being with Claudia Coppinger.

The glow spread out from the eyes, washed across the glistening skin until Uni was completely covered by it. Slowly, the creature took one step forward and then rose into the air, hovering several feet above the ground. The size difference between the two creatures was noticeable, Mykeltros had size and bulk, but it didn't count for much if they couldn't land a hit. With every inch Uni moved forward, Mykeltros was forced back and back, paws scrabbling impotently at the floor of the battlefield. The leopard roared its displeasure, tried to battle back against the oncoming invisible force, couldn't do anything to fight against it.

The change came when Uni dropped the barrier, caller and spirit watched as Mykeltros fell forward, unable to hold its own weight up. Uni hadn't stopped moving, thrust forward through the air like a blaster bolt before crashing down hard into the fallen leopard's spine, a brutal crack echoing around the arena. He didn't even wince, couldn't bring himself to. Very few things that had a spine enjoyed taking blows like that. Mykeltros' eyes went wide, the fight slipping out of it in an instant.

He wasn't finished. Crippled wasn't the same as dead. Uni was in motion again, reached out for the limp tail. He could hear engines in the distance, hoped that it wasn't more hostiles. Uni had to take both hands to the tail, muscular flesh tensing as it sized up the task in hand. Limp front paws tried to scrabble at it, claws extended but kissing empty air. If Uni was bothered, the expressionless face didn't show it. The only real thing he could see there was determination.

Mykeltros probably weighed ten times as much as Uni did, he couldn't see that little fact doing anything to stop the unialiv from the display of strength. First the leopard tried to fight, dug front claws into the dirt until it realised it was still being pulled regardless. By the time it left the ground, it was already too late for it, back legs waving uselessly as it hit the front row of seating and didn't get back up. Probably couldn't. The engines in the sky were getting closer, no time to worry about that now. He needed to take the thing down as fast as possible, so as not to get caught against two potential enemies.

They were so close now, Uni had rushed up into the stands at his behest, hovering above Mykeltros' head. Nick nodded, tipped his spirit the sign and smiled despite himself as Uni drove down, smashed its weight into the leopard's head, driving it hard into the solid flooring of the stands. A broken yowl fell from Mykeltros, the sound apparently only encouraging Uni who drove a fist into one of the saucer-sized eyes. The pop as it pulled the its clenched fist free of the membrane was a sound Nick wouldn't forget any time soon.

In a flash, he had his blaster out. Uni had that well in hand, he realised. The orders were there, not to let up, to make sure that Mykeltros couldn't interfere. He got the impression its interfering days were over for a good while now with the way Uni rained punches down on it, smashing the ruined face even further into the ground.

"Weronika Saarth, you are under arrest!" he shouted. "Under the powers invested in me by the Senate of the Five Kingdoms as an agent of Unisco, I command you to surrender now or suffer the consequences. You're a known Coppinger sympathiser, you're in big trouble for conspiring to commit murder using your spirits, as well as…" He glanced around the arena, saw the dying bodies in the front rows and felt his heart fall." "Multiple counts of murder. Lie face down on the ground or I will open fire."

He never got the chance to pull the trigger, he heard the distant pop, saw the expression on Saarth's face change as the scarlet flower started to bloom at her breast. She went down in stages, fell first to her knees, then forward face-first unmoving, not a sound escaping her. Good. He hated those who died noisily. So undignified.

An aeroship was hovering above them, rappel lines tossed down over the side. Already there were people on those lines, unmarked equipment and very much not that of Unisco. The ship itself was unmarked, that usually meant it had no real right of being there. He saw gunmen hanging from the sides, weapons pointed into the stadium, smoke still emerging from the barrel of one rifle where the shooter had pulled the trigger on Saarth. He didn't feel pity for her, couldn't bring himself to feel that way.

"Uni!" he shouted, giving the mental orders. Mykeltros wasn't getting back up, though the caller might if she was granted the mercy of immediate medical attention rather than being left to bleed out. "Get the ship, now!"

Someone was shooting at him, they'd hit Saarth and the second and third shots peppered the ground at his feet. He leaped backwards, turned and made a run for the tunnel. Uni had left the confines of the stand, rocketing into the air on collision course for the aeroship. His very own surface to air missile, he almost pitied the people aboard when Uni tore through them. He should have done this with the aeroship at Frewster's mansion, now he thought about it. The ear-splitting crash that accompanied the thought a second later was vindication, he picked up his pace and made a run for the tunnel. The blaster was still in his hand, the two rappelers falling the last few feet. Nick raised the weapon, blasted a hole through the head of the first while he had the shot, watched him fall to the ground before lining up on his companion.

The second one hit the stadium floor, rolled out the way of the shot that cracked impotently into the spot where his face had been seconds earlier. His rifle came up, Nick flung himself out the way as it spat crimson fire in his direction. Not the most dignified of landing, but screw that, he'd not been hit. As a pilot he knew once had said, any impact you walked away from was a good one. He wasn't going to miss a second time, not from this distance. His blaster sneezed, he watched the head snap back. No satisfaction. He should have nailed him at the first attempt.

Divines, what a clusterfuck this whole thing had turned out to be. At least it was over now. Uni landed next to him, the three-eyed expression something akin to pride. The aeroship had gone down in halves, hit one of the stands, but so far hadn't exploded. The flames would take it soon, licking merrily at the metal frame protruding pointedly into the air, its engines sputtering into death. Emergency response teams had to be on their way. They'd take it from here. Uni hadn't even struggled to deal with it, just flown through and smashed it into two giant pieces, watched them fall out of the sky under their own weight.

Spirits should not have that much power. It terrified him, just a little. And Coppinger had made how many more of them? One for him. One for the late Weronika Saarth. The one who'd wiped the team out in the labs. Too damn many.

That was a problem for another day. For now, it was over.

Nick turned, saw Frewster stood behind him, a look of surprise on his face. Red stains were starting to ripple across his chest, kisses staining his shirt.

"No!"

Oh, fuck no! No, no, no!

He ran towards Frewster, just too late to catch him as the old man sagged to the ground. Cradling him in his arms, he realised just how weightless he felt as the life gushed out of him. Nick was sure he'd never been that pale before now, his skin almost translucent with the stresses of age, his breathing heavy and laboured. Gradually they were becoming less frequent, he could hear that. Every movement brought fresh gouts rupturing from him, his expression beyond pain.

He should go get Ramsey, the doctor could treat him better than Nick could. He made to rise to his feet, a withered hand almost claw-like grabbing at his wrist.

"I know where you're going," Frewster said. "Don't. It's too late for me, dear boy."

"What sort of talk's that?" Nick asked, rocking back on his heels. He let out a sigh of disgust. "Brennan, you can't give up now. We can fix this."

"You could," the old man chuckled. He sounded like he was slipping away already, very little left in his tank. Tears dribbled down his cheek, leaking from the corners of his eyes. Blood was gushing from his wounds, Nick reached down and pressed his hand to it, desperate to slow it until he could find something more appropriate for the situation. "But I don't want that. I've had enough, Nicholas. My life has been grand, the best I could have hoped for and sometimes you have to say enough is enough. These wounds are mortal, I know that."

"Don't talk, you gnarly old bastard, save your strength."

Frewster hacked a laugh, spat up fresh blood. "That's fight. You'll need that, Nicholas. What sort of life will I have left even if they fix me up? None I'd want to experience, I'm broken now." He reached up to Nick's hand, the one that wasn't pressed against his gushing wounds, pressed something small and hard into his grasp. "Consider that your answers. Everything I need to tell the world. Make sure the story is heard." His eyes were sliding shut, he could barely keep them open. His breathing slowed, came out pained and broken. "They might not believe. But they need to. If they don't, it'll spell doom for us all."

He didn't say anything else. With that, Brennan Frewster, the last founding member of Unisco was gone. Everything he might have been in life ceased. Nick didn't say anything. Just stayed there, held him for a few moments longer. He couldn't bring himself to do anything more.

Finally, he looked at the item Frewster had passed to him, small, plastic and rectangular. A memory drive, an older model but still one that would suffice in most modern equipment. Stuff like this, they built to last, none of that replace it every year shit they tried pushing on consumers these days. It was slick with blood, he reached down and

172

wiped it against the old man's trousers. In death, he looked small and weak, his face losing everything that had made him such a remarkable man. The spark had gone, nobody would have recognised him now.

"Sorry," he said. "So bloody sorry!"

The sirens were getting closer now, the fires up in the stand burning merrily away. The Mykeltros still lay in the stands, skull caved in at Uni's hands. He let Frewster go gently, stood up and strode over to Saarth. She was still alive, but barely. With medical attention, she'd survive. Probably. Nick had seen people in worse conditions pull through.

Why should she?

He looked at the blaster in his belt, slid it free and pointed it at her prone form. Why should she get the chance to pull through? They could talk all they liked about trials and intelligence and wanting to prove that the system worked. She didn't deserve to live. She knew what she'd signed up for. She'd joined Coppinger and killed in her name. Why should she live when Frewster had died?

He couldn't think of a single good reason. He pulled the trigger, felt the power cells click dry. Her eyes widened, then relaxed, as much as one in horrible agony could relax. Even near death, she wanted to clutch onto life for as long as she could, a chance she'd never given those in the stadium. Nick shook his head in disgust. "Lucky bitch!"

That was all he wanted to say on the matter, found her summoner and dispelled the Mykeltros back into a crystal. It wouldn't be hurting anyone else. Not today. Not ever if Unisco had anything to say about it.

Some good should come out of this situation. You needed to find it in the unlikeliest of places, otherwise you'd go insane. He could testify to that. After a day like this, he felt like screaming until his throat hurt.

"We live in a time of tragedy, where sorrow is becoming a constant companion we must walk arm in arm with. In a time when strong leadership is painfully lacking amongst the Senate and Unisco, though for once the ICCC appears to be getting its act together, the question that remains on the lips of most of the people in our kingdoms, is Coppinger right? She's been the only one prepared to back up her beliefs with actions, not to parrot oft-repeated phrases with increasing tenacity while at the same time wringing her hands in an unwillingness to act. I'd welcome any sort of leadership she could bring to the kingdoms. Yes, her acts are extreme, but we have reached a point where after the actions seen in the stadium at Westwick today, I think extreme solutions are about the only path to true peace. If she wants to lead, I say we let her. She's a magnificent woman and one that could truly bring about the change she's promised."

Corbyn Jeremies, Canterage revolutionary and sympathiser to anyone actively opposing the current system, speaking to the media.

He'd gotten away with minimal explanations, hadn't revealed his true purpose here to the local police services and hadn't been too forthcoming with the Unisco delegation that had come out either. Wasn't any of their concern. Just made it sound like him and Frewster had been passing through, along with Frewster's housekeeper. It wouldn't hold up against severe interrogation. Not when you considered what had happened at Frewster's house. For the time being, it would do. Someone would realise there was something bigger at work here, Nick was right in the middle of it and he'd have some questions to answer.

Soon. Not now. He wanted the answers himself before he started giving them out. Hard to properly defend yourself when you didn't have all the weapons at your disposal that would be needed. They'd taken Saarth away, she was still alive but in critical condition. Frewster had already been bagged. He'd seen Ramsey and Helga leaving for hospital. Just him left now who knew what had really happened here. He stood, hands in his pockets staring at the battlefield. Wondered exactly how much of it all had gone out on viewing screens around the kingdoms. Too much for sure, probably more than enough. He needed to be careful, he hadn't even activated his muffler before storming out there.

He'd wanted Saarth to see who it was. He wanted her to feel fear. Whether she had, he couldn't say. All he did know was that she was near death and he was alive and kicking. The survivor once again.

This was turning into a habit he wouldn't want to break. Slip out of it and the end would come. It only took one mistake, he told himself, that was everything you'd worked so hard to achieve gone.

Recriminations like these weren't uncommon at the end of missions. The cost of mortality always felt heavy when you'd felt it coming for you. With that out the way, he'd stepped up into the heights of the stadium, had found himself in the commentary box. Secluded. Out of the way. No reason for anyone to come up here. Perfect. He glanced around the cluttered room, shook his head. Frewster had been here not too long back. He could still smell his aftershave lingering in the air.

Nick slid the memory drive into the bottom of his summoner, placed it flat on the desk and watched the holographic image of Brennan Frewster appear in front of him. Dead for less than an hour, this might have been his last act. It almost certainly was, Nick realised, given his clothing. Another reason to hate Coppinger, another bright soul taken from the kingdoms in her name.

"Hello, Nicholas," the hologram of Frewster said. It was uncanny, the same air of resignation that had followed him into death. He looked tired, more exhausted than he ever had in life. "If you're watching this, then I never got the chance to tell you the rest of my story. Some circumstances are beyond all our control. I wanted to tell you it in person, answer any questions you might have had. I did intend to tell you it all, you know. And I'm sorry I cast aspersions on your character for saying you'd run off without helping me once you heard it. You live so long, you get suspicious. It's not an ideal way to be, but you don't want to take chances if you can help it."

Nick found himself nodding in agreement. He didn't know why. The hologram couldn't see him. Wouldn't respond. "But it is important, so I feel like you should know the story." A pause. "Just one thing first. Have them burn my body as quickly as possible! Do not let any of my blood get loose!"

A strange request. Nick shrugged to himself, paused the recording and went to his summoner. He typed in the message, sent it to the medical team. He knew how to phrase it so that it wouldn't be questioned. If Frewster had felt the urge to say it from beyond the grave, it must have been important.

He could never have been described as the sort of man to be unnecessarily dramatic outside being paid to be so. When he'd been on the viewing screens, he could be dramatic with the best of them. Dramatic, funny, serious, official... He could be all of them and more. The man of many talents.

Frewster contagious. Infected by disease that killed dozens in the stadium. Dispose of body immediately! No samples left behind.

That'd do it. A warning like that, nobody would question it longer than they had to. In a hospital full of sick people, they wouldn't want to risk an unknown pathogen inflicting even more damage. They wouldn't take chances.

With that out the way, he went back to the recording. Part of him was aware a fair bit of Frewster's blood had stained his clothes, he'd burn them later. They were already ruined, might as well kill two storks with one big rock. He pushed play, settled back and listened.

"Okay, so as you recall, Amadeus King's home had just been invaded by a ruffian with a kjarnblade. I'd tried to shoot him, it hadn't gone too well. Such is life. We were cornered, I could see that in an instant. No way out. Amadeus had run, he had Maureen and Brendan to worry about. I pulled my trigger again and again, more out of hope than expectation. One shot might get through, he wasn't wearing armour and it might drive him off. I realise now what a fallacy that was, but I could hope. You know what they say about hope? If you can get it to grow, it will flower. If you kill it, it will never return. I hoped. My cells ran dry, I turned to run but in just a few short steps he was upon me. He grabbed me by the throat, didn't even touch me in doing it, just threw out a hand and I was thrown against the wall. I kicked and kicked, couldn't get free.

I thought that was the point where I'd die, if I'm honest. Clearly, I didn't, but what happened next was even more remarkable. The night man brought back his blade, ready to bury it in my chest, I'd made my peace with the Divines when another window smashed through. My attacker turned, I heard the hiss of another blade and I slid to the ground as his focus on me was lost. There were three of them in the room now, all with shining blades, two going for the night man with vigour and energy. You ever seen one of those swordfights where they're tapping at each other and nobody really wins? It wasn't like that. The two new arrivals, they went for my attacker, hammered their blades against his. It didn't even look like a fair fight, they were faster and stronger, and a lot more skilled. I've never seen a fight like it before and I still haven't today.

They killed him, Nicholas. One of them drove his blade straight up through his ribs and out the other side, damn near cut him in two. I breathed a sigh, not entirely of relief, but I felt a little more reassured. Not least because someone who'd tried to kill me was dead. I rose to my feet, looked at the two of them as they deactivated their weapons.

176

One was blond like the man he'd just killed, his hair buzzed short into little more than fuzz, his eyes filled with a wild look. I'll never forget that look, Nicholas. Some things just stay with you and a lot of this did. Clearly. He was powerful, muscular, looked like he could be an actor, but you'd never mistake him for one. There was too much danger about him. Some people just look like killers, you can tell it from the moment you meet them. The other man wasn't quite so remarkable. Dark skin, black hair also buzzed short, I remember he wore a blue scarf around his neck. Electric blue. Stood out from a mile, you know.

I looked at them, they looked at me. Thanking them felt like the prudent thing to do, so that was what I did. I strode forward, not displaying even a hint of ill-intent and pumped their hands. I'd made my peace with dying, didn't mean that I wanted to and with their timely intervention, I had been spared a fate I hadn't expected when I'd gotten up that morning.

They both looked more than a little uncomfortable, like they hadn't expected this. I always think that's good. Life should be about the unexpected. You appreciate things more that way.

"Good evening, gentlemen," I said, polite and courteous as is the style when strangers save your life. "As much as I appreciate your timely intervention, I'm going to have to ask you what you're doing here?"

Gratitude is nice, business is business. We all wind up with a purpose in these kingdoms and it's best to follow that purpose through its course. Besides, I was curious.

"What next?" the blond man asked. "Are you going to say you had it under control?"

I smiled at him, not afraid to admit to my own shortcomings in this matter. "Dear Divines, not at all. He was about to murder me."

"You appear remarkably cavalier about it," the dark-skinned man said.

"Everyone goes sometimes," I replied. "If you fear death, then it will come for you sooner than you think."

"Sage words," the blond man said. "Someone fancies themselves a philosopher?"

"Not in the slightest. Just that sometimes attitudes are the inches that make the difference between life and death."

"I like him," the dark-skinned man said. "You don't often hear someone so unenlightened speak with such passion and wisdom."

I didn't know what he meant, but he must have seen my hackles rise at being described as unenlightened for both burst out laughing.

"Don't take it so hard," the blond man said. "Not your fault. You can't be criticised for what you cannot change. Too many do that.

"Who are you both?" I asked. Introductions and answers both felt long overdue. "And what are you doing here? Other than saving my life, of course." A winning smile goes a long way. Sometimes you need to give a little. "My name is Brennan Frewster."

"Adrian Battleby," the dark-skinned man said. From Lahzenje? I wanted to ask, kept my tongue still. The Battleby family of Lahzenje were famous back then. They made weapons. Don't think they do anymore now. Demand went out of the window for it, I think you'll find if you look it up. Not entirely sure. Don't really care. A Battleby was a big deal. The other fellow, well I think you'll recognise the name even if you never met him.

"My name's Canderous," the other man said. "Canderous Arventino." He couldn't have been much more than in his early twenties at that point, a junior to Battleby for sure. I'm not sure if he's still alive today. You might be in a position to know that more than I, Nicholas."

Nick paused the recording, glanced out the window towards the stadium battlefield. He didn't know how to feel about that. He'd never met Canderous Arventino. Sharon had told him he was dead, had never gone into the details. This explained much. If she'd had the same powers as her father, then it was interesting. Maybe there would be something useful on this recording after all. Not that he'd expected Frewster's last words to be offering him closure about the family he could have had.

Honestly, he found it more intriguing than revelatory. Next time he saw Baxter, he'd ask him about Arventino, see what he had to say. That could be worth listening to.

"It was about that point that Amadeus burst back in, it must have made for an extraordinary scene, yet I will credit my old friend in that he showed no hint of distress or confusion. He just stood there and listen, as if dumbfounded by the stories he was hearing.

"We're Vedo," Arventino said, saying it with pride, like it was to mean something. I thought Amadeus' jaw might fall off his face. It meant nothing to me.

"Impossible!" Amadeus said. "You're supposed to be a myth!"

Battleby bent down, retrieved the dropped blade from the character I'd come to think of the night man, pocketed it. They both wore casual gear, the sort of clothing that wouldn't stand out in a crowd.

"I very much assure you, we're not myths," Arventino said. "We only let the kingdoms think that because it's easier."

"What's a Vedo?" I asked. Three pairs of eyes looked at me and I shrugged. "I never heard the name before, I think it's a reasonable question."

"You're happier not knowing, Mister Frewster," Battleby said. "Why did this man come here?"

"I don't know," I said. "Maybe if you'd interrogated him instead of stabbing him, we might know." My breath caught in my throat, I hesitated. Those eyes were back on me. "It's not the first time I've been attacked today though."

"Really?" Arventino sounded bemused, like he wanted to make a sarcastic comment. Vedo or not, I'd have punched him if he did. There is just no need for certain things.

"Yes." I decided to rise above it. "I was at the hospital earlier, my father died…"

"My condolences," Battleby said. I nodded at him, gave him a smile of gratitude. Felt like the least I could do. Normally I don't like being interrupted.

"But we were attacked there. Me. Him. They wanted to know about the Forever Cycle."

I heard Amadeus suck in a deep breath, saw him shake his head in disgust out the corner of his eye. I almost rounded on him, once again determined that he should tell me what he knew about it.

"Now that is a myth," Arventino said. "Allegedly anyway."

"And yet, I've been attacked twice in a short space of time which I don't believe is a coincidence. So, tell me, one of you. What chance that it's a reality?"

I was still reeling from the revelation that my mother might have been Divine, not something that I wanted to share with these two. Who knew what they might do, I doubted it would be good for my health if they found out. Divine blood. The idea was preposterous and yet people had killed for less. Religion was as good a reason as any to start shedding blood, especially when it led down the road to power.

"It doesn't necessarily need to be real or not for someone to believe in it," Battleby said. "For whatever reason or another, they've gotten it into their heads it is real and that you can help them with something. They attacked you at the hospital, they attacked you here. You are the common denominator in all of this."

He was right. I didn't like to admit it, but he was. The idea I was a target felt… I don't know how to explain it. I'd never played that role before. Always I was the hunter. Did it make me feel powerless? I don't think so. It pissed me off more than anything. Right there in that room, I felt the grin crawl across my face.

179

"Okay," I said. "They want me. We can work with that. We hunt them. We find them. We wipe them all out."

"This man had one of our weapons!" Battleby said, digging his foot into the night man's remains. "At the best, he's a rogue Vedo. At the worst, he's a sanctioned Cavanda. Either situation is cause to worry."

"I don't know what either of those things are," I said. "Ergo, I'm not worrying about it for now. Just saying."

"The Vedo are the guardians of knowledge, they search for understanding in the mysteries of life," Amadeus offered. "They have power, but they choose not to use it for their own gain. The Cavanda…"

"The complete opposite," Arventino said. "Selfish, unrestrained greed. They've been waging a silent war on the kingdoms for lifetimes, scheming to get into power and hold onto it. It's only through our efforts that they haven't succeeded."

At this point, I felt like pointing out that if they'd schemed for lifetimes and nothing had come to fruition, they couldn't be very good at it. Things change though, and nothing scuppers dreams more than people. Just because the previous generation had a goal of something doesn't mean that the next one would be any good at carrying it on. Any chain is only as good as its weakest link.

"I still think we should kill them all," I said. "Easiest way to wipe a scourge from the land. Find the source. Cut it out. Kill it."

"Easier said than done," Battleby said. "If it were easy to wipe the Cavanda out completely, we would have done it centuries ago. They're like cockroaches. Hard to kill. You think you've gotten them all and from the last one springs many."

"I'm not talking about them," I said. "I'm talking about him and his friends. He's got to have others. You said it yourself, if they're rogue then nobody will miss them. Let's arm up and…"

"I like how you assume that you'll be a part of this," Arventino said with half a smile. "Given you did so well against this one malnourished specimen." It was his turn to kick the body of the night man. "That's what happens when you abuse the Kjarn. It distorts and disfigures you, makes you a shadow of your former self. It's a common sign in rogues. We have more sense, the Cavanda have more sense. I don't like to credit them unnecessarily, but I must in this instance."

"Mister Arventino, Mister Battleby, I was unprepared before. But I am with Unisco." I drew myself to my full height as I said it. "One of the founder members no less. I fought in the Unifications War. I've killed people before." I saw Amadeus looking at me curiously out the corner of his eye at my revelation. "I will fight alongside you." I

180

shot the night man a look. "If there's more like this, you may need all the help you can get."

Nick considered the words. He'd fought a Vedo before, hadn't even come close to a victory. Wim Carson had been rusty, out-of-sorts by all accounts, his powers only recently back to him, and he'd very nearly killed him with minimal effort. If Frewster had willingly gone up against them, he had some balls. He felt something growing in his stomach, a new-found respect for the man.

"Anyway, I searched the body and found an apartment key fob in his pocket, though the key had been damaged when he'd been killed. That was convenient of him, it gave us a place to start and the three of us set out, all the while, I was pumping Arventino and Battleby for the best way to combat them if one wasn't skilled in the art of waving around an energy sword or fluent in magical mumbo-jumbo. Not that I described it as such. It's hard to be flippant about something when you've been on the receiving end of it. I still remembered how he'd thrown me up against the wall with little more than a flick of his wrist. Terrifying.

"Our blades repel other sorts of energy," Arventino said. "They're powered by crystals infused with the power of the Kjarn and because the Kjarn is in everyone and everything and everywhere, it has a deleterious effect on everything it meets. Kjarnblades will repel energy, split apart material on a molecular level. Very few things can resist it. Denser materials do fare better but only moderately. Best way to defend against it is with another blade, they repel each other. That's why we all carry them, though it is with the hope that we may never need to use them."

"Walk softly but carry a big stick?"

"Exactly! That said, energy blasts are repelled, but they do better against some types of impact than others. We've found out the hard way that stun blasts are harder to repel, more force behind them. Ditto for kinetic dispersers."

Now that was interesting, for back at headquarters we had plenty of those and as the boss, I could get hold of them with ease. I put the call in to my number two, ordered him to meet us at the apartment with kinetic dispersers. I could tell that Battleby and Arventino were unhappy about the situation and yet I could not bring myself to care. They'd brought their fight to me, they weren't the ones who were being threatened with death by enemies they'd never heard of.

The other worry was that for a secret organisation, they were being remarkably cavalier with their secrets. It made me wonder if there was something I couldn't see coming in store for me. Maybe they weren't planning on my being around after the event to tell the story. I didn't want to think that, both gentlemen had been nothing but courteous with me, but it is easy to think the worst in people sometimes. More so in the days that followed this event than ever, there've been plenty of them.

Joey was in place, he'd brought a holdall with the weapons in, I was pleased to see. Joseph Butcher always was a fine man, not necessarily a good one but the sort you'd want at your back. He'd do the dirty things without flinching. He was the sort of man for whom 'whatever it'll take,' wasn't just a trite soundbite. He really would go above and beyond for the kingdom. We served together in the Unity war, I recall all too well. We were caught under fire, I don't think I'd have made it out of there without Joey having my back. The man was a savage, but he was my savage and I wanted him here if we were going into hostile territory for the first time.

It might sound not particularly brave on my part to an unenlightened observer, but anyone who has ever experienced combat will know the value of it. I'm talking about when it's life and death, not just a bunch of drunkards laying into each other outside a fast food outlet on a weekend. If you can, you have people to watch your back whom you trust without fail.

Anyway, Joey divided up the weapons between us, Battleby and Arventino put their hands on their blades and we walked through the door into the apartment block. Dear Divines, it was a tip in there, like the last fading refuge of society leaving civilisation behind for good. I'm not sure what the building manager was doing, but it wasn't his damn job. The number on the key we'd found directed us to the fourth floor. More than once, people came out to ask us what we were doing. The first few times, Joey was polite, told them we were here on official business and to go back to their homes. The fifth time, a rather scruffily hirsute fellow got up in Joey's face, never a smart idea especially given that he stank, and Joey hit him in the guts with the butt of his gun. If Unisco these days has gotten a bad reputation for excessive violence and brutality, it probably devolves back from those days. It makes it harder for you guys today, but that was what we had to do back in the day. It was a different time. People were harder. Life was harder. Sometimes, just to get results, you had to be even harder than them. If they tried to fight you, it was important to ensure that they would break in the process.

I don't know if our two companions on the mission had ever seen anything like it. Maybe they hadn't, and they were shocked by the state of the world they found themselves in. Maybe, I personally believe this one, I think they knew what sort of world we were slouching towards and they'd already inured themselves to whatever bleakness may yet come. They certainly gave the impression that they knew things and given what little I found out about the Vedo after the mission, I wasn't surprised to find that the impression was correct.

We arrived at the door, looked at each other as if in silent debate as to who'd take the first step of knocking. I didn't want Joey volunteering, I wanted one of our companions to go first. If there were more people with laser swords on the other side, I wanted someone capable of at least doing something about it to go through the door to meet it. Eventually Battleby volunteered, put his hand on the knocker and rapped it three times before hustling clear.

Smart, I had to admit. That way, if anyone tried to ram a blade through the door, he'd be safe. Nobody did. Not a hint of life anywhere. I gave Joey the nod, watched him size the door up and then bring his boot against the lock with crushing force. It shook under his blow, stood firm until he kicked it again and again, each strike echoing down the corridor. Another door opened, a haggard-looking woman poking her head out. In another life, she might have been pretty. Here, she looked worn down and defeated, little older than a teenager but already beaten by the life she'd stumbled into.

"What the hells are you people doing?" she demanded. "Some of us are trying to bloody sleep in here!"

"My deepest apologies, madam," I said. Behind me, Joey kicked the door again, damn near broke it off its hinges with that final blow. I showed her my ID, gave her an apologetic smile. "We're here on official business with Unisco. Tell me, have you ever met your neighbour?"

"The one whose door you just kicked in?"

I nodded.

"Nobody lives there. Hasn't for as long as I've lived here, and I've been here four years next month."

I stroked my chin. Curious. Curious indeed. The fob didn't lie, I've always believed that if something cannot speak, it cannot lie, although the truth may not be the obvious one is always worth remembering. That he had the key to that apartment meant there was a link there.

"I wouldn't live there though," she said. "Sometimes I walk past it and you can feel it. You just feel dirty looking at the door. Like every bad thing you've ever done is on the verge of being released to the world. You ever get that feeling?"

Given my list of bad things was probably infinitely larger than whatever she had perpetuated through the course of her life, I nodded, not that I had experienced that feeling for myself, but because courtesy costs nothing, and a helpful witness is always more useful than one who wants you dead for wasting their time.

"Thank you, madam," I said. "You've given me a lot to think about here."

Things hadn't changed that much in fifty years then, Nick thought. The job was much the same as it always had been at the very core of its essence, even if the approaches had had to be relaxed. Talk to who you need to talk to for answers. If someone needs their head cracking, do that. Just a little more on the sly, definitely not with any witnesses. There'd been more than once he'd wanted to punch a suspect who wasn't talking. Wasn't in the Unisco rules to say they could do that. Even if they were, the Senate would probably have words about it. Human rights and all that. They got a little hung up on that.

A simpler time, simpler problems. Allegedly.

"I followed the rest of the team into the apartment, immediately struck by how bare and sparsely decorated it was. The walls had never seen paints nor papers, if there had ever been a carpet in here then it had long since gone and any touch of domesticity with it. It appeared the woman I interviewed had been right. Nobody lived here or had for a while. Back to my earlier point. What cannot speak cannot lie. I should have said it can't be wrong. Because while the neighbour had told me nobody had lived here for years, the five bedrolls on the floor told me differently. They told me that people had lived here. They told me that people still lived here. Some cans of food remained at the back of the room, still sealed shut. Labels hadn't faded. Still in date, I'd wager. Beans and preserved meats. Not the healthiest meal but sustaining.

"What the bloody hells is going on here, Director Frewster?" Joey asked. He'd lowered his weapon, a flashlight strapped to the side of the barrel. Arventino and Battleby both held out their hands, a touch of luminescence rippling across their skin. At the time, I thought it brought an entire new meaning to the phrase hand-held light and I must have laughed for all eyes went to me.

"Hells if I know, Agent Butcher. Hells if I know."

I never liked not having the answers. A good stance for one in my position for the answers are something they seek to conceal from us and we must ferret them out. I took that dislike as a challenge and used it to find the truth, to drive me on. Here, I couldn't even start to comprehend where to look. Not without more information. With no other avenue immediately obvious to me, I decided that searching the apartment was perhaps the best bet. Sometimes you'll enter somewhere, and they've left it instantly obvious what you need. A more stupid breed of criminal you couldn't hope to find, unfortunately they very quickly go extinct. Natural selection is not always a good thing, you'll find."

"I never worked out why Graham's Field is so popular. The Guypsians love it there. We know what happened a year ago. They might never do the carnival again thanks to that blatant bit of urban terrorism. I'm just glad Unisco caught the guy responsible. Makes me glad we pay our taxes. I sleep better knowing that guy isn't out there."

Belderhampton mayor Morgan McCarthy on his city's most famous park.

With four rooms and four of us, we split up. Joey took the bathroom, I didn't envy him because it made the rest of the apartment look well-heeled and kempt. I took the bedroom, found more bedrolls in lieu of any sort of bed, while Arventino and Battleby took the main room and the kitchen respectively.

I could only hazard a guess as to how long these bedrolls had been here and how recently they'd been used, but they had that human stink about that that is hard to miss. My estimation was that they'd been used frequently, enough for the smell of their occupants to rub off on them. I gave them a cursory examination to check none of them had anything hidden within them, yet I was disappointed. That said, the sparseness of the room required only a short search, the only feature of note being a cupboard which I opened to find some papers and handwritten notes. I pulled them out, started to read through them.

I know paper is rare these days, Nicholas, but back then not so much. Words on a screen are easier to read, but there's so much to be said for a delightful form of penmanship that has long since been lost to us. Perhaps the most remarkable thing about all this was that it was written in blood. Imagine that, if you will. Blood or almost certainly crimson ink. I couldn't tell from here. I wasn't entirely sure it mattered, other than to prove my point I was dealing with some wholesomely deranged individuals here.

After all that, I couldn't read the words, they were written in an unfamiliar tongue, so I retreated to the main room where Battleby had turned up something in the kitchen, a small bronze container about the size of a teacup, but with a sealed lid covering the top, a tiny tube protruding from the side. Doubtless it probably meant more to the two of them than it did to me or the disgruntled looking Joey. He'd gotten a truly shitty job, he knew it, I knew it and even though I doubted they cared, our companions knew it as well. To add insult to injury, he'd come up empty.

Arventino on the other hand, had hit a jackpot. He'd found a concealed section of the wall... How I didn't know... and removed some of the bricks. I suppose with a careful eye, it might have been possible to spot that the mortar was loose, that some of them were piled back in unevenly, all the other signs that they'd been recently removed. Easier said than done. Out of the cubbyhole, he'd pulled more papers, a wicked-looking knife with a hooked blade and covered in rust-coloured stains that might have been blood and finally, a mini-projector. They're so common these days, you don't give them a second thought. Back then, they weren't rare, but the average man on the street certainly didn't have them. It was probably comfortably worth more than everything else in the apartment and given the shit state of it, probably the apartment itself. This model was only set to receive, rather than transmit, we realised immediately as we placed everything we'd found atop a bedroll in the middle of the room.

Battleby and Arventino looked towards the papers, Joey and I looked at the projector. Felt reasonable. I had no reason to assume those two weren't tech-savvy, but many hands, Nicholas. Given neither of us could read the language on the papers, it was an easy decision. The cup remained ignored for the moment. I thought about asking about it but neither of them looked interested in talking for the moment.

"Got some messages stored in it," Joey said, running his fingers across the readout. "Hold on, if we can just access them, we can see what their orders were. Hells, maybe we'll know where to hit these guys then." He looked at me. "Director are these guys trouble?"

I looked around the squalid apartment, from the bedrolls to the food, to the door that led outside and how nobody had known people were in here. "I'd say they're the worst sort of trouble. They've not got good intentions for someone, that's for sure."

He inclined his head towards Arventino and Battleby. "I meant those guys."

If either of them was offended by his remark, they didn't show it. I only needed the trust to hold out a little longer, until we reached a conclusion and these guys were off the streets. Battleby even laughed as Joey said it, a deep, rumbling bark of mirth that started off like the complaint of thunder.

"Your partner is remarkably perceptive, Mister Frewster," he said. "If what we see is right, there's a few people in for bad days soon. These papers are birth records of children being born going back the last forty years." He paused, ran a finger across the page. "There's huge sections that have been crossed out though, which is interesting. Maybe one name in a hundred left. Bears further examination, perhaps?"

"And mine," Arventino said. "Are an examination of the parents of those one in a hundred names. Looking into the exact nature of the relationship, how it started, how long it lasted, how it ended. Usually in death. Adds weight to the theory that they're after the Forever Cycle."

"The what?" Joey asked. I suddenly remembered he'd not been in the room when we'd had that earlier conversation with Amadeus. Probably for the best. Poor Joey looked well out of his comfort zone, even more so as Arventino and Battleby went through the idea of half-breed Divine children out there in the kingdoms. I was out of mine too, but at least I'd had the chance to come to grips with that knowledge.

"Your name is on here too, Frewster," Battleby said. "I'd imagine that it is also…"

"That's correct," Arventino offered. "A complete dissection of the relationship between your parents."

I felt more than a little insulted by that, the knowledge that something so private had wound up in the hands of people like this. One more reason to ensure that they were eradicated quickly. They had the means to find things they shouldn't have. As far as I knew, what had happened between my parents was between them alone. So how did they know things like how long they were together and how they'd met? Because I was sure as the hells that my dad didn't tell them. I didn't know the whole story myself, it always came out a little vague and when I'd pressed on it, the reply had always been 'well that was how it happened, Bren.'

"Arse," I muttered, quickly realised that could have been taken the wrong way. Having a go at Arventino wasn't going to help things, he was only the messenger. He didn't look too bothered, I suppose that was a good thing.

"We got an address for where these guys are based?" Joey asked. He cracked his knuckles. "And what the hells is that cup for?"

"It's not a cup," Battleby said. "It's a receptacle."

Joey gave him a sour look, perhaps not the wisest thing to do to a man with a laser sword and the compunction to use it. Still, he had a great pair of brass bollocks did Joey, I'll give him that. Took no shit from Divine nor man and he wasn't starting here. "A receptacle for what, pray do tell?"

That sort of weary sarcasm made me smile, if only briefly. Felt like the day had been long and before the night was out, it would be even longer.

"Blood," Battleby said. "It's for holding blood. Inside one of these things, so the stories go, Divine blood can be preserved for years. Maybe it's the celestial nature of it, maybe it's something about the receptacle. I don't know, the theories are all a little hazy."

"Terrific."

188

"Settle down, Agent Butcher," I warned him. Bolshiness was okay, I could go along with that. We didn't want to show these Vedo that we were a soft touch after all. But outright disrespect was something I was not prepared to tolerate here. After all, we were on the same side and I doubted we could do the job without them. And maybe, just maybe, there'd come a point where they'd need our help too.

"Receptacles like this are placed within the Forever Cycle," Battleby continued as if neither of us had spoken. "Blood is power, it is a link to heritage and what came before. With that blood, the presence of the progenitor remains. The blood of seven will power the cycle."

"How many names in those pages?" I asked, looking at Battleby. "How many possible candidates?"

"We're just accepting this is happening now?" Joey asked. He was starting to look a trifle disturbed, I couldn't entirely blame him. A few hours ago, I'd found myself in his position. I'd come to wonder about things and the more I thought about them, the more I'd started to realise perhaps there was something to it. We all worship at least one Divine or another. I mean some of us worship them all, just to hedge our bets, some of us might only pray to one sporadically in a time of need, but I don't think faith has ever been a problem in the five kingdoms. We might lack it sometimes, but we never entirely lose it. There's too much wonder in the world. I wonder if that was what was running through my subconscious mind back then, that there had to be mysteries we'd never entirely understand. We might walk in the light but sometimes you must look for things in the dark where you might not want to venture.

"Six, including yours," Battleby said. "Six out of a possible thousand." He reconsidered the numbers in front of him. "Ish, anyway."

"So possibly five missing people?" I asked. "Joey, get those names, go talk to someone at HQ. See if we can find if they've been reported missing. Or dead. Or drained of blood. Anything."

"Okay, Director," Joey said, Battleby went with him to translate as they headed out of the room. Just Arventino and myself remained in, I looked at the knife and then at the Vedo.

"I take it this is what they use to cut people open for their blood," I said. The words felt hollow and dry. It was a statement of the obvious, but I needed confirmation, mainly for my own peace of mind. The knife was proof of intent. It was a statement that things had moved away from the theory and into the practical. If they had used the knife, they'd hurt, and they'd possibly killed, and they needed to be stopped. "There's stains on the blade."

"That would appear to be correct," Arventino said. "There are some deplorable human beings in the kingdoms. No matter how hard the rest of us try to rise above it, there are always those who seek to pull us down."

"So how about we find them and make damn sure they can't do this to anyone else?" I asked. "I mean, I assume you have an address."

"What makes you think that?" Arventino smiled. It was not a pleasant smile.

"I can read people, Mister Arventino. I know what people are like. I know they lie. And I know when they're hiding something. You don't want us to come with you when you go for them, do you?"

"This is going to be dangerous, Mister Frewster."

"And I'm damn dangerous as well, Mister Arventino. Don't think that myself and Agent Butcher can't handle ourselves."

"You've never handled anything like this before."

"Then there's no time like learning on the job now, is there?" I surprised myself with that comeback, snappy as it might have been. "These guys want to kill me. I'm very committed to making sure that they don't succeed."

"Then stay well back and let me and Master Battleby do our jobs. We do have a history of killing Cavanda..."

"That what these guys are?" I asked. "Cavanda then?"

He needed at me and I stubbornly folded my arms, difficult with the weapon I still held but I felt making the point. Targeted by magical maniacs who wanted to use my blood for some sort of ritual. Terrific. How great to be me? I did think that most mornings but rarely sarcastically.

"The equipment, the language, that would appear to be the guess," Arventino said. "Even this place. When the Cavanda pull an operation like this, they like to make a place a staging point, somewhere they can mount their attacks from and retreat to if they are routed. Secret places. Out of the way holes where nobody would dream to look for them. Everything about it hints at Cavanda training, yet I doubt it's the main body."

"Extrapolate," I said. He'd gotten me curious now.

"Most high ranking Cavanda, and of course, they're the ones who make the policies, couldn't give a fig about what happens in the next life. They're more concerned about doing something with this one and in a strange sort of way, I can respect the hells out of that. Wanting to make the most of the time you have rather than chasing the chance to extend your life when it might not even be worth it. Maybe some of the younger ones broke away or were expelled and wanted to strike back. I can only speculate."

I was stroking my chin in bemusement when Battleby and Joey returned to the room, Battleby looked thrilled by what he'd found out and I didn't see that coming. Battleby looked like the dour one.

"We've got a location, narrowed it down," he said. "Tell them Agent Butcher."

"Right," Joey said. "Five missing people. No bodies. What we could do as triangulate the position of their homes and we overlapped their cones of influence to see if there were any intersections."

"And were there?" I asked.

"Just one place," Joey said. "Right in the middle of Graham's Field." He triumphantly held the data pad up with the map on it. "That's where we'll find them. I'm sure of it."

Nick smiled. He knew that area of Belderhampton all too bloody well. Graham's bloody Field. The unchanging area of green in the middle of the city, the patch where they held that damn carnival every year. He should remember what that was like, he'd been to the last one. It was unlikely they were repeating it this year. Coppinger liked bombs as methods of crowd control, the more rudimentary powerful they were, the better. They'd proven that over and again, deploying them in crowded areas wherever possible. The purpose of terrorism was to inflict terror. It felt like if that was her aim, then she'd succeeded in fantastic fashion.

It just felt strange how some things just kept coming back around, how even in death people still had a part to play and places kept drawing people back to them however much they might want away from it all.

When you looked at it, he found it increasingly harder to doubt the presence of the Divine in a world whose mysteries were slowly running out. That there was something out there they weren't mean to understand just made it that more special. Something to aim for.

That and the theory that the philosopher James Michael Tan had always pushed, Nick didn't remember much in that line, but he always remembered this.

Those places that have seen blood will inevitably do so again, for the air of violence taints thoroughly.

"My one bloody consolation with this whole thing as we headed for Graham's Field was at least that there'd be none of the travelling folk involved. That just would have been inviting trouble, all them milling about looking like trouble. Honestly, letting the travelling folk into Belderhampton was a bloody bad idea. I mean, they had their uses at first but soon they started gambling and drinking and fighting. an endless series of horn-headed buffoons cropping up determined to prove themselves as the hardest. I don't mind them fighting amongst themselves but when they start to attack others, it gets tricky. We weren't allowed to discriminate against them, but the problems were there the moment they showed up. If we cracked a few heads, they cried foul. If they cracked a few of ours, they'd whoop and holler and party into the night. A truly unpleasant people, I can see why they were persecuted out of Serran.

Thankfully there were none of them about as the four of us made our way into the field. A security guard had tried to stop us, if you can believe he had the temerity to do so. Do these men not know who we are? I jest with this, Nicholas. I flashed my badge, Arventino and Battleby did something with their hands and I saw the blank looks flash across his face. I wasn't sure how I felt about that. They were only doing their jobs after all, it wasn't right to mess with them in so cruel a fashion.

Into the darkness we stepped, this time all of us with flashlights. Battleby explained that they dare not use their powers this close to the enemy lest they give their position away. The element of surprise would serve us well, I agreed with him on that. We couldn't afford to be found out until we were in position to strike.

In addition to the kinetic dispersers, Joey had brought more heavy weaponry. Mines. Magnetic grenades. High-powered blaster pistols, more potent than our regular sidearms. He knew his stuff. When we'd served together, he'd always said that overwhelming firepower was the best sort and I agreed with him on that. Never have too much of it when venturing into the unknown.

You've probably been there, Nicholas. You know what the Field is like. People see it all lit up come carnival time and they think it's a happy place. They associate it with joy. What they don't realise the rest of the year is that it's a dark and unforgiving place at night. You can die in there if you don't know what you're doing. There's no sort of light that you don't bring with you. The moon doesn't shine as brightly when you're in there. Something to do with the gases in the earth someone once told me. There could be all sorts of phenomena under the ground there, but of course, they aren't allowed to dig it up and find out. The laws protecting that field are very clear. You don't go there at night.

Someone hadn't told these gentlemen that, we saw them sat there around a fire of ebullient black light. Strange that the flames were the same colour of the darkness yet the radiance from them was more beautiful and brighter than anything else I ever seen. We saw it from a distance, yet I doubt they would from the city. The closer we got, the more uneasy I felt about this whole thing. Joey didn't look too secure himself, Arventino looked to the both of us and grinned.

"It's the aura of their Kjarn," he said. "They're casting malevolent intentions to keep people away not versed in their arts. It's what they did in that apartment unless I'm mistaken, I sensed the faintest traces of it in the stonework." I remembered what the woman said and nodded.

"How do we guard against it?" I asked. My hands were shaking on my weapon, I wanted them to be steady for when the shooting started. "Is there some sort of ward?"

"Nothing we can teach you in time," Battleby said. "Maybe you two should stay back, at least until the fighting starts. Last thing we need is liabilities in combat. If you're twitching, then you're not going to be helpful."

"Not a chance!" Joey said, his whisper harsh in the darkness. "We're going to kill these fucks for making us feel like this, fear or not!"

"Fear isn't the problem," Arventino said. "Fear can be conquered. This is more than fear. This is shear unabated terror seeping deep into your muscles and your bones, you don't realise how much it's affecting you. It's a slippery descent. The closer you get, the closer you find yourself to falling off the edge. And once you do, you won't make it out of there. This is black magic, not the sort you just walk away from unless you can ward your mind from its effects."

I kept quiet. As preposterous as it might have sounded, I had a feeling that they both spoke the truth. It's hard to lie about something like that and sound so serious when the words sound so fanciful. I doubted they were in the habit of producing falsehoods when it could get us all killed.

"So, what do we do then?" I asked. "Is there a source of it that you can remove, and we can come charging in to help you?"

"You come charging in, it'll be slaughter," Battleby said. "But when we break their parley up, it should disrupt their aura. How something like this works, you can have one man generating all the energy, but it causes a great strain on the system, especially in an area like this. In an enclosed building, it's not too bad but out here it would burn you up in hours, and even then, only if you carried an uncommon level of power. What they're more likely to be doing is splitting the effort, sharing it out amongst all of them. It takes a little focus to sync up that many minds, so when we attack, it should negate a lot of the effects. Fighting for your life tends to remove all other thoughts."

"We strike first," Arventino said. "You guys hang back. Maybe attack from a distance. Create confusion into their ranks. Just don't shoot me or Master Battleby for Divines sake!"

Nick's summoner trilled, momentarily interrupting the recording. He frowned, glanced at the ID. Icardi. He could wait. He wasn't talking to him yet, not without hearing what happened fifty years ago. It died out eventually and the dead man's voice resumed.

"I handed Arventino a magnetic grenade, he looked at me like I'd tried to hand him a pile of my own faeces. "And what is this for?" he asked.

"You know what these weapons are?" I asked. "Magnetic grenades work by creating a powerful magnetic field..."

"Obviously."

I ignored that. "Across a small area. The field draws in all ferrous materials towards it. Anything. Quite deadly in enclosed environments where there's a lot of metal. Works on all sorts. Weapons, for instance. Best way to kill someone is if they can't kill you back while they're doing it."

The look of realisation dawned on his face. I continued to speak. "They talk about honour and decency in battle. I don't go for that. I want to survive. Using a magnetic grenade on a group like this is akin to using a sledgehammer to kill individual flies. It'll get the job done, but it's massive overkill." He looked like he was going to open his mouth, I smiled at him. "In a situation like this, against foes like that, I think overkill is probably called for. Even up our odds."

"Director Frewster..." It was the first time he'd used my title and I felt a little swell of pride in my chest. "I think we're entirely in agreement on this."

"Throw it in the fire. The confusion should be worth a few extra seconds for us all to get into position."

He laughed. "I like it, Director. The sort of dirty trick I appreciate. With a mind like that, you'd have made a first class Vedo."

"I think I'll take that as a compliment," I said. I felt the need to return it. "And I'm damn glad that I've got you at my back. Could have done with a few more like you back in the war. Things might have gone a whole lot damn differently a couple of men like you in our company."

Arventino chuckled. "One day, Director, I may share the story of the role the Vedo played in the Unifications War. It may surprise you."

"I hope we live to hear it," I said. Another wry chuckle was my answer, and then it was time for us to go. We all looked at each other, nodded in sequence, me to Arventino, Battleby to Butcher, Butcher to Arventino, me to Battleby. You probably know what that moment's like Nicholas. That moment where you all stand together before the shooting starts, not entirely sure if you'll see each other alive again after. A moment to reflect with your comrades because there may not be another.

In this bit of Graham's Field, there used to be an overhang of hill which would shield anyone below from the elements. We decided between us that Butcher would be the one to hurl the grenade, his arm was more powerful than mine. We crept into position as Battleby and Arventino headed up the overhang. Given the chance, they'd spring their ambush. All we needed was a signal to commence. We'd worked it out. The night birds weren't uncommon round here, we'd simply set up a relay call to announce our movements. When one team was ready to move, they'd whistle. Anyone who gave one back agreed that they were good to move. Anyone who didn't reply, we all held back.

We both sat there, juggling with our terror until we distinctly heard the distant sound of the birdcall. Ka-kee-ka-kee. Great spotted diver duck. Not uncommon around here. Easy to impersonate. My heart was beyond pounding, it had become a constant beat of unease in my chest and I didn't want to think too hard about what might be coming if we got this wrong. I could see the outlines around the fire, maybe nine or ten of them. Not quite close enough to count for sure.

I thought of my life so far and the choices I'd made as I watched Joey pull his arm back and pop the pin out of the grenade, discarding it. He rose to his feet, hurled it as hard as he could towards the fire. From a distance, I watched it bounce off the grass and come to a halt just in front of the black flames. Some of the Cavanda were already on their feet, rising faster than I'd ever seen a human move. Weapons were already out for some, blades ignited. They were fast. Not as fast as the explosion that ripped from the grenade, tore weapons out of hands. More than one of them was immediately maimed as the base of their kjarnblade swung beyond their control. That had gone a lot better than I'd expected. The feeling of terror vanished, I watched as twin glowing blades fell out of the sky, Arventino and Battleby entered the fray. The fire hadn't completely gone out, I could see them moving around at superhuman speeds, weighing into the confused Cavanda before they even realised that they were there. In a matter of seconds, half their number was down or disabled and I genuinely found myself believing we could do this.

It wouldn't be that simple, of course. Weapons flew back to hands, lightning crackled from fingertips and fire hissed and spat out of palms and rather than stay on the offensive, Battleby and Arventino were forced to bring their own blades up to guard themselves, enemy blades striking harmlessly against their own.

We'd already formed a plan, Joey and I, worked on it ourselves in the last few moments of calm. I raised my disperser, made for the camp. The closest one I could see was little more than a lad, but he looked a real mess, like he'd overdosed on the bad stuff long since and was running on autopilot now. I pulled the trigger, sent a blast of hardened kinetic energy towards him. His blade came up, he blocked it but with great effort. I saw the blast force him back a few feet, Joey put him down with a trio of blaster bolts to the chest. I dropped to my knees, ducked under the strike that might have taken my head off had it connected before Joey's blaster roared out, shots hammering harmlessly off the blade. From my knees, I raised the weapon and blasted the Cavanda cultist right through the lower back, point blank range. I think he nearly hit sub-orbit. That accounted for seven, nine even as both Arventino and Battleby had torn through their opponent, leaving the pieces of the ground. They both had rounded on the last one, he had a modicum of skill with the blade, even I could see that, but it wouldn't do him any good. He got a few good strikes in, too late to do him any good before Arventino cut his legs out from underneath him. He hit the ground, Battleby buried his blade into his face.

I blinked. That was easy. The fighting was over before it had even had the chance to truly start. I looked at Joey, held a hand and gripped his, almost drew him into a hug. Not quite. Wouldn't have been appropriate. We hadn't done that even when we'd almost been killed by Serranians in the Battle of Hoag Island. Those were stressful days. This hadn't even come close, now it was over. Hoag Island, there were men getting shot down by the dozens, body parts everywhere. This had been a minor skirmish at best. Between friends, the simplest gestures will always suffice.

We stepped out into the carnage we had helped wrought, Battleby and Arventino had already deactivated their weapons. I made a mental note never to screw with either of them. I'd thought the earlier assassin was scary with his energy blade. Seeing these two cut their way through five of the same people in as many seconds was downright terrifying.

"This wasn't as tough as you made out," Joey said, surveying the bodies with casual disinterest. One thing that made Joseph Butcher such an effective man to have at your back was he'd never been overtly too bothered about the suffering of his fellow man once they'd been snuffed out.

"The element of surprise does have its fortuity," Battleby said. "Even so, you're right. This many of them, one of them should have seen us coming."

"Don't complain," Arventino said. "We caught a break here." I saw him kick one body in examination. "Although, Adrian, didn't some of them look a little green to you?"

"Green? I've seen less greener blades of grass! The cream of the crop these gentlemen were not." Battleby looked disgusted as he said it. "We were expecting ten Cavanda, we got maybe two of them worth that name. Master Arventino and I are a match for any two they have. The rest of them are just boys with blades they couldn't hope to control and forces they couldn't hope to master. Lads with ambition outweighing their talents."

I wasn't complaining. I wasn't an expert on these things, so I didn't want to pass comment. I've always believed in leaving that to the experts.

With little more to say, we searched the area, ran our hands across every single dismembered body until finally Arventino came up with what we were looking for. He found it in a chest towards the back of the overhang, right in the crevice. Perhaps not its final resting place but that was where they'd left it for the moment. The device wasn't huge, not at all but it reminded me of an old-time compass, a large bronze circle with an onyx-coloured face that had the consistency of glass and seven indentations around the edge of it. I took the receptacle we'd found from the apartment, held it against one of them. It fit neatly, would have been held there if we'd forced the two parts together.

"When the seven come together, the lock will turn," Battleby said. "The Forever Cycle itself. Hard to think that so much bad could come out of something so small." Arventino had come up with five vials, all of them filled with something crimson and sloppy. I didn't need to guess at what they were. It fed on blood after all. I felt a little queasy looking at it. Maybe my own blood was responding to it. Maybe I was imagining things. I hoped not.

"Why do they call it the Forever Cycle," Joey asked. "It's a strange name."

"It's a High Sidorovan variant word," Battleby said, looking at the device. "Originally was something like fuh-evar-sekel. The translation stuck. Means eternal lock, roughly translated."

Huh, I thought. How about that. Instead, I vocalised the question that had been troubling me ever since we'd put the last of the cultist Cavanda down. "What are you going to do with it now? Use it?"

Arventino shook his head. "Hells no, that's the last thing that we want. With the use of the Forever Cycle, it costs far more than you'll ever get. You can't hope ever to use it and remain the same. It would have burned these people alive." He threw a hand out towards the bodies of the men we'd killed. If there was any compassion left in him towards them, he didn't show it. They were just meat. End of. "Best thing we can do is lock it away, hope that nobody else ever gets their hands on it who might use it for ill purpose."

"I'm going to take it back to our temple," Battleby said. "I've got a ticket booked onto the Aerius a few days from now. Her first voyage. I'll get off in Serran and head north to our temple. Once we're there, our grandmaster can lock it away, we'll never hear of it again if we're lucky. But first!" He looked at the vials, extended a finger into each of them and I saw a brief flash of flame and a whisper of smoke from each in turn. "Just make sure what they gathered can't be used."

That was it then. I wasn't going to argue with them, they had the capabilities of dealing with it far better than Unisco did, they knew what they had, and I trusted them not to use it. There weren't many others whom I could say the same thing about. Of course, what happened next was disastrous. The Aerius disappeared, with it went Battleby and the Forever Cycle. I don't know if he ever made it back to Serran, but given the ship never showed up there, I assume he didn't. This is the story I wanted to tell you in person, Nicholas. The past has a way of coming back around. I watched what Claudia Coppinger said during her address of the Quin-C final, when she killed all those people. I have no doubt in my mind that the Cycle is what she seeks, she wants to fully embrace divinity the way those men did fifty years ago. In the aftermath of all this, I spent time with Amadeus King to understand the legends. Should something like this ever happen again, I wanted to be prepared. I knew that they would come for me. This is the reason why my body needs burning before my blood can be harvested. You need to find the other Divine-born and keep them safe. They might not believe that they are in danger, they might not understand what they are. But they are out there and Coppinger will be looking for them."

A resigned sigh broke from the recording. "I don't have much time left. She came for me, just as I thought she would. You've done your best to keep me safe, Nicholas. You went above and beyond. Not just for me but for Helga. Keep an eye on her. She's precious. I never had a better companion in all my years. The one true constant in my latter years, a gem of a woman. Talk to her, she might be able to help you with finding them. Good bye, Nicholas Roper. And above all else, thank you. I'm sure you did everything you could to try and save my life."

Not quite enough, Nick thought as it died to a close. He'd done everything he could and Frewster had still died. He hadn't been able to save him. A horrible thought struck him that just maybe the old man had committed suicide, walked in front of those blasts to get away from all this. Given the nature of his story, it wouldn't surprise him. It was fanciful, almost as fanciful as the idea that Frewster had managed to record all that while he was fighting Saarth? How long had that bloody battle gone on for then? Very easy to lose track of the time when fighting for your life, it would appear.

His summoner trilled once again, cutting him out of his reverie. This time he answered the call without thinking, saw the image of Davide Icardi on the screen in front of him. His boss. Nick winced inwardly. Terrific. This was going to go well, he could see it already. He never thought he'd miss Brendan King. The sooner Arnholt kicked Icardi to the kerb, the better. He could see the island of grey hair at the front of Icardi's balding pate all too clear, the repeatedly broken nose prominent. He'd once heard Wade say that it was a good thing the nose looked like that, it broke up an otherwise uninteresting face. Harsh but fair.

It told him Icardi wasn't the best fighter ever. To have had his nose broken that many times by his fifties, he didn't know how to duck a punch.

"My, my, Agent Roper. You have been busy, haven't you? I've got a steady stream of reports coming in about what you've been up to today, none of them from you first-hand. Now, I wonder if you can tell me why I find that deeply unsettling?"

"I suppose you know your own mind better than me," Nick said. "And I'd imagine that the lack of information upsets you because you like to feel like you have a grip on things. That's understandable. If I was in your position, I'd want to know why I've not heard from me either." He cleared his throat. "All I can assure you, Chief Icardi..." The title was only temporary, but nothing like mollifying an ego. "... I've been on the run, fighting for my life all day. I didn't get the chance to call in, lest my position be betrayed."

Not entirely true, but it sounded convincing enough. And there wasn't much Icardi could do to call him on it. No witnesses. Unisco protocol would back him up. It had been a dangerous circumstance.

"Can't you behave like a normal agent rather than turning everything around you into a disaster zone?" Icardi asked grumpily. "I want you back here, right now! I want a full report as soon as possible."

"Understood."

"Roper?"

"Yes sir?"

"What did Frewster want from us anyway?"

How best to answer that? The answer caught in his throat, a dozen possible replies and none of them felt like they'd do.

"Not entirely sure, sir. I've yet to examine everything he said and did and arrive at the conclusion he left for us."

He cancelled the call, determined to not have to answer any further questions. Icardi was going to want those answers sooner rather than later, he'd have to give them eventually. No point in repeating himself.

"Why do I trust her? She has a certain charisma about her, that's to be sure. A real find of a woman. Perhaps when someone like her takes their attention to governance, it should be discouraged. Too many business people have struggled in politics. I think she could make a real success of it. A shame that's beneath her scope. Why settle for kingdoms when she wants even more? I wonder sometimes if she can do it, then I realise that's not the question that needs to be asked. The way things are going, it's only a matter of when she does it, not if. And when she does, I'll be at her side. The Mistress will triumph."
Excerpt from Subtractor's private journal.

The man calling himself Subtractor came here every night when his day had finished and pondered, sat down with a glass of Black Briar beer on the balcony overlooking the city. Here, he considered everything that had happened, everything he had been in a position to affect and whether he had done everything he could to ensure things went the best possible way they could for the Mistress.

At the end of most days, the answer was yes. He'd done everything and would continue to do so, and not just for the fees that she paid him though exorbitant they may be. He'd gladly have done everything she'd asked of him for free, though he'd never let her know that. If people think you believe utterly in a cause, they tend to make unreasonable requests of you. If they think that you're only in it for the credits, things tended to remain a little more sensible. There were no suicidal requests they'd expect to be carried out under pain of death.

Not that the Mistress was like that. Far from it. Best employer he'd ever had, beat shades out of Unisco in that respect. They demanded secrecy concerning their employees, the Mistress understood the need for it but spoke of a day when everything he'd done would come to light. The organisation would be dead, and he would oversee her secret police, he would be the one who saw that the world set out to be what she desired it to be from a law and order point of view. Her vision was absolute, it was flawless, how many simply desired a painless transition, an idea of same shit but different boss? The Senate and the kingdoms had pushed that idea for years. Revolution was dead before it had even started. If you wanted change, you were probably going to be disappointed. Too many had invested in making sure things remained the same.

If you wanted things to change, you had to strip everything down to the bare basics and rebuild from scratch, it was the only way to do it, the Mistress had worked that out years ago. Only now were the kingdoms seeing the fruits of those efforts bloom. Not that most of them appreciated it, the ungrateful little oiks. They set to try and keep things the same, frantically defending what they had as if it were something precious instead of the squalid little thing it had become. Value faded but principle lasted only if they mattered and the principles of the five kingdoms had died a long fucking time ago. People didn't know what that meant any more. Subtractor remembered sitting at his grandfather's knee, being told what mattered. "Do what's right," the old man had said. "If you know something's wrong in your heart, it's probably wrong. Always be your own barometer, lad."

He'd tried. He'd joined Unisco because he'd thought it was the right thing to do. He wanted to make his own difference on the kingdoms, ensure that the law was upheld. Who he had been before didn't matter so much, just a boy with big dreams and the will to follow them. That boy would have looked at the man he'd become and… Well that was the question, wasn't it? Would he approve? Or would he recoil in dread? Yes, he'd done horrific things. He'd betrayed those he'd sworn an oath to. When they found out, his name wouldn't be worth spit. Any agents who were left would probably try to kill him out of spite. He'd put a big brass bullseye right on his forehead and for what?

Well, for the Mistress for one thing. If that wasn't reason enough, he didn't know what was or would be.

He'd graduated the top of his class naturally. He'd had the will, he'd had the application and he'd had interests in Unisco academia that had extended far beyond pulling triggers and throwing punches. Everyone wanted those jobs, they were glamorous, and they were romanticised as hell, the womanising, hard-drinking spy regularly saving the world. There were more shows and movies along those lines than he could count. He'd wanted more, especially when he'd finally found out what a professional career at Unisco was like. The first case he'd been assigned to, he'd seen the very worst of the agency in action. He'd seen slovenliness and laziness, corruption and wanton brutality towards suspects and witnesses alike. It had been some hells of a first day in retrospect. Only then had he realised the true size of the task ahead, realising that should he wish to rise to the top then it was up to him to stick his head above the parapet, to make them wonder about this junior fellow and how he was embarrassing people with ten times his experience.

Getting promoted was his aim. From the act would spring everything else and once he'd hit that target, he could move onto step two. He wouldn't be here in five years' time in the same position he was now. That would have been wasted effort. If he wished to enforce change, he needed to be in position to do that.

He'd continue to climb the ladder, he'd already made up his mind his time with Unisco would not be permanent. The spell might be temporary, he'd since encountered many fellow agents who'd proved to be cut from the same cloth as him in all ways but one, they would never betray the agency. They acknowledged that they'd made a commitment, they would honour that, and he could respect it in a strange sort of way. He didn't agree with it, but he respected them for it. Yet even with that number of clean agents he encountered, it took only a few to sour the reputation of the lot of them. Unisco's reputation was hurtling towards an all-time low even before Claudia Coppinger came onto the scene.

He'd met Claudia Coppinger long before ever going to work for her. Subtractor had always been skilled with his hands, some of his inventions had been famed back in the day before he'd been overshadowed by larger names in the organisation. Just because someone was a famed spirit caller apparently meant that their work was better. This sort of vile favouritism had always existed there, and he'd had enough. A job had come up at Reims, given the title of Head of Innovation and he'd applied for it. He'd put his resume through and he'd gotten the call to go for an interview. They sounded excited about him, more than his superiors who were masters at taking the wonders he'd made for them and stripping them down to the cheapest sum of their parts, mass-producing an inferior version. It was a wonder they'd moved him into the labs at all, that someone had allowed themselves the chance of seeing something past the end of their own nose to appreciate his value as an inventor over an assassin.

They hadn't even moved to give him Alvin Noorland's old job when it had come up, they'd handed it off to a fricking HAX mechanic. Of all the insults he'd borne, that ranked amongst the fiercest.

When he'd met Coppinger, spoken to her and revealed a little about himself, she'd seemed excited and given what he knew about her now, it was perhaps unsurprising.

"But," Subtractor had said. "I don't want to give you the impression that I'm a difficult worker. I'm not. Far from it at all. I know what I want to do, I'll move heavens and kingdoms to get it done. I just can't abide the tape holding me up, the constant penny-pinching."

Coppinger had smiled at him. The contract had been right in front of him, he'd taken it with him, determined to sign off on it and mail it back to her. The chance for his innovations to be marketed to millions, billions even and make everyone's lives better, it wasn't one he could ever have turned down. His heart told him that going to Reims was the right thing to do, and as his grandfather had told him all those years ago, he'd followed it.

He would have, at least, had the option been with him. Unisco had found out about his intents to leave, they'd told him he couldn't and thrown a new ironclad contract at him with promises and assurances about position enhancement and financial improvement laced with just enough penalties and threats he'd found it hard to turn down. That had been the nail in the coffin for his relationship with Unisco. He could have walked but they wouldn't have let that be the end of it. They'd have gotten something on him in the end. For all intents, he was trapped, locked in. Later, he'd had an uncomfortable conversation with Claudia Coppinger.

They'd met for drinks, no doubt cut an unusual couple, her elegantly refined and approaching forty with a poise that most women lacked. Him, enthusiastic with the scruffiness of youth that he'd never been able to shake off, clad in a suit that didn't fit him properly. She'd wanted to celebrate, he could see that, expensive champagne had been to come their way before he'd dropped his bombshell. He'd readied himself for what was to come, he'd expected the screaming and the shouting, he'd played down his own part in it and assured her that it was all Unisco's fault, that they were the only ones holding him back.

Right there, he should've seen the smile and realised something was running through her head, some sort of private plan only she was aware of. Instead, he was too filled with self-pity to feel insightful. The night could have been nice but all that had come out of it was the start of the simmering embers of resentment.

Subtractor finished his beer, cut the thought from his mind. There was such a thing as dwelling too much on the past, something he'd rather not do, he preferred to look to the future.

On his summoner in front of him, he could see the dataflow, he always liked to gaze into it when he needed to relax. There was something soothing about seeing it rush past, some of it encrypted, some of it not, some strands of information jumping out at him, some too fast to be seen. That didn't matter, there or not. There they would be, somewhere if only one would look.

He could see the shots from the stadium where Roper had finished his makeshift duel with Saarth, just more examples of his thinking. Nicholas Roper was a textbook example of what happened when Unisco agents thought they were above the laws they set out to enforce. How many times had he been suspended, cautioned, threatened with the sack? Too many. He'd gotten results, but they were atop a pile of skulls, a castle of infamy built on a sandpit of the morally reprehensible. He had his own problems with Roper, going back a year to the whole Belderhampton fiasco when he'd cost Subtractor a perfectly good assassin by sticking his nose where it didn't belong. Never mind that he'd been suspended while doing it either, killing an assassin and exposing a corrupt Unisco Agent-in-Charge justified the means apparently.

Hmmm…

An idea was starting to come to him, it might have been the beer giving him crazy thoughts, but this felt like a good one. A real prize of a thought and if he could pull it off, then it might solve a lot of problems, not just for him but for the Mistress as well.

He popped another bottle of Black Briar, took a swallow of the contents and let the sigh slip from him. The cat, as they said, would be amongst the pigeons if this was pulled off. If she wanted chaos, then he would give her chaos.

Do what you know is right in your heart, lad.

"I will grandfather," he said aloud. "She is the way forward, I know that in my heart. She is what the kingdoms need to thrive."

He liked these nights. He reached up to his temple, flicked the tiny switch there, hidden beneath his hairline. Invisible to the naked eye, he found it out by touch and let the mask retract from his face, his own spin on the muffler technology Unisco had developed to conceal their identities. Nobody saw his true face anymore. He'd even gotten used to not seeing it himself. He didn't own mirrors, had always considered them a luxury aesthetic for which he wasn't willing to pay. He didn't want to look at himself. Not when the memories would suffice. Everything he did, he did with a mask on. These times when he was alone, he could be himself and that was enough.

The thoughts were still on his mind the next morning as he set out, a clear plan of action in his head. The idea was simple, he'd run it past the Mistress earlier and she'd laughed out loud at the thought of it. If this idea wasn't a beauty, then he didn't know what else to call it.

"Do it, Subtractor," she said. "Make it happen and I'll reward you beyond your wildest dreams. Muddy the waters. If they're worrying about this, they won't be able to divert as much attention to me. An enemy divided is as good as conquered."

He always had an excuse to be wherever he needed, a face for every job and every job has its face. Today he wore the face of someone who'd have need to be here.

Unisco had always run a private prison within each kingdom, he'd found himself at the gates of the one in Canterage. Chessinghold, they called it, named for the small town a mile or two away. The main business there appeared to be catering for the families of those in there. Chessinghold wasn't a normal prison though

At the academy, they'd always told tales about these prisons. Maybe they still did, he couldn't say. Betray the agency and that's where you'll wind up. Traitors, murderers and cheats, all of them had worked for Unisco and all of them had been caught. There was no other way of putting it. The inquisitors had demanded that they get a place to put the specialist prisoners, those who had secrets they didn't want spilling to outsiders.

Security was tight, not that he'd have expected anything less. They liked to keep a monitor of who was coming and going and what they did while they were there. The inquisitors were nosey like that. Couldn't wait to stick their nose into the affairs of people who'd come to see the prisoners. Visiting hours were restricted, families could only get limited and sporadic access. That was why Chessinghold town did such a great business, the visiting hours were announced at random through the week to take the prisoners by surprise. Given chance to plan, your average Unisco agent was a dangerous beast and should be treated as such. The prisons had to be good, they trained them to be able to escape from places like this.

Granted, it was probably less than humane, but the inquisitors didn't care. Try and imagine the size of the fuck the average inquisitor didn't give about the rights of their prisoners and you might be right, Subtractor always thought.

He'd managed to bastardise up an ID card that would let him enter without leaving a name he didn't want investigated on the system. In what he'd consider later to be a rare moment of humour, he'd given the name of an agent on the Mistress' personal shit list just solely to be a bastard. He'd been using said agent's name a lot recently when it came to inquiries, it might bring a lot of trouble down on him eventually. Good. Anything Subtractor could do to increase his own value to the Mistress was worth it. And anything he could make Unisco do to sabotage themselves was worth it twice over.

They'd waved him through, hadn't even given him a second glance. His face didn't entirely match the ID. All they cared was that it buzzed him through. Thank the Divines for workers who spectacularly couldn't be bothered. This wasn't like it was national security or anything. Of course, this was only the outer layer. In theory, the deeper he advanced, the tougher the security should be. He reached up to the side of his head, fiddled with his optical mask. Just enough to fool a serious glance. When using a fake ID, everything had to match.

Checkpoint after checkpoint, they couldn't wait to wave him through. Every time, his access card beeped to show he was authorised to be there. It was almost pathetically easy. A job like this bred endroids, they wouldn't think for themselves if they didn't have to. The system knew best, the system couldn't be wrong, therefore why should they interrupt their day to question it? Probably just wasn't worth it from their point of view. Especially when they saw such a famous face as his walking through the building. He'd had a few of them fawn over him, move to let him through that little faster. He'd been a spirit caller before, a town champion but he'd never known adoration like these fleeting sensations. All because his access card said he was who he said he was.

Hacking never had been his strongest skill, he'd learned a lot and improved on it though over the years. He couldn't have gotten into the Unisco mainframe from the outside, not in a million years. Only the best could even hope to do that. Having access from within and being able to modify and implement his own protocols though, he could do that in a heartbeat. Okocha had taught him some of this stuff when they'd been stationed on Carcaradis Island, unaware of what he was about to unleash on Unisco. He'd liked Okocha, the man was just so damn trusting. He knew not what he could do with the power at his fingertips, not what someone with less than honest intentions could do with that knowledge. Naivety should always come with a price, he'd thought.

Eventually the cell block had come into view, he'd surrendered his weapons with the guard at the entrance to the block. No amount of hacking his access would change that. That was just prison protocol and immutable to the extreme. He doubted they'd check the serial number of the blaster against the agent it was assigned to. A momentary lapse he hadn't considered, but when filling the form out, he left it deliberately fudged. More than that, it looked like it had been considered and then screwed up. It would have looked more suspicious if he'd walked in here without a weapon. Unisco agents went everywhere with their blasters these days, it was a war zone out there after all.

"Have a nice day, sir," the drone behind the glass said, Subtractor watched as he went to put it away in a lockbox. "Enjoy your visit." It sounded inane even as the words left his mouth, Subtractor wanted to laugh sarcastically. He didn't, chose not to draw the attention to himself. That would be costly. Instead he just strode onto the wing, shut down his optical mask and activated the muffler in its place. Not the whole thing, just the part that fogged surveillance systems. When you knew what you were doing, it was amazing the extra levels of performance that you could get out of something compared to those that just took the technology at face value.

He didn't look at the faces, tried not to look directly at the videocams, they wouldn't pick him up, but it wasn't worth someone looking on and wondering why someone in the cellblock lacked a face. They'd know the answer, but they might come down to ask him some questions he'd rather not answer. The best lies were the ones that you avoided telling.

Subtractor knew which cell he was looking for, he'd checked it out before entering. It was only the smart thing to do. Nothing ruined an effective disguise more than looking like you didn't know what you were doing. A little prior research was priceless. He strode through them like he didn't have a care in the world, ignored the few jibes thrown his way from the cells. Reacting to them wouldn't do him any favours, he'd rather not reveal his identity before he had to. Honour amongst prisoners simply didn't exist, most in here would say anything to get an early release. Whether they'd be believed or not was another matter.

The man in the final cell had seen better days from when Subtractor had seen him last. He'd been one of Subtractor's first senior agents, a man whom always struck him as a tricky bastard with whom nothing could be taken at face value. How long had he fooled Unisco over his own betrayals, the harmless old duffer mask concealing the razor-sharp mind he surely must have possessed to get where he had. Unisco didn't hand out promotions based on sympathy. If you deserved the job amidst a field of qualified candidates, you got it. He had to hand that to them, there was none of the sort of favouritism you found in other agencies. There was a reason Unisco had risen to the top of the pile after all. If he'd been a distinguished grey before, it had evolved into the unkempt now, the sort of grey associated with the homeless. He'd tried to commit suicide upon his arrest, had failed and now they didn't even let him have the implements to shave with. A year-worth of beard lined his face, made him look like a vagrant in an orange jumpsuit. Those jumpsuits, dear Divines, was there any further symbol of how far the mighty had fallen? He'd always found them hideous.

Subtractor hoped he wasn't broken beyond repair and some sort of fight remained within him. The eyes opened as he approached, Subtractor saw them follow him all the way to his cell without blinking, a spooky effect.

"Oh," he said. Considering he was the first person in months to see Subtractor's real face, there was a disappointing lack of surprise. "It's you."

"It is," Subtractor said. He'd expected more of a reaction. A lot more of one than what he'd gotten out of the ageing man. "And how've you been, Nigel? Prison agreeing with you?"

Nigel Carling, former Agent-in-Charge of the Unisco operations in the Canterage city of Belderhampton rose from his bed and fixated Subtractor with a beady-eyed look. He looked like an abused eagle, his nose broken and crooked from where he'd resisted arrest. Larsen, if Subtractor remembered the reports correctly and there was no reason to assume that he hadn't. In most other walks of life, getting your face smashed in by a woman half your size would see your reputation take a knock. Here, it was the least of Carling's problems.

"Well, three meals a day, two hours in the yard and an unwanted wake-up call every morning aren't to be complained about, old son," Carling said. "It's like the retirement I never thought I'd get." The sarcasm in his voice was palpable, couldn't have been more unmistakeable if he'd held up a great neon sign announcing his mood.

"Not loving it then?"

"What do you think?" Carling said. "It's not going to make my career highlights, put it that way, old son."

"That's adorable. You think you still have a career."

"Well, technically they never told me I was fired." Carling's grin as he spoke had a certain ghoulish element to it, his lips pulled back across to show his teeth.

"You've been locked up for a year on charges of corruption, abuse of position and collaboration with an enemy of the kingdoms, as well as accessory to over a dozen murders that THEY know about." He emphasised the word, grinned as he said it. He liked the hint of threat. If Carling still had anything about him, he'd pick up on it. "I think they worked out that you were smart enough to get the message."

That was one thing he couldn't underestimate in all this. Carling wasn't stupid. The man had managed to string along both a highly skilled assassin and his own colleagues for a too many years. Only Subtractor had worked him out and he wasn't in position to throw him under a mag-rail carriage. Not when he might need to use them down the line. You didn't remove potentially viable future assets from the field.

Carling wasn't stupid, Subtractor knew that, but neither was he. If he kept his wits about him, this tiny dishevelled man wouldn't get the better of him.

"So, you came to see me?" It sounded like a question, Subtractor knew better than to believe it was. It was a statement, a process of fact and a clear demand to know why he was here. All the time in the world and yet he didn't want to waste it playing games. Subtractor could respect that. His own time was valuable after all. The longer he was here, the more chance it could go wrong.

209

"I did indeed. Can't I come see how my old friend is doing?" Friend was pushing it. Old superior might have been more appropriate. Never a good idea to remind people of how far they had fallen though. Once people remembered the past, it tended to stir up all sorts of emotions which didn't make them easier to bargain with. Broken people were always more pliable, they agreed to things they might never do in a thousand years before.

"We were never friends. You were just one of many beneath me. Don't even think I knew your name until you started building stuff."

Now if that wasn't the story of Subtractor's life, he didn't know what was.

"As for coming to see me, I've been here a year, old son and you're my first ever visitor. Even the family don't want to know."

The perils of being branded a traitor, Subtractor wanted to say. He chose diplomacy, kept his mouth set into a neutrally sympathetic position. If he was lucky, Carling would buy into it. If he didn't get many visitors, he might be more open to keep the one he'd got, rather than drive him away. Some people just wanted to talk. Loneliness was the best sort of interrogation tool. Leave someone on their own for long enough and sooner or later, they'd want to communicate, they'd want to hear a voice other than their own and they'd want a conversation. It was the reason the prison had been built like this. Each cell was soundproofed, the prisoners kept one to a cell and no communication with permitted one another. It must be, Subtractor had often thought, the worst sort of hells. The kind of place where you know there's someone six feet away from you and yet you can't talk to them in any way, shape or form.

He would kill himself before winding up in this place, he'd already decided on that. If things looked like they were going to go south in his quest to fulfil the Mistress' dream, then he'd pull the trigger on himself. He wouldn't talk, he'd make sure of that.

"Terrible," he said. "Well I'm here now, Mister Carling and…"

"I heard you died. At the Quin-C final."

Subtractor's face didn't change, just folded his arms and let him get it out of his system. He might have heard a story, yet he wasn't quite willing to believe the contents of his own eyes. He could clearly see Subtractor was stood here in front of him and yet he chose to speak of something not untrue.

"A lot of people did die at the Quin-C final," he said. "But as you can see, I very much was not one of them, Mister Carling."

"Aye, that's true." Carling gave him a sardonic smirk. "But look at you now. Still live, still kicking and still with a face like a diseased badger's shitbox and speaking the amount of fuck-dribble that'd slide out of there if it had been violated over and over."

"You learned some colourful language in here." Subtractor had been called worse, even if this chosen insult was a little harsh and not even remotely fair. "Interesting."

"Don't speak down to me. You've not got that right. Tell me what you want from me or I'll start screaming for the guard that there's a dead man walking here. Might put a few cracks in whatever you've got planned here."

"Who says I've got a plan?"

"You've always got a plan. You're crafty like that."

"I'll consider that a compliment, Nigel, from a man like yourself."

Carling puffed out his chest, drew himself up to his not overly impressive height and smiled at him. A couple of his teeth looked like they might have gone rotten, brown and yellow with decay. "Dear boy, there are no men like me."

Subtractor glanced along the length of the cell block, mentally counted the occupied cells, gave the old man a smile. "I can count about fifteen men like you right now," he said. He mentally punched the air. Payback for the diseased badger's shitbox comment. He wasn't letting that slide. Wouldn't have been right. Carling wasn't his boss any longer. He couldn't do a damn thing to him bar potentially exposing him, and he wasn't worried about that. He'd surrendered his blaster, didn't mean that he hadn't managed to sneak in a method of dealing with Carling should he prove uncooperative in his efforts. He hoped it wouldn't come to that. It would truly be more trouble than the efforts were worth. Coalition would always be better than concealment.

"These gentlemen and ladies were greedy. I was unlucky. I commit one minor indiscretion…"

There had been nothing minor about it. Subtractor had been the one to discover it, the one who'd set the blackmail by proxy in motion. The information had gone to Lucas Hobb who'd used it to coerce Carling into helping him. He'd even faked Hobb's death so that Unisco ceased searching for their disavowed sniper. Even then, the Mistress' agenda had been pushed. The more compromised Unisco agents, the weaker the whole thing became. With enough seeds of discord, it would collapse in on itself. That had been her plan and he had been its architect.

"… And it haunts me for the rest of my life. I don't deserve to be in here like these people do." Carling shook his head as he spoke. "The years of service go out of the window once you no longer have value to them. How they soon forget everything that you did. Once they hailed you a hero and soon you become a villain without so much as a cursory trial."

"Sucks, don't it?" Subtractor said. He couldn't do with self-loathing and recrimination, something Carling had managed to fill himself up with in the time that he'd been here. It grated on him. "If it's any consolation, the last contract you and Hobb had got fulfilled. I had to do it my damn self, but it was done."

Carling perked up at that, he hadn't expected those words and the look of surprise on his face was just simply delightful. "I wanted out from underneath Hobb, you know that?"

"I know. I just don't care. I don't think anyone does. In a situation like yours, you've always got a choice. You can come clean and take your lumps, you could have done that, but you didn't, you kept lying and kept facilitating in hopes that you could still make the best of it. You tried to con your way out of it, you failed miserably."

"I hoped Hobb and Roper would kill each other," Carling said. "But not after Hobb had killed Prince. It relied on timing that didn't work. Roper got to him first. Even my backup plan failed. I wired that whole damn thing to explode. Matthew Prince was going to die, one way or another that night and yet he didn't. He managed to get away with it. My life ended that night."

"Not necessarily, Nigel," Subtractor said. "Always there is a chance of redemption for even the lowliest of us, but when the opportunity comes along, we must seize it with both hands."

"You're not here on behalf of Unisco, are you, old son?" That mind was still sharp then, it had grasped the concept with very little prodding, he'd arrived at the conclusion a lot faster than Subtractor had expected him to. Good. It saved time.

"Indeed, I am not," he smiled. "But I'd at least ask for you to hear me out before you do what you're thinking about doing and screaming for the guard."

"I wasn't…"

"I won't insult your intelligence Nigel, if you won't insult mine. Some part of you is already considering whether the knowledge of what I'm about to ask of you could be exchanged for your freedom. Maybe it could. Maybe you'd spill your heart out, they'd thank you for it and then put me in the cell right next to you. I'd rather not find out and I'm sure you rather wouldn't either. Not knowing is always better. It's the same sort of logic that made you facilitate Hobb for all the time you did. You'd rather cling to an awkward secret than a painful truth. It's human nature and you're no different to the rest of us in that regard."

"Dear Divines, I'd forgotten how much you liked the sound of your own voice," Carling said with disgust. "But, regardless, I'm happy to hear what you've got to say."

That was music to his ears. This was it, the point of no return. Once he put his offer to Carling, they either parted as allies or as the living and the dead. There could be no middle ground, nothing left behind between them.

"How much are you aware of what is going on the kingdoms these days, Nigel?" he asked. "I'm not sure how much media they let you have access to in here."

"Not much," Carling admitted. "Is there some sort of war going on, I hear something like that. Some woman named Coppinger. That name I know." He shrugged. "Only what I can coax out of the guards. Some of them are remarkably chatty if you know how to get them to loosen their tongues."

That's atrocious, Subtractor thought. These prisoners were supposed to get the silent treatment from their captors, not give up any sort of information they asked for. Never mind Carling had been a skilled interrogator back in the day, the fact they'd surrendered any sort of information would normally be cause for a review. If this was the quality of prison wardenship these days, this entire undertaking might be easier than he expected it to be.

"She's trying to take over," he said. "She wants to remake the entire kingdoms into her image, fix everything that's broken and be worshipped like a Divine."

Carling said nothing, just blinked his eyes several times. His mouth opened and closed, like he now wished to say something. Then without warning, he turned back to his bunk and sat himself down on it.

"Goodbye," he said. "Let yourself out please, you'll understand if I don't get up to wave you off, won't you?"

Lesser men might have given up there and then, just sidled off into the distance and called it a bad job. Subtractor had never considered himself a lesser man at anything, nor did he entirely care as to the notion of giving up. He stretched out his arms, buffed at the lapels of his jacket and smiled at the prisoner.

"Mister Carling," he said. "I think you're rushing to a hasty decision here."

"Coppinger was the one who wanted Hobb to kill Prince, wasn't she?"

Ah, his memory was sharp then. Subtractor's own relationship with the Mistress could have soured over the fuckup and yet it hadn't. She'd kept an eye on him, he'd made sure to work to atone for what had gone wrong, even if truly he was blameless for it. No harm in making sure that everyone else knew it.

"Business rival," he said. "She's moved onto greater things since then."

"Didn't she attack the Quin-C someone told me?"

Subtractor had memories of that day, he'd been in the stadium when it had all gone down, not that he'd ever been in any sort of danger. He'd watched as the dogs had come and the men with the blaster rifles, he'd watched as people died and the Cacaxis had risen out of the ground. He'd even watched as Alvin Noorland had sacrificed himself, a brave but futile gesture. It might have saved the day, but they wouldn't win the war. When their best people made acts like that, it would only hasten their defeat. Victory via attrition was no sort of triumph.

"A statement of intent," he said. "She'd been exposed…" He'd been part of the assault team to her ship, he'd only just managed to warn her in time that they were there, he'd enabled her getaway. She'd had a few choice words about the delay of his warning but what else could he do? It had been crowded on that transport, it would have been suicide to do it under watching eyes. When they were running amok on the station, he'd found himself a few moments to warn her and had she appreciated it? Not truly. "And she wanted to warn people that she wasn't yet done. She might have taken a knock, but she was ready to punch back."

"Her strategy would appear to be flawed," Carling said. "That's not the sort of statement that will win hearts or minds. Wanting to make a change is okay, but ruling through fear ends badly, my old son."

"She took Vazara," Subtractor said. "Had one of her men kill Nwakili on the steps of his palace. She's already loved and worshipped there."

"Vazara has never been important to the scheme of things," Carling said, a look of disgust on his face. "I suppose if you wanted some slaves, you might go there. Most of the valuable minerals went years ago."

"Strong bodies win wars, you should know that." He knew how old Carling was, knew he'd been around in his youth for the last major war in the kingdoms. Little more than a boy, but he should still remember. Those who lived through wars and those who fought them were often the ones who sought to never see them repeated.

"Ah, so that's it." Carling's smirk lit up the room, he sat up in triumph. "She doesn't want people to love her, she wants them to die for her. Difference my foot. Leaders have been wanting their less-desirable subjects to do that for them for years. It's how you keep control. You put them on the front lines and hope they die before they realise how futile it is."

"And yet, she's willing to offer you a pardon. A full second chance."

Carling rolled his eyes. He was being strangely resistant to this idea, Subtractor thought. He found it unsettling. Most people in his position would already be looking to sign up. Perhaps he still clung to some noble idea he was a hero in a bad way, but things would look up for him and he would find redemption.

"This offer doesn't come along every day, Mister Carling. I would not resist it if I were you. That would be foolish."

"Just weighing up the cost, old son. See something like that, it's never done out of the goodness of the heart. Somebody always wants something, they never give it for nothing. You can't pull the wool over my eyes, old son, I've been around the block a time or two and I know how it works."

"There's no cost, Nigel." He decided to try a different tactic, something to get under his skin. "You know, when you first started commanding me, I did my research on you."

"You did?" He sounded impressed. Everyone liked to believe they were someone after all. If they thought other people found them fascinating, they made more of an effort to be that way. Simple psychology.

"I mean, you were so flamboyant with your language and all the 'old son's' and all those little quirks. I researched the family Carling, such as it was. I thought, who is this guy who swans around like he's a damn king."

The smile had faded from Carling's face. He knew what was coming, that satisfied Subtractor immensely. Getting under his skin was some hells of an achievement, he'd always had a reputation for being notoriously tricky with his wordplay.

"Not a lot to go on, is there? I mean, you like to behave and speak like you're some sort of minor aristocrat. You want us to think that you're so much better than the rest of us. And if that was the case, surely the name Carling would be up there." Subtractor smiled sweetly at him, savouring the moment.

"Is there bloody somewhere that you're going with this!" The accent had faded ever so slightly, that plummy grandfather style that he always favoured so much slipped and something rougher crept in.

"I know how much noble blood is in your veins, Nigel. Not a whole damn lot, if any, so we can cut through a lot of the crap. Lose the attitude, it really doesn't suit you no matter how much you try to make it so."

"Of all the things I've alleged to have done," Carling said, his voice rising. "Putting on a bit of an accent is hardly the worse. I never proclaimed to be royalty, if people assumed that by the way I spoke then they're missing the first rule of doing a job like this. We never are what we seem. I mean, look at you. How long have you been paying lip service to Unisco while whoring yourself out? What exactly do you get out of the arrangement with Coppinger, out of interest?"

"Credits," he said. "A lot of them. More than I could ever earn on a Unisco salary, but hells, I'll spend them like they're going out of fashion. A man has debts, not all of his own making."

"So, it's not about the cause then?"

"I never said I didn't feel a deep commitment to her cause," Subtractor said. "Just that if she wants a job doing properly, it's only fair that I should be adequately compensated for the danger involved."

"What would she want out of having me released?" Carling asked. "What would I have to do for her in exchange? Because I don't pay lip service to psychopaths."

"She's not psychotic," Subtractor said. "Far from it. She is glorious and beautiful and terrible, everything you could ever want in a leader. I can get you out of here, Nigel and give you freedom. You'll walk down the street a free man, nobody to stop you or harass you and you'll never have felt so alive as you do right then."

He reached up, tapped the switch at the side of his head, let the mask slide across his face. Now he bore the features of Nicholas Roper, the man whose identity he had borrowed to walk in here. He glanced back towards the videocam, let it get a good long look at him before turning his face back away and retracting it.

"I'd love to kill him," Carling said. "Bastard. I worked my socks off to get him into a decent position and he ruined everything by surviving."

"You can't kill him," Subtractor said. "The Mistress wants him for herself. She has special plans for him. He screwed her bad, he tried to kill her, he's on her shit list. She wants him ruined before we pull the trigger."

Carling snorted. "What about Larsen? Does she still work for the agency?"

"Natalia Larsen is a liaison these days," Subtractor said. "Effectively a bodyguard for the head honcho of the enemy army. We have no such limits on her. If you wished to eliminate her, you could. It'd do us all a huge favour if you did. That's what the Mistress wants from you if you walk out of here. You know the identities of Unisco agents. Track them, find them, eliminate them. Discredit and destroy wherever you go."

For the first time since he'd walked into the cell block, he got the impression that Carling's smile was genuine. All that was missing was him rubbing his hands together in glee. In that moment, he knew he had him. Carling was on his side in this. A partner in crime, they could do this in the name of the Mistress and everything she stood for.

Carling laughed. "Freedom and revenge? Now that's a boat I can get on board with, old son. Should have started with that rather than giving me the salesman pitch. We could have been done by now and already out for high tea and biscuits. So, what's your plan?"

"My plan?" Subtractor asked. "Is very simple, one that will require split second timing on your part, Nigel. You need to follow every word I say to the letter, listen carefully and act without hesitation. Can you do that?"

He'd have been amazed if he couldn't. Getting as far as Carling had in Unisco required a certain level of intelligence. Though he'd ultimately been caught out, it had been due to a particularly unfortunate lack of luck he might have gotten away with under other circumstances rather than any loss of skill on his part. Still, back on the streets, he could be a potent ally.

Subtractor stepped back to the guard post, wore the mask of Nicholas Roper as he did and gave the guard a big smile. It always felt weird when he did that, like the mask was a little out of sync with his facial muscles and so it reacted a split second later than the action. Weird but not uncomfortable.

"Hello again," he said, his voice nothing like Roper's, but it didn't matter. He saw the recognition dawn on the face of the guard, he'd worn this face to get this far, he didn't sense the danger that was coming his way. "So pleasant to see you."

He never saw the hand come up through the hole in the glass, snatch his tie and drive him hard against the blast proof sheet of plastic, blood smearing the transparent material. Again, Subtractor yanked him into it until his face resembled little more than a battered piece of meat, let him fall limply to the ground. It took a little effort, he reached through the hole, found the release button on the other side, and tried to ignore the screaming pain in his muscles as he thumped it down.

Within moments, he was in the post, not even bothering to give the man he'd knocked unconscious a second glance. He was unimportant now. He retrieved his blaster, ignored the stray thought about giving him one in the head to make sure he stayed down. Murdering him wasn't a priority. Instead, he found out the cell release switch and studied it for five long seconds. Part of him was aware he was humming as he watched it, before finally he reached down and pushed it. Ahead of him, dozens of doors started to slide open and as one, dozens of prisoners started to file out of their confinement.

Perfect. Everything was going to plan.

"I fear that one day, the kingdoms may change, and we will not change with them. To mire yourself in the past is to risk losing yourself in a future when you have become increasingly irrelevant and out of touch. Even now, my people lack the touch with the common folk. We try to set ourselves apart and yet I fear all it'll do is force us to stand alone."

From the journal of Adrian Battleby, Vedo Manifold.

Then.

Battleby only donned the robes for official purposes, visits, gatherings and devotions. The rest of the time he chose to dress like a regular human being. Admiring your heritage and the long tradition of your order was one thing. Keeping it secret was entirely another and he'd rather not stand out. Too many prying eyes, especially when one considered the cargo he carried. Although the compass-that-wasn't didn't look like much, he considered it perhaps the single most valuable object across the five kingdoms and to lose it would be to invite chaos. In the wrong hands, it could be lethal.

They'd just prised it out of the wrong hands, losing it again would be careless and Adrian Battleby did not do careless. The Vedo were not his only heritage, he was one of the last Battleby's of Lahzenje and they had not become the masters of all they desired through being careless. In the distant past, his family had been kings and emperors, rich men and conquerors. Now, the wealth might not be what it once was, but the name still had cachet. The Battleby name was worth something, it was a declaration of duty and integrity and honour and all those things that they'd stood for over the years.

He didn't talk to them anymore. Not out of his choice, nor out of the rules of the Vedo order. Should a child display gifts, he would be taken into the order, the younger the age the better. All full Vedo were required to procreate at least once in their life to ensure the bloodlines continued and yet the Kjarn always found ways to renew or reject the unworthy. Anomalies in the breeding line would emerge, surprises being the spice of life. Battleby had been one such anomaly, stripped from his family and wealth, although he hadn't missed them as much as he'd thought. He'd always felt out of place there.

What he had found was that he felt much closer to his new family than he ever had to his previous one, though the name Battleby would always be his to cherish. The last time he'd seen them, his father had told him his view of how the fortunes of the family had changed when the young Adrian had been torn away from them. Battleby always thought that perhaps where they'd gone wrong was with the sheer number of credits they'd thrown at the problem to try and get him back. If they'd shown that much concern previously for him, he might have wanted to go back. They hadn't, and he didn't. They'd hired mercenaries, bounty hunters, kidnappers and assassins all to take him back from the Vedo and all had failed miserably, taking their credits to the grave with them. Those men and women might have thought they were hard stuff before, they were unprepared for the combined might of the Vedo.

Ten years had passed between him leaving for the first time and leaving for the last time, he'd been dragged out as a boy and walked out as a man.

The compass felt heavy against his chest, he tried to subtly adjust the weight. He didn't dare let it leave his person. Not until he was locked away in his cabin. It was too important and there were too many unknown variables aboard the Aerius to take things for granted. If he let his guard down, even for a moment, that hesitation could be fatal for the kingdoms.

He'd picked the Aerius because of its size and reputation, a new ship yet to be fully tested to its limits. There was less chance of it breaking down, something comforting in the sheer size of the vessel. It would power through the skies with ease, so the flier said, delivering passengers in comfort and luxury to their destination with haste. He didn't know how many of those claims they could really back up, but they'd certainly won the hearts and minds of the adoring public with their bombast and enthusiasm. He'd seen a lot of press aboard the trip, eager to share their stories with their readers, many newspapers and broadcast shows represented, even some of those newer net-shows. People from all walks of life, all manner of colour and creed swarmed the decks as they sought to find their cabins. Once he might have belonged to this crowd, but now he felt like a predator amidst prey, never a part but present to see the whole picture. Look at the big picture, Adrian, his old master's voice in his head chided, and you'll never be lost for what to do. If you can work out the place for everything and everything's place, it's a start.

Dotty old woman. He was amazed recently they'd made her their leader, the highest of the high, the grand master. Back when Allison Teserine had been his teacher, he never would have seen her as leader material. She enjoyed her sleep too much for one thing, was too content never to do something for herself if she had someone else to do it.

They'd made her their leader, a council of senior Vedo had put together a shortlist and Teserine had snuck onto the list only as a late replacement. They'd liked what she had to say, they'd made her do was she was so reluctant to before. Few had really heard of her until that moment, she'd been regarded as a bit of a radical, a dangerous thinker. He'd learned a lot from her though, not just practical stuff with the Kjarn. He liked to think that she'd moulded him into a better human being than if he'd stayed with the family Battleby.

That name had its uses still. Acquiring a cabin aboard this vessel had not been easy, the clerk had been most unhelpful when Battleby had tried being polite. He'd taken his measure of the man, debated whether fogging his mind into compliance would be the best path to dealing with him or whether to take the route less travelled. Teserine had always insisted on that as well, she passed it on to all her apprentices from what he'd heard from the others. Never use the Kjarn to do something that you can do yourself with a little effort. You've got hands and a brain. Use them.

It turned out that a sense of entitlement was a better key than fancy mental tricks, Battleby had fixed the clerk with his most exasperated stare and what he could only describe as a flounce that felt ridiculous leaving his body. "Now, excuse me, my good man," he'd said, unable to hide his smirk. Old habits could be quashed but they were hard to kill. "I've tried to be reasonable with you, but you insist on being otherwise. Now do you know what the hells my last name is? It's Battleby and that means I can legally buy your arse. It means I could buy this whole damn company if I wanted to, I could put you out on the streets. Hells, I could have you killed if I wanted to. You really think that anyone would ask me about it? You think they'd miss someone like you?"

He found it unsettling how easy it was to creep back into the role after so many years, spoiled rich brat out to crush the little guy. Teserine would have probably been simultaneously disgusted and proud, a curious mixture but one his efforts probably deserved.

"But, I'm in a forgiving mood. Turf someone else out, send them the regards of the Battleby family…" That'd please his old man, assuming he was even still alive. "… and move me in, there's a five hundred credit tip in it for you." Not a life changing sum but not bad for him doing his damn job!

The joke would ultimately be on him. Finally, he did draw on the Kjarn, made the gesture and watched the greedy eyes light up as the cabin was confirmed. He never handed any credits over, just watched as the clerk extended out his hands, closed his fingers around something that wasn't there and slide to his pockets. He was going to be in for a nasty surprise later, Battleby thought with a smirk. He was going to be a kingdom or two away by the time the little trick wore off. Shame, he'd liked to have seen the look on his face when he realised he'd been had. Simple tricks were the most satisfying. The grand master wouldn't deny him the moment of satisfaction. She was the least tolerant of fools out of all of them. He supposed that came with age and with time.

He liked the cabin though, wide, spacious, everything his cell at the Vedo temple hadn't been. He felt uncomfortable in spaces like this when it came to personal quarters. Most of his early years with the Vedo had been spent in a room ten by twelve, three of them to the room. They'd had to fight for what scraps of comfort they could find. Training to become a Vedo wasn't meant to be easy, it was meant to toughen them up and teach them the value of resilience. If it were easy, the accomplishments would not feel the same. They would be cheapened by the lack of challenge.

Battleby liked the idea of challenge, of the contest between himself and the obstacles keeping him from his goal. He would never give up, he would never surrender, those had been the words he'd always tried to live by and by Gilgarus he'd done it. He didn't deny he'd made mistakes for that would be a fool's delusion and that was one thing he'd prefer not to be levelled at him.

The cabin he'd gotten wasn't much, decidedly unstatesmanlike but it would serve purpose. Yes, the décor was sparse, but it was designed to hold objects he didn't possess. No tragic loss there then. A place to lay low until they got to Serran. He'd jump off there, return to the Fangs up north. It sounded so simple the more he said it, the urge to remind himself that it wouldn't be so kept filtering through his head. He needed to keep an edge upon himself lest he be dulled by the trials of the journey.

Here though, he could allow himself a respite. The door behind him was locked, a wedge driven towards the base to grant him extra security. He felt, if not safe, then reassured by his predicament in here. They'd all been wiped out. Nobody else knew that he had the device. Just himself. Just Arventino and Frewster and Butcher. They all had seen what they'd seen. None would betray the others. Not with what had been shown to be at stake.

The Forever Cycle. He'd always thought it a myth. He withdrew it from inside his jacket pocket, tugged it free with great effort, felt the fabric sigh from the release of the heavy object. He was amazed he'd kept it in there for as long as he had without his pocket tearing under its girth.

He laughed to himself. If only it were that simple to smash it. The compass was a divine artefact of immeasurable power. It was doubtful one could break it by dropping it six feet to the ground. If it were that easy to destroy, someone would have done it long ago. Thousands might not be able to resist temptation, one person would have done it, even if they were careless enough for it to be accidental.

He tossed it on the bed, lobbed it underarm and watched it bounce lazily onto the mattress. A shaft of stray sunlight through the porthole window caught the reflective copper, caught his breath in his throat. That made it look special, he had to admit, the light framing it giving him a sense of what the fuss was about. More than that, he could hear it if he listened. It sang to him, words unable to be made out no matter how much he focused but an unmistakeable tune demanding his attention. Catchy. Seductive. It wanted his attention and it knew it had gotten it. More breath caught in his throat, he couldn't think, couldn't breathe or move. As spells went, it was better than any the Kjarn could cast over him.

His finger twitched, one of the pillows jerked at the motion and flopped over the compass, smothering it and the lull vanished into a distant buzz. Not gone but quieter. Enough to ignore. He blinked several times. He could remember what had happened, even recall the last echoes of seduction. The thing wanted his attention, the Forever Cycle was calling to him. If this wasn't a moment of scary realisation, he didn't know what was.

He made a choice then, something he'd already toyed with for and decided was finally worth the risk. The Vedo would like to see the artefact, no two ways about it. The council of nine liked rare and powerful objects, they liked them out of the way from where they could cause unnecessary damage. In the Vedo vault, there were enough rare and powerful artefacts locked away, that some Vedo had never even heard of them, never mind knowing what they'd do.

Ignorance was bliss but sometimes it could be its own punishment. It could truly be a prison, could lock you up and hide you from wonders that the rest of life were experiencing.

He took out his blade, studied the artefact and told himself again the choice would be the right one he could make. He had to know for sure. He thumbed the activation switch, felt the blade snap into life, the room bathed in the illumination. Battleby flicked his hand, the cushion slipped aside, and the compass dropped to the floor, landed on its side and rolled the rest of the way like a wheel until it halted in the middle of the room. He studied it like a predator, gripped his kjarnblade and went for it, drove the glowing sword down hard into the artefact.

He saw what happened, he could feel it, he truly couldn't explain what happened next. His blade swung towards the ground, the tip close enough to touch the compass and yet it wouldn't. Battleby's eyes widened, he put more of his strength into the efforts and yet it wouldn't shift, more than that it was trying to actively slip away down the side. If it went through the floor, there'd be some explaining to do. He didn't need that kind of notoriety now. He withdrew, turned and slashed at it, trying to bring the blade down on top of it. Again, it came up short and he felt his muscles screaming under the efforts of trying to force it down through the compass.

That wasn't possible! Nothing should be able to resist the kjarnblade like that. All while he struggled, he heard the humming of the compass bellowing through his ears, roaring like a mag-rail through his head. It was enough to make his vision swim, his head feel heavy, the room spun around him, and he had to steady himself against the dresser to avoid falling. His stomach lurched, threatened to purge the last meal he'd eaten but he closed his mouth and focused on the patterns threading their way through the carpet, pink backdrop with a line of black and white triangles.

He deactivated his weapon and tossed it onto the bed. It wasn't working, no point wasting his power cells. He might need it to defend himself as he travelled, best to keep it in working condition. Battleby walked over to the compass, picked it up and studied it. He'd kept the vials separate, left them in his pocket. The blood within them had been charred into a scorched mess, no longer viable but there was no point tempting fate. Anything that wanted the whole thing would have to take it from his body, as distressing as that thought might be, an opportunist sneak thief wouldn't make the take of a lifetime in one lucky swoop.

Precautions didn't hurt. He reached into the depths of his pocket, drew out the seven brass vials and clutched them in his grasp, not saying or thinking, just feeling. The easiest thing in the kingdoms for a Vedo to do was to feel, to open oneself up to all manner of new experiences and let them wash through you, soak into the very fibre of your being. It wasn't always a pleasant experience but always it was enlightening, even if perhaps that wasn't the feeling at the time. The breath caught in his throat, he clutched the vials together hard, so hard he feared he might crush them. His core sense of self screamed, he could feel them all, those who'd died to fill these vials. Not just the recent ones. All of them. Years and years turned into decades and centuries, always some being filled but never all, people died and yet their fall never mattered for always the same result would come to pass. Their torment and their terror would lie forgotten amidst stories and legends of something so potent it couldn't possibly be true. How many stories had Battleby ever heard about various artefacts around the kingdoms lined with divine power? The Chain of Fate, the Gilgarus Heart, the Cycle itself, not to mention the Spear of Griselle and the Orb of Rochentus to mention just a few. Most of them hadn't even been seen for centuries, only the Cycle ever came into whispers. Maybe it wanted to be found. He'd sensed everything when he'd opened himself up to it, more than fifty victim's dead in its name by his guess.

Divinity was a funny thing, only the gods above themselves could ever claim to understand it. When Gilgarus had stood on Cradle Rock millennia ago and proclaimed they were leaving humanity to its own devices, they'd taken with them a lot of knowledge and certainty, only scraps left behind for their subjects to fight over. Nobody could agree on a damn thing. Certainty was replaced with debate. He was amazed it never turned violent beyond the occasional skirmish between academics. People had enough to fight over in the kingdoms without throwing religion into it.

None of this was his concern. He wished Arventino had come with him, but he'd had other pressing business to attend in Canterage. Business that couldn't be avoided. Battleby was capable of this, he knew that. If he wasn't, then the Vedo had done a sorry shit-show of training him. He could murder a rival Cavanda in combat with little effort, yet this piece of bronze was getting under his skin with little effort. Not a pleasant thought.

Battleby didn't like touching it with his bare skin, but touch it he did, rolling it under the bed and out of sight. For the time being, that would have to do. He wanted to get out of here, get some food in him. The Kjarn could sustain only so much. The vials he slid back into his pocket. Keep them separate. They couldn't do harm that way. They might be tainted but at least they didn't make him feel sick like the Cycle did.

The dining room aboard the Aerius was more refined than he'd been expecting, given the way the people had been crowding aboard the ship before it took off, he'd been anticipating a zoo, a real fight for food and space. In truth, nothing could have been further from the truth. Pleasant atmosphere, not too loud. Perfect really. People were behaving themselves. Wonderful.

He couldn't help but grin as he strode through the room towards the counter at the back. Official mealtimes were set through the day aboard the ship, only then would hot food be served but there were a selection of sandwiches and candy bars at the back, crisped potatoes and packets of smoked chewable meat. Sustaining rather than substantial. The best sort of meal. The sort of meals they'd been raised on back in the day. It's not meant to be enjoyed, it's meant to give you strength, they'd always said, and by Gilgarus, they'd been right. Taste of food had always ceased to be a consequence for him, as unimportant as colour or texture.

All wasn't entirely calm in the room though, he could sense a few undertones of discontent lurking there, he let his eyes trail around until they fell upon a group towards the back of the room, white shirted men all hailing from Canterage or Premesoir by the pale colour of their skin. Process of elimination. It wasn't impossible they could have come from somewhere else, but it was unlikely. Vedo philosophy told them the simplest explanation might not always be the right one, but it was a good place to start with the search for answers.

He could hear them from across the room, their words bringing a curl of displeasure to his mouth. All an opinion they were entitled to, yet it couldn't help but leave something sour curled in the tip of his being. The speaker was an older gentleman, almost white-haired but for a few tufts of grey and strangely affectionate towards the three men around him, all of whom had a look about them reminiscent of the old man. His sons, perhaps? The more he looked at them, the more he considered it a viable possibility.

"You see, my boys," the man said with a jovial edge. Premesoiran then. Battleby could hear it in the accent. "We talk about the Vazarans like they're a good people at heart, they just had none of the opportunities. I mean, I like the kingdom. It's a significant one. There are more treasures in Vazara than in the rest of the kingdoms combined and I don't just mean the minerals and the diamonds. You just can't leave it in the hands of the savages. Can't trust them with anything of value, they'll just sell it." He burst out laughing, braying like a horse, a sound that set Battleby's teeth on edge. His family had been from Vazara once upon a long time ago. Very distant generations, but the heritage remained.

"I mean, we want to buy it, but we don't want to pay a competitive price for it. Competition is for suckers, you can't let the bastards have an inch or they'll want a mile. Your average Vazaran, he has a chip on his shoulder a mile wide. They want everything, but they don't want to work for it, they want it all handed to them. I mean, don't get me wrong children, you might get one in fifty who grafts but the other forty-nine would rather drink and snort and whore their way through life. They'll take any chance of taking offence, look to stab you in the stomach when they get the opportunity. They have no love for you or me, nay that's wrong. They don't have the respect. They don't know their damn place; the fucking savage bastards chat their jibber-jabber in their own damn language and they could be saying anything.

They could be threatening you, they could be telling you they're going to cut your damn throat or rob you. Doubt they're telling you your suit looks nice." Another laugh. Battleby paid for his pack of meat, popped it open and placed a piece in his mouth as he headed back towards the exit.

"Gives me a damn headache, love to cut their damn tongues out and listen to their silence. It's gold. Gold's about as rare as a silent Vazaran sometimes, I mean they do like to hear their own voices. On and on and on and on."

The feeling was mutual, Battleby conceded. He didn't feel anger. Doubtless a man like that would lump him in with them, at least until he heard him speak. The generations had been far enough removed that any trace of a Vazaran accent had been lost. The Lahzenje accent was far more subtle, rich and cheery. Growing up in the temple, he'd long abandoned any notion of one race being perfect over another. They were all human after all. Rich and poor were the true divide in life, he'd always found, not the colour of skin nor accent or language.

He pitied him, felt sorrow that life had pushed him to the point where all he could feel about his fellow man was a sense of superiority. He wouldn't like to hear it, but he reminded Battleby of his father. A man who couldn't see ahead of for the shape of his nose.

Back in his cabin, he locked the door behind him and resealed it with the Kjarn, a tricky little defence against anyone who tried to force their way inside. They'd be in for an explosive surprise if they did. Security out the way, he sat down on the bed, the packet of meat resting across his lap as he picked at the scraps inside. They'd been pre-shredded, cooked in hickory that left a wonderful taste in the back of his throat. As much as flavour wasn't a factor, sometimes it was nice. Sometimes you found something you could appreciate, and you clung on like a torpelo lizard. It was something you sought, you wanted it, you felt like you needed it and your body wouldn't be sated until you got it inside you.

He blinked. Where had that come from? He'd never felt that way before. Not about hickory. Not about hickory at all. He blinked again, slid the packet of meat from his knee, got to his feet. Things felt vivid. Very vivid. He'd never known meat smell that good, he'd never felt this relaxed under circumstances like these. He just wanted to take a break, let himself slip into the gentle embrace of slumber and sleep until he awoke refreshed. Ignore that little voice at the back of his mind nagging away and away, it wasn't important, it was an irrelevance, one didn't need those in life.

227

Was it warm in his cabin? He tugged at his shirt, thought about removing it. His legs felt heavy, although not as heavy as his eyelids. The ends felt leaden, like they couldn't wait to fall. He dropped to the bed, let his body fall back until his head was caught in the grasp of the mattress. Mmmm, bliss. Beautiful bliss, rushing up to surround him. If only that humming would stop, he'd be just fine. Stupid bloody Cycle screaming for his attention…

His eyes jerked open, he rolled to the side just as the blade swept through the space where his face had been seconds earlier, the kjarnblade burning through the mattress. The fugue was gone, he thrust out a hand and the Kjarn came to his rescue, rushed through him and hammered the assailant hard in the chest. Battleby watched him sail through the air as if fired from a blaster and smash into the shelving, blood gushing from his nostrils as he tried to pick himself up.

He wasn't alone. Two more of them came at him with kjarnblades of their own and Battleby brought his to meet them. His blade came up to push theirs aside, he knocked one away, swung out a swipe at the other that would have taken the top of his face off had it connected. Things made sense now.

It had always been regarded amongst Kjarn users that there were seven different specialities. Seven applications for the power. Be they Vedo or Cavanda alike, they agreed on that, what little Cavanda lore they recovered told them that. Everything made sense. He hadn't been prepared for a psychic attack from a Cognivite and it had caught him unawares, gotten in under his defences. Almost. They just hadn't been good enough. Cognivites were masters of the mental attack and should a master get their hooks into you, it was hard to shake them off. He was lucky. This one, whichever one of the three it was, was not a master.

Blades hammered at him, he ducked under one, slashed out at the legs of another attacker. This wasn't going to work; the room was far too small for three of them to have a drawn-out confrontation. Not when the one who'd initially tried to kill him was getting back up, wiping his nose. He looked mad. Real mad.

Keep them fighting with the blade. Don't let them focus on bringing their powers to bear. He didn't know who or what they were, other than they were better trained than the cultists he and Arventino had faced earlier. Wouldn't be hard. Those jokers couldn't have conquered a raffle. And yet, he had wondered whether there was someone else above them. Some sort of sponsor. Getting them organised must have had someone else's hand in it. None of them had shown any hint of leadership nous, judging by the way they'd been routed.

"Do not suppose we can talk about this, gentlemen?" he asked, moved his blade to cut aside a strike at him. A third blade had activated. His door remained closed and sealed, he could feel the faintest hint of power there about it. They hadn't come in that way. So how... "Which one of you is the Farwalker?"

A gambit but a reasonable one to make. If they'd come to rob him, remove the Farwalker first. Amongst the seven aspects of the Kjarn, Farwalkers were the rarest of all, far from the most powerful but their power did have its uses. Farwalkers weren't confined to traditional time and space, their location was only relative to where they thought they were. A Farwalker cared very little for walls as obstacles, half a kingdom away was nothing to one, they could take one step and be where they needed to be. True masters of the skill could move not just themselves but others. That explained how they'd gotten in here.

They looked at each other, he chose the moment to strike, tore amidst the three of them in a blur of blade and energy, electricity crackling from his free hand. It hit one in the chest, the recognition starting to filter through him. He'd seen them before. In the dining room. He wondered where their senior was. Maybe he was their master. Not important right now. Only survival. The one he'd shocked had gone down but wasn't dead, rose as if he'd been kissed rather than tried to be killed. Elementalist perhaps? Or an Enhancile. Either would explain the survival of the hit. Enhanciles were rare as well, not as rare as Farwalkers or Manifolds such as himself, but unique amongst Kjarn-users in that their powers were passive rather than active. All other specialities could affect the world around them, an Enhanciles power only affected themselves. The Kjarn made them damned near unkillable. Elementalists controlled the elements, lightning wouldn't do much more than annoy them.

The temperature had lowered in the room, the lightbulb above his head blinked and his danger sense screamed out, louder than before. He turned his head, felt the invisible blow crack him on the jaw. Before he could recover, he felt the same force on his throat, hurling him into the air and against the wall, his head brushing the ceiling.

The old man was there, a bemused look on his face and a hand outstretched. "Amusing," he said. "As much as watching you play with my boys is, I'm afraid I must cut in, son. I mean, you might hurt them and as much as we all know what sort of lesson pain is, I've got uses for them yet."

"Bastard!" Battleby spat. He struggled against the invisible bonds, tested his strength against them. Nothing. Willpower always trumped physical strength, this old bastard looked like he had it in spades. He hadn't seen it before, maybe he hadn't wanted to, but there

229

was a composure there within him. A fire of certainty that burned bright within him.

"You know, we all recognised you for what you were the moment you walked into that room," the old man said, too matter of fact for his liking. "You people think you can hide in plain sight, but we can smell the Kjarn on you. I mean, you think all that power you wield doesn't affect you? Hence the distraction. All that stuff about Vazaran inferiority. You see what you want to see. We all do. It's the failing of humanity."

He tried the Kjarn against the invisible force holding his throat and his arms, again to be disappointed. It was never so simple. The bonds were never the pivotal point. It was like hammering at the strongest link. Go for the weakest. And no matter the circumstances, the weakest part of the Kjarn was always the one who wielded it. They could be broken. The Kjarn could not. He fixed his glare on the old man.

"You can fight all you like but it makes no difference. You got something we want. You got something we had, before you stole it. Could feel it from a kingdom away, ready to bring it into play we were and then you interfered. Got here just in time."

"You've got a Farwalker," Battleby said. "Should have come sooner."

"Son, I'm the Farwalker," the old man said. "Amongst other things. About the only one in existence by my reckoning. Where's the Cycle? You're not living through this but at least you'll get a dignified end if you hand it over. It'll be swift. Fast deaths are the best sort."

So, a Farwalker and a Cognivite for sure, one either an Enhancile or an Elementalist. One unknown. He couldn't say for sure, nor even which was which. Restorers and Alchemites weren't much use in a fight. This old man wouldn't have brought one of those with him unless he thought they'd have a use. A Manifold would be dangerous, not just to those in the room but everyone else aboard the ship.

Battleby knew first-hand just how dangerous Manifolds were. He had some experience in that area. Second rarest skill after Farwalker. Even then, one in a thousand Kjarn users developed Manifold abilities. Farwalkers were categorised at one in half a million, bare minimum. He had the figures, estimated by the grand master long since. Four specialities were common. Three were not. Those were the thoughts in his head, he didn't want the Cognivite catching any stray impressions from him about what they sought.

He knew how dangerous it was. He'd considered every option, thought them through and his situation looked hopeless. He was outnumbered, probably overpowered. The old man alone had everything on him. Experience and age counted for a lot where the Kjarn was concerned, it brought new perspectives and knowledge, the comfort to try new things. Battleby had reached his forties, he should be coming to that point of his life. Right now, he had to acknowledge that he wouldn't reach it at all unless he did something.

"You know, I was raised never to quit," he said. He could feel his voice shaking. "I was always raised to do what is right." He couldn't let the Cycle fall into their hands. They were dangerous. Whatever the price was to not let them get away with it, he could already tell it was worth paying. Terrible for everyone else but he couldn't do a damn thing about it.

They were all a victim of circumstances.

"A fine speech," the old man started to say before Battleby cut him off.

"And you know what else I am?" he asked. "One in a thousand." He gave him the grin and opened himself up to the Kjarn, not just the Kjarn within him but the power he'd felt ever since he'd come to possess the Forever Cycle. Since first contact, he'd felt it calling to him, trying to seduce him into using it. It had power, more power than anyone could hope to contain, a little piece of divinity there for the taking.

Those skilled in the art of the Manifold could affect the environment around them in all manner of ways, the power was only limited by the imagination of the one controlling it. Battleby had never done this before, he'd always respected the power too much to entertain any thought he could control it. His body was only the conduit to something so much greater, yet the flesh was fragile. The Kjarn was eternal, all powerful, everything and anything that ran through life was a part of it. Something so fleeting as mortality couldn't hope to stand against it. The power in the Forever Cycle was the power of the Divines, a gateway to the heavens, and he felt their power beneath his skin, bubbling flesh into solid cancerous lumps. Battleby screamed, not a human scream but a roar of agony that shattered his teeth in his mouth, the words stripping the paint from the ceiling of the room, cracking the plaster beneath. Flakes fell to the ground, dusted the burned mattress.

"Master..." one of the young men said, the old man fixed him with a stare.

"You cannot control this power," he said, his words gentle and polite, the change in demeanour might have startled Battleby if he was capable of surprise any longer. He couldn't see it. The words were like floss in his ears, soft and meaningless. If he twitched his head, they would fade.

"Control…" It came out not as a word but as a Word, a single burst of power formed into sound, he could see it through bleeding eyes as it struck the old man hard in the chest. His clothes started to burn, his face remained unfazed. "Control is not something I seek!" With each Word, the cabin shook, flames erupting into life. Some parts of the wall simply ceased to be. He could see people outside the room looking in, fear and shock on their stupid cow faces. They were unimportant, they were already feeling the effects of looking at him. They wouldn't survive it. They couldn't. The flesh was fading but magnificence was eternal. He could hear their screams as their eyes caught alight, the azure fire spreading to their skin, engulfing flesh and bone. They were already a memory, only the ashes would remain.

"Control!" Battleby could no longer stop himself from speaking, wasn't sure he could do anything. His body wasn't his to control. Training against mental attacks had been a basic requirement for Vedo, the only reason his mind hadn't gone. That knowledge hurt, more than realisation, it was acceptance. Acknowledging his life was over, no going back from this. The life of everyone aboard the boat was over, that truth just hadn't caught up yet. It would come in a blaze of fire and death, no time for regret. Any pain would be fleeting. In a way, he'd betrayed a vow to preserve life. If the only way he could preserve it was to take it, a thousand for a billion, it still felt like a betrayal. "You don't want control. You want power. And this is power you will not take."

This was why they were Vedo. Because someone needed to make the hard decisions for those that couldn't. He was laughing, he thought, could hear the roaring of blood escaping his body. Every little sound and sensation were his to observe. Thoughts and feelings, the terror and the fear and the surprise all echoed in his body, sapped at every iota of his essence.

Alone. So alone. He was connected to everything and everyone, one tiny neuron in a giant brain spread far across the kingdoms and he felt alone. His body hurt, he looked down through eyes that felt increasingly alien, saw the blade protruding from his chest, one of the younger men… Claridge Coleman, his name was. He knew; therefore, it was… holding the hilt with an almost sheepish look. Battleby blinked and Coleman no longer existed except in memory, fine ashes falling to the floor beneath his feet. The other two young men, Timothy Massa and Simon Tomasi, both looked worried. Their master was gone in a flash of light leaving them alone. The looks on their faces as they realised he'd farwalked without them might have made the vessel smile once. That consciousness was gone and only the wrath of the Kjarn remained. Massa and Tomasi were not long for the world, they died painlessly. The fire and the fury were working their way through the ship, adding new fuel to its flames every time it touched something organic, cradled the life in its embrace before snuffing it. Every warm soul had a story, sadness and light, joy and pity.

The descent was starting. They were falling through the air and would hit the ground shortly, lost amidst the mountains. The entity within was fading, the vessel had expired. Gone. Self-sacrifice. The entity could appreciate that. The right thing over the easy thing. A sacrifice to make sure what had been found was lost again, it could not be forced into the wrong hands. The entity had been born only to die again, did not know right from wrong, only that they were words that had meant something to the vessel from whose conscious it had been birthed from. To the entity, they meant nothing. The importance behind them had been stressed, it could appreciate how important life was to these pitiful fleeting monkeys.

The first explosions ripped across the bow as the hull of the ship met mountain peak, not a soul remained alive aboard. All the entity could do was honour those final wishes. Nobody would find the Forever Cycle. Not until one worthy came. The entity knew that day would eventually come, couldn't fight fate. Until that moment, this location would remain hidden. Wherever the Aerius fell, it would lay, undisturbed until the time for revelation. It hoped the vessel knew peace, wherever he had gone. Those were not the mysteries for the Kjarn. Those were the times beyond. All was connected and yet connections were not all that mattered.

"Farewell, Adrian of Battleby," the entity said through the vessel's own lips. Any words of power were gone. Lost. The power had faded and with it, any urge the entity had to go on. The vessel hit the ground, rolled with the ship as it fell into the mountain, deep into the crevices and the gaps between peaks.

For a few long moments, commotion. Then nothing but silence, the Aerius came to rest against the base of the nearest peak, all the energy of movement lost to it. The hull cut a distressed figure, broken grey against the backdrop of white. As if nothing had happened, the snow continued to come down and down, their flakes kissing the shattered hull.

Now.

They'd searched every inch of this thrice-damned ship, finally found the cabin in question. The thought they'd never find it had crossed her mind, made her question her motives, wonder if this was all just a foolish errand. Doubt was the greatest enemy you could have. Once you ceased to believe, questioning yourself followed, and should you start doing that, you might find uncomfortable answers. She'd decided her own answers so long ago, to weaken now would be disastrous. She'd tried so hard, come so far and the end was near. She could feel it. She could almost taste the potential success. The Forever Cycle had to be on this ship somewhere, they'd searched the hold and almost all the passenger cabins, she'd picked this one as the next. The manifesto had left little clues, only how the inhabitant had been a late arrival who'd thrown credits at the situation and a corrupt clerk had supplied him with passage. A Battleby. A dead name now.

Her information, if it had been accurate, had suggested the only reason he'd not been removed from his position for taking bribes was only because no actual credits had changed hands. A strange story, even if the minutiae of fifty years ago were an irrelevance. She didn't need to know how they'd wound up here, only that they had.

She pushed the door, felt it swing open under the slightest of touches. Her brow furrowed as she took in the view of the lock, it had been burned completely away by something she couldn't explain. The wood around it had rotted partially but there was no other sign of damage. The smell of spoiled wood filled her nostrils and she wrinkled her face at the odour. There'd been damp in here at some point. Strange, the rest of the ship had suffered no such damage.

None of the other rooms had taken such a beating as this one, there'd been some strewn debris as to be expected with a crashing ship but this one looked like it had been hit by a cyclone. If it could have been dislodged or broken, it had been. The bed had been upturned, the closet doors ripped asunder and shelving laid across the shower facilities. There was a dressing table at the back torn into two pieces, neatly bisected across the middle. The rip was smooth as well, sheared clean with no ragged edges.

"What happened here?" she said aloud, not really expecting an answer, before she saw the piles of ash. They weren't the first they'd seen across the ship either. An explanation hadn't come to mind.

"I'd say murder," Domis said from behind her. She hadn't heard him enter the room, but she could sense him. She could always sense his presence, like a second shadow. Even before she'd stepped in the chamber, she could sense him. Before he'd whispered to her. Now he positively screamed, she could no more have ignored him if she'd tried. It was always good to know when her bodyguard was near. She trusted him with her life, secure in her certainty that he would never betray her. He loved her too much. His desire was to see her desires come to light.

234

Without him and his support, she wouldn't have made it this far and that was the undeniable truth.

"Murder," she said. Domis knew far more about these things than she did. How many times had he killed in her name, if perhaps not with her express permission? He didn't take words against her lightly. Her enforcer as well as perhaps her only friend. She didn't have much time for that word and yet with Domis, it applied well to the situation more than it did to most. "Who was the aggressor though and who was the defender?"

"Does it matter?" Domis asked.

"Perhaps," she said. "Unless you feel the urge to go rooting through their remains, it is perhaps the best policy to study the scene and work out what happened here. If the occupant had what we seek, it may be hidden somewhere within the room. If the attacker had it, then we are wasting our time. Yet it is here. I can feel it."

Not entirely true perhaps, but she could feel something. In the same way Domis resonated with her senses, she could feel something else in the room calling to her with a low hum of energy, something drumming into the deepest, darkest corners of her being. Drumbeats in time with her heart, she felt like they were slowly starting to sync up and she wasn't sure she liked that. If the drumbeats stopped, would her heart cease to beat with them?

Now she was being ridiculous. She shook her head, tried to clear those thoughts. She'd been aboard here for too long. The eeriness of the Aerius was starting to get to her. She didn't scare easily. Not with what she'd seen ever since her time in the chamber. Hells, not even with what she'd done. She'd put things into motion that would make a garden-variety psychopath shit himself with fear. How many had died because of her crusade? How many would continue to die? The answers were always the same. Not enough and too many.

People were always the problem. Even the ones who wanted to help often did little more than ache their jaws over the subject, indecision and inertia winning out over desire for action. Those who had died since she'd started the project. They would still perhaps be alive if she hadn't. But their presence wouldn't have changed a thing. They'd had their chances and they hadn't taken them. When they came into these kingdoms, everyone had the opportunity to leave a mark on them. Some marks were bigger than others admittedly, but a mark was a mark regardless. Too many marks were fleeting and didn't benefit anyone other than those making the statement. Man kills woman, is imprisoned and executed, it affects his life, her life, the life of everyone who they might ever touch and not in a good way. A true waste of potential.

An old friend of her fathers, her first ever advisor as the owner of Reims had always told her that he believed everyone had but one destiny in life, all the variables inevitably pointed to one outcome. He was long dead now, but she wondered if he'd always considered her destiny to waste away at the peak of Reims, a queen of industry or to reach for even higher peaks. Might he be surprised if he saw where she stood now?

Domis did his part in the search, she saw him turn up something gleaming and silver in his hand, she dismissed it out of hand. It wasn't what she was looking for. Even as the blade erupted into life in his hands, she gave him barely more than a cursory glance. A new toy for him to murder with. She'd seen Carson with one, that girl assassin months ago doing the same. Didn't that feel like a lifetime ago, like it had happened to someone else. A different woman then. A weapon like that would give Domis a new murderous edge to his being. The Senate and Unisco had Vedo on their payroll now, Vedo entirely unlike Carson as he'd been in a hurry to point out. She could recall the scorn in his words.

"These, Mistress, are not Vedo. They are what Ruud Baxter thought the Vedo should be. Only a subtle difference in theory but it might as well be a mile."

Maybe they'd come around, see things her way and she could bring them into the fold. Maybe. Or they could all be wiped out. Carson was in Serran, searching for another artefact for her. He was looking for students of his own, men and women powerful in the Kjarn but he'd already conceded they wouldn't be ready for years. If it came to a war, Baxter would have the edge.

That was when she heard the voice outside, high and eerie and the commotion that came with it, her guards already giving orders to cease movements. She knew the voice, she knew the shape of the shadow she could see outside.

"Easy you shitwallocks," the mincing voice said, she turned and saw Rocastle barging his way in past the guards, with only Domis' glare halting him from approaching her further. His false leg thumped against the door frame. "Heh, sorry Mistress but I come bearing news from… Get the fuck away from me!" Two of the guards had come up behind him, he rounded on them. "Messenger! Don't harass me, bitches."

"What do you want," Domis said, no hint of threat in his voice, just cold words hard with anger. "You were ordered to remain aboard the Eye."

"Yes, well dearie," Rocastle said breezily. More cheerful than anyone ever should be when talking to Domis, she thought. His fuse

236

was short where anyone who wasn't her was concerned. "As I already said, I bear a message for the Mistress and one that won't wait. It's from Premier Mazoud."

That got her attention. "And? What does Phillipe want now?"

"War," Rocastle said. "He said he's ready to move on Serran."

She felt a stab of annoyance. That wasn't supposed to happen. Not yet. She gave the cabin one final look around, pursed up her lips in annoyance. Fucking Mazoud, determined to ruin things with his wild impetuousness. Much more of it, she might have to look at replacing him in Vazara. A tricky task and one she wouldn't relish but if it became necessary then she would. The efforts to get him on the throne had been massive, removing him would surely be easier.

Except he still had the Suns at his beck and call and she couldn't fight them and the rest of the kingdoms at the same time. She wondered if Mazoud knew that and was deliberately sabre-rattling. If that was the case, he was perhaps more dangerously intelligent than she gave him credit for.

"Search the room," she said. "It's in here somewhere. Leave nothing unturned and we will find what I need. Domis, stay here and oversee. I'm returning to the Eye." She reached to her bodyguard, took his giant hand in both of hers. "I know you won't fail me."

"I will die first, Mistress," he said.

True words indeed. She'd seen some of the wounds inflicted on her dark scoundrel. He could hurt but he couldn't be broken. He'd suffered wounds that would have killed anyone else, had shrugged them off and kept on coming. What it would take to kill him, she did not know. That he should make such a vow to her only underlined his certainty.

"I know you will," she said, patting his hand. "Good luck, my friend."

"And to you, my Mistress."

They parted, she gave Rocastle a suitably withering look. Make sure he always knew his place, lest the ideas in his head make him think himself better than he truly was. "With me, Harvey," she said. "We're done here."

"I will have revenge on my enemies, those who defy me will be dealt with, be it today, tomorrow or the day after. Society bears insults which must be born, but I will not let it slide forever. These kingdoms need a firm hand, one which will slap them down if they seek to rise up."

Claudia Coppinger.

Domis had returned, one moment he wasn't there and the next he was, a presence across her senses. She hadn't even heard the door open, lost in her thoughts. A good thing he wasn't an intruder wishing her harm. She spun her chair, turned to face him. She should have guessed he'd made his way back to her, she'd heard the engines and the return of his shuttle. Now he was there in front of her, Sinkins behind him and a box in his hands. The tiny and the tremendous, the mountain and the mole.

"We found it, Mistress," he said simply, his voice little more than a throaty growl from the cold. It had been biting down there, she'd recalled. They couldn't have brought the Aerius down in much more of an inconvenient place if they'd tried. "We found the object of your desire."

It was more than desire, she thought as she studied the box. A lot more. It was lust and envy, a waking dream she didn't wish to wake up from. Everything in her life had led to this moment, finding this box upon the Aerius and laying claim to the power inside it. She could feel it from where she sat, raw power resonating with her senses, throbbing with its very presence. The answers were there, she could smell them, rich and coppery, the odour of power older than she could comprehend. It was hers as well.

"Under the damn bed if you can believe it," Sinkins said, shaking his head. "I don't know what the hells sort of hiding place the original owner thought that was, but there it is."

"Might have made more sense at the time," she mused. "Could have been any number of reasons." Why was she even contemplating this? The why was irrelevant, all that mattered was the when and the how and both times were approaching.

"We've found it, Mistress," Domis rumbled. "What are our next orders?"

She said nothing, still intently focused on studying the box, running her eyes across every edge of polished mahogany. It looked new, she had to admit, perhaps a little too new. The realisation flooded through her, knowledge hitting her this wasn't the Forever Cycle but

238

rather the receptacle they'd chosen to hold it. Their choice had been exquisite, she pulled it towards her, fingers fiddling with the clasp. The anticipation made her heart pound inside her chest, bounce harder and faster than it had in years. Her fingers closed around the lock, pulled it aside and gasped at the sight awaiting her inside the wooden confines.

"Ah, it wasn't us that broke it," Sinkins pointed out quickly as she reached into the box, withdrew the bronze compass-like artefact and held it to the light, disappointment tugging at every fibre of her being. The face had been marred, a terrific crack running down the centre. She danced her fingers across the surface, felt the power flow around the stricken area but not through it. There was potency there, potential for chaos unrestrained if only she could tap it. The mysteries it could solve remained just out of reach, a lock for which she didn't have a key and it frustrated her. Like this, it was useless to her.

"Sinkins!" she barked. "What the hells do you get paid for?" She didn't wait for him to answer the question. "I want you to use all your contacts, anyone you might know who can do this job. I want it repaired now!"

"Mistress Coppinger," Sinkins said, his voice servile and creeping. The sort of voice that made her want to punch him in the face. If she hadn't gotten used to people treating her like she was an afterthought before, recent times had changed her, the trials and tribulations of life catching up with her. "It is not that simple to repair an artefact like this. Not simple at all. It is not a case of using some glue and a new lens. It is complicated machinery, from a simpler time admittedly but designed by beings whose nature we can't even start to comprehend."

"No excuses, Doctor. I want to hear how it can be done," she said. "Not about why it can't be. If that's how you feel when faced with challenge, then perhaps it was a mistake to promote you."

"I did examine it thoroughly on the way back here," Sinkins said quickly, the determination to rectify his earlier mistake plain on his face for all to see. "It appears to be all in working order." He reached into his coat, withdrew a handful of brass that jingled as he handed them towards her. They looked like little shot glasses, she thought, the choice of beverage of the hardily inebriated. She'd never seen the attachment towards them, though she studied the bronze cups with interest. A layer of faded black hung to the bottom of some of them, she scraped at it with a fingernail, black ash came away. Something had been burned in there, long ago but burned regardless.

"Any ideas?" she said. "You're the expert, Mister Sinkins."

Sinkins only shrugged. "Going through my notes, going through the ones Blut left behind before his timely demise, I'm concluding that by the court of agreement, that that is indeed the Forever Cycle. Blut made a few references to it, it's where we got our link to Mister Frewster, of course…"

She would have loved to have known how Blut had made that connection. Blut had been an information gatherer extraordinaire. Nobody had been able to touch him in that regard. His death had been a setback, she often wondered who'd struck the final blow in putting him down. Sinkins was adequate in the task. Nothing more. When she'd needed something investigating fully, research carried out to the hilt, Blut had turned coal into diamonds too many times. His mind had been a weapon like no other. He alone out of everyone she'd ever brought to this quest had found Wim Carson, her own pet Vedo. He was hers, he just didn't realise quite how much just yet. If push came to shove, he would kill for her.

They all would. That was the truest mark of a great leader. Would your followers kill for you without you asking them to? Would they take the greatest act of theft against another human being, steal their life, upon their own initiative?

"Unfortunately, that lead is no longer viable," she said. "Subtractor informed me Frewster was killed. He's trying to get access to the investigation file, but information is coming through slow."

"I do not trust Subtractor, Mistress," Domis rumbled. "A man who will sell himself to the highest bidder will never be truly yours. Not like me or Mister Sinkins."

"He will if you outbid everyone else," she said. "Domis, as valued as you are, as valued as Dale over there is, there are tasks out there you are horribly inadequate for. Don't make me question Subtractor's loyalty for he has betrayed everything and everyone that once meant something to him. He betrayed it for me, whether it is for the ideology or the wealth, I do not care. Provided that we all pull within the same direction, then all will be well, for my credits will continue to roll into his account until the day he decides to betray me and then he'll cease breathing."

Once Domis looked suitably chastised, she returned to the examination of the compass, brow furrowing as she ran her eyes across the golden-brown surface, fingers probing every little flaw and imperfection. She found the holes quickly, tested the bronze cups against them, found that all seven of them fit neatly in. The prongs that held them, she quickly noticed, were more than that, they were pipes. As she studied them, she saw the holes leading into the depths of the compass, subtle small but recognisable once discovered.

If only it hadn't been broken… She wondered what could have done this. Tales of artefacts like this always said the same thing, that they'd be a constant in this world and the next, unchanging, unbreaking. They could not be altered, they could not be smashed, their power immense. She could feel that power towards the centre of her being, not as vast as she'd imagined but present regardless. The jewel embedded in her wrist sang as she placed it near, hot and cold juxtaposing at the same time, an unusual feeling but not unpleasant. Even with her wrist facing away from her, she could see the glow, the same swathe of light casting a pall across the surface of the device, tiny plumes of smoke rising off the metal. She blinked, yanked her arm away. That wouldn't do, not at all. It might already be broken beyond repair, the last thing needed was to cause further damage. She studied the underside of her wrist, her flesh around the jewel reddened and swollen, though it did not hurt.

Further examination of the Cycle revealed one further truth to her, one in her haste she had initially failed to notice.

Where the light had cast its pallor earlier, from where the smoke had started to rise, the words had started to appear, exhilaration dancing through her spirit as realisation dawned. Back she brought the jewel, chose not to react as the smoke started to rise this time, it wouldn't do the compass any lasting damage. It had survived thousands of years, it would survive her as well. Finally, she could read them, several long agonising minutes passing before they were legible.

Just because she could read them though, she quickly realised, didn't mean that they had to make any sort of sense.

The blood of the seven touched by Grace shall restore the way of the Divine

She held out the compass for Sinkins who read the words upside down, mouthing them to himself through thin lips as he perused them. Several times he repeated himself, considering every possible word, even resorted to mentally ticking a checklist off on his fingers, though as to what he was ruling out or counting, she couldn't say.

"Blood," he said eventually. "Blut makes too many references to it. Divineborn. There's reference to those as well. I think that's what they mean by being touched by Grace."
"Talk to me of Divineborn. Who is Grace?" she asked. "I want more than that, Dale." Something about it sounded familiar, maybe an inkling of remembrance from her time in the first chamber slipping back to her.

"More a metaphor than a person, Mistress," Sinkins said. "The Divineborn are the children of the Divines." He curled his lips, a touch of insolence maybe, perhaps he wanted to add sarcasm to his words. If he did, it might well be the last thing he did. Domis would break him in two if she gave the command. The insolence had been unsaid, she needed his experience for now. "Every hundred years, each Divine comes back to our level of existence in regards of procreation. Not at the same time, obviously…" There was that word again, he'd vocalised it this time. "They will spend time here, they will fate, parent an heir and then expire, returned to the heavens from which they came."

"Why?"

"Nobody seems to truly know. A lot of academics dispute it as little more than a legend, rather than a basis of fact. Blut believed it to be true though."

"Blut believed a lot of things," she said. "And a lot of it was at least partly accurate. The man had a mind like which we've never seen before." And he was also a violent, abusive drunk. Genius had its price.

"These offspring don't inherit Divine powers, well not on the level you might think. Maybe some slight abilities, nothing noticeable. They'll still bleed if you cut them. And blood is the important thing. Their blood is special, it is the sole solid evidence of the Divine in existence. Irrefutable proof of their existence. And it is that blood which powers the Forever Cycle. A gateway to the heavens themselves, if some of the stories are to be believed."

"But why?" Two words, two small words but they were important ones.

"As far as I can tell, there have been a number of different tales told as about why. One says it is a contingency, a back door in case any of them getting stranded here without a way back. They could find the children of their kin, bleed them and get back."

Made sense, she thought. Anyone worth their salt had a backup plan in case of failure. Why would Divines be any different? It made a lot of sense.

"Although, there's another one I find intriguing," Sinkins said. "Apparently they didn't create the Forever Cycle. They simply found it and managed to make it work for their own ends. They twisted it into something used to ascend to omniscience, they didn't create their home, they merely appropriated it for their own use. Their blood powered it the first time, hence why it works now. Neat theories, Mistress Coppinger, I think you'll agree. The truth is, we don't bloody know."

She didn't like that second suggestion as much, too many unanswered questions, too many variables that she couldn't even conceive an answer to. If Sinkins, the closest thing she had to an expert in these times didn't have the answer, then she sure didn't.

"I don't expect you to tell me what I need to agree on," she said. "The point is, Dale, where are these Divineborn now?"

Sinkins smiled at her, a face flecked with nerves. She could see it in his body language, the sheer fear at what response his answer might give. He thought he was doing well, his shaking only slight but present.

"Spit it out," she said. "I need to know before getting too excited. Tell me the problem."

"Well nobody knows exactly," Sinkins said. "There are billions of people in these kingdoms, narrowing down those with very specific blood is going to be problematic, I think you'll find." He grinned at her, his eyes flickering back and forth as if looking for a way out. His bravado was astonishing, she had to admit. Domis straightened up, anticipating an order. She shook her head at him and he relaxed.

"What can you tell me about Divineborn," she said. "Historically, what have they done that might narrow them down? Any tell-tale signs? Marks? Psychological ticks? There must be something."

"A lot of this is only theoretical at best, Mistress," Sinkins said quickly. "None of it has ever been proven one way or another. What one man takes as gospel, the other man dismisses as lunacy. I've spent my time analysing every writing I can on the subject, cross-referencing everything I can. I could spend the rest of my days on the subject, a thousand more than I'll ever live, ten lifetimes even and it may never be enough to say definitively. We could find them. We could bleed them and even then, it might not work."

She tapped her nails on the desk, considered his words. Of course, it had all crossed her mind before. It might be useless. She might go to all this effort, it might turn out to be one wasted venture. She could have been putting her time into subjugating the kingdoms via force and technology instead of chasing ultimate power. It might be a waste. It might lead to failure and death.

All paths have failure as one potential route. It is the roads you never walk out of the fear of what lies at the end of them which often lead to the greatest rewards.

Her father had said that to her once. She'd wondered what he'd make of her if he could see her now, what she'd become. The gem embedded in her wrist throbbed, sending an ache up her arm. She rubbed at it, didn't even notice the alien sensations.

"What can you speculate at," she said. "If nothing else, do that. Make an educated guess, Dale. You have information, what do you glean from it?"

He paused, looked first at her and then at Domis before ploughing ahead with his answer. "Okay, so suspected Divineborn over

243

the years, maybe someone can put together an algorithm to search for ideal candidates. Maybe Subtractor." He paused again, looked at her as if hoping for some approval. When none came, he continued regardless. "Lose a parent usually before the age of ten in mysterious circumstances. That's always the case. The Divine comes, enters the life of an ideal partner, spawns and leaves when their time is up."

"Narrows it down, but not by much," Domis said. She looked up at him in surprise. It was an all too easy mistake to think that silent meant stupid. She should know better than any how that mind worked beneath his face, sharp and supple when he chose to apply it. So much less wasted potential than that ungrateful little bitch of a daughter. She could have had everything and what had she done with the choice? She'd chosen to reject her mother and pick that grasping harlot Lydia.

Okay, tipping Unisco off to a sighting of herself at the wedding so they'd break in and ruin it had been spiteful, but what else was a scorned mother to do? Perchance it might have made her see sense. And maybe wild horses would willingly accept captivity, she thought. Stranger things had happened but not by much.

"He's right," Sinkins said. "Parents dying in unusual circumstances aren't so much of a rare thing any more. I mean, Mistress, you yourself…"

She shot him a glare and he halted mid-sentence, determined suddenly not to carry on speaking. He wasn't wrong, but it also wasn't his place to comment on the events of her life. They weren't here to talk about her.

"Ahem," he said quickly. "Forget that. Of those who have been rumoured to be Divineborn over the years, there's one thing they all do have in common though, according to the sources I ran through. They all achieved great things. They reached for it and grasped it with both hands. History remembers their names, though I feel the need to wonder if their greatness started the rumour of them being Divineborn or if it was their blood which gave them that extra push towards greatness."

She said nothing, ran her eyes back and forth across the compass, distaste marring her lips as the crack glared up at her, spoiling what could have been perfection.

"Well you certainly achieved greatness, Mistress," Domis said. Only he could insinuate what he was and not risk her wrath, whereas Sinkins would wilt under her ire, Domis would stand tall in the face of it, secure in his position. "You've taken what most would have seen as a silver birth-right and you've made it your own, improved it in every way, all on your own."

She had, hadn't she?

She studied the Forever Cycle again, couldn't keep her eyes off something so beautiful and precious, something now hers and hers alone. For as long as she drew breath, nobody else would ever possess that hunk of bronze.

"Summon the cabal," Claudia eventually said. "Get them together in one room, Domis. I need to address them." Especially Mazoud, she added silently. To have done what he'd done, moved his troops in position to attack Serran, was lunacy. He didn't have the numbers to keep Vazara secure and launch an offensive, he'd pointed that out himself. All her earlier verbal barrages had done little to bring him to heel and he'd moved regardless. Why? She didn't know, had a feeling it might be worth asking him.

It was time to put him in his place. The rest of them as well. Remind them who their leader was. "Sinkins!" He snapped to attention. "Continue your research. Talk to whoever you need to, just make sure that you narrow down a list of targets. We need their blood and fast." Another thought occurred to her. "Start with every non-replicated individual aboard this ship. Maybe we shall find ourselves in luck."

It was wishful thinking, she knew that. But any possible way of making the job easier was welcomed. Things did slide for you sometimes, if only you knew the best method to tilt the table.

She'd watched him for days now, keeping him in her sights but never interacting. Those orders had been very specific. He was not to know she was there. He was not to even get the slightest hint of her presence or he would flee. Remember, her handler had warned her, if he sees you, he will know. He has insider intelligence of the entire operation, he might not know what you can do, but he is aware of what you could do. That sense of danger will see him flee for his life.

She'd been designed for one thing, stripped of her humanity and rebuilt from the cells up into an implement of death. Knowing it was one thing. Forcing yourself to care when every sense of self had been stripped away was entirely another. The lights, the pain, the voices in her ears as they'd broken her. It felt like it had happened to someone else, a dream in which she watched herself move on strings, guided by hands that weren't hers, whims that weren't her own.

Every thought she made, she questioned whether it was one of her own or just one they wanted her to think. Not being able to trust your own mind was terrifying, wondering whether today's the day your thoughts pushed you over the edge, threatened to make you do something truly reprehensible. Was it the day they turned her against a friend? A former lover? Family? As much as she hated the blood on her hands from what she'd done, better it be someone she didn't know than someone she cared for. Strangers, it was easier to shut them out when you didn't know their faces. Didn't have to dwell on the look of horror as they realised who'd pulled the trigger or beaten them to death.

Why the Mistress wanted him dead, she didn't know. Only that he was her next target. They'd dumped it all in her head, mixed it all in with her memories. Sometimes she remembered her old life. Sometimes she had memories of the new that couldn't possibly have juxtaposed with her old life. These days, she'd found herself wondering more and more if this was what insanity felt like, maybe the first stages sweeping through her, unnoticeable at first before it became full-on madness. Before, she'd always thought awareness of going mad was a sign that you probably weren't, now she wasn't so sure. She wasn't sure about a lot of things any more.

The house stood in front of her, one solitary room illuminated, the rest dark. She didn't know how many were in there, not that it mattered, just that there was only one she cared about. He would die by her hands tonight. She bore him no ill will, but the Mistress did, and it was all that mattered. The windows were tempered, she wasn't getting a shot through them. Had she brought a rifle, it might have been an option she'd considered. Maybe one of those old projectile weapons. That'd have gotten through an energy protected window no trouble. Nobody used them any longer, only the massively skilled and they were becoming fewer and fewer. When you were a sniper of that capability, either you were already part of an organisation where your skills would be utilised, you were a private contractor able to charge whatever you liked for the hit, or you were a target yourself. All of this she knew now from the information they'd put in her head. The woman she'd been before, the spirit dancer, wouldn't have known this. She'd have been clueless, would have been terrified now. As it was, she felt nothing other than cold resignation the task had to be accomplished.

Ever since they'd had their way with her, she could see in the dark. It had terrified her at first, the way her vision had switched from normal to everything cast in black and white as the darkness had surrounded her. Not just rudimentary vision either, as perfect in the night as the day. As perks went, it was one of very few. Being largely unkillable was also pretty good, before you considered what they'd made her do with that gift. She'd been shot, she'd been stabbed and blown up and poisoned, all before they'd let her out into the field, deeming her regenerative abilities satisfactory. She didn't know what her limits were, she was unsure as to whether she wanted to find out. Just because it'd heal didn't mean that the pain didn't exist, in fact it was worse. When bones knitted back together in instances, wounds closing shut, suturing themselves so neatly, it hurt a damn lot compressing it into seconds.

She could see two guards by the door, both holding BRO-80 assault rifles, a new model, thirty shots to the charge pack, exceptional firepower over short-to-mid range. She didn't consider them a threat. They'd have to be dealt with, she knew that, but there was a way to do things. The impulses in her head, they were mysterious, that she'd failed to yet work them out yet was probably deliberate on the part of her captors and conditioners. If she'd worked out how they made her act, she could twist them around, work within the parameters while at the same time retaining a measure of rebellion. That sometimes it let her get away with a mild beating while in others, they made her punch them with her enhanced strength until the target was little more than a fine mist was scary.

It was the diode on her chest, she knew that. Underneath her leathers, she could feel it pressed against her skin, the claws dug into her, the chemicals flooding her system. Those chemicals could be pleasurable, narcotics fed into her to keep her docile and submissive should that be what they desired of her. Or they could be not so pleasurable, amphetamines fired into her to increase her aggression and bloodlust. Even worse, sometimes she wanted it so badly, she craved that feeling. She was an addict, she knew, she couldn't help it and she found it so very hard to care. She needed them, no matter how much she might hate herself for realising that simplest of truths, caring about it became a chore.

Just do it. Do the job. Kill him, leave.

No! Kill them all.

He's the only target though.

They will kill you if you don't.

They'll try!

Yes, they will. And you'll have to kill them to stop them.

There must be a better way!

Not with the time you have.

Arguments raged through her head, she could feel the faintest twitches at the edge of her conscious mind, her urges begging to be twisted by the drugs, she could feel her nails scraping back and forth against her sleeve, her teeth silently chewing empty air. Her hands were shaking, it was a good thing she didn't possess a blaster.

She didn't need a weapon. She was a weapon.

A final long exhale and she leaped from the bushes, took off across the lawns at a run. No sign of motion detectors, which meant nothing, there always were some. Freshly disturbed patches of lawn, uneven lengths of grass where it had been torn up and put back down to hide the surprise below. She was fast, faster than any human had a right to be. One of her spirits was a gazelle, she'd clocked herself running a race with it and could easily keep pace, even if perhaps killing was a different proposition with opponents like these.

By the time they realised she was there, it'd be too late for them, she knew that. The lawn wasn't massive, about standard size for the large detached house looming above her, all white bricks and old wood to try and make it look a little more rustic. She'd never appreciated effects like that, even when she was a spirit dancer. She was done with that part of her life, not by choice admittedly, but that was the rub of things. For Unisco agents, their reactions weren't anything special, she was on them before they could get a shot off, thankfully. The place being on high alert following the discharge of a weapon wouldn't make the mission harder, but neither would it make it easier. She'd prefer to avoid being shot if she could help it.

One of them got a weapon up, she took it from him, bent the barrel up into a U shape and smashed the butt of the rifle into his face, watched him go down hard under her blow, damaged but not dead. She knew exactly how much force needed to be applied to a human bone in to smash it, and how much it'd take to turn a painful blow into a fatal one. The other, she flung out a fist and saw caught him in the chest, saw him crash through the door, smashing straight through. He lay on the other side amidst the wooden remains, a pile of twisted limbs and broken lumber.

If they hadn't known she was here before, they did now. She kicked one rifle out the way, the damaged one, picked the other up and checked it over with practiced hands. Might as well make things easier for herself now, as much of a workout as beating them to death with her bare hands might turn out to be.

She'd seen the architect plans for the house before coming here, had done her research. Fail to prepare and prepare to fail and all that. She needed to know about any possible escape routes she hadn't considered. A simple enough point of entry, a front door and a back, one flight of stairs and the only route out up at the top being the windows. If she cut off the stairwell, it'd effectively corner the target. Between main door and stairwell, she had a single large entrance hall, doors surrounding it on all sides and a small corridor leading to its base. Already the doors around her were starting to open, Unisco agents sprinting out with blaster pistols up and aimed at her. Some of them even got close to hitting her with their shots, she ducked down, retaliated with fire of her own the moment she got the first hint of movement, her superior vision picking them out with ease in the dark.

By the time she reached the stairs, she'd drained her charge pack and didn't give the pattern of bodies around her a second glance, so many dead in so short a space of time. She'd become a master so quickly, had been put through her paces on the shooting range, even if so much of it felt natural. When the cells ran dry, she flung it aside, picked up her pace and ran, put her shoulder out in front of her and decided she wasn't stopping.

A quintuplet of blasters pointed at her as she tore through the door leading to the meeting room, six shocked faces staring at her, not entirely registering her presence. Only her target hadn't drawn, he'd studied her with first curiosity and then shock on his broad face as they took her in. She wondered how she looked, a small woman covered in blood not her own and dressed in worn speeder bike leathers. If she could see herself, she'd probably have been terrified by the spectre she'd become.

They went to pull triggers on her, didn't realise she'd be just a fraction too fast for them. By the time the blasts left the weapons, she'd already moved, flung herself onto the table and slid across the surface, kicked out and hit one of them in the throat with the toe of her boot, saw him fall away gagging. His weapon fell from his grasp, and she snatched it out the air, emptied it into the one furthest away from her, put five shots into his centre mass, two down in as many seconds. Her arm snapped out, drove an elbow into the solar plexus of another, she felt him double over, adjusted her shape to grab him by the collar of his jacket and violently yank him down into the table, face first. A shattered skull made a distinctive sound, she'd always found.

The fourth got lucky, blasted her straight in the face four times, heat and light cutting off her vision. The first time it had happened, it had terrified her, sent her pulse hammering and a liberal dose of narcotic had flooded her system to keep her calm. They'd done some tweaking after that, aware that loss of her vision made her less effective and the eyes were a weak point. Though they'd heal, it would still take a few minutes and in the heat of battle, that wasn't the sort of time an enemy would allow her.

The second her vision was torn from her, the rest of her senses kicked in, enhanced way beyond even the norms she'd had bestowed upon her, she could hear a pin drop a hundred feet away and point out the direction. She could smell sweat and fear, almost taste it in the air as well, cloying thick and sickly on her tongue. She'd never admit it aloud, but this was almost better than sight. She could hear his pulse rate rise and he must have been terrified to see a once-beautiful woman with a ruined face still coming for him despite suffering injuries that would have dropped anyone else. In a split-second, her hands closed around a neck and she squeezed hard, driving her thumbs into the soft flesh under the jaw, locking them in so he couldn't break her grip. Judging by the sounds escaping him as the air was crushed from him, the pain had to be excruciating. More pressure, she guessed, and his neck would break. The crack confirmed it, the unmistakeable sound of vertebrate splintering and shattering under forces they weren't meant to absorb.

He had a knife on him, she could smell it, polish and old blood, the odour of the latter masked by the former but still there. She plunged her hand towards it, closed fingers around the hilt of the blade and she threw it behind her without looking, caught the fifth shooter with it, no hesitation, no trouble. By the burbling sounds he was making, she'd hit him in the throat, he'd be bleeding out right about now, his last moments spent in agony. She liked the throat. As targets of weakness went, it was quite a good one. Hit it hard enough and anyone, no matter how big, would go down and not get back up. Her vision was starting to come back, the rest of her senses fading with its return, the edges of the black replaced by red gradually. Soon the red faded into an array of colours and shapes, everything coming back to her.

She heard the click of the safety being removed from the blaster, turned to her target. The last man standing. She couldn't see his face yet, but she could hear his rapid breathing, sucking in big gulps of air, smell the odour of his body.

"If you think it'll make any difference," she said. "Then go ahead. I didn't want to kill everyone else, but they didn't give me much of a choice."

"I know you," he said. He didn't sound puzzled or afraid, more just resigned. "I saw you in my sister's lab. You were asleep in a tube. She told me who you were and what she'd done to you. What Harvey Rocastle did to you."

She blinked. She could almost see his face now. She didn't normally talk to the target, it made it harder to drop them if you had a nice little chit-chat with them. It made them more human, too easy to empathise with and she didn't want that. Just because the drugs took the edge off didn't mean that the rest of the feelings couldn't cut her given the chance

"You know it's not too late," he said gently. "The kingdoms are looking for you. You're only useful while you're my sister's secret assassin. You get pictured, everyone knows you're alive and what she did to you. It's been a year; your name is old news now but that changes so quickly in these kingdoms."

Even at the point when his death was about to come, Collison Coppinger was trying to talk his way out of it. She could see him, could see he still pointed his weapon at her, although the inclination for him to use it wasn't in his eyes.

"I know it's not going to kill you if I shoot you. That's not why I don't want to," he said. "You know you're just as much a victim as anyone you murder in my sister's name. I'm amazed you can remember your own, Ms Stanton."

"Stanton?" She said it to herself, tried the name out in her mouth, realised how natural it felt to her as she spoke.

"That's your name," he said. "You don't remember, do you? Selena Stanton. Spirit dancer. One of the best. Damn good one. Former friend and mentor to Harvey Rocastle. You were the price he paid to stand alongside my sister. They needed a subject to do this to. I guess you were unlucky. I guess we were both unlucky, huh? Can't help it sometimes."

She said nothing. Selena Stanton? Had that been her? Every so often when in the field, she'd see the name crop up in the news, see the pictures. The resemblance ended past the face. Stanton was healthier, happier, not broken like her. Her hair had been the colour of copper flames, hers was the colour of oil-soaked soot.

"She's pulling your strings," he said. "I know that. My sister does that. She grabs control of whomever she can, makes them dance to her tune. You can't fight her. She made sure of that, I'll wager." He sighed, took a step closer to her. He was in reaching grip now, she could crush him if she wanted. Take his blaster from him and fire it into his face. He wouldn't survive it.

"You don't want to do it, do you?" he said, almost an accusation. "I can tell it in your eyes. You just want this to be over. We all want it to be over. How does my sister make you dance? What hold does she have over you?" His voice was soft now, smooth and hypnotic, that weird blend of Premesoir deep-south and almost aristocratic Canterage drawl. "Work with me here and I can help you."

Unconsciously, she thrust out her chest... Stanton had had a magnificent chest... pushing her breasts to straining point against the leather, hoping that it'd emphasise the curve of the control disc there. Maybe, just maybe if he shot it... She couldn't tell him about it, her mouth wouldn't let the words form, but the subtlest of gestures might save her life.

His eyes went there, she saw the recognition, saw the way his arms tensed, the muscles in his fingers going to pull the trigger, his aim adjusting...

Her reactions kicked in, she hit him hard, a vicious backhander with all her back and shoulder muscles thrown into it, Collison Coppinger sailed through the air like he'd been yanked back by a speeder, hit one of the oversized windows at the back of the room and went straight through it, his head bent back at an awkward angle. Her blow had broken his neck on impact, she realised that with a sense of cool pleasure rupturing inside her.

Mission complete.

She stepped towards the back of the room, looked out the window into the night, saw him laid out on the path below, his body broken and contorted into angles the human body had never meant to experience.

She hadn't wanted to hit him, she'd had no control over herself, seen every emotion and reacted as if it were a threat, rather than a genuine attempt to help her. So far, Collison Coppinger had been the only one to make the effort and not try to fight her, not try to kill her. And it hadn't done him a damn bit of good, she thought, trying not to look at the body. Inside she was weeping and not even the flow of sweet, sweet narcotics straight into her system was enough to cut out that grief.

She'd completed her task. That was the long and short of it. No matter the cost.

"I'm sorry," she said under her breath. A pointless sentiment. Nobody remained alive to hear it. Whatever it took to save her soul, she'd do it. She feared that might be beyond her at this point, but she knew what'd happen when someone found the means to kill her and where she'd be going. In her past, she'd never been especially devout. Now, though? It had taken her free will being stripped from her to realise just how far she'd fallen. The Divines must have had a plan when they'd given it to humanity and now it had been torn from her.

Truly, she'd been forsaken.

"Threads. You assume all of what I did came together overnight? Not so. Not even close, I've been sewing this tapestry for years now, putting everything together to make my victory assured. A case of when, Subtractor. Not if. You're a late arrival, I'll forgive your lack of faith."
Claudia Coppinger in discussion with Subtractor.

The first shots had been fired, the transports moved to moor just off the Tsarco islands, a trio of landmasses between Serran and Vazara, the decision made to use them as a staging point. Hovertanks rested across the decks of giant transport ships, aerofighters fuelling, ready to go at the command. Mazoud had made his choice, the attack on Serran was about to commence. He saw it through his tiny window, saw the fighters fly past and them all moving into position. Maybe ten miles to land, ten miles across open water. His geography had gone to hells, wasn't his strongest subject at the best of times but now he couldn't bring himself to care. In the distance, he could see the opposition moving into position. They might have been doing it for minutes, might have been hours. Time had ceased to be something he could gauge, he only knew night hadn't fallen since they'd started.

He didn't know how long he'd been in the cell, only that it had to have been months. Months since he'd had contact with any of his family or his friends or anyone with Unisco. He didn't know what had happened to the outside world in the meantime. They could all be dead, this ship he'd been locked up on cutting him off from them all. The only voices he heard were those of his captors, his jailors and his torturers. Vazarans, all of them, big black bastards who'd all appeared to have studied at the same school of wanton brutality. He could have gone insane, the only reason he hadn't was because he remembered his mission. He remembered that no matter what happened, he needed to make his time here matter. He'd gotten out once, had almost made it free but for a tremendous bit of bad luck. They'd caught him, just one more beating amidst the many.

He had to give them credit in one regard though, they'd seemed determined he didn't die on them. When the beatings had finished, they'd made sure that he was patched up, kindness and cruelty in equal measure. He never faltered though. He remembered the mission. The mission was paramount. It was his sole guiding light, the whole reason for keeping on living when others might have given up.

Escape. Get the fuck out of here. Survive.

Unisco agents didn't die easily and he'd gone through a lot of hard times for the agency, he'd drawn on every experience and memory to keep him on that path. They wouldn't break him, he would not falter. And yet, they'd not asked him any questions, not asked him to betray those he worked with. That stunk of terror for him. It meant they were torturing him for torture's sake and there was nothing worse. Those asking for information could be temporarily appeased by some small titbit that might take time to verify one way or another. Here, they just wanted to inflict pain, break him down, build him back up and break him down all again. He could admire the sophistication of it, a level he wouldn't expect from primitive bloody savages like these men. Without reprieve, the pain became manageable, a constant companion. When it was taken away, the memory faded into oblivion, only to come back when the torture resumed.

Someone else had to be behind it. He couldn't attribute something like that to people like this. That he was in the hands of skilled madmen troubled him little. Those with skill had restraint. Those without, didn't. And you were often in far more danger from unskilled lunatics than their better trained counterparts. Trained torturers kept you alive indefinitely, amateurs killed you by accident.

They'd come to feed him, left the door hanging open and he'd picked his moment. Only one guard, normally the door shut, maybe they thought him broken and tame. They'd grown lax and that was what he needed. His cell might have been just that, a cell, but he'd seen worse. When the pain had subsided, he'd worked to keep his muscles in shape, determined how when his moment came, he would take it. They had to have known and yet they'd let him carry on. Maybe they didn't care. The flicker of hope remained in him, perhaps they didn't want to crush it just yet. A hopeful prisoner could be broken. One without it wasn't as fun. He was under no illusions. He'd tortured in the past, for Unisco, he knew what they were doing. Didn't mean he could do much about it.

A single guard? Close quarters? Easy. He rose from the bed, smashed his foot into the base of the tray, sent the shit they served as slop flying everywhere, drove the tray into his head. As the guard went down, he snatched the tray, left a huge face-shaped dent in it as he clubbed his captor. He went down like he'd been shot and the Unisco agent was out of there, the first steps of freedom. He didn't know where he was going, only that he needed to get out fast. He didn't even know if this was the same ship he'd been secured on before. All cells looked the same on the inside.

Out of the jail, he heard voices ahead and ducked into a room, his face lighting up as he realised he'd happened across a uniform storage closet. He stripped out of his prisoner's rags, the clothes left faded of their natural colour and stained with his blood, slid on garments that should at least let him pass a cursory glance. In the mirror, he caught sight of his face, he didn't look good. He almost didn't recognise himself, he looked older than his years, the months caught up with him.

No matter. When he got out of here, he was due some serious R and R. No two ways about that. He'd seen security guards wearing the blue jumpsuits, his skin might make him stand out. Try as he might, there was no way he was passing for Vazaran. This damn ship couldn't be populated solely by them, could it? He'd be in for a world of trouble if it was, be picked out in a minute.

Deep breath, deep breath, keep calm. He bent over, rested his hands on the bench, determined not to let the hammering of his heart break his concentration. Too long since he'd been free, too long since he'd faced pressures like this, he needed to get his head back in the game. It'd have to do. If anyone called him, he'd have to bluff his best. Just like playing Ruin. He could do that. This would be his last chance to escape. If he didn't, the consequences would be dire.

Failure was not an option. He'd already made the choice that if it came down to discovery, he'd try to force them into killing him. Better to die free than live a prisoner. Nobody would ever know what happened to him, at least not yet. It'd come out one day and Unisco would avenge him.

So far, so good. Nobody had looked at him twice, well not in a suspicious way, his worries that his skin colour would betray him unfounded. Just the occasional Vazaran who gave him a dirty look, typical chip-on-their-shoulder darkie with an inflated sense of their own superiority. Every time they did, he met their gaze with a challenging one of his own. Never show weakness. That would be fatal. It'd show that he had something to hide.

In a situation like this, what basically amounted to an undercover experience, it was important to look like you belonged. People sensed more than they realised, if even one minor detail was out of place, they'd pick up on it on a subconscious level and react, however delayed it might be. With that in mind, he'd made his way as quickly and as inconspicuously through the ship as he could, even taking one detour through what looked like some sort of giant laboratory. In this sterile room, his professionalism had taken a knock and he'd found himself looking around like a wide-eyed child, determined to take in every little detail. He'd never seen a lab like it before, it looked like the textbook definition of cutting edge, he couldn't even begin to work out what they were doing here. In a moment of ingenuity, he picked up a pile of discs and, confident he was alone in the room, slid them into his jumpsuit. Hopefully there was something on them they could use.

Not a moment too soon either, for he heard the door open at the far end of the room and a pair of white-coated scientists' stride in like they owned the place. Perhaps they did, this was their domain after all. Neither of them was Vazaran, he moved to go past them. One blocked his way, fixed him with a cold glare. "What are you doing here?" he demanded. Serranian by the accent, he'd have guessed. "This area is off-limits."

"Disturbance," he grunted. The less information he proffered the better. "Had to check it out."

"I wasn't notified." The man had whitening hair and an expression that suggested he didn't take kindly to his workplace being violated by the presence of a stranger. "This is most irregular!"

"It'll be on the way," he said. "Bureaucracy, right? "

If he hoped for some sort of conspiratorial acknowledgement of the problems they all had to deal with, he was to be sorely disappointed. "What's your name? Who's your supervisor?"

Crap!

If nothing else, Unisco training encouraged them to think on their feet. "Hang on! I'm doing my job here. I know you don't want me in here, but I think you'd appreciate your property being damaged or stolen even less. Something showed up on the videocams that looked suspicious. I came down here to check it out."

"What sort of suspicious thing?"

He decided to throw caution to the wind. "A prisoner got out. They don't want to advertise it. Don't want panic. Dangerous man. I came down because they didn't want you getting attacked in your lab. You're one of their most valuable assets after all."

He could see the white-haired man swell with pride. You prodded someone's ego enough, they'd forget their anger. Everyone liked to believe that they were important, being told it was one of the best ways to assuage their pride. Pride trumped anger every time.

"Don't tell them I told you though. We're supposed to keep it quiet. You're good anyway, he's not here." He gave them both a grin. "I'll get out of your hair right now. My deepest apologies, gentlemen. Good luck with all of…" He waved a hand towards the lab equipment. "… This, I guess. Whatever you're doing."

Not looking back, he made his way to the door they'd come through, breathing a sigh of relief. He'd gotten lucky there, he couldn't rely on that trick working again. Best to maintain minimal contact for the time being, do it only where he needed to. At least they hadn't asked for ID, he'd seen the badges they wore on their chest. Outrage had prevented them from asking immediately, mollifying them had done the rest. The next person might not be so amenable in their complicity.

He heard the roar of engines outside long before he got there, sticking his head out through the bay doors to see the fighters warming up. Typical Vazaran Sun assortment for their squadron, anything and everything that was airworthy and packing ordnance. Dark Wind fighters mixed in with a few ships that looked reminiscent of a striking eagle. Not the most elegant of design he'd ever seen but it left all hells of an effect on the retinas. Far out in the distance, he could see the coast of Serran. Ten miles. That had been his estimate before. He saw no reason to change it now.

In addition to the aerofighters, he could see jet troopers warming up, he considered them an interesting option. He couldn't fly a fighter worth a damn, by the time he'd worked it out, he'd have long since been shot down. He'd never had an aptitude for it, but a jetpack... He could manage one of those, surely? How hard could it be? The troops wore heavy black uniforms, gloves and goggles that must have stifled horribly in the heat. Their packs were heavy and clunky, armed with rotary laser cannons. They weren't the sort of things that would win a battle on their own, but their presence might well turn the tide in the favour of their side. He'd seen them used before, not often admittedly, fast, agile and heavy firepower. The downside? Those suits might be good for protecting against the elements in the sky, they wouldn't do a damn lot to stop blaster fire. He couldn't see too many better options though. Fuel might be a problem. They only carried limited reserves, nowhere near enough to hit the mainland of Serran. Ten miles was too much of a task for them. If he got halfway there on one of their tanks, it'd be fortunate.

It was a problem, he knew that. One he didn't have an immediate answer to, and yet he didn't have the time to peruse one. Behind him, the alarms were starting to jangle, it didn't sound good. Clearly, they'd discovered he'd escaped, and he'd just run out of his anonymity. They'd be on alert now and he couldn't afford to be stopped again.

He made his choice, once more threw caution to the wind and made a break towards the pilot's area. He'd seen the troops filing in and out of it, not a way in the hells he was trying it without protection. He didn't have that much of a death wish. Nobody stopped him, hells nobody was paying him attention as he shoved his way through the door, found the room to be about the same as the one he'd pilfered the security uniform from. His heart was pounding now, must have been the air. It stank, sulphur and oil, not even close to being pure but it was the first of its kind he'd had for months and that meant something. It was a sign freedom was close and yet so far away. He could touch it, but it could still be snatched away from him if he wasn't careful.

The room was empty but for two other jet troops, both of whom gave him bemused looks as he entered. Bemusement turned into scorn. Typical darkies, looking down on someone they thought beneath them. They didn't rate ship security by the looks of it, neither were they the smallest. Being a jet trooper required a certain amount of physical strength, he'd heard, to control the jetpack. They didn't take weaklings, only the best got given the training, the sort of experience where failure usually meant death.

"What do you want?" one of them asked, words he could barely understand above the accent. The alarm couldn't be heard here, thank the Divines. It might give him a chance. Might.

"Just checking," he said. "A prisoner got out…" It was the same excuse he'd used before, he was skating on thin ice, but he had no other option. Both were looking at him closer than he'd like, it might give him an opening but nothing more. He was a man in his forties, looked at least a decade older, they were both half that age, looked tough and fit. They surely couldn't view him as much of a threat. "Just checking he's not here."

He took a step towards them as he said it, wondered how much force he'd need to knock them out, hells to knock them both out before one called for help or punched him unconscious. Probably more than he could muster right now. Getting into a fist fight wasn't a smart idea. He hadn't been in one for years, not since his promotion to section chief. It didn't afford a lot of opportunities for violence.

"Hey, we see someone who shouldn't be here, we kick his arse, aye?" the other guy said. He was marginally easier to understand, the Unisco agent was grateful for that, even if he didn't fully appreciate the words. "You fuck with the Sun-Coppinger Alliance, you get what you deserve."

That is a terrible title, he thought. He didn't know what it meant, didn't want to know. No doubt when he got back to civilisation it'd be explained to him. "Thought that'd be the case," he said. "Thanks gentlemen. You see anything or anyone suspicious, don't forget to holler."

"Where's your ID?" the first guy asked, the one with the barely understandable accent, it did little to hide the menace in his voice. "Who are you?"

He grinned at the speaker. "Damn, you're the first to notice it. Lost it, waiting a new one. You know what they're like for issuing new ID, right?" He twisted a finger around his head, didn't like the way they were staring at him. "Lax, right?"

"You ever had any problem getting new ID, Demetrious?"

"Not at all, Cassius. I think this man's in the wrong place at the…"

He didn't let him finish, hit him hard before he could complete the sentence, felt the pain shoot up his arm, jar into his shoulder as he caught the big negrus in the throat, saw his eyes widen as he went down in pain, hands around his crushed windpipe. Already he was choking, he'd be dead in minutes unless his friend got him help. Judging by the look on his fucking ape face, that wasn't in his thoughts. He wanted to crush the attacker, came at him like a wounded bull, a fist the size of a Winterheight ham swinging at his face. He ducked, didn't even try to block it. That fist was the size of both his arms put together, greater maybe. He wouldn't fare well in a punching match, he'd gotten lucky with one of them. His gaze danced across the floor, the walls, the shelves, anything he could use as a weapon.

Nothing. He ducked again, weaved out the way of a second giant punch and nearly tripped over the bench behind him.

The bench!

He rolled backwards, flung himself over it, felt the air move as giant hands closed over the space where he'd been stood a moment earlier. He hit the ground, kicked the bench out towards the giant negrus who stepped into it and tripped, stumbled to one knee. The Unisco agent was on his feet in an instant, drove a foot into his nose. Pain shot up his leg, he gritted his teeth, never the best idea in anything less than steel toed boots and these were shamefully inadequate. Still he heard the crunch and the bellow of pain, the negrus was trying to rise and he leaped onto his back, wrapped his arms around that fat neck and locked them hard, trying to cut off his air. He struggled, that much he expected, he couldn't allow himself to be thrown free. If he hit the ground, it'd be over. This big black freak would stamp him into a fine paste and that'd be the end of his story. That knowledge drove him on, forced him to clutch on tighter. He imagined there was guys who wrangled cows in Premesoir who'd never experienced this, he felt hands beating at his locked arms to break his bones, powerfully at first and pain screamed through his nerves, though he felt them weaken with time.

It took five minutes for him to stop struggling, five minutes he wouldn't have thought he could spare but he didn't have a choice. If he let go and the flow of air returned, the negrus would rise and kill him.

259

By the time the attempts at breathing ceased and the giant had keeled over, his pulse ceasing to move, he let go and rose to his feet. His muscles were sore, tender from the efforts. It didn't matter. He'd done it and a little discomfort was worth that. He glanced about the room again, saw one of the uniforms and started to slide into it, pleased to discover that they had a built-in airloop. That might make things easier. The plan was starting to slide into place now. Maybe, just maybe, he could glide the last five miles if he used the fuel supply in his jetpack to go as high as possible. Upward thrust meant he went both forward and high, if he continued in the same direction on his descent then he might be able to pull a few more miles out of it than he would otherwise.

A fine theory, although he had only a rudimentary knowledge of physics and it remained just that, a theory until proven otherwise. Only one way to test it and he wasn't looking forward to it.

A jetpack awaited him as he stepped out of the changing room, clad in the uniform, the stiff gloves and the bulbous goggles that made him look like a human fly act. Two of them, to be precise. The mounts of the two black fucks he'd murdered in there, he'd wager. Shame he couldn't take them both, combine their fuel. It wasn't going to happen, unfortunately. Now, people were looking at him. If he'd been inconspicuous before, the opposite was true now, in his ill-fitting battle suit. He tried not to meet anyone's gaze, hustled towards the closest jetpack, made a show of examining them. The rotary cannon wasn't out, collapsed into the rear of the compartment. It gave him a thought though, maybe a distraction. Security guards had stepped out onto the deck, he could see them and there was nothing fake about them. They had everything he'd lacked in impersonating one, from the identification to the blaster rifles in their hands.

The Unisco agent picked the one with the most fuel, pulled it over his shoulders, clipped it across his front. The guards were heading for him, they'd already given an order for all activity to cease. One aerofighter ignored them, already taxiing to leave, rotating into a departure position. Another idea slipped into his head, he knew he was crazy for considering it, but the aerofighters were heading in the very direction he needed to go. Couldn't fly one, but that wasn't his plan. All other activity had ground to a halt, silence was pervading, he could hear them shouting for him to cease moving and he threw out a hand, hit the rotary cannon activation switch on the spare jetpack, threw himself to the ground as it erupted into life, spat laser fire in the direction of the two security guards. Their weapons rose, made no difference as their bodies were chewed up by the acid green fire, torn beyond recognition. That was the point all manner of hells tore loose as jet troopers turned to see the source of the shooting, the motion sensor in the cannon picking up on them, the deck a flurry of activity and one solitary rotary blaster trying to pick a target one after another. He'd read something once, that the sensors recognised other jet troops through the detectors in their packs, chose not to fire on them. He hoped and prayed to any Divine listening that was true, or this'd be the most epic failure of an escape attempt ever.

He didn't have a choice. The Unisco agent hit his thrusters, what he hoped were the thrusters anyway, accelerated across the hot tarmac of the deck, kicked himself into flight, saw the aerofighter rising the same moment he hit it, his hands closing around the edge of one of the wings, his ribs complaining in agony as he banged them into razor-sharp fins. If it weren't for the gloves, he might have lost fingers, especially as the acceleration kicked in and he had to close his eyes behind the goggles. Below him, the shooting continued, a dozen or more streams of blaster fire moving to mow down the rogue cannon. One shot hit the fuel inside, he saw the explosion out the corner of his eye, couldn't afford the distraction. The fighter had hit top speed now, all he could do to hold on. Any hint of weakness and he'd fall, be lucky if he wasn't sucked into its engines. He could see the pilot looking out the cockpit at him, shock on the face beneath the helmet. The Unisco agent tried not to acknowledge him, not until the fighter went into a sharp dip, a series of hairpin loops that left him gripping for dear life. He was lucky he hadn't fallen, he had an idea that had been the pilot's intent. He didn't like the idea of having an impromptu passenger.

Bastard.

He didn't let up, the pilot had more tolerance for this than the agent did, was all he could do to avoid vomiting, sharp twists and dives testing his muscles to their limit. He felt something give in his shoulder and his grip slipped, the pain like fire in his upper body. With one arm out of commission, he knew it was futile. He couldn't lift it back onto the wing, he could activate his own rotary cannon though and he felt it spring to life, laser fire ravaging the aerofighter at close range, tearing giant holes into the fuselage, gaping black gashes staring accusingly at him, spray-firing into the cockpit, he saw the pilot slump over his smoking controls and the fighter started to fall.

He let go, relaxed his grip and fired his thrusters as he did, shooting high above his mount, almost high enough to touch the clouds he felt. He'd never had an experience like this, simultaneously exhilarating and terrifying, he didn't know if he wanted to cheer in glee or piss himself in abject terror. Maybe he did both, he didn't know, time seemed to stand still as he rose like the eagle. Behind him, the ship he'd escaped from looked so small, Serran below looked even smaller.

His face relaxed, frozen into the rictus of a smile. It was cooler up here, the winds not as turbulent, they coughed, rather than howled as they whipped at him.

Those weren't winds, he quickly realised, suddenly he wasn't rising any longer, but falling, his thrusters coughing impotently. He'd spent his load, he didn't know how far he had to fall but hoped it was enough. The agent tried to point himself like an arrow, aim for the patch of land below. A terrifying thought struck him, he hoped he'd not gotten turned around and it was Serran below him. It'd be bad if he landed in Vazara, they'd have him locked back up in seconds.

He ejected the thought from his head, even as he cut through the air like a human-sized bomb, falling faster and faster through gravity's embrace. He was going to hit the ground and leave a small crater if his airloop didn't activate. Another thought he didn't even want to consider. That was assuming he hit the ground, there was an awful lot of water between him and Serran. At this height, it wouldn't matter what he hit if his loop didn't activate. He'd splatter across the water just as well as he would across the dirt.

Falling like this, it wasn't unpleasant. Considering the months of torture, it was downright desirable. Just him and his thoughts, the hopes he'd achieve his goal and get out of this alive. He'd done well so far. Even getting to this point had looked impossible minutes ago, when those two blacks had faced him down and he'd thought he was going to get his face smashed in. Fight hard and fight dirty. Two lessons he'd always taken to heart.

When he dropped below what had to be a thousand feet, he started to believe he'd make it, he could see Serran below, the waterfront town of Latalya and that mountain behind it whose name he couldn't remember. His altimeter in the jetpack was beeping, warning that he was approaching low altitude. Another five hundred feet and he'd punch his airloop, slow his fall temporarily. That'd be the moment of truth, if it failed then, he wouldn't have too long to regret it. He'd been to Latalya before, found it a picturesque town with the occasional roughneck who fancied a fight. Now though, it had been turned into a military staging point, hovertanks and anti-aircraft defences built into the sea wall. He really hoped he didn't register as large enough for a target. They'd track him, blow him to pieces no problem. Something he hadn't considered before starting this hairbrained plan.

He held his breath, punched the button that sent the electricity coursing through his airloop, stiffening the material to form a cape-like sheath and his fall slowed, the wind catching beneath. The updraft caught the cape, pushed him further forward, past the sea wall and before he knew it, he was over the makeshift military camp, close enough to see the dark specks below he knew were people, shapes growing larger the further he fell. This was as good a place as any to land, he figured. He pulled himself out of glide formation, tucked himself up into a ball and started to drop the last leg like a stone, only throwing himself out into a starfish shape as he came within a hundred feet of the ground, pushed the button again, this time held it in for the cape to keep its shape, all the way to the ground, he rolled with it, his back jarring against the useless jetpack

This hadn't gone unnoticed, he realised all too quickly as he looked up. He'd been too busy focusing on his descent to see them swarming beneath him, a dozen soldiers pointing blaster rifles at his head as he threw up his hands in surrender, laid on his back like a giant turtle.

"I'm Section Chief Raphael Barthomew of Unisco!" he shouted. "I've been held prisoner! For the love of the Divines, don't bloody shoot!"

The meeting room had seen some use recently, she thought as she made her way in, gliding across the floor in what she felt was a regal enough manner to draw every eye to her. So much of life, she'd found, was psychological. If you acted the part well enough to make them believe your claims, they'd believe it without you having to repeat yourself. Here, she might as well be a Divine to them, so that was the role she chose to play. She gave them all a big smile as she entered, Domis pulling out her seat. One day, she'd get a throne and receive them all in the proper fashion, but for now, she'd stay in the same seat as the rest of them. The battle wasn't won yet, and she needed to keep them onside. Holograms of Mazoud, Carson, Subtractor and a small-ish man next to him she didn't recognise, sat staring at her. Alaxaphal, Fuller, Rocastle and Costa stared at her in person.

"Welcome, gentlemen and lady," she said. She liked having Fuller around, in playing her part removing Ritellia from the rigours of life, she'd earned her eternal trust. A cacophony of polite greeting echoed around the room, not at all convincing but she couldn't have everything. They'd been summoned at short notice and they'd come to her. That mattered. It mattered a damn lot. "Thanks for attending this urgent meeting, and without further ado, I'd like to ask Premier Mazoud what the hells he thinks he's doing."

She gave him a pointed look and a nod, permission to speak granted. Mazoud looked like he'd gone around the twist at long last, not a surprise. She always suspected it was the heat in Vazara, it set their minds a-spin given the chance. Most of them were crazier than wild rabbits in a heated sandbox. He wore a military uniform that had gone for grandeur over practicality, pure white with golden trim and enough medals to provide the gold to fund a small town's economy for a month. Some of them looked almost genuine, others she was sure that he'd made up to grant himself sole receivership of them. She'd ask Alaxaphal later as to how genuine they were.

"Mistress Coppinger," Mazoud said, his voice oily and unctuous. "Thank you for dragging us all to your presence, I must say. It is an honour to once again take time out of our busy schedules to be here at your whim."

He must be feeling brave, she thought. His own soldiers from the Suns were mixed in with her own. All it would take would be one word from her and the next time he thought he was safe, he'd take a blaster bolt to the back of the head and that would be the end of Phillipe Mazoud. She could do it. Right now, she would give the order without hesitation. His words were measured enough to hint at insult without outright acknowledging it.

"And I am grateful you did, Premier Mazoud," she said. Politeness cost nothing, even when the first urge had been to have his head torn off his shoulders and mounted on a spike for a warning to the masses. Only the difficult task of anointing a successor so soon had stopped her. Vazara was too volatile as it was, stabilising it had become a priority and removing an outspoken leader within weeks of him taking charge would be another step backwards. "Invasion of Serran at this time was not the plan."

"It was your plan," Mazoud said. "I stepped it up. Unisco taunted me, they sent a ship into my kingdom under the guide of a rescue mission, straight into the jungle. My forces are ready. Even now, we are staged and capable of launching attacks across their shoreline at my command. They move to mount their defences, and…"

"You are aware that one of your prisoners got away, aren't you?" Subtractor said, silencing Mazoud mid-comment. "Straight off your flagship and into Unisco custody. They're talking to him even as we speak, who knows what he's going to spill about this."

Inwardly she smiled. That event hadn't been unforeseen. Agent Barthomew had been pumped for months now, Unisco hadn't even been looking for him, a section chief himself scooped up and they'd done nothing. Further example of how Unisco needed to go. The organisation was too ineffective to function any longer. Parts were swallowed up. Hells, she'd even had a part in making sure Barthomew had been given a window of opportunity to flee, one of her own had put it into place. He might follow Mazoud's orders for now, but he danced to her tune. They all did. She'd considered threatening to withdraw them from Mazoud's ranks, see if he still wanted to attack with a fraction of his forces, yet she kept her tongue. If she made that threat and failed to follow through, he'd make sure anyone with even a passing association with her would be moved to a place they couldn't be of any use. Better to keep her powder dry and her cards in play.

"Don't worry about Barthomew, Subtractor," she said. "That problem will resolve itself. He knows nothing that will benefit them. Probably the opposite in fact."

The man sat next to Subtractor let loose a bark of laughter, his voice polished like stone. "I have to say, my dear, that's marvellous. Sow the seeds of discredit. A master tactic."

"Subtractor, who is this?" she asked, smiling despite the seriousness of the situation. There was something about the dapper man, a sense of levity that she'd found missing from times like these of late.

"Nigel Carling, Mistress Coppinger, late of the Belderhampton branch of Unisco," he said. "I'd kiss your hand if I weren't worried my lips would go straight through it, so instead please accept my sincerest gratitude."

Carling... That name sounded somewhat familiar. "Carling and Hobb?"

"I had a life before Lucas Hobb, my dear. You associate with one murderous bastard and you're tainted for life." He grinned as he said it. "I have no fancy nickname like my associate next to me, but Subtractor..." He made a face as he said it, clearly wasn't keen. "Subtractor says he broke me out under your command. You want me to do something for you, name the price and it'll be done double quick time. I honour my debts."

"Shame you didn't come with Hobb," she said, breaking her gaze away from Carling and moving across to Mazoud. "He had a good record of killing problematic Vazaran rulers who got above themselves."

Subtractor snorted with laughter, he'd heard the story by the sounds of it. Carling grinned, though nowhere near as wide. If Mazoud saw the funny side, he didn't show it, rose to his feet with outrage on his face.

"I must protest at comments like that, Mistress," he said. "I've been nothing but loyal to you and to hint at anything otherwise insults us both, my character and your intelligence. I moved my forces into an attack position for you. You've been out of contact for days..."

And you thought you'd try and make a play for power. Don't try to fool me, Mazoud, you can't kid a kidder.

"We all worried that something terrible had happened to you. We desired to follow on with your dream and subjugate the rest of the kingdoms as quickly as possible." He looked worried now, she couldn't blame him. He'd be a lot more worried if he could hear what she was thinking. He'd be cutting the connection and holing himself up in the palace he'd stolen from Nwakili.

"I never spoke to him," Subtractor said, quick to ascertain his loyalty. She'd never doubted it. Costa made the same proclamation, as did Fuller and Alaxaphal. Carson remained silent, resting his chin on his hands as he leaned back in his seat, yet he shook his head. Carson owed her a lot, he wasn't going to disappoint her just yet by breaking their agreement. She hadn't seen him for weeks, he was in Serran, miles away from the battlefield Mazoud wished to set up. Rocastle was the final one to deny any sort of contact and Mazoud managed to go pale as he looked around the room. He was worried, she could see that, could read it in the way he held himself, like a rabbit ready to flee.

Poor scared little man. If she chose to crush him, he'd be crushed.

"Sit down, Phillipe," she said. "Withdraw your fleet. Nobody's needlessly thrown their life away so far. We can resolve this without shots being fire, right now that's what we need."

"Mistress Coppinger," Mazoud said, his eyes blazing with defiance. "I have my forces sat on Serran's doorstep. If I do not attack now, I show the sort of weakness that will halt my rule in its tracks. If I retreat, they will follow me across the sea. They'll use my launching point against me, I'll be hunted like a beast as they try to take back their precious kingdom."

She shrugged her shoulders. "Tough at the top, Phillipe. I told you not to attack, to wait for my command. You've shown your hand, don't be surprised that they know what cards you're going to play."

"Mistress, you cannot make me do this. We must press the advantage now before we lose it."

She fixed him with a glare, the sort of pointed stare that would have cowed a dragon tamer in his tracks.

"I'm sorry," she said. "I believe you just told me what to do. I'm going to let you in a little secret, Premier Mazoud. I own you. You have your crown because I gave it to you. You'd still be a third-rate mercenary prince if I'd not elevated you to something more. I gave you your crown. If you really think I can't take it back from you, then you are sadly deluded." She continued to smile at him. "That is the burden of rule. You do what you think you must until you can't. And when you can't, you need to face the consequences of your actions. If you wish to press this attack, then go ahead. But do not expect my forces to fight with you. Do not expect any further help from me."

That was the stick. She liked using the stick, though sometimes they needed some carrot too to help them make the right choice. Some people backed down when they felt like it was their interest. "But," she added. "Step back now and our relationship can continue. More than that, our alliance remains intact. Mutual benefit, Premier Mazoud. Win this battle and you'll lose the war. But stick with me and you'll win many battles after."

She had him then, she knew it with the way the defiance fell from his face and he let his head tilt almost imperceptibly.

Getting back into her office with the bronze compass, she felt relief the meeting was over. Mazoud was turning out to be too much of a problem. The sooner she could replace him, the better things would be. If Leonard Nwakili had turned out to be more amenable, they wouldn't have found themselves here at all. Nwakili, for all his perceived faults (her propaganda machine at work during the initial stage of the invasion,) had been a much better leader than Mazoud ever would. He'd had an aura about him, the feeling of a wise man tempered by his experiences. Mazoud was a thug, he'd been a thug while a foot soldier in the Suns, he'd been a thug when he'd led them, and he was a thug now. No other way of looking at the situation. She'd brought him to heel this time, he'd promised to cease his assault, but it would only be a matter of time before he tried again.

The words lay heavy on her, the insinuations that had come from both Sinkins and Domis earlier. Her mother had died before she was ten. She had grasped for greatness, developed an obsession with Divine lore, what came before and after life. It was certainly food for thought.

She poured herself a firebrandy, sipped the contents thoughtfully. Claudia knew she'd never truly considered her mother as important before, hadn't known much about her. In childhood, you never saw your parents as human, they were more as Divines themselves. All-powerfully prominent. Only with the wisdom of age did you start to realise their fallibility. Past a certain point, you began to revel in it. Every failure became a victory for you, a building brick in the steadfast certainty that you were going to do things better than they ever could.

All she remembered about her mother, a woman dead for more than thirty years, was she'd been beautiful, even if sometimes there had been a cold indifference about her, a trait she'd been accused of more than once. Cycles really did come around then, if that were the case. She'd always wondered how the two of them had gotten together, her and her father. The sort of family they'd been, there weren't any sort of nostalgic family sit downs, no 'this is how I met your mother' stories. They'd never been like that, but now she wondered about the attraction.

She had to be crazy for even considering it, she'd almost snapped at Sinkins earlier for suggesting it. Could he be wrong? Possible. Could he be right? It wasn't impossible. What if he was right? What and if were only two small words but the potential impact they might have were staggering.

Claudia looked at the compass on her desk, the Forever Cycle, saw it stare silently back at her through its broken face. The little bronze cups next to it lay untouched and alone, she leaned forward and placed her glass next to them before sliding them into place, attaching them through the holes delicately threaded into the sides of it. Something about the act felt soothing to her racing heart, a chance to relax and reflect, work with her hands, a task all too alien in recent years. She even brought out the polish and the duster, did her best to buff away the burns and the stains filling each of the cups, wondering how they'd come about. It was tough to shift them, her muscles ached by the time she'd finished yet she didn't falter in the task. Doing this felt like the most important thing she could do at this moment, a simple first step on a long road.

When she was finished, she had to admit but for the crack that marred its face, the Forever Cycle was the most beautiful thing she'd ever seen. Perfection in pocket size. Attachment to an object was irrational but she knew she'd kill to keep hold of it. Looking at it, she got the feeling that she and it were meant to be together, that it was hers by right.

"Stupid," she muttered, and yet it felt less so the more she considered it. She slid open the drawer in her desk, drew out a knife, silver and pearl engraved into the handle, a family heirloom she'd not been able to let go of despite it belonging to the past. Her grandfather and great-grandfather had used it to open letters back in the day, yet she maintained it well, knew it was one of the last few historical Coppinger treasures. They weren't big on sentiment, never had been, likely never would. One day, she might have handed it to Meredith. That wasn't happening now. Maybe she'd hand it off to Domis, any descendants he might have. That idea wasn't without its charm, though for as long as she'd known him, he'd never shown any sort of inclination towards sexual relationships with either men or women. She couldn't entirely trust someone who lacked those urges, not normally, but they made for reliable associates. Domis got a bye in that respect, she'd put her life in his hands on more than one occasion. That sort of trust was difficult to erode without tangible reason.

Claudia looked at her empty hand, the knife in the other and the Forever Cycle on the table. Divineborn. Blood. Fuel. Cycle. Forever.

Only one way to find out, to be sure. And it was going to hurt.

Pain didn't bother her, not if there was purpose to it. If she cut herself and it was for nothing, she'd be annoyed. Maybe she shouldn't do it. Once more, she considered the knife, kept sharp across the years. It was good steel, not a hint of rust on it, sharp enough to cut through skin without much trouble. She didn't look down as she pressed the blade against the palm of her hand, felt the pressure almost immediately. Claudia wished she had something to bite down on, anything to distract her as she…

Ouch!

… did that. She felt her eyes widen, swallowed the yelp threatening to break out, only then did she look at the wet stream of scarlet pooling in the palm of her hand, the tear glaring accusingly at her. She moved her hand towards one of the cups, careful not to spill a drop on the carpet or the desk, tilted the appendage at an angle, watched the first few droplets fall into the bronze receptacle with bated breath.

It took a few minutes to fill it to the brim, she withdrew her hand and wrapped a tissue around it, anything to stop her dribbling everywhere, all while making sure she didn't move her eyes from the cup. So far, nothing. She wasn't sure what she was expecting to happen, maybe it wouldn't work. Maybe there wouldn't be a sign. Maybe something only happened when all seven sets of blood ran through it. Maybe she wasn't what she thought she was.

Too many maybes and not enough facts. She wished she had more to go on, that Blut was still around. She'd taken him for granted at the time, had never appreciated the true depths of his knowledge until he was no longer here. Sinkins was an acceptable replacement, but he was still just both of those things and more, a poor imitation of the original.

She tilted her head to the side, looked at the Forever Cycle at an angle. Something was happening, she was sure of it, though what she couldn't say. It looked like the level of blood in the cup was depleting, running through the pipe into the compass itself. And with every millimetre it sunk, something was happening to the main component, the faintest hint of light poking up from it at first before gradually it increased, warmth radiating out from the Cycle, hot enough to bring a sweat to her brow. Before her very eyes, the Forever Cycle was coming to life, repairing itself, the crack across its face sealing up. Within moments, the face of the compass looked flawless, like it had never been broken in the first place. She picked it up, studied it again, running her admittedly inexpert eye across the item. It looked fixed. More than that, it felt different, a hint of warmth to it. It felt... Alive? Was that the wrong term? She didn't know. It appeared to have accepted her blood, she knew that much. Which meant...

"You're still out there somewhere aren't you, mother?" she said aloud. Under normal circumstances, she might have felt foolish for the question, not least because she was alone. "You're probably watching me as we speak."

No reply. She hadn't expected one.

"You know, I'm going to follow in your footsteps. I'm going to bring these kingdoms to heel. I'm going to piece back together everything broken about them. And then I'm going to take my place at your side. You will be proud of me. You brought me into this world and I intend to change it."

Still no response, yet the satisfaction that flooded through her was enough to make her think that it had been the right choice. With that out the way, she got to her feet and made for the door. The medical bay beckoned to fix her hand. Somewhere amidst the pain, she felt the excitement dancing in her heart, an unfamiliar feeling.

Things were well in motion, moving towards her conclusion. In time, she would achieve everything she'd set out to. If at the end of one's life, they could say that, then they could die happy. Not that death was in her plans any time soon.

Certainly not her own anyway. A brief laugh escaped her as she closed her office door behind her, the two guards on her door giving each other surprised looks as the lock clicked into place. Only she could open it, herself and Domis for emergency purposes. Nobody else was entrusted with access to it.

"It's okay, gentlemen," she said. "I've had the most magnificent of news. We're going to win. We're going to bloody win!" The laughter was coming out in full now as she moved down the corridor, those words echoing through her soul.

"We are the knife behind the throne, a threat never uttered. We never rule, but we hold the reins. They might not know our names, but they will bow to us, for to lose our favour is to lose all they cherish. That is who we are."

Master Amalfus to Kyra Sinclair on her first day as his apprentice.

She'd not been to Zalchak in Serran for a while, the old city didn't hold much mystique for her. Still, obligations were obligations and duties were duties. Pree hated the city, had too many bad memories of it. The sort of memories that'd make a lesser person wake up in the middle of the night screaming in terror. Ascension had taken place here. The moment she'd ceased to solely be Prideaux Khan and started on the path to becoming someone else. Something else...

She didn't like to think of it like that. Some of them did. They liked to think of themselves as beyond humanity, no longer part of it, what they could do setting them apart from the rest. The building looked abandoned, condemned, not suitable for purpose. They wanted it to look that way. In any other city, in any other circumstance, it would have been torn down long ago. Nobody here in Zalchak dared, those who even suggested it soon found themselves tooting a different tune. Even the homeless avoided it, they took one look and found themselves wanting to be elsewhere. Woe betide anyone who entered who didn't belong.

Did she belong? Absolutely.

Was she going to be welcomed? Possibly. It was too early to tell. Either she'd be welcomed as a hero or left an outcast for the rest of her very short life. Divining the future had never been her strong point, there were few Cavanda out there skilled at it. Some skills did veer more towards one path rather than the other. Those aligned with the Vedo, those supposedly with light in their heart turned out more Cognivites and Restorers, seers and healers, while the Cavanda, the darker side, allegedly produced more Manifolds and Enhanciles, destroyers and brawlers. Her own speciality was testament to that, as a Manifold she was capable of so much more than any other speciality. A curious thing, to be sure. Alchemites and Elementalists were common on both sides, only Farwalkers remained an enigma among both sides alike. It wasn't to say that a Manifold would never emerge amongst the Vedo, or a Restorer amongst the Cavanda. People were who they were, those who sought power didn't gain it in looking to help others or divine the future. They worked for it, relied on themselves.

271

She placed her hand across the door handle, let the Kjarn rush into it, a sign identifying herself. Anyone not knowing the specific spell to enter would be vaporised, she'd seen it happen. It was the reason she'd left Wade behind. His time would come, he would be magnificent, but only would she be permitted to teach him when she'd gotten this task out of the way.

At her side, the bag bumped against her leg and she tussled again with the idea behind bringing it with her. Getting it out of Burykia had been a hassle, it'd taken all the power of the Kjarn she could muster towards warping minds and her Unisco badge to bring it along. But it'd have the desired effect when she revealed it.

The doorman stood on the other side of the door, a huge Enhancile with a pair of kjarnblades hung at his waist. She'd come unarmed, neither blaster nor blade on her waist. Best to present the right impression, show she had nothing to hide. The Dark King of the Cavanda and the princes were all about the right impression, especially in an organisation where everyone had secrets. Secrets was what the Cavanda did. They had people everywhere, every organisation, all feeding back information to make the group stronger. The doorman didn't look at her, continued to stare past her as if she wasn't there. If she wasn't welcome, he would have let her know by now. One didn't get past him if he didn't want them to. The black armour he wore repelled all but the strongest of Kjarn attacks, his gifts made him a fearsome foe blade to blade. The single greatest swordsman in the entire order, barring King Vezikalrus himself, as the rumours went. The king hadn't crossed blades with anyone for decades though, surrounded himself with the darkest aspects of the Kjarn. To challenge his dominance was to accept death was only a breath away and that was if you were lucky.

"Good evening," she said. "Blade Telles to see the royal council. I have an announcement to make immediately." One king, two princes and eight lords. The Royal Council of the Cavanda. Those that she'd have to convince her claim was lawful by the rules long ago laid out by the first Dark King centuries ago. Well, the seven lords right now. Tarene wouldn't be making it after all.

"Blade Telles," the doorman rumbled. "They are expecting you, I think you will find." He stepped aside. "Go on through and if the Dark King rules, you will come out again. Should your favour not be found, it has been nice to have seen you one last time."

Well those words didn't bode well. The doorman certainly had a way about him.

"Thank you," she said. "I appreciate your candour. More than that, I know you're right in what you say."

Behind him, the doors swung open and she drew a deep breath. "If you want to offer me some good luck, I'd take it."

"You don't need luck, Blade Telles. You need a small miracle."

Nothing sinister or sarcastic or cruel, just cold fact in a hard voice. The doorman didn't take sides, he didn't favour or discriminate, he just was a constant presence in the residence of the Cavanda. No matter who came and went, lived or died, the position remained filled. Regardless, the insinuations of his words lay heavy. She knew the odds weren't entirely in her favour. The Royal Council were automatically inclined not to trust those who'd murdered one of their own out of fear they would be next. It was self-interest of the highest order, but the laws were the laws. If her claim was valid and true, and they'd know if there was even a hint of deception, they couldn't punish her, only grant her what she'd won by right of victory.

"Stay well," she said. A pointless thing to say to an Enhancile, she knew that, but there you go. Enhanciles were at the peak of human conditioning, the Kjarn affecting them on a physical rather than spiritual level. They couldn't do any of the other stuff, control the elements or telekinesis but they were unbeatable in physical combat, their bodies healing naturally any damage caused to them at an extraordinary rate. She had a theory she'd not managed to prove one way or another in her other life, knowing for sure might have made things at Unisco a lot easier but better to stay silent for now.

"And you, Blade Telles."

Pree took the side door, didn't dare venture through until she'd changed into her robes, black and ankle-length with splashes of colour across the armbands to designate her speciality of Manifold. It was a good job she liked the colour purple. She'd heard that Vedo made it a point not to reveal what they were skilled at, the height of rudeness to inquire casually. A strange way to be sure. No wonder they'd all been thought wiped out long ago and only recently returned from the dead. Five years wasn't a long time and she had to wonder about the quality of the job that had been done. If they hadn't all been killed, then whomever had been in charge had done a piss poor job of it.

That was a story for another day. For now, she had her own job to do and the cost of failure would be immense. She slid her own mask on, black and purple and red stripes with ghastly protruding teeth. The doorman would know who she was. The Royal Council would know who she was.

Appearances. Keep them up. Obey protocol.

The Cavanda, for a secretive mystical group, wasn't too dissimilar to Unisco in that respect, as strange as it might sound.

She strode through the door, made the deliberate decision to do it like she owned the damn place. A risky stratagem but it came back to appearances. Those who looked like they had something to hide inevitably did. Those who looked guilty and suspicious inevitably were. Pree was neither of those things, she saw ten bodies staring at her and she dropped into a bow, her head low. All of them wore masks, the simpler the mask the higher their rank. The lords wore intricate designs of colour and pattern, horns and spikes and piercings. If the effect was to terrify, it would succeed on a lesser being.

The masks of the princes were less so, no protrusion or exaggerations, only whorls and swirls against otherwise plain backdrops of monochrome shades of blacks and whites and greys. The Dark King himself bore the plainest mask of all, just a simple shade of black that looked to suck you in, engulfing you. Looking at him made her heart want to flee her body and run for cover. He wore no crown, but the aura was there. Of all the Cavanda, he was the only one not to wear the coloured armband that signalled his speciality. Nobody knew what it was, nobody wanted to ask lest it be directed against them in devastating fashion. King Vezikalrus didn't suffer fools gladly.

"Arise, Blade Telles," he said, his voice like the wind across dried leaves. "Your show of respect has been noted." She got to her feet, looked around the room at the seven lords with their missing member and his empty seat, the two princes studying her intently. She didn't break the focus in her stare back at them. If they wanted to gawp, then they could. She had nothing to hide. "At this time, anyway. Though it is the opinion of this council that perhaps your respect has not been noted in other areas, particularly concerning our missing member, would you not say?"

One of the lords chuckled at the insinuation, she didn't break her stare. Vezikalrus' eyes flickered to the side and the sounds of mirth died away. There was no laughing in this chamber, the same one used for full gatherings but empty and devoid of all life but the ten men and women in front of her. It was a solemn place, one where cruelty became reality.

"I would say that my respect has been where it always has," she said, considering her words carefully. A false step would condemn her, even if it were an innocent slip. The council did not forgive mistakes lightly. They could be fatal, for mistakes led to exposure and exposure to a loss of the secrecy they prided. All who entered knew that would be the cost they'd have to bear should they need to pay the price. "I respect not just the Cavanda itself, but the rule of law passed down from generation to generation. Ever since the first Dark King laid down the decrees, I have sought to follow them, I have aimed to use my skills and my aptitudes to ensure the prosperity of the Cavanda. Where there has been an advantage to benefit, I have been there to take it. Through my acts, the Cavanda grows stronger. I respect the laws and the traditions as I respect my king and all those he chooses to enforce his will."

"Then pray do tell why you removed Lord Tarene from the land of the living?" Vezikalrus said. "I find this…" He paused, almost silently considering his words before he spoke. "Disrespectful."

Her breath caught in her throat, she took a moment or two and let it out. "No disrespect has been offered to you, highest of them all. A challenge was made, a challenge was accepted and Lord Tarene was slain in combat." She almost said single combat, enough of a distinctive untruth to catch her out, had caught herself in time. That would have been fatal. At least one of the lords was a Cognivite, she knew that much and to lie in front of him, no matter how small, would be a mistake.

"No challenge was recorded by our keeper as delivered or accepted," Vezikalrus said, casting a glance about those in front of him. "Unless someone wishes to update me with something I am hitherto unaware of?"

None spoke up, the king looked back at her expectantly. She couldn't see his face for the mask, didn't know who he was under there, but she almost got the impression he was waiting for her to justify herself. He didn't care, she realised, whether she lived or died, or was raised to the vacant lordship position. He wanted her to prove that she was worthy of it and that meant surviving this interrogation.

"No challenge need be recorded," she said, moving to prove she knew the laws. "If special circumstances behold it."

"What special circumstances were this?" Prince Samandir spoke up. "Please do inform us in as great detail as possible."

"As the Royal Council is aware, we all do our part in organisations around the kingdoms to ensure a flow of information is retained for future use. My role as an agent of Unisco currently involves the hunting of the terrorist Claudia Coppinger. An investigation into one of her associates…" She paused, was that the right word? She'd gotten their attention by mentioning Coppinger. Coppinger was the biggest name in the kingdoms right now, a figure to rally around or to defy and she wondered which side the Cavanda would choose if they deigned to get involved. Coppinger had a Vedo on her side, yet so did Unisco and they had many. This could get interesting.

They wouldn't though. They'd fail to get involved. It didn't concern them. They'd take the advantage wherever they could from the conflict though. That was their nature.

"Led me to a building which contained a number of vaults. Secure vaults filled with the greatest treasures of the strongest and the most powerful of the five kingdoms. Entirely through accident, we found our way into the Cavanda vault. All our greatest treasures."

"Who is this we?" Prince Tabukah asked. "Has your partner been dealt with?"

She chose to ignore the question, she knew what dealt with meant in this context and she didn't want to answer it just yet, didn't want to prejudice their opinion early. Not until she knew for sure what her own fate would be. If they killed her, they'd kill Wade as well. She held no sentimental value for him, other than he'd probably give his own life to save hers. They were partners after all. The Unisco lessons might feel like a lifetime ago but their roots had sunk deep. Partners looked out for each other. A strange battle between what she should do and what she wanted to do, she could feel the two warring sides clashing inside her.

"I didn't realise it at the time, but we had tripped an alarm and Lord Tarene came running. I don't know how he arrived so quickly, but he did. I did wonder if he was a Farwalker, but…"

"Idle speculation without foundation or purpose," Vezikalrus said curtly. "Carry on."

The reaction was perhaps excessive, but she chose to ignore the tone in his rebuke and did as he ordered. "I don't think he recognised me. He had a bloodlust going on, he didn't want word of what was in that vault to reach the outside world. He attacked both of us, I declared a challenge and we fought."

She gave the room a crooked smile, held both her arms out at her sides as if to emphasise she had nothing to hide. None of the Cognivites had called her on what she had to say, that had to be a blessing. It wasn't a lie. None of it was. The truth was mixed up in there just enough to muddy the issue. Cognivites could do many things where the human mind was concerned but they weren't fool-proof. They were capable of error just as much as the next man or woman, perhaps even more so because they had an air of smug arrogance in their faith in their abilities. They were only human, despite what they professed otherwise, and they held most of the same faults.

"Lord Tarene was the keeper of that vault," Prince Samandir said. "I hope you didn't allow the local police to get a look inside. Assuming you reported it at all."

"I know the law, your highness," she said politely. "I moved the body far away and then called it in." She held the bag up. "A few items for your consideration." Inside the bag stank, she knew this was a stupid idea the moment she plucked Tarene's rotting head out of its black depths and tossed it onto the table in front of the Dark King. All eyes went to it immediately, she saw them water and recoil at the smell emerging into the room. She had no problems with it. Unisco dealt with too many bodies for it to faze her beyond mild discomfort. "I have the autopsy report. I have his mask and his kjarnblade."

"Those latter two are more traditional, you do know that?" the Dark King said, baring his teeth behind the mouth hole in his mask. "Not that thing for starters."

"I apologise for entering the vault," she said. "It was an honest mistake and I am aware ignorance doesn't make it right. If you wish to punish me, I will accept it and hope only that you realise we are all fallible at the times, especially where our other lives are concerned."

"You did not answer my question, Blade Telles," Prince Tabukah said. "What happened to your partner?"

"He lives," she said, letting the words slide slowly out of her mouth. In any other sort of meeting like this, there might have been sounds of outrage and disgust at her admission, here the silence was worse. She could hear the cogs turning in heads as they considered what she'd just said. Already they might be toying with punishment to make sure that nothing like this ever happened again. "I wasn't the one who picked out the Cavanda vault. He did. He picked up on something inside and chose that we should enter." She looked around the room, dared anyone to even suggest it was luck. She didn't believe in luck, not entirely. She'd always thought that it was something you made yourself. "He has potential himself. Lots of it. Ruud Baxter has tried to convince him to join the Vedo and yet he declines."

The aura of the room turned ugly at the mention of the name of the oldest living Vedo, she couldn't blame them. Ruud Baxter had survived where all the others had died, and that level of insult could not be permitted to go unavenged. He would get his one day, he and the rest of the weaklings he had trained would all be wiped from the face of the kingdoms. She'd met Baxter once or twice since he'd returned to Unisco, didn't know how much longer it'd be before she went for him. His very presence tested every iota of her self-control, she desired to lash out and to hells with the consequences of that action.

"You wish for him to be recruited?" Vezikalrus asked. "Intriguing."

"The Kjarn is strong in his family," Pree said. "His cousin is what passes for a full Vedo these days. I ask to be granted the time to work at him, to see if I can convince him to join our cause. He and I are friends, at least he believes us to be. I believe that he would see my way of thinking within time."

"Our way of thinking, Blade Telles," Prince Samandir said. "Always remember the motto of the Cavanda. All before self."

"I have never forgotten our mission," she said. "I apologise for what happened to Tarene, but in the oldest of ways, I have proven he was weak and unfit for his role. I humbly ask that I be considered for elevation to his vacant position, as has been the tradition of elevation for centuries."

"Your skill is not up for dispute," Vezikalrus said. "Your judgement however bears cause for worry. However, you are correct. We have a vacant position and as the cause of that vacancy, you have a case for filling it." It was his turn to let his gaze drift idly around the room. "Because of your indiscretions of invasion, insubordination…" He gestured to the head on the table, clicked his fingers and it exploded into flames, foul-smelling smoke filling the room to mask the rot. "And your assumptions that you may decide on acts affecting the secrecy of us all, we will first vote on whether to enact punitive measures and the depths of those measures. Should you not be put to death…" He didn't even sound like he was joking, and she didn't believe he was for a second. Secrecy was their greatest asset, she'd thought more than once today already. "We will vote upon your ascendancy."

The Dark King clicked his fingers and the fired died away, leaving a fine carpet of ashes across the surface of the table. The first time she'd seen a trick like that employed in here, she'd been shocked. There was a reason they all met within this room, every Cavanda meeting for the last four hundred years had happened within these walls. Someone, nobody remembered who, had placed runes across the surface of every brick, ancient Kjarn runes never since replicated. They only had one purpose, to nullify Kjarn abilities within the room. Later she'd discovered the king and his princes were in possession of bracelets that let them activate their abilities despite it. Because of their rank, only those three figures were permitted to wear them, three out of hundreds, one story said there were only three such bracelets in existence, she wasn't sure if she believed that or not.

A vote though. This could get tricky. She'd seen Cavanda votes before and they were notoriously unpredictable. The lords would vote first, all seven of them silent throughout and she couldn't see herself making too many friends there. Who'd vote for someone who'd just killed one of them to get away without punishment?

Then again, Tarene had never been popular. If she became a lord, killing another lord for their position was no longer an option.

Samandir and Tabukah might be called princes but neither of them was the child of Vezikalrus. The title was a rank of honour, not a hereditary one. Any lord could claim it the way a blade could claim the title of lord. Killing a prince was harder than killing a lord though. Samandir and Tabukah hadn't lost the roles in nearly four decades, Vezikalrus had been on the throne even longer. With ascension came access to new knowledge, but always it was worth remembering those above you had knowledge you did not, that they'd seen the same information you'd had given to you and considerably more time to learn how to use it.

Normally eight lords could lead to a tied vote. If the vote was tied after every lord voted, the votes would go to the princes and they'd be able to either continue the deadlock or break it at their will. Should they oppose each other and continue the stalemate, the Dark King had the final say. With seven, it would be over here and now unless one of them broke tradition and abstained. She glanced around the room, set her mouth into a grimace behind her mask and folded her arms.

"If that is the will of my king," she said. "Then I submit to the wise judgement of those I wish to join." Pree bowed her head, didn't wish to meet the eyes of anyone out of fear for what she might go on to see.

"In accordance with our traditions, I will ask each lord for their reasons and their decision, while Blade Telles gets right of reply. Decisions are hitherto optioned as life or death. Any who pick another of their own choosing shall be ignored. Should the verdict be death, then it will be administered immediately. Should the verdict be life, then I will decide her punishment myself. Are we clear?"

Nobody in the room was going to argue with him, Pree thought. At least he'd laid it out. If he let everyone vote on their own unique punishment, she could be declared dead with two votes and that wouldn't be good at all. "Lord Celej," Vezikalrus said. "What do you feel?"

Lord Celej was a Serranian, a short one but broadly built in his robes, filling them with impressive muscle. She could tell by the accent flowing from behind his mask, blue and white stripes with bull horns in silver. "My king," he said. "I desire to see the harshest punishment possible imposed. I vote death."

Lovely. If they were all like this, then she was in for a world of trouble.

"Blade Telles broke the rules, she endangered the secrecy for us all and when a Cavanda starts acting like this, it has to be snuffed out as quickly as possible. Should we turn a blind eye to this in hopes that she becomes a great lord? I think not."

"Blade Telles, do you wish to reply?" Vezikalrus asked and Pree shook her head. Questioning what Celej had done for the Cavanda in his time as a lord wouldn't bring her much aid, as fun as it might be. "The vote stands at one for death. Lord Hoey?"

Hoey was taller, his mask pink and green in a hideous blend, scar-like grooves cut across the eyes and the nose flat and pig-like. By his accent, she'd mark him as a man from Canterage, maybe Guypsia. Those people were everywhere, very distinctive. The hair she could see above the mask was coal black, flecked with shades of iron grey. "Hey, everyone makes mistakes and I'd rather have someone who makes a mistake trying to benefit the Cavanda than who doesn't and sits on their arse doing nothing."

She fought the urge to smile. Typical of the travelling folk there. No fucking around with their words.

"I've known Blade Telles a little, I've seen some of the reports she does from her work with Unisco. I think the Cavanda is better off with her in it than out of it. I vote life."

"Do you wish to reply?" Vezikalrus asked her and she shook her head again. Effusively thanking him for something that might not yet do her any good felt premature. If she got away with it, she'd thank those that had sided with her then. "Good. The vote stands at one to one. Lord Amalfus, if you please?"

She caught her breath in her throat, watched the lithe man out the corner of her eye. Amalfus gave the impression of great grace as he rose, his mask orange and gold with protruding red eyebrows and viciously pointed teeth. Another Canterage man but from the south maybe, his words clipped and his accent almost posh she would have said.

She knew something about Amalfus that he might not want repeated, might bring it up if he voted against her. It took her back to that day when Unisco had attacked the Coppinger airbase and how she'd gotten off that damn thing. He might not want to be so quick to condemn her when he heard about what his own damn apprentice had gotten up to up there. It'd wipe a smile off his face for sure. Maybe get his head removed from his shoulders if they were feeling as righteous with him as they were.

"Secrecy is prime," he said. "It is the only reason we have gotten away with what we have for as long as we have. No matter Blade Telles' intentions, good or bad, beneficial or not, she did what she did. Every action has consequences. I vote death."

"The vote stands at two to one in favour of death," the Dark King said. "Blade Telles, do you wish to respond to Lord Vezikalrus."

280

"Actually," she said. "I wouldn't mind that. Just wondered if he knew about what his apprentice was getting up to months ago if he's that concerned about the veil of secrecy. Because I've never seen such a wildly public display of Kjarn abilities as I did from her then." She was pleased to note Amalfus looked like he'd been slapped. Good.

"If you have an accusation to make…"

"I'll save it for after," she said. "Assuming that this ends well. If you send me to my death, just consider that one of your own will be as culpable for a much worse breach of secrecy."

She was considerably relieved Kjarn powers didn't work in here, not without those bracelets. Amalfus would probably be moving out of his way to make her as dead as possible with it if he could. A risky stratagem around this many powerful Cavanda but decidedly less so than having her spill her guts.

"Lord Barrass," Vezikalrus said. "State your piece."

She was sure Barrass was a woman, couldn't say for certain, for the voice was muffled around the mask, brown and grey with hundreds of pockmarks chipped into the surface of it. What impression she did get was she was Vazaran, her clothes leaving her shapeless in body, but dark skin could be seen at her wrists and neck.

"I find it hard to fault Blade Telles for her actions," she said. "As reckless as they might have been, she's given good reasons for the way she acted every step of the way. She risked exposure, she did her best to push it all back into the bottle after. Given there are none at our door, I have faith she'll learn from her mistake without consequences that will doom us all. I vote for her to live."

Yes! Over half the votes out of the way and there was still a chance. Two more in her favour and she'd be granted the reprieve she deserved.

"Two to two," Vezikalrus said, after offering her the right to reply which once more she chose to decline. Speaking her mind wouldn't do her any good, as often as the offer was made. She'd already made herself look weak by casting aspersion on Amalfus, even if the seed needed to be planted. "Lord Jeziorek?"

A Burykian like her, Jeziorek cleared his throat with a sound like paper being sanded off a wall. His mask had a brilliant golden beak, black and white patches across the face like a myriad gameboard. Like Celej, he was short, but his arms were thick and beefy. She wondered if national kinship would count for everything. Somehow, she doubted it. From an early age, all loyalty was twisted towards the Cavanda rather than family or friends or national identity. They didn't want their apprentices to feel divided loyalty. If anything, it might reinforce Jeziorek against her to avoid the accusations of favouritism.

281

"Secrecy is our oldest tenant," he said. "I vote death. We don't want our blades thinking it is optional rather than necessary. A sorry end here saves tears later. The next one might just think twice rather than doing something rash."

Huh, she thought. So much for the suggestion of kinship then. He'd thrown any hint of that straight out the window. She couldn't blame him. Not really. In his shoes, she might have done the same thing. Sympathy was a hard broom to shake in the Cavanda and you avoided it by not having to do it in the first place. If you didn't have to face the accusations, you didn't have to deal with the fallout.

She shook her head again, declined the right to comment as Vezikalrus announced the decision as three to two against her. Pree looked to the last two members, Necid and Fekir. Both were from Premesoir, she knew from experience, Necid the fat one with the rainbow coloured human hair billowing from his mask, Fekir the averagely built one with the half and half mask, half a normal face and the other half vivid reds and browns and purples like a burn victim. She didn't trust Premesoirans entirely. The kingdom had a dubious record of people doing unnerving things when they achieved a little bit of power. They couldn't be trusted. Some of the Premesoir presidents had been some of the worst people in history in the name of advancing their kingdoms, they'd started wars and done their best to finish them often, though the fallout left behind was often catastrophic. They'd never gone into a situation and made it better than when they arrived.

And what did that mean for her in the here and now, she wondered.

"Lord Necid," the Dark King said. "Please render your verdict."

Necid was fat but his voice was deep and stern. He got the impression he was bald behind the mask, one of the rumours she'd heard was how his own hair had been used to make it. "I believe that Blade Telles showed remarkable behaviour all throughout this. She showed initiative in letting her partner live, because he has the gift. A potential asset that could be ours one day is always worth taking a risk for. She should be punished, but I believe after her initial slip, she did everything to rectify the situation, she moved the body, the vault wasn't scrutinised, and nobody knows we were involved at any point. I don't believe the nature of the situation warrants death. I vote to let her live."

She didn't realise she'd been holding her breath until it all rushed out of her in one deep sigh of relief. Three to three as Vezikalrus quickly reminded them all, as if he needed to. One more vote and it could swing her either way. This was her moment of truth, perhaps the last few minutes she'd live unless things went her way. The Dark King would murder her on the spot if Fekir said to kill her. She was sweating now, it wasn't warm in the chamber, but she could feel her heart hammering, her adrenaline levels spiking, her fists clenched.

"I decline the right to comment," she said, keeping her voice strong. "I just await the words of Lord Fekir."

Fekir chuckled, rose to his feet and cleared his throat. "Blade Telles," he said. "I've heard what my fellow lords have said, and your future depends on your answer, for I wish to address you directly if it pleases his grace?" He looked to the Dark King who nodded briefly. She wondered what was coming. "Blade Telles, of your partner who knows a little of our ways now and you hope to convert. Give me one answer to my question and your fate shall be decided. I care not for your reasons, the depths of what you did or didn't do. I just desire to know if your heart remains true to our cause. Should Wade Wallerington have sought to expose us, would you have removed him, your partner at Unisco and perhaps even your friend?"

She was glad she could hide her surprise behind her mask. That was unexpected, she thought, wondered how Fekir knew of her professional relationship with Wade. Perhaps he too worked for Unisco, though she had no idea who he might be. Perhaps he was a skilled Cognivite and the Kjarn had told him. Either way, he knew too much and that unsettled her, not least for the way he'd just blurted it out in front of the rest of the Royal Council.

Regardless, there was only one answer she could give, and she was surprised as to how quickly she'd come to it as it arrived on her lips. She'd shield Wade the best she could but if he wasn't compliant, it wouldn't even be a choice. "A potential asset he might be," she said. "But should that asset not be worth the fruit it might bear, then it should be removed. If he had sought to expose us, he would no longer be with us. I would not hesitate to remove him. My loyalty has been to the Cavanda. It always will be. It is because of the Cavanda that I am where I am. Make no mistake of that."

"And why should we kill such a loyalty?" Fekir asked. "Mistakes are there to be learned from, especially when the fallout is nowhere near as bad as it might have been. We have avoided a minor catastrophe. I vote for her to live. I doubt she'll make such an error of judgement again."

"Four to three," Vezikalrus said. "In the absentia of Lord Tarene, the vote is decisive and Blade Telles, you are to be punished at a pre-determined date in the future rather than executed. Consider yourself lucky." The Dark King cleared his throat. "Now, with that out the way, it is time for another vote. With Lord Tarene's seat emptied, we will all vote by show of hands whether to permit Blade Telles to fulfil his position and his duties. By right of law, she has a claim to it, it is the duty of you all to honour that claim." He looked at the nine men and women underneath him, the seven lords and the two princes. "Failing that, we will meet again in the future to discuss future candidates. The Eight need to remain whole, to leave an imbalance will have disastrous consequences. All in favour of elevating Blade Telles to the rank of Lord of the Cavanda, raise your hands now."

She didn't know what to expect. Just because something was her right didn't mean said right would be honoured when it came to pass the motion through. What was right and what would eventually be done were two entirely different things. She'd need six out of nine available votes to be ascended Maybe the Dark King had even avoided punishing her yet to see the outcome of the vote. A punishment for a lord carried a different measure as a punishment for a blade. Lords weren't usually put to death for breaking secrecy, although the cynic in her felt the need to point out that they usually had more sense than to do so by the time they got the opportunity to ascend.

Yet, she was surprised, felt the tingling sensation flood through her as hands raised to approve of her, both the princes, well over half the lords. Only Jeziorek and Amalfus didn't raise their hands. Given they'd both voted to have her put to death, she wasn't entirely surprised. Amalfus had to know that halting her ascension wouldn't get him out of the shit his apprentice had gotten him into. Although, now she thought about it, the word of a lord would be taken more seriously than that of a blade. It was perhaps the only reason she'd sat on it until now. That and she hadn't been here for a while. Cover. Maintaining the secrecy, they were so proud of. Those were her reasons and she'd stick to them.

Jeziorek though, appeared to have no reason not to vote against her unless there was something going on she was unaware of. Maybe he and Amalfus had compact, perhaps he wanted to be the sole Burykian on the council. It didn't matter. Those two had failed in their bid to halt her. "That concludes the vote," Vezikalrus said. "And with a majority vote of seven for and two against, rise to your feet Lord Telles and look your fellow councillors in the eye for the first time."

Lord Telles. That had a nice ring inside her head, she thought. She could get used to that title and maybe more. Prince Telles sounded even better.

She chided herself for the thoughts before they exited the conception stage. Best not to be greedy right now. The nature of a Cavanda was to covet power, it was instilled in them from their first days. She'd been a lord for all of ten seconds. There were others on the Royal Council with decades of experience with power she could only now start to discover for herself. It was a long game, to be sure, and she'd need to play smart rather than fast.

Pree rose to her feet, tried not to react as she found the Dark King in her face, he'd made it from his throne to next to her in the time it had taken her to raise her head. Not a great distance, maybe ten feet at most but still a great distance to cover in a fraction of a second. He gripped her arm and a curious sensation whipped through her, one not unfamiliar in its feeling but strange in its execution. Early in her Unisco days, she'd tried to cram herself through a pipe just a fraction too small, had spent several agonising minutes attempting to force herself through the gap.

It reminded her of that, the room around her suddenly gone and cold whipped at her face, bitter winds making her grit her teeth. She doubted they were even in Zalchak anymore, it didn't look like any part of Serran she'd seen before. Mountainous and cold, perhaps up north. Or maybe elsewhere. The peaks she could see didn't look familiar.

Vezikalrus in typical fashion didn't appear perturbed by the cold, fixed her with a stare, eyes unblinking behind his mask, even in the gale. Her robes weren't the warmest, she wrapped her arms around her and felt her teeth threaten to chatter before she realised that she was no longer under Kjarn restrictions. It was like a light had been switched on inside her, she felt the fires rise, she fanned them mentally with the buffering winds that crashed into her, used that energy to make them rise, let the heat seep through her entire body. It took a few seconds, but she was soon able to straighten and compose herself with dignity as she looked at the Dark King.

"You wish to know where we are," he said. "Or how we got here. Both questions are an irrelevance in the scheme of things. Always we have places we need to be and how we get there is a matter only for the minor details."

"You're a Farwalker," she said. "I've never travelled like that before." She knew how rare Farwalkers were and it worried her the most powerful Kjarn-wielder in the kingdoms was one. Farwalkers made for deadly enemies, no door could keep them out, no lock could deny them. If they wanted you dead, they could get to anyone from anywhere.

"Few have," he said. "I don't take passengers often. Only at times when speed and privacy is a must."

"You wanted to talk to me in private?" She glanced around, realised that she couldn't imagine a much more private place than this. Realisation flickered through her. "You don't trust your own underlings not to have you bugged, do you?"

"This is easier," Vezikalrus said. "To spy on someone, it always helps to know where they are. You work for Unisco, you should understand this. It's difficult to do to a Farwalker, I assure you."

She could believe it. Following someone who could vanish from right in front of you and relocate to anywhere in the known kingdoms they could think of, in the time it took you to put one foot in front of the other was a thankless task.

"If where and how are pointless questions," she said. "Then I can assume that the best one to ask is why?"

"Perhaps," he said. "I brought you here to swear your oath to me and to the Cavanda. I brought you here to inform you of your duties as a lord and your punishment for your previous transgressions. More than that, I want to hear what you have on Lord Amalfus. I wish to hear it before the rest of them do."

"Your highness," she said. "It will be done. All of it."

"Repeat after me," the Dark King said. "I, Lord Telles..."

"I, Lord Telles," she said. That prefix of lord still felt new and exciting in her mouth. More than that, it felt damn good to be able to use it.

"Hereby proclaim in front of the eyes of my one true king..."

"Hereby proclaim in front of the eyes of my one true king..."

"... To uphold the traditions and the laws of the Cavanda as laid down by those that have gone before..."

"... To uphold the traditions and the laws of the Cavanda as laid down by those that have gone before..."

"... To seek out knowledge that will benefit our kind and destroy our enemies..."

"... To seek out knowledge that will benefit our kind and destroy our enemies..."

"... Proclaim only to think of the whole rather than the individual..."

"... Proclaim only to think of the whole rather than the individual..."

"... To take triumph over glory..."

"... To take triumph over glory..."

"... To accept supremacy over acclaim..."

"... To accept supremacy over acclaim..."

He paused, looked her up and down. "Those who have gone before observe your oath, every blade and lord, prince and king. Do you make it in their eyes, always to honour the lessons of the past and use them to shape the future for our own ends?"

"I do honour them."

"Do you pledge to use the new power and knowledge available to you to benefit only the Cavanda, seek only to make us stronger in our unity, rather than weaker in our squabble for power."

"I do make that pledge."

"Do you vow to forsake all others but your brethren and your kin from this point on? Blood is blood, but we are united in spirit and that trumps all. Should you be ordered to exterminate your family and your friends, what would your answer be?"

"It would be done," she said. "Always the Cavanda. Never anyone else."

"On your knees," he said and there was a flash of metal in his hand. She stiffened up, knew what was going to happen but she let herself drop regardless, the snow at her feet rising up her thighs as she sank into a kneeling position. Above the wind, she couldn't hear the Dark King's kjarnblade activating.

"When your shoulders are touched with my blade, your confirmation will be complete, you will be born anew as Lord Telles of the Cavanda. Your past sins will be forgiven if not forgotten. Together, we will forge a path that will set the future aflame with its fallout."

She nodded, mentally trying to gather herself. She wasn't sure that she was ready to be touched with a kjarnblade like that. Best not to wriggle. She'd seen what they could do to limbs, even the faintest of touch would leave grooves that would never fade, he'd be scarring her for the rest of her life. Still, if it needed to be done and it was the price that had to be paid then so be it. There were worse things in life than a little pain and permanent damage. A lot worse.

"Your life as a Unisco agent has left you with many desirable qualities I would look for in one of my lords," Vezikalrus said. "I demand ferocity and tenacity, I always look for the ability to follow orders and the competence to carry out what is demanded of them. I follow your career with interest, Agent Khan. I would like one of your first duties to be a complete review of Cavanda security, as well as quiet investigations into some of your fellow lords. I have faith none of them are plotting against me, but faith will only take you so far. Trust but verify."

"How can you be sure?" she asked. "You never know what goes on in the heads of those that covet power."

"Very true, Lord Telles. I like to feel I have the measure of my... What did you call them? My underlings? I know what sort of people they are and given a choice I'd like to replace them all. Amalfus is competent but I worry about his ambition. He recently acquired quite a big job in his other life without the approval of the Royal Council and I worry it might affect his duties as a lord. Should a vacancy appear amongst my princes, I fear he might be the one to make the claim and fill the void left behind. Others have too little ambition, they grow sated and stale where they are, strong enough to maintain their position against any challenge that comes their way but never powerful enough to rise against those above them."

"You sound like you want it," she said. "You want them to challenge you?"

"I want them to remember they are Cavanda. It is in their tradition to rise, rather than grow complacent. Perhaps one of them will surprise me one day." She could have sworn he had smiled at her then. "And this is your punishment, Lord Telles. You've been given an opportunity that could easily have gone the other way for you. Had you not been so fortunate, you would be dead by now. Take that fortune and use it to build it all. I expect you to be more than an acceptable lord, I expect you to be magnificent. I hold you to the highest of standards and I demand you fulfil them. It will not be an easy life, but I believe you can do it. Nothing worse than wasted potential."

She considered his words, wondered what sort of punishment he'd just inflicted on her. Nothing she wouldn't do anyway, perhaps. Except, was that true? She'd never turned anything down from those above her, either in Unisco or the Cavanda. Always there'd be a first time. Demanding the very constant best from someone didn't sound like a traditional way of punishment. Pree knew she had to consider the fact that Vezikalrus had been alive a very long time, he knew more psychological tricks than a team of torturers and how to apply them with infinitely more skill. If he was challenging her, did he truly believe that she would succeed? Or that failure was a case of when, rather than if.

That thought killed the good feeling inside her. Constant questioning of herself, unhealthy paranoia over her own ability? The urge to have her worth proved greater than her judgement? Was this what her life was to be like now? She didn't know, but the title suddenly didn't feel so grand and good any more.

"Now," he said. "Before we get out of this cold, tell me more about what you said earlier. Amalfus and his apprentice. Gideon Cobb?"

"Kyra Sinclair," Pree said. "And several months back, I had an encounter with her while I was part of a Unisco operation…"

"Pull out every stop, every dirty trick. I don't like the way Jacobs and Jameson sullied the good name of this academy, if they're going to pass, they can do it the damned hardest way possible. They want their sins cleaned, they're going to work for it like no cadet ever worked before."

Nandahar Konda regarding the upcoming trial for academy graduates.

It felt like they'd come full circle. When first they'd approached the Unisco academy, they'd been thrown from an aeroship with nothing but an airloop for company, forced to sink or swim from the first whistle. Pete hadn't appreciated it at the time, he'd never used one before, wasn't something that had ever come up in his days of being a spirit caller. And yet, he'd managed. He'd swam rather than sank, the relief as he'd touched the ground nothing short of bliss. Had he realised at the time what would follow, he would have questioned the feeling. It might have been an accomplishment at the time, not dying, but he'd quickly come to realise if he wanted to survive his time as an agent of Unisco, it'd have to become a regular thing, the norm rather than an isolated experience.

Maybe, anyway. If he survived this final test, then it was to the inquisitors with him. He'd been told that chance of an early death in the inquisitors was unlikely, that there were more chances of being injured by your own side than an enemy. He'd already been hit with a bowl by Theo, it had to get better than that. The reality was it probably wouldn't. He'd had the talk with another inquisitor they'd sent over at Konda's request, Inquisitor Sweeney who'd been charming enough, had that lilt that came to those hailing from the west of Canterage, the emerald islands and all that. Guypsia. Sweeney had told him it all, made it sound like it was the best option. Of course, every recruiter did that. They wanted recruits. Konda had done it all, but he'd told him to get a second opinion. It's only professional, he'd added. Never take someone at their first word.

Privately, he'd doubted how much Konda knew about it, overseeing the academy. It wasn't the same. It was like hearing from someone who used to be a spirit caller talk about the latest techniques without them having any recent experience.

"Because, my lad," Inquisitor Sweeney had said. "The inquisitors are the last bastion of morality within Unisco. If Unisco are the secret police of the five kingdoms, then we are the ones who police the police. We keep agents in line as best we can."

"Doesn't it make it harder for them to do the job?" Pete had asked. "According to what people have said?"

"These people, they cling to the old ways. Maybe back in the day, you could smash an answer out of a suspect. Now though, it's a different world. It was, anyway. Now it doesn't even closely resemble the same. People have rights, or at least they think that they do. What they don't realise is it don't make a damn bit of difference what some bill says if nobody can see it get broken. We make sure it doesn't get out of hand. Can't get them all, that's for sure, but we get enough when we have to."

Pete had said nothing, just considered the words. "I imagine it's a lonely job."

"Hey, nobody joins Unisco to make friends, my lad. It's a tough life. Most other Unisco agents hate you. Inquisitors make up the highest percentage of disliked groups amongst the organisation. Others include snipers and pilots. Nobody likes them either."

"Pilots?"

"They do a lot of training and they get to fly around in state-of-the-art machinery looking glamorous," Sweeney said. "It inspires jealousy amongst some. Don't matter that they'll occasionally crash and ninety-nine times out of a hundred, a serious crash is fatal. It's about what happens before the fire. And of course, nobody likes snipers." He got that. They'd all had a few rounds of sniper training in the second month here, getting a practice rifle and shooting at a watermelon sat a thousand feet away, a crude face drawn on it with its tongue stuck out at them. Someone setting up the course had a weird sense of humour, he'd thought at the time.

Nobody in the group had gotten close to hitting it, the instructor overseeing it had made some notes and they'd never been invited back to try again. That was fine, nobody liked snipers or the idea of being killed from a thousand feet away by a foe they couldn't see or hear. First impressions counted for a lot in Unisco training. He'd thought it strange at the time, just like the airloop thing. Later he'd realised, they wanted people who could instinctively grasp at something, natural talent they could develop. And apparently, his natural talent was to keep the peace amongst those who were meant to keep the peace themselves. He didn't know what that said about him or what impressions he'd been giving off. Maybe keeping peace between Scott and Jess for all those months had rubbed off on him, playing peacemaker by stopping them from killing each other. Maybe. He'd never considered it that way before. Sometimes experience brought clarity.

"You understand we need to do what needs to be done," Inquisitor Sweeney said. "We always do that. Nothing else. It's our motto. Whatever it takes."

Looking back at that day, only a matter of hours ago now, he could understand it. Whatever it took to get there. Now he had a goal, rather than a target of graduation, he'd found himself ready to dedicate himself to it. First though, the final test, the last practical. He and Theo had jumped from the aeroship first, airloop's fastened across their upper bodies and he'd heard his heart hammering in his ears, fighting for supremacy with the roar of the air as they fell. A few thousand feet up, the city sprawling beneath them, once they hit the ground, they'd need to survive, evade the other team who were giving them a five-minute head start. Him and Theo against the rest of them.

Wouldn't be easy, but he'd been assured countless times nothing worthwhile ever was. Theo had been his usual unflappable self while they'd been ready to jump, giving off the impression it didn't bother him at all. Maybe it genuinely didn't. As annoying as that smug sense of self-worth was, it was preferable to him flapping like crazy and panicking. He got the feeling Theo didn't panic. He'd never seen it. Didn't mean that he couldn't be broken mentally. He wouldn't have hit him with that bowl if he couldn't. A real loose cannon, if things didn't go his way.

There had to be more to him than that. Had to be. Either way, their test awaited, they had to work together to get this done. He looked down, saw the ground rushing towards them and he yanked his loop. He felt the electricity crackle through his cape-like coat, felt it stiffen and catch the breeze, wind whipping at his face, he squeezed his eyes shut. The first time he'd done this, terror had flooded through him. Now though, he liked it, felt the rush and he let out a cheer taking him by surprise. He hadn't expected that. Pete could feel Theo's eyes focused on him, drilling into his falling form like laser beams.

Then he heard the shout, a yell of shock that hit a crescendo into terror. Pete craned his head back, saw Theo clawing at his cape. What had he just been thinking about the lack of panic in him? Moving through air was hard, it was like swimming but without the water, no sort of forward propulsion and the idea of the ground coming ever closer was a touch distracting. "To me!" he yelled, his voice lost amid the roar of the air. He repeated it, kept his eyes on Theo as he tried to keep pushing himself forward to his partner. Theo had given up clawing at himself now, was scanning the ground, his eyes widening in fear. He knew he was going to die, for whatever reason his airloop wasn't working and he knew that the end was near.

Not a chance!

Pete didn't like him, he wouldn't go out of his way to be nicer than he needed to with him, but he'd be damned if he was going to let him die on his watch without doing every little thing that he could to save him.

"Theo!"

He screamed it at the top of his lungs, wondered if some of it had gotten through. He thought he saw the other man's head twitch in the breeze, just slightly in his direction. The urge to tug his own airloop ring was overpowering, he had to move his hand away from it, a definite no-no he'd been warned. You let go of it, you might not get hands on it again in time. If he slowed his fall, Theo would continue to move at the same speed, would hit the ground before he had the chance to catch him.

Instead, he aimed down, pointed his body like a missile and tried to get some leverage, kicking with his feet at an angle. He could feel water leaking from his eyes, tears streaming down his cheeks as he pushed and pushed, squeezing his eyes shut, didn't want to look at the ground. It'd have them both shortly unless he pulled it out of his ass. He flailed about with his arms, allowed himself to peer through wet vision.

Close! So close. Theo had seen him now, was doing the same thing as he'd tried, his face still laced with the fear but at least he was fighting. Divines knew it was one thing Theobald Jameson could do when the cards were down, he could fight, and he wasn't going to go down without one. Their hands were inches apart, their fingertips almost touching, the ground incoming and now they were in amongst the skyscrapers, could see the lights of the early morning traffic far below. If he didn't pull it off, some commuter was going to have a truly horrific morning. A savage grin swept across his face, nothing like gallows humour to get the blood pumping. At times like this, a short fall could feel like a lifetime in a second. He kicked his legs, tensed his muscles against empty air, he felt Theo's fingers graze his and he thrust his arm into them, caught each other in an embrace. His airloop kicked, he felt the electricity run through it, saw it in Theo's hand. He'd found it! He'd bloody done the job for him and they'd slowed almost to a halt before starting the fall again.

By the time they kissed the ground, the final pull had snapped the string, propelling them the last few feet into an untidy heap, a jumble of arms and legs.

"Don't ever tell anyone about what we just did," Theo muttered, wriggling to dislodge himself. "I mean it, Jacobs. That was… My bastard loop snapped off when I went to pull it that first time." He craned his head up at the aeroship high above them, waved his fist in anger. Pete fought the urge to smile as he picked himself up, dusted his legs off. They'd hit grass, damp with morning dew and he was glad for the chance to experience the soak stains across his clothes. Better than the alternative. "Sabotage!"

"Oh, grow up," Pete said. "Got to test us somehow, don't they?" He straightened his jacket, hadn't had the chance to throw much else on over his black clothing, t-shirt and trousers. They looked like exactly what they were, trainee agents on an exercise. His jacket was the only thing covering the Unisco logo on the back, the unicorn head and horn he'd seen on the identification shields before. His jacket was black like the rest of the gear, it blended well. Theo's was blue and purple, he looked a little out of place, like the kingdoms most pissed off jogger.

"I don't call nearly killing us testing us, I call it sadism!"

"Hey, we didn't die though, did we?" Pete said, shrugging his shoulders. "All about teamwork and that, I guess. We pushed through. You're lucky I heard you shout, I'd hate to be having to try and scrape you off the ground right now."

Theo scowled at him, his face temporarily flushed red with anger. It wasn't a pleasant image, he had to admit. Maybe he'd pushed it too far with that comment, few people liked being reminded about their mortality and he doubted Theo was much different. Instead he was surprised as his partner offered him a hand, looked more than a little uncomfortable with it as his face returned to its normal colour.

"You can be a real pain in the ass sometimes, Jacobs," Theo said. "You don't know when to shut up, you don't seem to have a filter in what passes for a brain. But…" He paused, shrugged his shoulders uneasily. The words looked like they tasted poisonous to him. "But, you saved my life up there. You didn't have to. You could have let me drop. It might even have been easier for you to pass this whole thing on your own."

"Doubt it," Pete said. "Two against the rest of them isn't exactly a fair fight. One would stand no chance."

"Speak for yourself," Theo said, that cold grin back with its obnoxious presence. He showed his teeth, hand still outheld. Pete made his choice, gripped it and moved to hug him. He felt the recoil, didn't let him break away from it. He didn't care how uncomfortable Theo was by it, he wasn't going to let him forget this moment.

"I do," he said, almost whispering it in his ear. "Believe me, I saved your life because I couldn't picture myself letting you die. I

293

risked my own life to make sure you carried on living yours. I could have hit the ground as well, you know. I joined Unisco to preserve life. Don't think I forgot the bowl."

He broke away, straightened the lapels of his jacket in what he hoped was a suitably intimidating look. In truth, Theo had probably been threatened more across family breakfasts, yet he still looked shaken up by the ordeal. This was probably the ideal time to make a point.

"I expect you to do the same now. Work with me. We can beat the rest of them. Hells, we'll probably make top two in our class if we make it through this. Konda told me, they've never tested cadets the way they're testing us. The teams are always equal. They made an example just for us."

"They want us to fail, don't they?" Theo said, some of the fire returning to his voice and Peter Jacobs had never been so glad to hear that level of condescending arrogance before. He grinned at him.

"Sure do," he said. "You know what, partner? Let's go disappoint them, shall we? Make them regret ever betting against us."

The moments of doubt had gone, the fear and the uncertainty he'd seen since they'd hit the ground wiped from Theo in an instant. He looked ready to kill now, Pete thought, and he hoped he wouldn't regret pushing him to this point. Last thing they needed was for another cadet to get seriously hurt because Theo lost the plot.

"Fuck yeah!"

Something hit the ground between them, tore out a chunk of concrete the size of an eyeball, Pete felt it bounce off his leg. Instinctively, they both stared to the sky, saw another streak of laser fire homing in on them and they moved simultaneously, throwing themselves aside. It hit the ground mere centimetres from its partner.

Some bastard was shooting at them. Live shots as well by the looks of it, he'd seen the weapons they used for training purposes and they didn't leave gouges in solid concrete like that. Best case scenario, they were stun blasts. Wasn't particularly better as an alternative to deadly force, both would leave them on the ground. At least though, they'd be able to eventually walk away from a stun blast. They'd fail the exercise though.

"Run!" Theo bellowed, Pete gave the sky one final glance as he stumbled to his feet, saw the outline of figures falling through the air. The rest of them were coming, three, four, five, six, seven he could see. Number eight had to be giving them covering fire. That was simultaneously worrying and a relief in Pete's book. They didn't have a decent sniper amongst them, probably the only reason they hadn't been hit. Over three thousand feet from a hovering aeroship buffeted by wind…

Cheating bastards! They had to have had a professional Unisco sniper on that aeroship for a shot like that. Pete wasn't an expert but there wasn't a chance in any number of hells you could find of a trainee capable of shooting like that. Either way, it'd made the message clear. They needed to get clear and fast before they got company. Getting into a fist fight down here wouldn't end well. It wouldn't be the smart play. Neither he nor Theo had weapons, he didn't doubt that the hunting team did. All it took was one of them to get lucky and land a stun blast to them while they were distracted, and it'd be over.

He didn't know where they were running to, dipped back and let Theo take the lead. He looked like he had an idea where he was going, like he had a plan. That was a relief. Pete didn't even know if he was sure which city they were in. They came on a fence, hurdled it with ease. They'd jumped bigger fences back in the academy for fun. A few people milled about, Burykians, all of them. He couldn't see a single face drastically different to the rest of them. At least they hadn't left Burykia then, they couldn't be too far from Iaku. That made sense given their travel times. No way they'd go to another kingdom, not when Burykia had perfectly good urban environments of its own. Their cities were distinctive compared to those in other kingdoms, they had a real sense of development about them, like the architects had looked to the future and imagined what it'd look, then putting their own spin on it. Greeting the future right now and all that stuff. The traffic across the road was dense, thickly packed together, a hint of a thousand different fumes in the air, deadly sweet and noxious on the back of his throat. He fought the urge to shove his arm up against his mouth, wouldn't do to stand out.

Looking around, he could see some pedestrians wore face masks, not the worst idea he'd ever seen for the health reasons, but neither he nor Theo had anything on them bar the clothes on their back. No credits. No weapons. Not even a summoner. They'd still not been given them back yet and that rankled. He hadn't seen Mermari or Basil for too long. They couldn't miss him, that'd imply a sentience long since lost but it didn't change the fact he missed them. He knew there'd have to be some sacrifices made in the line of duty, this was one such sacrifice, didn't mean that he had to like it. Just that it might be the first of many.

"That way," Theo said, pointing ahead. They'd stopped running now they'd hit a civilian area, dropping to a brisk walking pace. Another thing he didn't like. They needed to put as much distance between them and their pursuers as rapidly as possible but there was a way to do things. A running target caught the eye far more easily than a stationary one. Best they could do was walk quickly and keep their heads down, avoid catching the eyes of anyone close by. It wouldn't be perfect, but it'd do.

Pete saw what he was pointing at, didn't quite know what to make of it. A mag-rail station was a fine idea, at least it would have been if they had any means of accessing it. Most stations around the kingdoms were card operated to avoid letting the homeless have access to them. Especially in Burykia, they liked their stations clean and their vagrants out of both mind and sight. If they couldn't be seen, then they weren't a problem.

"I've got an idea," Theo said. "Come on, we can do this. Trust me. Partner."

Hearing him say it like that didn't reassure him much, the word partner sounded alien coming from his mouth, he even saw the twitch as he said it in the corner of his eyes. Theo didn't like the word either. He made it look dirty, soiled on his tongue. He'd always thought his partner would be a little more reassuring. It wasn't like there were too many more options though.

"Okay, lead the way," he said. "Partner."

The crowds built up a little more, the closer they got to the station. They would, Pete supposed, people had places to be and jobs to get to. The trains were good, they'd been brought in to try and reduce speeder congestion, make the air cleaner to breathe, move a mass of people around in comfort and haste. Maybe all the boxes hadn't been ticked all the time, but it was a better system than it had been when he was growing up. Back then, public transport both clean and efficient had been little more than a dream, a life where the dregs of society still saw the trains as their own personal bathroom, a place for them to sleep and harass the respectable on their way to work. His dad had always had harsh words about the way they moved from carriage to carriage, shuffling along and screaming angrily at people trying not to meet their eyes, trying not to think of them as people. John Jacobs wasn't normally that sort of man, Pete had always found him kind and understanding, a lot more so than his mother's first partner if the things he'd heard were anything to go by, a union that had produced Sharon and not much else. It wasn't something that got discussed much at home, he couldn't say he was surprised why, especially since what had happened to Sharon.

"Follow my lead," Theo muttered out the corner of his mouth. Pete saw him edge his way through the crowd, sidling through the busiest throngs of people and he wondered what he was up to. More than that, he drew a few dissatisfied looks from those around him, mutters of discontent.

If he hadn't been part expecting it, part looking for it, he might never have seen his partner's hand snake into pockets, checking for lapses in security. Fondling someone without them noticing was a tricky skill, even more so when it came to sneak something out of their person without them catching on. He wasn't even sure they'd taught them this at the academy, doubtless it would be a handy skill in the field, but they'd elected to avoid it. Wherever he'd learned to do it, Theo hadn't picked it up in any official way.

Seeing him come back with two tickets and a grin on his face, he wondered why he found it so surprising that he had a trick like that in his armoury. Everything about him spoke of troubled childhood. And what do children do when they're troubled? They act up, break the rules, get away with what they can. They either grew out of it or they went further down the spiral into trouble. He still wasn't sure which one Theo had moved into. Sometimes he looked like a reformed criminal trying to do good. Sometimes he looked like a barely functioning good guy trying to avoid bad. That first one may be harsh, he quickly realised, hating himself for thinking it even as the thought passed across his mind. Theo might be many things, but he'd never given off the impression that he was a truly bad guy. Not like his father. Pete had heard too many things about John Cyris over the years to not wonder about his son and where his loyalties lay.

The rail pass was pressed into his hand, Theo's eye twitched for a moment, the corners of his mouth turning up as if he wished to grin. Maybe he was proud of what he'd done. Maybe he wanted recognition. Pete didn't know. He'd given up trying to recognise what he was thinking. He didn't do emotions the way other people did, he'd learned body language reading or at least the basics of it, but Theo didn't even carry himself like a normal human being sometimes. The only conclusion he could get was the bastard truly was broken inside and that unnerved him.

Should they pass, he wondered as they made their way through the ticket barrier with stolen cards, how long before he was called to bring some restraint to Theo and his like. Men who believed in violence as an answer, who were prone and quick to it almost as easily as they breathed. Combat specialists. Unisco had plenty of them, people who were trained to be able to kill in as swift a manner as possible with all number of different weapons. The only thing the inquisitors had going for them, both Sweeney and Konda had reminded him, was that to apprehend a violent killer, you needed to be capable of even more violence, be even more ready to kill. He didn't know if that was him, but he wasn't sure when he'd get the chance to find out.

Their tickets buzzed them through without a hitch, Theo continued to lead the way towards the nearest train and not for the first time, Pete wondered what he had in mind. The whole point of this test was that they couldn't leave city limits so getting a mag-rail carriage out of here was out of the question. He didn't know how big the city was, but compared to some around the other kingdoms, most Burykian cities were small affairs, more contained within themselves. You could walk across them in less than a day, even accounting for other factors. The bigger Premesoir cities couldn't be gotten across by speeder in a day.

Inner-city one then, Pete thought, spying the arrival and departures board. Maybe head to the other side of the city, see how long it takes for them to track us down when they don't know where we've gone.

He doubted it'd be that simple. The hunting team had every advantage afforded to them, they'd been told. They would get all the backup, all the support, whatever they needed for that would be the way in real life circumstances, while those being hunted had nothing but their wits. Pete glanced around, saw too many black eyes high on the walls and the ceilings, video surveillance capable of picking a face out of the crowd with ease.

They'd already know where they were in a case like this. All they could do is keep on running and try to keep one step ahead for as long as possible, try and go where those looming black eyes couldn't follow them. Hard. Very hard indeed. Ever since Coppinger had arose, over a million new pieces of surveillance equipment had been installed across each kingdom. Cosmin Catarzi had called it a brilliant piece of acumen, at the time, pointing to how they'd be able to have eyes on all manner of new places and react accordingly. Nobody would be able to get away with whatever heinous deeds they had planned, any hint of Coppinger sympathy and they'd be swept up in a manner of violence.

Pete had thought it a huge waste of time. He'd not heard anything about any Coppinger sympathiser being caught on videocam, even with the restricted media at the academy. Any sort of triumph for the system was a triumph for Unisco, those they had heard about. He'd supposed at the time that it had been meant to build their moral, foster a spirit, make them feel a part of this great machine. It had worked at the time as well, he'd felt a sense of pride at that revelation. A moment of togetherness he'd never had before. They were all in it at the same time, they'd win as an organisation or they'd go down fighting in the same way.

"Theo," he said, jerking his head towards the videocam. "They're watching us."

"Don't point, it draws attention to us."

"Yeah, I know! I was in the same class as you. Pointing at the cams is a big no-no." Pete felt a rush of irritation rub through him. he didn't need Theo stating the obvious to him. He wasn't stupid, he'd been listening and if it had been good enough for his instructors, it should have been good enough for Theo.

"Just saying!" Now it was his turn to sound aggrieved, like Pete was in the wrong, he fought the urge to poke him in the back of the head. That wouldn't solve anything, worst case it might bring a reaction of violence and throwing down for a brawl here would be about the dumbest thing they could do.

"Just get on a train," Pete said, glancing around. He couldn't see anyone heading for them, anyone pulling blasters. His neck was twitching back and forth, and he knew he was involuntarily doing the thing they'd warned them against in the academy, trying to look in every direction at once. It wasn't possible, all it achieved was to make the observer look suspicious and to give one a sore neck. Better to keep your head still, the lecturer had said, glance about only when you need to. Sparingly. Less was more. "Any train."

"You don't give the orders here," Theo murmured, looking around at him. "Remember. Partnership."

"Long as you do first," Pete shot back. "Do that and we're fine and dandy."

The corner of Theo's mouth twisted up in a scowl of displeasure. He looked like he didn't appreciate what he'd heard, had chosen to ignore it. "I'm doing this for me, Jacobs," he said. "If I help you out along the way, that's just a coincidence that I'll just have to live with. See if you can keep up with me."

"Oh I'll do more than keep up," Pete said. He saw a mag-rail carriage stood nearby, people already boarding it, he glanced at the readout above it to check for its destination, saw it as Chipaox Square. Huh, he thought. That would mean that they were in Shawzang, if he'd made his guess right. He'd never been here, but the city was legendary as a bastion of prosperity in Burykia. One of those cities where the wealthy got wealthier every day and even the beggars were a little more affluent than their counterparts elsewhere, a social ladder everyone sought to climb, and nobody desired to slip down. When Scott and Jess had come to vacation in Burykia like a year ago, he vaguely remembered they'd come here, at least he thought so. He wasn't sure. He didn't care. Those two were long away from each other now. Probably for the better.

They'd slipped onto the mag-rail, flashed their tickets and moved between the throngs of people, looking for a spot out of view of any videocams. Last thing they wanted was to get into a fight in a place like this. Too many innocent bystanders, too many potential have-a-go heroes who might interfere and no easily accessible escape route. Once it started to move, it'd be a difficult thing to get out of it. There was the emergency stop cable, but it didn't change the fact that once the magnetic rails were engaged, the carriages could float dozens of feet above the ground across a pre-determined track. Jumping out would be suicide, they'd hit the ground hard, both their airloop's already damaged beyond repair and useless in saving them.

Neither of them chose to look at the other, Theo purposely staring out the window, Pete choosing to focus on the shapely legs of a nearby commuter, he watched her sit studying a data pad, one smooth limb crossed over the other, her heeled shoe almost dangling from the tops of her toes.

He'd long ago decided there must be something in the water that helped make Burykian women that way, at least from the east side of it. They tended to have paler skin than those from the west of the kingdom, the people of Western Burykia were almost as dark as the average Vazaran, albeit dark brown rather than ebony. The women from the east tended to be physically lovely, he'd found, often sensual faces and understated bodies that hinted at so much and rarely disappointed when the clothes came off. His solitary experience with a Burykian whore had been one of the highlights of his sexual life, a list not the length he'd like it to be but otherwise he couldn't complain. He'd never told anyone he'd had a go with a whore from each kingdom, not even Scott. For an oblivious egomaniac with a barely deserved sense of accomplishment at times, Scott had remarkable success with the ladies. From Jesseka Blake who hadn't been bad looking and decent between the sheets, but what she'd had in appearance had been marred by her truly atrocious personality, to Mia Arnholt, Pete had often wondered what Scott had going for him that he hadn't.

"Can you stare at that woman any harder?" Theo muttered in his ear, jerking him from his reverie. He hadn't been aware it was noticeable, quickly realised she'd put both feet flat on the floor and was glaring at him with stern intent in her eye. She might be a schoolteacher with a look like that, he thought. He'd seen a look like that in the eyes of an educator before.

"Jeez, what's not worth staying at?" Pete asked.

"You're drawing attention to us," Theo growled. "She's going to remember what you look like."

"Yeah, she is," Pete grinned at him. He quickly let it fade as he saw the angry expression flashing across the scrawny features. Oh yeah. Right. He wasn't with Scott anymore. Scott would have found it exasperatingly funny, would have laughed even as he'd shook his head in disbelief. That sense of kinship wasn't there between him and Theo, he doubted it ever would be. He'd thought it before, but he couldn't work out what motivated him to do what he'd do. He didn't appear to have any hint of fun or joy in him, he didn't appear to like women, he didn't drink. What did Theo do? Pete knew he was a spirit caller, a pretty good one given his performance in the Quin-C, he might even have beaten down Scott in the final if the bout had gone on another five minutes. Talking to him about spirit calling felt a little too obvious, beyond the joining of Unisco, it was the one thing they had in common. But how to phrase it? He doubted Theo would want to share techniques with him, there weren't any bouts on to talk about, not that they'd have seen any.

"Get off the first stop we come to," Theo said. "That's the plan. You get off then, I get off at the next one and we meet somewhere in the middle." Pete saw him looking up, followed his gaze towards the map stencilled on the ceiling. This part of Shawzang was like a rat's warren, a maze of streets and roads, alleys and back streets that looked like a bowl of flaccid spaghetti had been mashed across the ceiling. Looking at it hurt his eyes, made him want to cover them, walk away and work it out for himself. Theo didn't appear too bothered by the way it had been designed, ran his eyes across every inch of the map, studied each contour and line before nodding his approval.

"I see it now," he said. "We'll meet there, right in the middle. Akata Road, we'll find a place to shack up. If you can lift a wallet, do it and get us some food. We'll need supplies and better someone else pays for it."

"You're loving this, aren't you?" Pete said. "We're supposed to uphold the law, you know? Making sure people don't do what you're planning on having us doing so we can survive."

"I take no pleasure in being hunted like an animal," Theo said. "If you can't do what you must to survive, then you don't deserve life. Let it be granted to those who will fight for it. Wasn't that what Gilgarus said long ago?"

"Probably. I don't do scripture." Privately, Pete hadn't expected Theo to either, the surprise in his voice had been genuine.

"And these aren't normal circumstances, Jacobs. They're hunting us. We won't graduate unless we get a great score in here. I think we're doing this the best way we can, you know." His tone of voice told Pete that he wasn't happy at having to explain himself, he fought the urge to fold his arm and fix a pointed gaze on him. "Just listen to me, damnit! We can do this if we follow my plan!"

"You came up with a plan like this in all of two minutes!" Pete exclaimed. People around them were starting to look at them now, he found quickly he could care less. They didn't matter to him. He wouldn't likely see any of them again, realised all too late they might know him, but he couldn't help that. Maybe they didn't speak the same language. Burykia was a proud kingdom and they liked their dialects. They wouldn't speak anything else unless they had to, foreigners be damned. "Excuse me if I don't hold a massive amount of faith in your scheme."

"Jacobs, I've been planning things like this for years! Trust me on that, I know what I'm doing."

"How though?" Pete asked. "Come on, Theo, talk to me. You're asking me to go a lot on trust."

"I'm what?"

"You're asking me to trust you and you're giving me no reason why I should. I mean, what have you really done recently other than hit me with that bowl. It's not exactly the foundation for a good relationship."

"I only hit you with it because you wouldn't leave stuff well alone!" Theo hissed. "I'm not your buddy, I'm your partner and not by choice. I had you thrust upon me like a giant hairless cock and I'll be happy once I never see you again. You want me to trust you? I don't even know who you are, Jacobs."

"We might be spending a lot of time together very soon," Pete said. "I get the feeling we'll be finding out all about each other before long."

Theo made a face. "Divines, I hope not."

A little hurtful, Pete thought, but as his mother had always said, it was impossible to change people who didn't want to be change. Redemption was possible, but you had to work for it and it wasn't always something that people were willing to put in. He'd long since arrived at the conclusion talking about change was easier than making it truly happen.

"Okay, we'll go with your plan," he said. "Seeing as you seem determined to make sure it happens, and you've put all this apparent effort in it." Making air quotes with his fingers would probably have earned him a smack in the mouth the way Theo was looking at him and he couldn't be bothered with the confrontation. Up in the distance, the first stop was coming up, his according to Theo's master plan and he needed to get out of it. "We'll do it then. I'll see you on Akata Road."

"Make sure you don't be late," Theo said. "Don't disappoint me with this, Jacobs."

"Never underestimate John Cyris. The man's like a rat, he might have gone silent since we pardoned him, but don't automatically think he's given up. Wouldn't surprise me to hear he's up to something naughty even as we speak."

Terrence Arnholt in private conversation with high-ranking Unisco officials.

The cool air hit him like a breeze as he stepped out of the carriage amidst the dozens of commuters who worked nearby, he took a moment to relish it, pulled the collar of his jacket around his ears. If there'd been videocams at the main station, there could well be some here, though it wasn't a certainty, he didn't like the idea of taking a chance. Maybe the collar around his ears would give him enough of a cover for them to miss him. Maybe.

He glanced back into the carriage as the doors slid shut behind him with a swooshing sound, saw Theo slide into a seat, legs sprawled out in front of him, hands in his pockets. Their eyes briefly met, he saw the faintest hint of a curl of the lips, a barely imperceptible nod and then the mag-rail train tore away into the distance, following the track of magnets on its path across the city.

For a few long moments, he watched it vanish into the distance, eventually moving out of sight around a corner and out of his mind. Pete turned, slumping his body a little to make himself less noticeable with his height and wandered off towards Akata Road. He wondered how this was going to turn out, realised he genuinely didn't know and that terrified him. How much time had passed while he'd been scared that when it came to this moment, he'd be out of his depth and would fall flat on his face. When you start anything new, the end always felt like such a long way away, it was almost an impossible task to comprehend. Yet here he was. Here they both were.

He'd been wrong, so very wrong, and it felt painful. Mag-rail stations out in the city were built high up to avoid the space that would have been monopolised by stations on the ground, instead they'd been erected atop poles by which the only point of access was a spiral staircase winding around it all the way between top and bottom. Normally, he'd have avoided it like the plague. Not a chance the old Peter Jacobs would have gone in there. Now though, he felt empowered and given the shit going on in recent months, the beatings and the bullying at the academy, it looked like a piece of piss. Plus, he noticed, it was sealed inside a wire cage, so any misstep wouldn't send him tumbling over the edge like yesterday's rags. No, he'd be fine. He'd get

304

down there, he'd made his way to Akata Road and he'd try and get Theo to admit he was making it up as he went along.

Not that he needed that, not really, he just wanted to see that stubborn confidence take a bit of a knock. Theobald Jameson had a world class ability to rub anyone up the wrong way, he didn't know if it came naturally to him or if it were something he'd had to work to develop. Either way, it was a scary thought of him working to develop that level of abrasiveness.

Pete reached the bottom of the stairs, privately glad his descent was complete, anything to mask his thoughts of it as he'd taken them. It wasn't that he didn't like heights, more the spiral was one hells of a head trip, walking down it was like twisting into a rainbow abyss, all the sights and sounds of the city swirling around him as he took the steps one at a time. He didn't normally, always he'd be a two or three at a time sort of guy, here he couldn't take the chance. Shawzang had seen rain in the last few days, losing his footing might be, if not fatal, then exceptionally embarrassing should anyone catch it on videocam. He didn't want his reputation ruined before he'd even started.

Okay. Akata Road. He remembered from the map he needed to go west as he hit the ground, he turned left, still hunching his shoulders up, forcing the neck of his coat around his ears, hands crammed into his pockets. Look like any other down and out, don't focus too heavily on me. He glanced back and forth, twitching his neck furiously on his shoulders as he tried to see if anyone was following him. Satisfied there was nobody he could see, he carried on walking, tried not to think about the ones that he couldn't see.

He was being ridiculous again. Fully trained agents might be able to follow him without being seen. Ones in training with the exact same education as him wouldn't. There'd be some hint. Of course, if he'd had more counter-surveillance training, he might find it easier to spot them. Admonishing himself came easy, he couldn't help but think of all the things that might have been.

Theo had mentioned to get supplies, he remembered, not that he had any credits to do it with right now. That hadn't stopped them before, they'd still be working out how to get on the mag-rail if it had been left up to him. Theo had gotten them through it then, all it had taken was a little light-fingered action. Too bad he didn't know how to do it.

Didn't meant that he couldn't learn to understand the theory behind it. Because the two really are the same thing, he thought to himself sarcastically. Knowing how something should theoretically be done and how it's really done are two entirely different things. Just because you know something should work, doesn't mean that it will.

What had he seen Theo do? A large crowd, people jostling each other so a casual bump didn't look out of place. When there were so many of them about, it was only natural and not everyone who walked into you wanted to lift a wallet. Some people would be on their guard, others wouldn't. They'd be so preoccupied with going about their day they wouldn't expect it to happen to them.

That had to be the second step. Pick a target, someone who looks like they've got plenty and won't miss anything beyond the inconvenience. Someone distracted. Someone careless. Someone busy.

Who though? People were few and far between here, easier back up on the platform for there had been many options there. When they were getting ready to travel, the concentration of the average person always lulled, in Pete's personal experience. Everything else was forgotten and all thoughts went to the imminent journey.

Screw it!

That thought came to him violently, he rejected the notion of what he was thinking about almost immediately. What the hells was he thinking? He wasn't a pickpocket, he didn't know the first thing about it and therefore should leave it to the professionals. Disgust contorting his face, he picked up his pace, Akata Road the first thought in his mind. More than that, he was finding it easier to make it the only thought in his mind. He didn't want to consider anything else, just getting there, meeting up with Theo and they could take it from there.

The further he got from the mag-rail station, the faster he picked up his pace, in short order he'd moved into a jog, stopping just short of a flat-out run. That would draw attention, not that anyone was looking around here. This area looked like the sort where people didn't put up videocams in case they were stolen and stripped for parts. Trust Theo to pick an area like this. Just went to prove even the most gleaming of metropolises could have their dingy bits, the parts people chose not to see unless they wanted to. This area lacked some of the gleam and polish of the others, a hint of grime shining through it. A young man running through here wouldn't draw attention, it'd be considered the norm. He wondered what Akata Road looked like, a question answered in short order as he turned the corner and saw the sign. He came to a halt, looked up at it. The main wording was in a local dialect, something that he couldn't read, but the translation underneath he could. They might like their local languages, but they were at least helpful to those that didn't speak them. Not every place Pete had ever been could say that. It was the places in Serran that were the worst, he'd always found, they were way more insular than they needed to be. Plenty of places there, people would like to vacation, only to be put off by stroppy locals who'd take your credits and then set fire to you cheerfully.

Theo was sat waiting for him on a wall, a look of impatience emblazoned across his face, arms folded. That was the one thing you could say about him; his face was never hard to read when he was angry or upset. All the other times, you had no chance.

"Took you so long?" he asked. A bag sat at his feet, a bland generic convenience store logo emblazoned across it. Pete tilted his head, tried to read what it said. That he couldn't meant nothing, images and branding were far more important than words. He recognised that he should know what it said, even if he couldn't read the language. Food and water, the things they'd need to survive. If they could lie low somewhere, they'd be fine. The less they exposed themselves to the public, the less chance they had of being caught on a videocam, the less chance of them being tracked down by those hunting them.

"Well there's just so much to see," he said. He made the choice right then he wasn't going to take much more shit from Theo. They were partners in this, they failed, or they succeeded together. It wasn't 'Theo does all the work and Pete just tags along for the ride,' he was determined to bring his own skills to the table. Cutting the crap out before it became an issue might just be one of those things. "I mean, this is one of the highest rated cities in Burykia and how many other chances am I going to get to run for my future through it?"

Theo gave him a disgusted look. "At least try and take this seriously, Jacobs. We've got a lot of work to do if we want to even have a hope of success and you're treating this like some sort of massive joke. Where's the supply run I sent you on?"

"You don't own me, I'm not your bloody servant. I'm your partner. You show me how to lift someone's wallet and I'll do it. I'm not about to jeopardise everything by getting into a scuffle that I don't have to when I don't have the skills."

"We all have the skills, Jacobs. We just need to know how to put them into play. You need to know how to think like a criminal to do, well this." He threw an arm out. "You think Unisco agents just happen overnight? I don't. I think they're forged in times like this. I think it's another circumstance like the simulator. It's not about winning. It's about what you take from it."

"Are we sure we're not in the simulator?" Pete asked, the thought striking him. The pain that shot through his face as Theo popped him on the jaw rapidly answered that question.

"Yeah, I'm sure we're not in the simulator," Theo said, rubbing his knuckles.

"Oww! Bitch!" Pete favoured his jaw, wondered if punching Theo in retaliation would improve his mood. He desisted. Just. If he was going to make a go of this, he'd occasionally have to work with people he didn't like. They'd really thought through every aspect of this. Nobody ever had a one hundred percent ideal relationship with everyone they ever had to work with. Given the problems the two of them had had, it was clearly deliberate. Force them to work together, learn the value of teamwork... A children's entertainment network could have written the script and put it on the air.

"Yep. Don't ask stupid questions." Theo jerked his head up the road. "Come on, this way. I've got an idea."

"Do I really want to know what sort of shit you're going to get us both into with this?" Pete asked, watching the smaller man turn to stride away.

"You can stand here moaning or you can follow me. If you want to do the former, tell me now because I don't want to fail this because you wanted to find every excuse under the sun to fail."

"I don't want to fail!" Pete almost snarled, kept the true venom he wanted to let rip in his words back. "I'm not going to fail. I just think we need a better plan than running around in circles."

"They always said to keep moving. The longer you stay in one place, it's easier for you to be discovered."

"Yes, and the more we move about, the more chance we've got of being seen. We need to hole up some place where there's no videocams. Some place private. It's easy to track us if they can spot us every time we walk in front of one of their eyes."

"That's why we're staying here," Theo said. "This area is a lot less gentrified. They don't like to acknowledge places like it exist. They're blind spots in the city surveillance network. You can get up to a lot of trouble in a place like this and they're none the wiser."

He shot him a sullen grin, the sort of expression that'd make someone who didn't know him question what was going on inside that head. "Besides, I know what they said in the lectures. Who says I am just wandering aimlessly? That's your thought, not my plan."

That took him aback, he hadn't expected that. His face must have gone red, Theo laughed. It wasn't a sound he was used to hearing, harsh like the sound was scraping against sandpaper in his throat. "Surprised?"

"Yeah, a little," Pete said. "It's just, you've got to give me something, man. A little trust goes a long way."

"Trust is earned, not given. You see if you can keep up with me and then maybe we'll see where we end up."

He couldn't argue with that. He didn't like it, but he wasn't able to call him on it. "Where are we going?"

"There's a few old apartment blocks around the corner, I don't know what they call them in the local tongue, but they're the sort of place you go if you don't want to be found."

"Isn't that the first place you'd think they'd look for us though?" He felt his own logic was sound, saw the glare at him and felt the satisfaction stab at him, quick jabs in the gut but satisfaction regardless. "And how do you know so much about this city?"

Theo glanced back at him, shrugged his shoulders uneasily. He looked like a man who didn't want to answer the question posed to him. "Not my first time here. Not by a long way, okay?"

Huh. That answered absolutely nothing. Most people who came to this city didn't end up in places like this, not unless they were up to something they shouldn't be. The sort of people doing things not entirely... Oh! Things clicked into place, he looked at Theo and nodded.

"Okay. Okay, I follow you. Lead on. Show me the way. We'll lay low there a bit. Can't hurt, can it?"

"I'd certainly hope not," Theo said. "Maybe they're not there any longer, it's been at least ten years."

"And you remember it?"

"Kind of hard to forget it really." He didn't say anything else on the subject, Pete wanted to press but decided to let it drop. No point pissing his partner off unnecessarily. He clearly didn't want to talk about it and sometimes you needed to respect boundaries, let them work it out by themselves until they were ready to reveal. Everyone had a time and a place in which they felt comfortable. Forcing them to do otherwise only built resentment and there was enough between them so far without letting more build up.

"Okay," he said again. "Show me the place." He looked around, saw the roads abandoned, a speeder crashed into a garden ahead, only the back half visible, its inner workings exposed where the locals had stripped away everything they could. The house next to it looked abandoned, the windows papered over with months old newspaper. If someone lived there, they were keeping quiet about it. None of the homes up the road were in mint condition, he'd not noticed it at first but now he had the chance, he was starting to realise Theo was right. This area was the sort people would rather didn't exist.

Strangely enough, he found that he wasn't overly concerned with safety. They'd had six months of training, both self-defence and offence, unless a gang of locals came at them with blasters, between him and Theo they'd probably have a chance of not winding up in the nearest hospital. He hadn't even seen anyone since he'd come away from the good streets, the mag-rail high above them both. He wondered if people were looking down on the area and curious as to the how and the why, the whom and the what were down here. From so high up, it was hard to imagine what happened down this low.

That said, he hadn't seen anyone. Glancing around, he felt like they were being watched, eyes everywhere following them. That couldn't be good. People only watched when they couldn't interact, snooped because they couldn't confront. Idly, he wondered how many unlicensed blasters were floating about in this area and his armed mugger theory suddenly didn't seem so farfetched.

The apartment block was everything he'd expected it to be, and not in a good way either. Calling it rundown was giving it too much credit, it looked like the building time had forgotten about, hadn't been touched since it was built while the world around it had crawled on.

"Doesn't look like much," Theo said. There was almost a hint of pride in his voice as he looked skywards to the tower block. "But there's a room up on the top floor owned by someone who doesn't come here anymore." That pride faded in an instant. "He's above it now. Doesn't mean that he's not a sentimental old fool who likes his memories of the past."

"You're talking about your father, aren't you?" Pete said gently.

Theo said nothing, pursed his lips and folded his arms in front of him, hugging himself. "Let's see if the door code still works."

He was amazed to hear the door had a code lock, was less surprised to see that the box in question had been ripped out, only a few stray wires left dangling down impotently to show their sadness at being left alone. The door itself swung open lazily on its hinges, creaking as it failed to shut. "Guess we don't need it," Pete said. "Looks like the people around here are a destructive bunch of bastards."

He didn't say it to infuriate whoever might be listening, more stating a fact as he saw it. Anyone who could leave something in that sort of state was missing a few screws in the head. Senseless destruction wasn't good for anyone, it hurt everyone in some small way. The door did look like it might have been moderately secure under other standards, thick metal driving it back and forth under its own weight, now though it offered as much protection as a condom on a knife.

"Yeah but what better deterrent than a hundred possibly armed criminals between here and where we're going," Theo said. Again, almost a grin that managed to mutate into a scowl before it fully developed ghosted across his face. "Anyone would struggle getting through that."

"I'm worried we might struggle getting through that, fuck anyone else," Pete said. "We don't exactly fit in around here, do we?"

"We're on the run from Unisco with nobody to turn to. I think we fit in just fine," Theo said. He cracked his knuckles, pushed the door open. "Come on, where's your sense of adventure?"

"I think I left it at the door."

"This is why they don't want you in the field," Theo said, Pete couldn't miss the sneer in his voice. "Inquisitors play it safe."

"Yeah, they really don't," Pete said. "I'm not sure walking into a place like this is the smartest play we could make."

"It's not the smartest play we've got, it's the only play we have," Theo said. "Trust me, nobody knows about this safehouse. Even that bastard I've got for a father forgot about it long ago. We hide out here and play the game to the finish."

"This isn't a game, Theo!"

"That's exactly what it is," Theo said, giving him a cold smile. "It's a game you play to win, or you might as well go home. What's the point in not winning? And don't give me that shit about taking part."

"I think that's the most words I've ever heard you use at one time."

"Better to use too few than too many, Jacobs."

Pete rolled his eyes at the back of Theo's head, wondered if they'd fail the test if he shoved him down the stairs. Why wasn't he surprised to see the elevators out of action, he thought as they ascended the building, one flight of steps after another. Any notion the Unisco life was a glamorous one had long since been knocked out of him, but this felt like a fresh new level of grime and squalor. Graffiti stained the walls, weirdly in a language he could understand. Someone had spray-painted the words 'She Will Come' across the stairs, multicoloured, multi-sized letters, uneven words left wonky by an unsteady hand. Some of them had been underlined, a thick black smudge emphasising the message. He wondered who She was meant to be. Coppinger, perhaps? That was paranoia moving to an entire new level. When the people in a place like this were throwing up tribute, it made things unsettling to say the least.

Final flight of stairs, the top floor and if there'd been a carpet here, it had been stolen long ago. There were things on the bare ground he couldn't even start to describe, wasn't sure what they were or what they'd been at their conception. So much had been ground into the stone that he couldn't tell where the stains started and ended, a myriad patchwork of colours and crusts that made distressing sounds beneath his boots.

"Apartment five-twenty," Theo said. "The last door on the left."

"You remember that after all this time?" Pete asked. His partner craned his head around, gave him a sour look.

"Clearly."

"Really? I can't remember stuff like that. I struggle with what I had for dinner a few nights back."

"Every time you open your mouth, you surprise me less and less. I'm amazed you've lasted the six months to this point."

Asshole. He pushed the ire back down. He knew what he was like by this point, he could suffer through it a little longer. Where Theo had developed the superiority complex in his life, he didn't know but it had been a trip they all could have done without him taking.

"I know where my father kept a lot of his safehouses across the kingdoms," Theo added. "Not going to forget those, if it sounds like I'm bragging."

"Yeah, because it's really the sort of thing that normal people brag about."

"I paid the price for this knowledge, Jacobs. He used to make me lead him to them, fastest possible route. I got the address wrong or took too long, I'd get a whack round the head."

"Divines, that's awful!" Pete meant it as well. As much of an abrasive asshole as Theo could be, he didn't deserve that. More to the point, it explained much if that was the sort of parenting he'd received throughout his life.

His partner's face flushed red as he heard the words, like he hadn't expected and wasn't comfortable with it either. He scowled, shrugged his shoulders like he'd said too much. "Was a long damn time ago."

Something had started to slip through Pete's head as he saw the door in question, apartment five-twenty, he saw the mat on the floor in front of it, watched as Theo bent over, pulled it aside. The glint of metal underneath caught his eye, he nodded to himself as his partner picked the key up and slid it into the lock.

"Nobody here'll touch it," he said. "Buildings like this have long memories. There's always someone here who'll speak for the rest of them, a nominative leader. They don't have much power, but they'll make sure certain rules get followed. One of them is don't fuck with John Cyris' rooms and you'll not have your legs broken."

"Nice to have that sort of power."

"Only if it's not being directed against you," Theo said, turning the key. He threw the door open, the light burst out and Pete wondered if the lights were meant to be on. The second thought that struck him was the immediate realisation upon entry they weren't alone in the apartment.

It had a lived-in look, he had to give it that. A home-like vibe he hadn't experienced in a while since leaving home. Most temporary residences didn't have anything like it. People came, and they went, they didn't have the chance to leave their mark. Probably for the best. Nobody wanted to live in a place that felt like it still belonged to someone else.

Three men and a woman stood towards the back of the room, four pairs of eyes on him and Theo immediately, an extra pair of black eyes coming up out of coats as blasters were levelled at them. Neither Cyris nor the woman went for weapons, the men with them were the ones holding them. If he had to make a guess, they looked like bodyguards, maybe hired muscle, big men cut from a similar cloth, shaven heads, beardless and youthful muscle not quite run to fat yet but were fighting a losing battle with time. Cyris, he recognised from the news.

"Close the door," one of them said. Pete thought about running, wondered about it for all of a second before deciding against it. He wasn't the greatest of runners, far from the worst but he wasn't faster than a blaster bolt. These two men looked like killers, like they wouldn't hesitate if a choice was to be made.

"Close it," Theo muttered out the corner of his mouth. "Don't fuck around here."

Pete nodded, turned, was halted by a cough from muscle stood closer to the woman than Cyris. "Slowly, asshat!"

"Theobald?" Cyris asked, surprise in his voice. "What are you doing here, son?"

He could see Theo bristle at the endearment. "Don't call me son," he muttered, pulling his jacket tighter around his body.

"Fine. Where's your girlfriend, my boy?"

Seeing someone else aggravate Theo might have been the highlight of his week, the way his partner looked like he wanted to leap on him was priceless. The cost was too high, it had kept him stationary for the time being.

"Somewhere else," Theo growled. "What are you doing here?"

"Bit of business. I could ask you the same question, lad." The smile on Cyris' face lacked anything approaching fatherly warmth, it held suspicion and anger, the expression of a surprised enemy. "You'll have to excuse me, Madame Tao, but…"

The woman had risen to her feet, Pete took her in for the first time. Burykian, small of stature but undeniably lovely, there was a certain sense of agelessness about her that brought about a great deal of confusion in his heart. His first impressions of her was she'd barely left her teens, yet he looked closer at her, narrowed his eyes to study here and he wasn't entirely sure that he liked what he saw. Her eyes hinted at her true age, they juxtaposed between wisdom and cruelty. Not a woman he'd like to get to know better, her hands curled like claws across her knees.

"Son?" she asked, studying Theo. "You know, the family resemblance I do see."

Theo didn't blink. "People always said I took after my mother."

"Yes," Madame Tao said. "They would."

If things had been priceless before, the shock that flashed across Theo's face like he'd been punched was beyond that, truly a treasure beyond measure. Pete guessed it was some sort of measured insult, something designed hardily to get at him.

"Gentlemen, please have a seat," Cyris said. "Step away from the door, our business is just about concluded here."

"Mister Cyris," Madame Tao said, a warning tone in her voice. "I don't know what these two men have seen or heard, but…"

"Nothing!" Pete piped up. "We heard nothing. Just wandered in here entirely by mistake."

She gave him a withering look. "I doubt that. Nothing happens by chance in this world. You had a plan to come here and I want to know why."

"Looking for a place to crash for a bit," Theo said. "Didn't know anyone was here. Used to come here with him when I was a kid all the time." He pointed at Cyris. "Usually for meetings not a million miles away from what this looks like."

Pete winced, wished he hadn't added that part. Tao's expression moved from thinly veiled anger to outright outrage. "Search them," she said, gesturing her head towards her goon. "Make sure this isn't more than it appears."

"Does our upbringing affect who we are? Nay, more than that, does it affect who we become? These two competitors, they couldn't have had more drastic early lives. Matthew Arnholt has a paragon as a father. Theobald Jameson has a complete bastard. Now, if your life was to depend on one of these two fighting for it, who would you pick? Circumstances shape us, they affect the world around us. We can no more fight against them than we can nature herself."

Professor David Fleck about the same time Theobald Jameson fought Matthew Arnholt in the Quin-C, six months ago.

It hadn't taken them long to discover the Unisco logos on the backs of their shirts, Pete had tried to brace himself for it, had found his resistance broken as the first punch had driven him to the ground, pain shooting through his body, legs no longer able to hold him up. Theo had seen the same treatment, he was sure he'd seen a look of consternation across Cyris' face as his son hit the ground.

Fuck though, the muscle was huge, he'd felt every ounce of weight driven into his kidneys, wasn't even sure he could move to muster a resistance as he felt huge fingers grab his arm, yank him towards the middle of the room, he could hear Theo moaning too.

"There's no need for this, Madame Tao," Cyris said. "I'll deal with it. My problem after all."

It was his turn to receive a withering look, she folded her arms, tapped her foot on the floor for a few seconds as she looked him up and down. "You invited me here to make a deal," she said. "You assured me that nobody knew about this place."

"Nobody does know about this place. Unisco certainly doesn't."

She gestured violently towards the two of them, Pete saw a manicured nail driven in their direction. "There's two of them on the floor and you're trying to tell me something entirely inconsistent with that fact."

"My son has always had a somewhat rebellious nature within him. Now that, he does get from his mother," Cyris said. If he was perturbed by her reaction, he didn't show it. "You can only try to beat it out of them so many times, especially in these days. People get so very upset when your son shows up with bruises."

"I don't want excuses, Cyris. I don't care if he is your son. I want this problem dealt with or our arrangement cannot take place."

Theo stuck his head up, spat blood out onto the floor with a rasping sound that might have been a laugh. "So much for going straight, old man. A full pardon for everything and you jump straight back into dealing with people like her."

His response was a boot to the stomach, cutting off his words violently, his body wracked with choking. Still he tried to laugh, his face contorted with pain as he shuddered. Pete had always guessed he was a little crazy, this was downright unsettling.

"People like me," Madame Tao said, a lilting laugh seeding her words. "Maybe he doesn't know what's going on here."

"It wouldn't be the first time," Cyris said. "My son often thinks he knows more than he truly does. He never quite seemed to grasp the concept ignorance and bliss are twin sides of an identical credit."

"Fuck you, dad," Theo groaned. "I got tired of hearing your voice a long time ago and it's not improved with age."

"Think those beatings never took hold," Madame Tao said. "Discipline and punishment, Mister Cyris, discipline and punishment. Two things missing from today's youths."

"He always did like to rebel," Cyris said. "Joining Unisco though…" He looked at the Burykian woman. "I'll deal with this. You and your man, leave. It won't come back on you. Nobody will ever see them alive again. Him or Jacobs."

Huh… Cyris knew who he was. That wasn't particularly reassuring. He had a famous face and they hadn't fitted him for one of those Unisco facial implants yet. Mufflers or whatever they called them. He'd been looking forward to that, he'd had this wild thought about using one to screw with Scott next time he saw him. All manner of mischief could be gotten up to with one. Mess with immediate memories, screw with videocams, he'd looked forward to it all. Somehow, he got the feeling they'd walked into the end of their brief Unisco careers right now. All because he'd listened to Theo.

"I'd like to believe that, Mister Cyris. I really would. Never trust a man to turn on his own blood," she said. "That bond is not so easily broken, bent yes, strained absolutely. Broken though is difficult."

"You've seen what my relationship with him is like," Cyris said. He looked to his own goon. "Rodolfo, restrain them both. Make sure they can't get away." The portable mountain stood next to him walked towards them, boots thundering against the floor, Pete tried to get up, fresh waves of pain washing through him. He rose partway, collapsed in agony. Tao's own bodyguard had done a number on him.

He didn't know where they'd pulled the rope from, but being lashed to a chair wasn't pleasant, he'd tried to break free and received a backhander for his trouble. "Less of it!" Rodolfo had barked, his voice lighter than Pete had expected for someone so big. Behind him, he could see Theo was in the same predicament, could see him out the corner of his eye.

They'd planned badly. He'd hoped and hoped they'd be able to survive this test, now he just wanted to live through this. They'd hidden here, out of the way of those hunting them and they'd never find them. The irony wasn't lost on him.

"I try to be a father to him, he doesn't want to be my son. You cannot break what has never been whole to start with, Madame Tao," Cyris said. "As much as it pains me to admit it, perhaps the best thing to do is remove the black mark from my life, start over anew. This deal is important to me."

"Then prove it," she said. "These two are famous. I ever see them again, my people will be looking for you, Mister Cyris. Our compact will be broken. Kenzo Fojila never forgets. It never forgives betrayal. Your life will be forfeit. You'll die broken and alone, nobody will ever see you again, nobody will ever give you a second thought. Such is the nature of our vengeance where betrayal is concerned." She straightened herself up, nodded to her muscle who opened the door for her. "I'm choosing to test you here, John. You get one chance and one alone. Do not make the wrong choice."

Kenzo Fojila? The assassins? Everyone knew about them, the famed Burykian killers for whom much had been spoken but little truly confirmed. Most of the stuff came from the media, sensationalised for drama and entertainment but it didn't change the fact that they existed. Why would Cyris want assassins? He didn't know. He doubted it'd make much difference. Tao had been right, it was hard to shoot someone you were related to. Which'd mean he was probably going to die first.

They were alone, just the four of them, as the door closed behind them and the sound of Madame Tao's humming slowly faded down the corridor. Cyris shook his head, Pete was sure he could almost see a look of sorrow on his face. He had to be imagining it. If Cyris was anything like his son, he wasn't even sure he'd have emotion beyond extremely pissed off.

"Well, boys, you've put me in a rather unfortunate situation here," Cyris said. "Theobald, I never got the chance to congratulate you on your achievements at the Quin-C…"

"You can shove your congratulations where the sun won't touch them!" Theo said, the fury heavy in his voice. "I don't want them. If you're going to bloody kill us, get the fuck along with it so I don't have to listen to your self-agonising bullshit!"

"Theo," Pete said. His mouth felt sensitive, delicate even. Maybe the blows had knocked loose a few teeth. He ran his tongue across them, couldn't immediately feel anything. Maybe not. "You might be in a hurry to die, I'm not."

"There are worse things than death, Mister Jacobs," Cyris said. "A lot worse, believe me. Death is the end, pain is just the start. I think the manner of your death depends on my son, you know that?"

"Oh, fuck me!" Theo swore. "You're going to turn the chance to kill me into a fucking torture therapy session? What the hells is wrong with you?"

"That's what the hells is wrong with you, father," Cyris said, wagging his finger. "And less of the foul language, I didn't raise you to talk like that." Pete heard Theo exhale sharply, his breathing heavy and rapid. He was glad he couldn't see his face for he doubted it'd be a pleasant sight. "I never got the chance to tell you before how proud I was when I saw you last. Going to Carcaradis Island, it was clearly good for you. That girl, I never thought I'd see that side of you. The way she stood up to me for you, that was impressive. So much fire for one so tiny."

Theo said nothing. Pete was aware painfully of Rodolfo stood between them, too much weight of muscle and flesh for him to not be noticed.

"Answer me, boy!"

Still Theo said nothing, Pete saw Cyris nod at his goon and the fist swept out, caught him in the side. Pete bellowed in pain, thought he felt something snap, fire lanced through him. He hoped he'd imagined the snap, he'd never felt pain like that before.

"Your friend suffers for your insolence," Cyris said. "You know that. Neither of you die until you say what I want you to hear."

Theo laughed bitterly. "He's not my damn friend, just someone they forced me to work with. You want to whale on someone, might as well do it to me. Come on, father. Let your fucking ape at me. Maybe my screams will convince you I said what you want to hear."

It was Cyris' turn to laugh. "You know, boy, I never doubted that stubborn spirit in you. Should have guessed you'd pick that up. Your mother had it. I had it. You're worse than both of us. If I told you the sky was blue, you'd disagree with me just to be contrary. This isn't a game, Theobald. You defy me here and it will grant you a painful end. I don't have a choice in that matter. You've tipped my hand. Your only option is to make it as easy for both of us."

Pete snorted, sent fresh pain lancing through him. That had been a mistake. "You ever met your son? He's not going to make it easy, is he?"

318

"You know," Cyris said. "For someone who isn't your friend, Theobald, he seems to know you remarkably well. And he's right, I think it's unfortunate to say."

He nodded his head, Rodolfo's fist swept out again. The blow probably wasn't anywhere near as hard this time, little more than a slap to Pete's already injured side. It didn't need to be, even the slightest touch hurt like the blazes and he screamed in pain.

"As a son could go, you are the most stubbornly unhelpful fruit of my loins you could possibly be. Tell me what I want to hear."

Rodolfo hit him on the other side this time, Pete flinched, tried to twist his body away, only brought fresh new sensations of agony through himself, pained whimpers slipped from his mouth and he hated himself for it.

"Interesting thing about Mister Rodolfo right there. Good muscle is hard to find. Almost all my people are gone. Silas, he died. Jenghis, she died. Mara, well I don't know. She's lost to me forever now."

Pete heard the crack of laughter break from Theo, pure mirth undiluted by the seriousness of the moment. Cyris' face furrowed, a look of bemusement and then he lashed out himself, cracked his son across the jaw.

"What's so funny, son?"

Theo spat, Pete heard something slap harsh against the ground and another growl of laughter. "Wouldn't be funny if I told you, would it? Dad." The last word came out almost mocking.

"As I was saying about Mister Rodolfo. He has a vested interest in preservation, mine, and pain, yours. Claudia Coppinger set a standard, you see. Apparently, nobody takes you seriously unless you've got three hundred pounds of psychotic muscle at your beck and call."

"Nobody takes you seriously anyway," Theo growled. "Not anymore. You used to be a big fish and look at you now. You're hiding in this shithole apartment, you're not a grand figure any longer. People got you worked out, sussed you're a fucking coward!"

"Nobody has me worked out, Theobald. Not the people out there, not Unisco and certainly not you. You don't know me half as well as you think you'd like to." He smiled coolly at his son. "And I'm certainly not a coward. I prefer opportunist."

"I've known you most of my life and I've got no damn interest in extending it. What do you think that says about you?"

"That I've got an ungrateful little bastard for a son. Should have drowned you at birth." The words were laced with venom, Pete heard, Cyris almost hissing like a kettle now. "I would have done. I wanted an heir, someone to take my place when I passed but the Divines gave me you. No, your mother gave me you."

"Don't talk about her. She was worth fifty of you."

"Your mother never told you the truth about herself, did she?" Cyris hadn't let up on the venom, now he laughed. "She told me. She told me a lot, more than I wanted to know. I think I was happier not knowing. Made so much sense in the way you turned out. You could have been grand, but you chose to be mundane."

"What're you talking about, you crazy bastard?" Pete had to concur on that, even in his pain fogged state. Cyris sounded like he was rambling, the only thing missing was wild eyes and flecks of drool slipping his mouth. The old man didn't answer, flung out a fist and clocked his son again, Pete saw Theo's head snap to the side, rolling with the blow.

"Charlotte. I loved her. How do you think it feels to know the only woman you've ever had feelings for just saw you as a means to an end? As someone to take advantage of? You've never had that, Theobald because you're incapable of love. Just like her."

Theo snorted. "You know, I hoped you were going to tell me she'd had an affair and you're just some stranger to me."

"Mister Rodolfo?" Cyris said. "Hurt his friend considerably until he civilises his tongue. Despite what he wishes, he is still my son and I will not have him speak to me like that." Rodolfo looked down at him, grinned through cracked lips.

"No hard feelings," he said, looking Pete in the eyes. "Business, eh?"

"Get on with it if you're going to do it," Pete said, privately amazed by how much he sounded like Theo in that moment. "Don't apologise for it."

"Wasn't intending to," the big man said. The first blow hit him in the unguarded stomach. "I don't do that. Never have." Another one, Pete would have doubled over if the ropes hadn't held him upright. A third came raining down on him, followed by a fourth and a fifth, punches not thrown in flurries but carefully placed, considered and deliberate. Each shot landed close to his injured ribs, which if not broken had certainly been fractured. Every movement hurt, his mind all over the place. If he'd ever experienced worse pain, he couldn't remember it, it dominated every synapse of his brain, every feeling, every sense. He couldn't remember what it felt like not to experience absolute agony.

"Damnit, father!" Theo shouted. "What do you want me to say?!"

"You know what I want from you," Cyris said. Pete barely heard it, too busy trying not to throw up. His mouth tasted coppery, he'd bitten his tongue hard when that last blow had hit him. "What have I always wanted from you?"

Theo said nothing, Cyris coughed and the rain of punches died away, Rodolfo stepped back and caressed his knuckles. "I don't want to have to pay someone else to beat my own son, Theobald, but if your tongue doesn't loosen then that might be the case."

"Go for it," Theo said. "I'm through with you. Been through with you for a long time but you never seem to want to hear it. It's all you're going to get from me. I'm not going to give you a moment, not going to tell you I love you because I don't. If I outlive you, I'm going to piss on your grave."

"Man," Pete said, slurring his words through his injured tongue. "You two could make a therapist real rich, you know that? He could retire to Carcaradis Island and live out his days in luxury after trying to fix your relationship."

"That'd mean him spending his credits where they'd do some good, Jacobs," Theo said, scorn heavy in his voice. "And the thing about him is, he doesn't do that. He'll find some extravagance that does nobody any good at all. A monument to his ego. Because Divines fucking know, there's enough of it to sate him for the rest of his days without adding more."

"You give me too little credit, son," Cyris said. "I'd love to spare the both of your lives, but I can't. You're making it easy for me, I hate to say. Kenzo Fojila will kill me if I don't take care of you."

"And if you were any sort of father, you'd take that risk!" Theo spat, the anger rising in his voice. It'd been there for a while now, Pete had noticed, now it was threatening to bubble up and over.

"If you were any sort of son, I wouldn't hesitate. Neither of us have been perfect in our relationship Theobald so you can't point the blame at me in that regard. Maybe I'm responsible for how you've grown, but you're just as responsible for my own failings. A vicious cycle doomed to repeat forever, I fear. The sins of the past plough the inadequacies of the future, I'm afraid to say. I'd hope you'd understand but you're both young, you're only children after all."

Cyris reached into his coat, drew out a blaster and shook his head. "It'll be quick, I can give you that. One final gift from a father to a son."

"You're talking about killing me as a gift," Theo said. "Just consider that the next time you look in the mirror. You can't take it back. You kill me, and I hope it haunts you for the rest of your life. I hope you see me in the corner of your eye every time you look away. I hope you have nightmares in which the reality of what you're about to do sinks in. Just remember, I'll be gone but not forgotten."

"You really think you'd be my first ever kill, Theobald?"

"I don't doubt I wouldn't be. I think your crazy bitch killer friend was right. I think you'll struggle to pull the trigger on me. You think you're strong, but you've always been weak. You chose to raise hands to a boy who couldn't defend himself when he was growing up because it was the easiest available option. Why show him a better option when you could take out your frustrations on him? You think I know what you want me to say? I know what you're going to hear and you're not going to like it."

Pete saw the muscles holding the blaster twitch, saw Cyris' face go black with anger as he raised it and he decided to act, no matter how much it was going to hurt. Frantically he started to jostle away, trying to break the ropes, smash the chair, anything, legs rocking back and forth. A giant hand came down to him, Rodolfo shook his head. "Not going to happen, boy. You can't break that."

Behind him, Pete heard sounds of wood splintering, the snap of rope being torn apart, and he tried to turn his head to see what was happening, couldn't quite see. The shriek that broke from Theo was almost inhuman as he hurled himself at Cyris, pushing the levelled blaster aside. Cyris swore, tried to throw a punch, a blow Theo easily batted away with his forearm, no hesitation. He spun, threw a roundhouse kick into his stomach and Cyris went down. Rodolfo let Pete go, turned to face the much smaller man.

"How'd you break that?" he asked, bemusement in his voice. "Little man."

Pete tried to crane his head around, see what was going on, saw Theo looking mussed, blood around his face, his hair covering his eyes, a flicker of steel in his hands. He saw the look in his eyes and just for a moment he could have sworn they had a reddish glow to them, he blinked, and it was gone. Must have been his imagination, he thought, as he saw the light gleam off dull metal. Theo flung himself at Rodolfo, blade pointed at his face, all his weight behind it. The bigger man caught his wrist, drove a fist into his stomach, Theo doubled over and staggered back, Rodolfo followed up on him, grabbed him by the scruff of the neck. Theo rose, stuck the knife in his side and Rodolfo bellowed in pain, tossed the smaller man aside like a ragdoll. As Theo hit the ground, the big man yanked the knife out of his side and tossed it away, didn't see it land at Pete's feet.

Come on Theo, Pete thought as he watched his partner rise to his feet. His legs were wobbling, their training hadn't exactly covered this.

You can do this. Don't trade blows with him, he's bigger and stronger than you. You won't win that way.

Regardless, that looked to be exactly what Theo was going to do, dipped in and hit Rodolfo on his injured side. The roar of pain shook the walls, Rodolfo threw out both hands, fingers trying to grab Theo who ducked under them and hit the huge man in the stomach with a shoulder barge. Pete winced as he saw it hadn't had the desired effect, Theo bounced off and almost lost his footing. Rodolfo grinned at him, brought back his foot, winding up for a kick and Theo jerked his head out the way, the blow catching him in the shoulder instead. He yelled out, the force propelling him to the ground, Pete watched him roll out the way as Rodolfo followed up with driving a fist into the floor where he'd been a moment earlier. Theo reacted, spun out with a kick to the bigger man's head, jumped back to his feet, hands up in front of him in a defensive stance. Blood spattered the floor, gushing out of Rodolfo's side, the carpet slick with it.

Pete braced himself, threw his body forward, rocked the chair on its legs. Fire blazed through him, fresh agony trying to halt him in his actions. A whine slipped his lips, he tried to push it down, brush it off and just fall forward. If he could get to Theo's knife, he could cut himself free. How useful he'd be in fighting Rodolfo, he couldn't say, but he'd give Theo a better chance even if he was just distracting. Unable to guard his face, he tried to turn it aside, so he didn't land nose first, his body complaining at the manner of his landing. Not the most dignified position he'd ever been in. He tilted himself to the side, trying to fall on his uninjured half, his hands missing any sort of way to get the knife. Even twisting hurt, he just wanted it to be over but the part of him that was a realist knew that wasn't going to happen. His hands closed around the hilt of the knife, a flush of triumph ripped through him as he tried to adjust it to sever his bonds.

Always a way to get yourself free. Always an opportunity will prevent itself. Those days when they'd all been secured at the academy, forced to find a way free, they suddenly felt like they hadn't been wasted. The blade met rope and he felt triumph as he started to saw away at them.

Rodolfo had risen again, his face contorted with ghoulish anger and stained with blood. He didn't look human, an ogre of old rising to face a warrior eager to slay him. The big man hurled a fist at Theo, he ducked aside, threw a kick to the back of his leg, missed his knee by inches. Rodolfo barked with pain, grabbed at him again, Theo ducked back, weaved out the way and drove a foot into his stomach. Pete didn't see, continued to saw away at the rope, determined he was going to get it off him before long. Good rope, he had to admit. He didn't know how

Theo had done this so easily and quickly, not when Cyris had been hitting him.

Speaking of Cyris, he could see him trying to rise over the other side of the room, his face woozy with pain. How hard had Theo hit him? More to the point, how much had he enjoyed hitting him that hard? The irony Theo had probably launched his best punch against someone he probably didn't need to hit that hard wasn't lost on him.

Come on, break! Break!

One rope snapped, he felt the twinge of triumph, the rest of them loosening. Come on!

Rodolfo had lost any sense of tactics or skill now, his face warped with fury and he'd abandoned finesse in favour of going after Theo, throwing punches left and right to try and get him. Theo, to his credit, had gone on the defensive, weaving and ducking out the way, trying to evade anything that came too close to him. One blow bounced off his arm and Pete heard him gasp with pain, all he could do to sway out the path of the follow-up blow that grazed his side.

Come on! His muscles were starting to complain, he sucked it up and ignored them, continued to work and work, not giving up, determined not to fade. The snap of the rope breaking had never felt so satisfying, the crack and the release as it tore the best feeling he'd experienced in a long time. He pulled his arms free, rose to his feet gingerly. Rodolfo hadn't noticed him, still trying to beat Theo to death. For once, his partners stubborn nature was working for him, he looked terrible, but he hadn't given up. Giving up would be the easy thing, accepting death.

Who really accepted death in a situation like this? That thought flashes across his mind as he lumbered towards Rodolfo, not even entirely sure what he was going to do as he approached him. There were plenty of ways to disable him non-lethally, sever the tendons in his legs so he couldn't walk, stab him in the spine for the same effect. So many choices and not enough time to make them. Theo had already stabbed him, and it hadn't taken. More than that, Rodolfo had realised he was there, Pete was already on him and he was just too slow...

Instinct took over, the knife swept up into his throat, metal triumphing over skin and cartilage and Rodolfo's eyes widened in shock as the blood started to gush out of him.

Just like that, he'd killed a man for the first time. Rodolfo wasn't dead, not quite yet, but he wasn't getting up from it. Reality hadn't caught up with the fact yet, Pete wasn't going to rush for medical help for him. He'd be dead by the time they got here.

Theo coughed. "About bloody time you did that."

"You're welcome," Pete said, watching him pick up the blaster. "Where the hells did you get the knife from?"

Theo said nothing, pointed the blaster at Cyris who'd made his move, heading for the door. "Oi! Where do you think you're going, father dear?" The tone in his voice worried Pete more than he'd like to admit, it was the tone of a man who'd given into sadism, he knew he was going to have to do something horrific and he was privately looking forward to the idea.

"Theo!"

He didn't hear him, just let a shot go right in front of Cyris, his hand on the knob. "I'm not the best shot ever. Not yet." That probably passed for humility from him, Pete thought. He took a step closer to him, not entirely sure what he was going to do yet. "Might hit you, might not. Might kill you, might just cripple you for life. Hard to say but do you really want to take that chance, dad?"

"Theobald, you wouldn't shoot your old man, would you?" Cyris said, turning away from the door. He put his hands up slowly, an uneasy grin on his face. "I mean, we've got so much history…"

"All of it bad."

"Not all of it terrible," Cyris continued, his voice taking on a soothing tone. Pete could tell he was wasting his time, it didn't even look to be having the slightest effect on his son. "I mean, I didn't do too bad. Look at you. You were nearly a champion. You've got the power of life and death in your hands here. What I did as a parent can't have been that bad."

Theo said nothing. The blaster wavered in his hand.

"I mean, like you said earlier. You can't take this back. You pull that trigger and it's over. I'm gone from your life forever. You'll have to live with it for the rest of your days."

"Are you trying to dissuade me or encourage me?" Theo asked. "Because you're doing a terrible job of persuading me not to."

"Theo, I'm appealing to your better nature. Don't do it for me, do it for yourself. Do you really want to kill me and taint your soul forever? You do it and you'll be broken inside."

"I already am," Theo said, resignation in his voice. "You did that. You made me what I am and that's not something you should be proud of. I'm your greatest success and your biggest failure. That's your legacy, you know that? One of failure at the very basic level."

Cyris smiled at him. Pete slowed down, he truly didn't want to put himself between father and son. It'd be suicide. Theo looked like he'd been waiting for this moment his entire life. Cyris looked like he'd been part expecting it.

"Down on your knees," Theo said. "Put your hands behind your head."

"Dear me, are you really going to try and arrest me? Do you have the authority for that? I see no official identification, no declaration of purpose. You barge in here, I was well within my rights to defend myself. Mister Rodolfo got a little overzealous, but you can't argue with a man like him. Well, you couldn't. Even if he didn't have that gaping wound in his throat, he wouldn't be doing much talking now." Regardless of the words, he complied, slumped to his knees slowly and placed his hands behind his head, interlocking his fingers.

"You've got a history…" Pete offered up, he didn't even believe the words that came out of his mouth as Cyris laughed.

"Everyone has a history, Mister Jacobs. Do you recall a certain dragon in the town of Threll and your associate, Mister Taylor? He still owes me that beast, I wanted it for myself. I never forget my history, Mister Jacobs for it is a memory of debt that separates us from the beasts and the savages."

"You should write motivational speeches," Pete said. "I reckon you'd make a killing at that."

"I did at everything else. As to my history, full pardon for services rendered to the kingdoms. It was a nice ceremony, they gave me a medal for my part in providing intelligence on Claudia Coppinger and her associates. Very shiny. I keep it in pride of place at home. I was a Divine-praised hero."

"Home invasion is not trumped by torture, father," Theo said. "They're going to lock you up again. You think a pardon means they forgot about you? It just means the moment you give them a reason to, they're going to throw away the key and about fucking time too. You won't get away with it this time."

"Theobald," Cyris said, looking up at his son, their eyes meeting. His voice remained steady as he spoke, not a hint of emotion there. "Your mother… I wish I'd never met her."

Pete saw what he was going to do, even before he did it, saw the hardening of his partner's mouth, the fury screaming across his face, the twitches in his muscles and the flash of the muzzle as the blaster discharged. Cyris' head snapped back, and he hit the ground, a pair of unseeing eyes staring at Pete, a third bloody one glaring at him accusingly.

The shout died in his throat. He couldn't speak, his mouth felt dry, horribly stale and he couldn't take his eyes away from Theo. His partner looked at the weapon in his hand, blew on the barrel, knocked the smoke away from it before sliding the safety up and sticking it in the waistband of his trousers.

"Do you think," he started to say, "this is going to affect whether we pass or fail the test?"

"You might want resolution, but I'm afraid, boys and girls, life doesn't work like that. Not everything gets tied up in a neat bow, no matter how much you might hope it so. Does one story end? Absolutely. Does another start? Of course. We are all a part of life's great picture, we each play our part, and, in a way, our stories never truly end. They carry on through our actions, those we leave behind. Remember every new beginning is some beginning's end."
Brennan Frewster.

He'd been sat in the hospital for two days now, finished typing up his report on the whole Brennan Frewster fiasco to give it the official label it had been granted by Icardi when Nick had been pressed for the whole truth. He could still hear the disbelief in his boss's voice, not quite able to accept what he'd been told, no matter how true or false it was. He couldn't see past the sensationalism of it all. Icardi was a solid enough choice to cover for Brendan while he was on leave, but he lacked any sort of imagination to be truly great at the job in Nick's opinion.

Not that he could comment. Brendan had tried leaving him in charge, even Nick had to admit with hindsight it hadn't been the best decision. He'd done the best he could, he lacked the experience and Walter Swelph had moved Icardi into the position until Brendan returned from Vazara.

Those memories haunted him, that failed operation felt such a long time ago. For a long time, he hadn't been sure about his place at Unisco and where he fit in. When Sharon had been alive, he'd felt he'd wanted to leave, a feeling that had developed first when Montgomery had nearly been killed, had simmered for the following months, to Wade getting hurt at the Quin-C, to his investigation for the suspected unlawful killing of Jeremiah Blut, to that undercover operation he'd agreed to go on following Sharon's death.

No. Her murder.

Those two words burned bright within the centre of his being, felt the heat rush through him at their meaning. Harvey Rocastle and Wim Carson. Those two had been responsible, neither of them was blameless. He'd had them both in his sights at one point, Carson had ended badly for him, he might be a target beyond him. That was why the Vedo were here. To deal with Carson ostensibly. Rocastle though, if he'd been willing to sacrifice the rest of the pieces, he could have killed him. Instead he'd made him suffer but it hadn't done a damn bit of good. He'd gotten away.

Back then, he'd thought about leaving Unisco for pastures new, a new challenge in life that wouldn't make a little more of him die inside or hurt the people he loved. Now, with everything happening, he couldn't see himself anywhere else. There was nobody left he cared about to make a long-lived life sound a viable possibility. He'd failed Frewster, thrown all his efforts at him and still he'd died. He'd heard that Saarth was still in critical condition, not quite dead but not quite alive either. They didn't know when she'd wake up, they weren't going to be getting any viable intelligence from her any time soon. Not that he expected her to crack. Ulikku hadn't, after all. They weren't breaking. Maybe something in the process that had turned angry, oddball spirit callers into hardened killers who didn't fear anything. He didn't know.

Carlow was waking up. He'd made the choice to be here, hadn't really had anywhere else to be before his investigation was complete. Icardi would be furious with him, but screw Icardi. He wanted every fact before he went back, lest he need them to defend himself with. First rule of Unisco. Never leave any weapon behind you might need, and he'd always considered information to be one of the ultimate weapons. Hardest to acquire, trickiest to use, but always the most useful.

Her eyelids trickled apart, she managed a smile at him. "Hey," she said, her voice little more than a croak. He'd seen her medical records, had noticed too many discrepancies for her to be just a normal butler. Whatever Frewster had used her for, it wasn't solely for cooking his meals and pressing his suits. Not unless that left broken-and-healed bones and noticeable scarring.

"Ms Carlow," Nick said. "Welcome back to the world of the living. You gave us all quite a scare."

He watched her eyes, suddenly alert again, scan back and forth across the room, searching and seeking, he saw them fall as she realised that he was alone with her. "Master Frewster?" she asked. "Did he make it?"

Nick shook his head, was about to apologise, only to be cut off by the wail she gave, primal animal, sorrowful and broken, every decibel a testament to her grief. He reached up, patted her hand. "My sympathies, Ms Carlow," he said. "In the end, he died a hero. You were down for the count, you didn't see it. He saved thousands of lives…"

"But he couldn't save himself, could he?" she said, moving her hand away from him to wipe her eyes. She looked older since she'd woken, twenty years transplanted onto an already hard-lived life. "That was Brennan all over. He'd do the right thing, no matter the cost. He never did consider the price he'd pay one day."

"I don't think we ever do," Nick said. "Not until it comes to us all. Heroism is not a common thing, Ms Carlow. We talk about…"

"Helga," she said. "Call me Helga."

"Helga, we talk about heroism and what it means…"

"Brennan wasn't a hero, he'd have been the first one to say so. He had his faults and his deficiencies just like everyone else. He wasn't perfect, you had to look at his personal life for that," she said, interrupting him again.

"Nobody is perfect," Nick said. "That's the only thing that's true about life. Someone once said, the older you get, the more you compromise."

"What he did do though," she said. "He tried to at least do the right thing. If there was an injustice he had the power to change, he would go for it. He might not always win, but he always made the enemy work for it. How did he die?"

"Shot," Nick said. "Wasn't even meant for him." It was meant for me, he wanted to say, the words caught in the back of his throat and wouldn't come free. "Stray blast punched straight through him. It would've taken a lot to save him and he ran out…" He swallowed. "He just ran out of time. I wanted to try and save him, he told me not to, more or less made me let him go."

"We always want more until we don't," Carlow said. "Sometimes we know when we have to let go. Life though, the most beautiful thing that you'll ever spend." He wasn't surprised to see the tears flowing from her now, for a woman in her fifties, she gave the impression of a little girl lost, not knowing what the future held.

"I know," Nick said. "I know. I'm sorry. It was a bad situation. People were going to die. People did die. They're talking about giving Brennan a posthumous medal for bravery and service to the kingdoms. Some sort of honour."

"He'd prefer to be alive," she said. "I know that much."

"I think we all would," Nick said. He was thinking of Sharon again, thinking of how Ritellia had stood up in front of the media of the kingdoms and proclaimed that in honour of her memory, the Quin-C trophy would be named for her. Nobody had won it, ironically. The champion of the competition remained Ruud Baxter since it had been unclaimed by either Scott Taylor or Theobald Jameson. Given a choice between a thousand meaningless accolades named for her and having her back in his arms, he knew which he'd pick in a heartbeat. Accolades didn't keep you warm at night. Didn't love you back. You couldn't stare at an accolade and see the spring in their step, the way they walked and talked, the way they laughed and cried. You looked at an accolade and you knew you were never going to see them again. The dead were gone, no bringing them back and only the memories lingered, the pain and the pleasure. You looked at the accolade and you felt the black hole where they'd previously existed in life.

"Look like you're having some tough thoughts there," Carlow said. "Do you need a moment."

"Just thinking," Nick said. "You're right, you know. We never can tell how much time we have. We both lost people to this whole Coppinger thing. Too many will before it's over. She needs to be stopped and fast."

"Then what are you doing here?" Carlow asked simply.

"Because not every battle is won in a day," Nick said. "And only a fool disregards vital intelligence because it sounds fanciful. Frewster didn't die for nothing, I intend to make sure of that. He died because he knew something, he died because Coppinger wanted him. He spun me a story that, if it weren't for some elements of it, I would find fanciful. I wanted to see how you were."

"And you were going to pump me for further information, weren't you?"

"I certainly thought about it," Nick said. "Forewarned is forearmed and this isn't the sort of game you want to go into without all sorts of plans."

"I'm glad I got out of it," she said, resting her head back. "It's not a life you enjoy after a while."

"Why do I know the name Carlow?" Nick asked, his interest piqued with her answer. "You can't leave me hanging on that."

"I had a bit of a past," she admitted.

"Don't we all," he said, smiling at her. He knew it lacked warmth, he just wanted a damn answer rather than the games. Standard question evasion. "Were you Unisco?"

She shorted. "Hardly. I was a bit better than that, Agent Roper."

"Arknatz?"

Carlow yawned. "Darling, I wouldn't be seen dead associating with those individuals. Thugs, the lot of them. No finesse. No refinement. Brute force and battery. I always found you got more results with silk and lace than with steel." The particular implications of that statement hung in his mind, he tried to brush them off. Carlow wasn't an unattractive woman, if carrying the trappings of a hard life. In her youth, he'd have wagered she'd been a real head turner.

"Nicholas, the organisation I worked for no longer exists," she said gently. "Thirty years ago, it was good. Twenty years ago, it folded. Life never quite is what we think it will be. Still, if you hadn't heard of us, I'd be surprised." He said nothing, she smiled at him. "Coldstone," she said. "We had our highs, I'll give the good old days that."

Of course, he had heard of Coldstone. "Okay, now I'm impressed," he said. "What the hells happened to you all? You went from everything to nothing in ten years."

As he remembered, Coldstone had been a small intelligence operation, only a few on its staff but it specialised in deep infiltration, putting people where others couldn't get them. They'd freelanced, taken up jobs where hired by those that couldn't do it themselves. Today, they'd probably have been called mercenaries. Back then, there'd been a certain romance about them, not least because most of their operatives had been attractive women. There'd been a drama made about them a few years back, he wondered if they'd taken poetic licence with the storylines and their choices of actresses.

He chuckled. Maybe he'd been right about Carlow in her youth. "Seriously though, you ladies were legends," he said. "No wonder I thought I'd heard of you before. Helga Carlow. The Thorned Rose herself."

She'd gone red, the touch of colour rushing through her cheeks. "Nobody ever called me that. That was made up for the drama. You know, they interviewed us all?"

"Incredible, they managed to track you down for it?"

"Some people forget the first rule of keeping your mouth shut," she said. "Just because we're retired doesn't mean that we like to talk."

"You're talking to me," Nick said.

She gave him a bemused look. "Only because you saved my life. I didn't talk to you before like this, did I?"

He had to give her that one. "No," he said. "No, you did not."

"Didn't just save it, you fought for it. Brennan would have let me die and I'd have been fine with that." She shrugged as he raised an eyebrow. "I had a good life. Brennan knew it. He wouldn't have regretted it."

"I think he would," Nick said. "It was a tough day for us all."

"Why?"

"Well, there was the attack and the shooting and…"

"Why did you save me? You and Brennan could have dumped me and carried on running, just leave me to die."

"First of all," Nick said. "He was a ninety-year-old man, how much running do you think he could realistically have carried on for?" Carlow smiled at that. "And second, well it wasn't really much of a choice. I don't like leaving women to die when I can do something about it."

"Do you miss her?" Carlow asked suddenly. "Your fiancé?"

"What do you think?" Nick replied, leaning back in his seat, folding his arms behind his head. "Every damn day I'm awake, I think about her. I remember the good times, I try not to dwell on the not-so-good. That won't do anything well for me."

"Hindsight always makes things better," Carlow said. "Love is what it is. It can create, it can nourish, but it can also destroy, I'm sorry to say."

"And yet without it, where would we be?" Nick said. "I once heard someone say if there was a drug with a comedown like love, nobody would take it. Thought he sounded like a wise man."

"I don't think you're over her, are you? A part of her still beats within your heart."

"I think a part always will," he admitted. "I know everyone says it, but I always feel that what we had was special. We could have had something wonderful and it was torn from us in pretty bad circumstances."

"When a love is torn in two, it is never in good circumstances," she said. "Be sad not that it's over but be glad that it happened. Those are words that I tried to conduct my life by."

She was right. He wasn't sure he felt better about it, but he didn't feel any worse and that was a good thing. Nick grinned at her. "Thanks, Ms Carlow.

"Saving my life grants you the right to call me by my first name," she said, managing a weak smile as she said it. "You know that, correct?"

"Does it also grant me the tale of how a deep cover intelligence operative ended up working for Brennan Frewster?" he asked. "Because that story might be interesting."

She laughed, looking better and better by the second. The deathly pallor he'd gotten used to across her skin had rescinded, she gained a little bit of colour right across her face. "Not really, I'm afraid. I needed a job. He initially wanted a bodyguard. He knew his onions, Brennan did, and he had a great respect for Coldstone. He threw a lot of work our way when he was the head of Unisco. All us ladies knew him by sight, and although it's irrelevant, but by all Divines, he was a handsome bastard back then."

They'd continued to chat for an hour, anything and everything, Nick's questions remaining forgotten until the end and finally she brought her speaking to a halt as she looked around the room.

"I thought he'd be here when I woke up," she said. "I know it was a dream before, but you've still got to believe, right?"

"I'm not sure what to believe in any longer," Nick said. "I don't think the kingdoms are getting better. Probably the opposite in fact. The more we do; the more things start to tear apart underneath us."

"We all have days like this," Carlow said. "Nicholas, you don't let them get you down too much when you lose, you don't let your victories lift you too high."

"Victories, huh? What do those feel like again?"

Her chuckle made him smile in turn. She had that way about her. Reassuring. Easy to talk to. A great listener. She'd probably been a great spy and an amazing butler. That she was using her experience to draw stuff out of him now wasn't something he was unaware of, he wasn't giving anything away compromising to Unisco. "Don't doubt yourself, Nicholas. You still have more to offer than you think. We all do. It isn't over until we're all dead, and the last one alive can switch the lights off."

"Everything Frewster said about the Forever Cycle," Nick finally said. "It's true, isn't it?"

She nodded. "He believed it was. He told me the tale he told you long since, of Canderous Arventino and Adrian Battleby and his adventure with them. I didn't believe it at first. He spent years researching it as a side project, he had great stock in what it said. The amount of times I came in early and saw him pouring over family trees and genealogy records and Unisco backgrounds of possible Divineborn, I lost track."

"Frewster was tracking the Divineborn?" Nick asked. "Did he get anywhere identifying them?"

"His notes are back at Withdean," she said. "When I get out, I can find them for you. He spun you his tale, didn't he?"

"Finished it post-mortem unfortunately. I got the whole gist of the story. Interesting. I think there's elements of lunacy there, but Frewster didn't strike me as not being entirely in control of his faculties. If he was struggling, he did a good job hiding it."

"Frewster came from fine genes," she said. Nick had to smile at the pun there, given the questions springing up around Frewster's parentage. "He didn't hide things when he didn't have to."

"Divines, but Unisco was the wrong line of work for him then," Nick said. "Until you're better Helga, then I'd like that research."

"It is just names and lists, none of it truly helpful," she said. "But if you desire, then I'll aid you. Brennan brought you into his life to help him when he was troubled. He would have wanted his death to be avenged, his enemies brought to justice and my assistance to be granted."

"Even the smallest of insignificancies can have surprising revelations," Nick said. "We never know what's going to be valuable, so we try to take it all." He rose to his feet, was surprised to find her hand on his arm.

"Not everything dies, Nicholas Roper," she said. "The dead carry on living in our memories. If we can recall them, they will never leave us. A lot of people knew of Ms Arventino. She was loved, she was adored by the masses. That counts for a lot. She'll live on forever. She'd have wanted you to be happy. You can't wear her memories around your neck like an anchor, they'll drag you down if you're not careful."

"Then I'll need to be careful," he said. He didn't want this discussion right now, he'd already reached his limit for the day. More than that, he wasn't ready to let her go yet. She had too much of a prominent role in his memories to just be forgotten like that. "Or learn how to swim."

"Make your report, Nicholas. Play it straight. Wordplay isn't your forte and you shouldn't treat it as such."

He laughed as he headed for the door. "You know, you're not the first to say so, Helga. You're not the first one at all." He allowed himself a look at her as he reached the exit. "I'll be back to see you again." She smiled at that, he thought she might damn near purr for a moment.

"Don't dally, Nicholas. This is a lonely place and the healing is slow. Someone to talk to would just while away the time nicely."

"Get well soon, Ms Carlow," he said, his choice of name for her slipping out beyond his best efforts to halt it. "Try not to let this place get you down. Farewell."

He didn't look back as he closed the door behind him, strode down the corridor like he didn't have a care in the world. Not a thousand miles from the truth either. All his cares had long since faded from the forefront of his mind, he could feel their weight pushing into his back and he looked forward to the day he could shed them all. He supposed it was time to go and face Icardi, see what music he had in mind for him. It wasn't a pleasant thought, but about his only viable option now. Too much had gone by for him to do anything else.

"Stupid," he muttered to himself. He shouldn't have hung about like this, risked awakening the ire of Icardi, a man prone to outbursts of temper at the best of time. He'd have to ride it out. He'd faced down Claudia Coppinger, routinely went blaster to blaster with people who wanted to kill him.

What was one pompous bureaucrat? Unfortunately, he was the sort of pompous bureaucrat that might well turn out to be a thorn in his side which he couldn't afford right now. The job wasn't done yet. Coppinger was still out there and he needed to be the one who found her and her crew of psychopaths.

She needed to go down. Nobody could dispute that. It was the single greatest truth that anyone in the five kingdoms would ever speak in either the recent or the coming months. Coppinger had to be stopped. She needed to be defeated.

As always, he thought, that was easier said than it was done.

It felt good to be back behind the main desk at Unisco, until he'd sat down in his old seat and felt the contours of the wood, he didn't realise how much he'd missed it. Terrence Arnholt had run a long race with death and staved it off for the time being, triumph a temporary reprieve. He knew that it'd come to him one day, but that day hopefully wouldn't be any time soon. The shooting hadn't been fatal, he'd wanted to come back to work a lot sooner than his doctors would allow him to, but they hadn't permitted that. They'd prescribed rest and recuperation, lots of it, even as he'd tried to explain the job needed him, yet they weren't having it.

He couldn't be overtly critical. What was the point in expensive and highly qualified doctors if you didn't follow their professional opinion? Unisco allocated a considerable amount from its budget to make sure proper medical care was available to anyone injured in the line of duty, it was the least he personally could make sure they did. It had been maddening though to see the way things had unfolded. He'd been distraught when Nwakili had died, the man had been a good ally to have in the past. When he'd been invited to speak in the Senate, Nwakili had always spoken highly of the need for a strong Unisco and his belief in law and order and how it needed to be applied.

There'd been a part of him that had considered not returning to the job. Nobody would have blamed him, he'd had a good run at it, Unisco was running its highest rates of mission success for the last twenty years, albeit statistics not including the Coppinger crisis. Nobody could have seen it coming, nobody at all and that they'd been ill-equipped to cope was hardly a surprise. Complacency had crept in amongst some agents, they'd gotten softer as they'd gotten older and that wouldn't do. Maybe they'd thought the kingdoms were getting safer, that they didn't need to be as sharp. That was the attitude that'd get an agent killed. Between Brendan and Swelph, they'd done the right thing when he'd been shot and unable to lead the agency, they'd immediately opened the door for new recruits. He would have done the same thing. Training them took time and the sooner they started, the sooner they could get them out into the field.

Now though, he'd had a message from Tod Brumley regarding the testing of two of the earliest cadets and Arnholt had to admit to mixed feelings as he'd read about Peter Jacobs and Theobald Jameson, one the friend of his daughter's boyfriend and one the son of the most notorious criminal in Premesoir in recent years. Said criminal had been killed on a training exercise, his son and his partner in their final examination had blundered into a meeting between Cyris and a Kenzo Fojila operative. They didn't know what he'd been hiring an assassin for, though Jameson had suggested it might be to kill someone, in what Brumley had described as 'typical abrasive fashion' according to instructors at the Iaku academy. The report from Inquisitor Konda said that Cyris had been shot through the face, his bodyguard stabbed in the throat. He'd seen the pictures of Cyris' dead guard, that a pair of cadets had managed to take him down was impressive. Most seasoned agents would have struggled with a fellow his size.

Both cadets had taken beatings, but they'd live. He was troubled by the idea of Cyris hiring an assassin but if he was no longer in the land of the living, Kenzo Fojila weren't going to get paid and they weren't a charity. If he hadn't paid, they wouldn't make the kill. Still, he'd forwarded it on to the Unisco task force intended to keep an eye on the assassins. Worth keeping an eye on. More of a struggle was the decision what to do with Jameson and Jacobs. Technically, they'd failed their examination, but he had to admit that the circumstances were exceptional.

It wasn't common for something like this to happen, but it was a possibility always considered. Right back to the foundation of the agency under the now-late Brennan Frewster, the wording in the rules had stated that circumstances like this came to fall under 'the discretion of the appropriate parties.' That meant Inquisitor Konda at the academy in this circumstance, he'd signed off on it and passed it up to Tod Brumley who'd also signed off with his consent. Now it had come in front of him. As far as he was concerned, the kingdoms were a better place without Cyris in them, the two cadets had behaved well in astonishing circumstances and he was happy to bestow upon them the rank of agent and continue their training in their chosen field. An inquisitor and a combat specialist, according to the reports. He had a feeling they might need plenty of those in the coming months.

Next, the Brennan Frewster thing itself. There'd been too much video footage of Nick's duel with Saarth on the viewing screens, it hadn't looked particularly good, especially considering they'd recorded Frewster's death. The whole situation had turned into a bit of a fiasco, Frewster was dead, his housekeeper in the hospital and they weren't sure if Saarth was going to survive for interrogation, he wasn't sure he'd have blamed Nick for it personally, but Icardi was doing his best to make sure he took some of the fall for it, criticising every aspect of his decision making throughout the entire process. No doubt to distract from his own part in it. Arnholt didn't rate Icardi, he wasn't overly impressed that he'd been moved into Brendan's job until he returned from Vazara, another decision he wasn't happy about. At a time like this when the kingdoms were going to the hells, Brendan could have made a different choice. One did simply not chew out a man like Brendan King in theory, but Arnholt was ready to do just that when he returned. The sooner Icardi could be shunted away, the better. As far as Arnholt was concerned, he wasn't trustworthy. There'd always been insinuations about him, the inquisitors had never found anything, but the director went with his gut. He always had. Instinct may be misplaced but they were rarely wrong.

Then Carling. Another embarrassment that Unisco's most high-profile traitor of recent years had managed to escape jail during a riot, videocams suggesting it had been staged especially for that purpose. So far, the identity of the instigator remained unclear, but techs were working on it. Surveillance had been damaged during the riot. Carling was lost, he hadn't been seen since, but he'd wondered if Coppinger had any part to play in it. They'd had connections, a recent fresh examination of the double act Carling and Hobb had put together had revealed the last contract had been paid for by Coppinger. The finances matched records Agents Khan and Wallerington had pulled from Harvey Rocastle's family in Burykia, though an investigation into the building had ultimately pulled up nothing according to Khan. A dead end. The two of them were in Serran now, chasing a fresh lead according to her, though she hadn't said what it might be.

Still, one positive. Raphael Barthomew had returned with a truly fantastic story of being held prisoner by the Vazaran Suns for a year, tortured and healed only for the cycle to begin anew when he'd recovered. The story of his escape would go down in agency folklore, he felt, not many escaped in that fashion only to be arrested and subsequently bailed by the military. Any story that involved jetpacks immediately had the making of legend. And those files he'd snuck back from his prison... They were being deciphered even now, hopes that they could glean some sort of tactical advantage from them, Okocha and his team going through them. Everyone was praying to any Divine that would listen they'd find something that made Barthomew's year of captivity worth it. He hated to think that things had gone the way they had. Barthomew had started out on a leave of absence, that leave had turned into weeks without contact. Anyone who'd gone looking for him hadn't found him and now they knew why, and it unsettled him. Things had been unsettled around Unisco lately, what the restructuring and most of the senior agents being unavailable for one reason or another.

A message flashed up on his monitor, he glanced at it. Okocha. Two words and an attached video sent to him and to Swelph. He read them aloud, not entirely sure what they meant until he clicked on the video. "Look familiar?" he asked. "Who should look...?"

He pressed the play button, watched it click into motion. Wasn't much to see, quite grainy, a glowing blue tube in the background, the camera panning closer and closer. There looked to be something in there, resting in the water. It could be water, it might be some sort of umbilical fluid. Curious. That something was a someone, their back to the camera but judging by the shape of their body, they had to be female. Very womanly shape, though he had to wait until it panned around to have that confirmed from the view of her front. Long strands of blond hair billowed about her face, enough to make it difficult to recognise her but not at all impossible. The only impossibility about it was her identity. It just couldn't be real. It was impossible. He could see her breathing, her chest rising and dropping in the fluid, a mask covering her mouth and nose as she slept.

No! No! Not possible!

He was gripping his fist together, he could feel the nails digging into the flat of his palm and he brought himself from his reverie by slamming said fist into the desk. Pain shot up through his arm, he winced and exhaled sharply. Could it be...?

No. It had to be a trick. There was no other way of looking at it. It couldn't be her. She'd died. He knew that face, he'd met her on more than one occasion. He'd dined with her, he'd interviewed her, he'd even fought her. He pushed the button on his summoner, found Okocha's number and dialled it, heard his voice come through loud and clear. "Okocha."

"Will," Arnholt said, unnerved to find he couldn't keep the shock out of his voice. "Is this video accurate? It's not doctored in any way that you can find?"

"Doesn't look it. It doesn't pass any tests for any of the regular themes in forged footage. I've seen plenty of them in my time, Director, and if this is a fake then it's the best I've ever seen. Maybe the best made ever, full stop."

That didn't bode well. He swallowed, glanced back and forth as if an answer might present itself. None came. The scar where he'd been shot ached in his chest, he had to fight the urge to rub at it.

"Your opinion Will?"

"It's not a fake," he said. "There are too many consistencies for it to be one." He carried on at length, started to list through all the factors rendering him so sure the video was genuine, Arnholt wasn't listening, found himself tuning out as he continued to watch the woman

339

in the tube. She looked better than she had done the last time he'd seen her, when she'd had half her head blown away and a burn straight through her chest. Though she slept, her mouth had that same arrogant slant to it, a smirk telling everyone around she found something funny and they didn't know what it was. He'd always found her a little arrogant on the battlefield, though most top callers had that in their armoury. It made things interesting. In private, she'd been much more hospitable, a pleasure to engage with. She'd done a lot of good things, though given what they now knew about her, perhaps it was atonement rather than charity.

"… there's always a level of fuzziness around the edges, it's a distortion of quality, not really anything anyone can do about it…" Okocha continued, oblivious to the thoughts running through his head.

"Will!" Arnholt said loudly. "I understand. Verify it as best you can. I need to know."

"Understood, Director." All business now. He no doubt had a chagrined look on his face at being interrupted in flow. Okocha was a genius but he could be touchy if you got on his wrong side. Still, people seemed to like him and there weren't many geniuses out there who could say that.

"This could be terrible if it's true," he continued.

"Understood, Director." He was definitely annoyed, Arnholt guessed. Tough shit, Will. We all have jobs to do.

"And Will?"

"Yes, Director?" he said.

"You told me, and you told Swelph. I'll talk to Walter. I don't want you telling anyone else. Not if it turns out to be fake and absolutely not if it turns out real. I'd prefer it if you just forgot the whole thing, but I guess that isn't likely. Keep it to yourself."

"Understood, Director. Don't tell anyone."

"Especially not Roper," Arnholt said. "And definitely not Baxter either. The last thing we need is one of those two going on some sort of suicide mission for answers. Guilt does funny things."

"If they do hear it, it won't be from me," Okocha said. "Anything else, Director?"

"No," Arnholt said. "Thanks, Will. Be well. Stay at it."

"Always do, Director."

He hung up, settled back in his seat and studied the video for one final time, before closing it down. He didn't need to think about the consequences of what he'd seen. Things were getting bad and this could be the firework in the melting pot that started the fire around them all.

They couldn't get much worse, he assured himself. The melting pot analogy felt disturbingly accurate. The kingdoms were being pushed, Coppinger was winning it would appear. Every day she was out there, she gathered new people to her cause. She spoke of another way, a new world with herself at the top. She'd already taken Vazara. The attack on Serran had begun, Mazoud declaring war and then beating a hasty retreat without a shot being fired back in anger. They were being pushed harder than they ever had before.

Another report, this one from the Unisco base on Galina Island that a distress beacon had been activated, the one Brendan had taken with him and a ship despatched to pick him and his academic team up. That had temporarily lifted his spirits until he'd read the next part, seen contact had been lost with the ship several hours later, in the part of the Vazaran desert known as Ferros' Arsehole. They were trying to get a recovery team out, but the locals weren't making it easy. Another setback but worth the efforts to get Brendan and David Wilsin back. They were wasted out in Vazara, he needed them here and bloody fast.

He heard the knock, glanced up as Ms Luccisantini stuck her head around the door, dear Lola, former Unisco bodyguard now enjoying her time safeguarding him. She was no ordinary secretary, that was for sure, he was lucky to have her. He grinned, it was quite fortunate he had some pull within this agency. She'd been quite the beauty in her younger years, still was a head turner into her forties, that beauty tempered by the wisdom of age but all the better for it.

"Director Arnholt," she said. "Your daughter is on the line. She's demanding to talk to you."

That caught his attention. Mia had never called him here before. She didn't know what he did, didn't know what he'd done throughout his life. She thought all his time was taken up being a city champion. As ruses went, those were running thin. The demands of two jobs like that just grew and grew, soon they'd all have to pick between one or the other.

"Okay, put her through on the holocom," he said, settling back in his seat.

"You might want to see the live news as well," Lola said. "I think the two might be related. I'll patch her through."

She vanished back behind the door, and he thumbed the remote for the viewing screen towards the back of the room, watched it flicker into life. He found the FiveK channel, the rolling media coverage for Five Kingdoms Media and leaned forward to get the best view. The scenes were coming in from Serran, he'd half expected it to be linked to Mazoud's aborted attack. Instead it was coming somewhere inland, a village out in the middle of nowhere, local police and uniformed

Unisco agents wandering all over the screen. His heart fell, hurt in his chest, a twinge bursting through him. The words at the bottom of the screen read 'Live from Donavio.'

What the hells had happened now?

His holocom buzzed, his hand unconsciously went to it as he read the tagline on the screen, one caption to sum up the story and he realised that he'd tempted fate badly and he'd spoken too soon.

The picture on screen was of a brown-skinned man, probably in his early-to-mid-twenties, a mixed-race kid grinning at whoever had taken at the picture. Arnholt knew who he was. Everyone who had even a passing interest in spirit calling knew who he was after he'd made a run to the final of the Quin-C some months earlier. No doubt the caption would push the kingdoms even further on the brink.

Competitive Centenary Calling Challenge Cup Finalist Scott Taylor Goes Missing in Serran. Coppinger Involvement Suspected. No Ransom Demand So Far…

No!

Even as the holographic image of his daughter appeared in front of him, an accusing glare on her face, he knew he'd been right in his earlier initial impressions. He wondered which she was more upset about, finding out the truth or her missing boyfriend?

"You bastard!" Mia said. "You've been lying to us all these years!"

He thought they couldn't. But they had. Things had managed to get worse.

A lot worse.

To Be Continued in Paradise Shattered…

Coming Soon.

A Note from the Author.

Thank you for the time spent reading this book, taking the time to spend your days in this world I created. I hope that you enjoyed reading it just as much as I did when I wrote it. Just a quick note, if you did, please, please, please leave a review on Amazon for me. Even if it's just two words, it can make a lot of difference for an independent author like me.

Eternal thanks in advance. If you enjoyed this one, why not check out other books I've written available at Amazon.

If you wish to be notified about upcoming works, and even get a free short story from the Spirit Callers Saga starring Wade and Ruud some twenty-five years ago, sign up to my mailing list at
http://eepurl.com/dDQEDn

Thanks again. Without readers, writers are nothing. You guys are incredible.

OJ.

Just another quick note. Special thanks to everyone involved in helping put this book in front of you from my cover designer to my beta reader for the series, Ethan DeJonge, to the people who tolerate me on Twitter and Facebook.

The Spirit Callers Saga.

Wild Card. – Out Now
Outlaw Complex. – Out Now
Revolution's Fire. – Out Now
Innocence Lost. – Out Now
Divine Born. – Out Now
Paradise Shattered. – Coming Soon

Tales of the Spirit Callers Saga.

Appropriate Force. – Out Now.
Kjarn Plague. – Coming 2018

The Novisarium.

God of Lions – Coming Soon
Blessed Bullets – Coming Soon
Spirit and Stone – Coming Soon

The Unstoppable Libby Tombs (A Novisarium Series).

Family Tradition – Coming Soon
Memory Lane – Coming Soon

Born in 1990 in Wakefield, OJ Lowe always knew that one day he'd want to become a writer. He tried lots of other things, including being a student, being unemployed, being a salesman and working in the fashion industry. None of them really replaced that urge in his heart, so a writer he became and after several false starts, The Great Game was published although it has recently been re-released as three smaller books, Wild Card, Outlaw Complex and Revolution's Fire, now officially the first three books in the Spirit Callers Saga, a planned epic of some sixteen books. He remains to be found typing away at a laptop in Yorkshire, moving closer every day to making childhood dreams a reality.

He can be found on Twitter at @OJLowe_Author.

38558426R00195

Printed in Poland
by Amazon Fulfillment
Poland Sp. z o.o., Wrocław